ADVANCE PRAISE FOR *GOLDEN DELICIOUS*

"The page is cracking, is breaking. We all know it. We've known it for some time. At least someone finally *said* it."
—*Haily Dampshire Mazette*

"This book is very strange, but there are some good parts about auctions, and a lot of biographical information about the Auctioneer. When you understand where she came from—the obstacles she overcame—you'll raise your bids even higher." —*The Auction Times*

"_____ is a promising worrier. If only he could *write* as well as he can worry!" —*Worry Illustrated*

". . . [B]ut not in all my wheelings have I ever seen a book shaped like an apple." —*Western Mass Trader*

"A pair of pants, a shirt, a tie, some shoes."
—*The Memory of News*

"The book does offer historical information about Johnny Appleseed, some helpful prayer schematics, and the first and only accurate map of Appleseed." —*Heartfjord Current*

"Volkswagens are one thing; apples are an entirely different thing. They are different in shape, size, and function."
—*Studies in the Avant Garde*

"I hear a burrowing. Can anyone else hear that? Like, a deep scratching?"
—*First Thought, Best Thought*

"The cheek, the axis, the apex, the cell, and the stalk."
—*The Book of Soil*

"All I know is, I'm glad to have the Mothers on my side. Those Mothers kick ass!"
—*Tornado Monthly*

"Now. Right NOW!"
—*The Daily Core*

GOLDEN DELICIOUS

GOLDEN DELICIOUS

A NOVEL

CHRISTOPHER BOUCHER

MELVILLE HOUSE
BROOKLYN · LONDON

GOLDEN DELICIOUS

Copyright © 2016 by Christopher Boucher

First Melville House Printing: April 2016

Melville House Publishing		8 Blackstock Mews
46 John Street	and	Islington
Brooklyn, NY 11201		London N4 2BT

mhpbooks.com facebook.com/mhpbooks @melvillehouse

Library of Congress Cataloging-in-Publication Data
Names: Boucher, Christopher, author.
Title: Golden delicious / Christopher Boucher.
Description: First edition. | Brooklyn : Melville House, [2016]
Identifiers: LCCN 2015047811 (print) | LCCN 2016000947
    (ebook) | ISBN 9781612195100 (softcover) | ISBN
    9781612195117 (ebook)
Subjects: LCSH: Families—Massachusetts—Fiction. | Domestic
    fiction. | BISAC: FICTION / Literary. | FICTION /
    Humorous. | FICTION / Family Life.| GSAFD: Humorous
    fiction.
Classification: LCC PS3602.O8875 G65 2016 (print) | LCC
    PS3602.O8875 (ebook) | DDC 813/.6—dc23
LC record available at http://lccn.loc.gov/2015047811

Design by Marina Drukman

Printed in the United States of America
1   3   5   7   9   10   8   6   4   2

For Lisa

CONTENTS

ENFIELD, CONNECTICUT

APPLESEED, MASSACHUSETTS

VOX

ROYAL JUBILEE

That afternoon I took the Reader to see the Memory of Johnny Appleseed. We left right after school on my customized Bicycle Built for Two, the Reader on the backseat and me on the front. We pedaled through the paragraphs of downtown and across Highway Five to the deadgroves near the west margin, where I figured we'd find the Memory planting stories in the soil.

That was the year that my Mom left us—sharpened the blades in her skirt, winged up her blouse, and flew off—and it was just me, my father, and my sister in our home in Appleseed. It wasn't a surprise when she left; she'd been planning to leave, telling us she was leaving, for months. And everything else that she'd predicted had come true— the blight, the loss of meaning, all of it.

Even so, we were shocked when she actually went through with it. There was no official goodbye, no pep talk. My sister and I were in the TV room that afternoon when my Mom appeared in the doorway, wearing her flightskirt and goggles, a suitcase at her feet. "Well, I'm all packed," she said.

My sister looked over at her from the couch. I pulled my headphones off.

"I'll see you both soon, OK?" my Mom said. Then she saluted us and walked out the door and into the backyard.

My sister and I ran out after her. "Wait—right now?" said Briana.

My Mom lowered her goggles over her eyes and lifted off the ground.

"Mom—*wait!*" my sister said. "You can't—what about— when will you be back?"

My Mom didn't answer—it was like she couldn't even hear Briana.

"What about *dinner?*" my sister shouted up.

My Mom looked down and made a face. "You'll figure it out," she called back. "Make some. Or have _____ make some."

"Who's going to do the *grocery shopping?*"

My Mom huffed. By then she was twenty feet high— then thirty, then forty.

I didn't say anything. I was pretty sure that this was my fault—that I was the reason my Mom was leaving. I'd done something wrong, but I didn't know what.

I was sad watching her go, though, and I missed her in the days that followed. I missed the obvious things—our trips to the Library and to the Bing for movie matinees— but also the things I never thought I'd miss: the sound of her footsteps as she vaulted up the carpeted stairs two at a time; the way she leaned over the kitchen counter while smoking a six-foot cigarette; the sound of her working out—practicing martial-arts moves in the worryfields, hitting the heavy bag in the garage, perfecting flight techniques out back. The house felt empty without my parents' arguments—their subtle barbs, their all-out shoutfests. I even missed being yelled at—the way my Mom spat out the words *spoiled* and *selfish*, and, more recently, *brat* and *blabbermouth* and *badseed*, and in the days before she left, *piece of crap*, and *piece of shit*. I *was* all of those things—I *was* a spoiled, selfish piece of shit. I ruined everything. That was probably why I didn't have many friends—why I rode my Bicycle Built for Two alone.

Then, a few weeks after my Mom flew away, Mr. Santos assigned us—you and I—a project in History about the founding of Appleseed. I told you maybe we could go see the Memory of Johnny Appleseed and interview him, and you looked at me funny and said, "I thought Johnny Appleseed was a *myth*."

I considered that. "I don't think so," I said. "His Memory works with my Dad sometimes."

"And he knows about the founding of Appleseed?" said the Reader.

"Sure," I said. "He planted, like, every apple tree in Appleseed. I think that's why they call it—"

"Does he know what happened to them?" asked the Reader.

"He says he does," I said.

You—the Reader—shrugged. "I'll go with you," you said, "if you're sure you know where to find him."

"He doesn't technically have an *address*?" I said. "But I can usually track him down."

Truth was, I wasn't sure I could find the Memory of Johnny Appleseed by myself. Usually *he* found *me*. I'd been on dozens of drives with my Dad, though, when he was trying to locate the Memory for one job or another. Sometimes we spotted him hitchhiking on Old Five; othertimes he was riding his treecycle past Wolf Swamp or standing outside the Big Why, handing out brochures. Once we spotted him turning cartwheels on the Town Green. The last time we needed him, we asked at the Recycling Center and they said they heard he was up on Appleseed Mountain. When we got to the base of the mountain, we saw Johnny Appleseed walking through the trees with an armful of ifs.

There were also those times, though, when we didn't find him at all—when my Dad drove around for an hour or two, pounded the dashboard with the heel of his hand, turned the truck around and went home.

The Reader and I pedaled past the Amphitheatre, the Arcade, the Library—there was no sign of Johnny anywhere. Soon, we'd crossed the off-white pages of Highway Five, bumping over prints and railroad tracks. In the distance you could see Appleseed Prison, the Mental Hospital, and back behind that, the beard of Appleseed Mountain. It was a tough ride, what with the extra weight of the Reader and all, and out past Jonquil I had to stop and catch my breath. At one point I turned around and looked back at you. "Are you pedaling?" I said.

"Of course I am," said the Reader.

"It doesn't seem like you are," I said.

"I am," you said.

I stood up from the seat and bore down on the pedals.

Finally I saw Old Colton Road, and, up ahead, the Colton deadgroves. When we reached the edge of the groves we laid the bike down in the grass and walked through the fields. My thoughts were clamoring; I leaned over, opened the top of my head, and let the thoughts spill out and run free on the dead pages. "Woo!" shouted one of my thoughts, sprinting forward. Another thought began digging.

"Don't get lost!" I shouted to them. "And think right back here if you find the Memory of Johnny Appleseed."

A third thought ran up to me. "I have to pee," it said.

"Go over there by that tree," I told it.

The Reader looked out across the page. "Should we shout for him or something?" she said.

"Shouting won't do much good," I said. "These groves go on for years."

We trudged across the marshy ground. We saw some memories and scenes; a few wild sentences crossed behind a treeline. Soon I spotted a figure in the foggy fields; he wore a satchel around his waist and he was kneeling in the soil. When he heard our footsteps approaching, he stood up and put his hand to his forehead. "_____?" he said.

The Memory of Johnny Appleseed didn't look good. He was wearing jeans that were too big for him, a green corduroy hat, and someone's old Converse hi-tops. His white beard was patchy and his eyes were tired. "Who's this?" he said.

"Reader," I said.

"I can see *that*," he said. He smiled a near-toothless smile. His face was stained with ink and soil. "What's she doing *here*?"

"School project," I said.

"About the founding of Appleseed," said the Reader quietly.

In the distance, two of my thoughts ran past, one chasing the other with a tree branch.

"We were hoping we could interview you for it," I said.

"What do you want to know?" said the Memory.

"About the first pages," I said. "The planting of the first apple trees."

The Memory stood up. "Sure," he said. "I can go through it for you. How 'bout you help me with what I was doing—pulling out these stalks?" he said, leaning over. "And then I'll give you the history."

I looked out at the field. Five or six rows of black, spiny clumps stuck out from the ground. I could see the Reader studying the stalks. "What are you growing here?" you asked.

"Only thing that *will* grow in the deadgroves," said Johnny Appleseed. "Those are stories."

"I didn't think anything could grow in the dead-groves," the Reader said.

"Stories will grow anywhere," the Memory told the Reader. "You can grow stories on the bottom of the ocean floor! In a tree! On the back of a song! These rows," said the Memory, "are overripe. They need to be told *today*. So how 'bout it?"

I looked to the Reader, who nodded.

The Memory positioned himself over a stalk. "This inky part here? You grab it and *pull*." He pulled, and up came a story. We looked at it; it was the story of Cora Morris, one of the first Mothers.

"See? There's some history right there," said the Memory of Johnny Appleseed. "Now you guys give it a try."

I knew I didn't have a choice about the stories we were harvesting: they were already fully formed. But if I'd had a choice? I would have grown more of the small, dumb stories that I'd lived and lost: family of four goes out to Appleseed Pizza for an extra-large pie. Family of four has enough meaning to pay the mortgage. Family of four never has to worry about bookworms, meaning-losses or blights. There were never any problems and nothing bad ever happened. Were those even *stories*? Anyway, that's what I wanted.

The Reader and I leaned down and took hold of a storyroot. We pulled, but the root held firm.

"It's stuck," I said.

"Oh, come on," said the Memory of Johnny Appleseed. "Pull! With your arms!"

We tried again—you put your back into it; I dug my feet into the fibers. The root finally budged, and loosened, and gave. Together, we pulled the story out of the page.

GOLDEN NOBLE

As far back as I remember—page 11, even—I used to kneel on the margin with my Mom and send out prayers: thoughts, honed and directed. Prayers, if you don't know, can be sent to other people—the dead, the memorized, the far-away—or, with the right words and codes, directly to the book's Core.

Some prayers are public, like the prayers you get from Town Hall or announcements from the newspaper, but most of them are private—"holy," my Mom would say—between you and another person or you and the Core. My Mom liked to pray out loud sometimes, though, so I'd hear snippets of her psalms to my grandfather, Old Speaker, or to her mother the GameMaster, or a quick hi-prayer to her brother in Baltimore. "I miss you *so* much," she prayed to Old Speaker once.

"Are you exercising?" he prayed back.

"Yes," she prayed.

"How's your eating?" he prayed.

"*Fine*," she prayed through clenched teeth.

"You're not throwing up?"

"No," she said.

When I first started praying, I just prayed to people I knew. Like, I prayed to my friend Large Odor: "Hey."

"What?" he prayed back.

"Nothing," I prayed.

But my Mom taught me how to pray better: how to make a thought in your mind and send it *up*, off the page and into the night. "Prayers are just sentences," she told me once as we knelt in the worryfields, the wet page cold on my knees. "Sometimes you can direct them, sort of shape them in your mind. But they can also get away from you—" Just then a small sentence scampered across the page. My Mom lunged at it, picked it up by the scruff of its verb and tossed it into the margin. "—wander off," she continued, "like a thought. You understand?"

"Sure," I said. I didn't. I wouldn't for a long time.

"If you want to control your prayers—really direct them—you've got to *practice*. Pray *a lot*. Pray even when you don't have to."

When I got better at praying, I'd send out prayers almost as far and heart as my Mom did. When my sister broke her leg in gymnastics? I prayed for it to heal. When my Dad went into debt? I prayed for more meaning for our family.

When we finished praying, my Mom and I would stand up and brush the page from our knees and walk back home. "You're a good praying partner," she told me one day. "Where'd you learn to pray like that?"

She was so nice then.

"I have a good teacher," I said.

But then the language rose up and the rot set in—into my mind, the town, our hearts—and my Mom stopped bringing me out to the margin; it was just too dangerous.

Then my Mom left altogether. Months after she floated upward, though, I started going back out to the margin again to pray. I didn't care if it was safe or not—I had a missing I couldn't meet. I'd pray out as far as I could, and sometimes my Mom prayed back. But it was always a cursory response—"Tell your sister and Dad I said hello!" or "Hope you're having a nice day!" or "Do your homework!" Once I didn't hear from her for a whole month, so I submitted a Missing Persons Prayer to the Core. All it did, though, was generate an automatic response: "Thank you for praying to Appleseed—we appreciate your prayer, and regret that we cannot answer every prayer individually."

When I couldn't reach my Mom I'd pray to someone else: my Dad at work, my friends Chamblis or Berson, the Memory of Johnny Appleseed. Sometimes I'd send out psalms to the dumbstars. Once, just to see what happened, I tried praying to myself. I thought the prayer would just boomerang back and feedback my thoughts, but it didn't; it went—somewhere—and reached a me on a different page. "Hello?" said the other-page me.

I prayed to myself that I was here in Appleseed, basically all alone with no one to take care of me. That I needed help. "I just don't know what anything means anymore," I prayed.

"And you're *where*?" the me prayed back.

"Appleseed," I prayed back.

"I've never heard of that place," I prayed to myself. "Is it near Norwich?"

Somewhere, in a stuck drawer in my mind, I think I always knew about the blight. I probably knew about the bookworms, too—where they came from, what they wanted, who brought them. Some thoughts rise into the sky, but others are just too heavy—they sink into the page-soil, where they fester and rot. One person's imagination can cause a lot of damage—destroy a whole town, even!

Before you read any further, though, I want to apologize. I'm really sorry—I am. I didn't mean to hurt anyone. If we work together, though, there might still be blank pages—room to fix all this.

Reader: Work *together*?

Maybe I could carry these stories, and you could carry those.

Reader: That whole stack? What is all that, even?

"This is most of my childhood right here," I said.

"I'm not sure I can even *lift* that many stories," you said.

No, no—you can store them in your mind. Here: I'll—open the top of your head, move some thoughts around—

Reader: Ow.

—and we'll stuff as many stories as we can in there.

Reader: They smell like cigarettes.

Those are my Mom's. Don't smoke them! They're special MotherSmokes, six feet long and strong as Baz. Once I tried one and my mind started coughing and hacking and it almost puked into my skull.

Reader: That all of them?

Just—one more. There. Now we'll just close up your skull good and tight, and you're good to go. Hey—what page are we on?

Reader: 17.

OK—let's go. We're late already.

Reader: Go where?

Forward. To try to fix this. We've got to try to save Appleseed.

FIESTA

Turn the page, step onto the margin, and you're at the edge of Appleseed, Massachusetts, standing right on the Connecticut-Massachusetts border, next to the Connecticut River. See? You can see Appleseed City—the smokestacks of Bondy's Island, the Meaning District—off behind you. To your right is the town: the Amphitheatre, the Town Hall, the Appleseed Free Library, the Shoppes. Back behind them, but before you reach Appleseed Mountain, are the Prison and the Mental Hospital.

I wasn't born here in Appleseed. We lived off the northwest margin until I was three, and moseyed here the way most of my friends' families did, as part of the Housing Boom of '77. That year, droves of houses—two-stories, ranches, Victorian mansions, cottages—stumbled across New England, looking for a space to settle. The boom began as a murmur in Vermont and bombasted into New Hampshire and Massachusetts. Houses started crossing the Connecticut River in March of '77, marching through Greenfield, Easthampton, and Agawam. Our house walked that entire summer, carrying my family inside it every step. My parents spent all day steering from the porch while my sister Briana, who was four at the time, sat in front of the TV and I slept in my steel case.

By the time the houses reached Massachusetts, my Dad said, every major road was blocked. "The old highways were literally *clogged* with houses," he told me once, on a drive out to visit The Ear. The Ear was a handyman, like my Dad, except he always had much better tools. "What's sad is?" my Dad said. "Some of those houses—"

"Died right there on the road," said a thought lying on the couch in my mind. I'd heard this story a hundred times before.

"Died!" my Dad said. "Right on the road! Their foundations cracked from all that idling!"

"Those are the suburbs now," said the thought, shoving some crackers into its mouth.

"And they closed down the roads and made *those* the new suburbs!" my Dad said.

By the time my parents made it into the Pioneer Valley, most of the towns along Old Route Five had closed their exits. You'd see signs, my Dad said, reading NO PLOTS AVAILABLE.

"It was nervewracking," said my Dad, driving us through the Meadows. "You know how your Mom gets. And the TV antenna broke somewhere around West Springfield, so your sister was so bored."

"What about me?"

"You were," he said, "you. Quiet. Thinking in the Vox."

At three, I had not yet made a single sound—not a gurgle, not a bleep, not a screech. I used to just sit still and stare like a reader, my Mom said, with a terrified look on my face. Sometimes tears would run down my cheeks, my Dad said, but no sound would accompany them. My parents thought that I might never speak, that I was mute, that I might not have been born with a voice. My thoughts kept repeating the same words, over and over: "You won't," they'd say.

Reader: Won't *what*?

Won't anything—won't talk; won't *be*. My parents took me to see a doctorcoat who specialized in early speech, and he sent us home with something called "the Vox"—an iron-lung-type case which was designed to help with vocal development.

I remember that box—the hours, days, years lying awake inside it. Speakers inside the box filled it with sounds: squawks, yipes, zoops, words, and sentences. "The capital of North Dakota is Bismarck," the speakers would say. "B-I-S-M-A-R-C-K."

"I'm not," I thought to the Vox.

"Water freezes at thirty-two words per second.

"You live in *America*. A-M-E-R-I-C-A.

"You have one nose and two ears. Ears rhymes with years. Years rhymes with fears."

Slowly, I learned more words. "I'm lonely," I thought to the Vox.

"Everyone is lonely," the Vox replied. "At least you have the Reader."

Which was a good point.

"I want to get out of here," I prayed.

"No, you don't," said the Vox. "You wouldn't survive a year in Appleseed."

"Why not?" I prayed. "What's wrong with me?"

The Vox looked me over. "Where to even *begin*," it said.

That box became my first cage. Remember looking through the foggy glass and seeing the sunlight shouting through the window?

Reader: Who—me? I just got here. I just now arrived in Appleseed.

How I'd send my thoughts to run around the neighborhood so they could tell me what it looked like? How, sometimes, my sister would peer down through the glass at me, her curly blond hair obstructing almost all of the light?

"Help!" my thoughts would say to her.

"_____?" she'd say. "Can you hear me?"

"Get me out of here!" I'd think.

I remember my Mom's visits, too: how she'd open up the Vox to feed me food or vitamins. If there were tears on my face, she'd wipe them away. If I still didn't stop crying, she'd lift me out of the Vox and cradle me. "This is only temporary," she'd say. "OK?"

"OK," my thought would say.

Then she'd put me back into the Vox, lock it, and leave.

"We were getting desperate," my Dad said, as we neared The Ear's neighborhood. With the house inching along Five, my parents started to panic: how far would they have to go before finding a plot? "We were starting to think that we might have to live in *Connecticut*!" my Dad said.

Then, just a few miles from the Connecticut border, my house spoke up. "What about that one?" it said, and pointed to a banged-up sign. I knew that sign—it sang, APPLESEED, EST. 1775, and below it, ALL NEW WORDS MUST REGISTER AT THE TOWN HALL.

My parents had never even *heard* of Appleseed. Was it a real town? When they checked the map, though, they found the word "Appleseed"—a tiny round quell in the corner of the state.

Just at that moment, my Dad said, he and my Mom heard a sound from the other room—a "chirp," my Mom called it. They ignored it at first, but then they heard it again. My Mom once told me that it sounded like a baby bird.

They followed the sound through the house—"Chirp! Chirp!"—and into the TV room, where Briana sat next to the Vox. "What's making that sound?" my Mom asked Briana.

"That's _____," said Bri, matter-of-factly.

My parents looked at the Vox. They heard the chirp again.

"See?" said Briana.

My Dad opened the steel case. I have a foggy memory of this moment—of everyone standing over me, and of opening my mouth wide to make the biggest sound I could.

"Appa," I said.

My parents looked at each other.

"See?" said Briana.

"Appa," I said again.

"He's saying *apple*," my sister announced.

My Mom once told me that tears appeared on my father's face when I made my first sounds. My Dad, meanwhile, said my Mom ran back out to the porch and steered the house off the winding ramp and into Appleseed. "Your Mom thought it was a signal or something," my Dad said.

"So it's *my* fault we ended up here?" I said.

"It's no one's *fault*," my Dad said. "We'd just been praying for so long for you to speak. We took this as the reply."

It was another two hours of house-traffic before our house actually crossed the line into town. My Dad steered us past sentences about schools, a town hall, a town green, a small downtown, an amphitheatre, and long stretches of wilderness.

"And apple trees everywhere," my Dad said, turning onto the old dirt road where The Ear's shack stood. "So many different kinds!"

"There are different kinds of apples?" I said.

"'Course there are," he said. "Dozens. Don't you remember?"

I shook my head.

As my parents steered the house through the town, though, they became discouraged: there were plots available with FOR SALE signs on the lawns, but all of them cost far more meaning than my parents could borrow. It wasn't until they drove the house over to the Northeast Side—down Bliss Road, past Laurel Brook, and onto Converse Street—that they started to see houses in their range of meaning. The houses in that corner were shabbier, my Dad said: one had a stain on its pants; another drank from a bottle wrapped in paper.

On the far corner of that street, right across from some worryfields and the margin, was a plot marked forty thousand truths. It was the smallest piece of available land in Appleseed—the house had to scrunch up its elbows to fit on it—and still it was more meaning than my parents could afford. But that was the best option, my Dad said; it was there or back into the month-to-monthing in the margins. So my Dad picked up the FOR SALE sign, drove the house to Appleseed Town Hall and signed a Promise of Truths with an interest rate of thirty percent.

"There—Ear's abode," my Dad said, pointing to a wooden shack with a dirt driveway. "Now let's see if he's home."

"What does that mean, thirty percent?" I said.

My Dad pulled into the driveway and honked the horn. "It means," he said, "that if you borrow ten ideas, you pay back thirteen. If you borrow twenty? Pay back twenty-*six*."

"Holy crap," I said.

The Ear came out of his shack. He looked older than I remembered him; he had lambchop sideburns and some sort of skin irritation. "Ralph," he said. He peered into the cab. "Bring your assistant with you?"

"Teaching him the business," my Dad said.

"Oh yeah?" The Ear turned to me. "Going to be a landlord, like your Dad?"

"I'm going to be a movie person," I told him.

"Hoping I could borrow your steth," my Dad said to The Ear.

"Two-meter?"

"Four," said my Dad.

The Ear motioned for us to follow and we stepped out of the truck. The Ear led us into the shack. There was all sorts of recording equipment inside: tape decks, microphones, wires, and dozens of other devices I couldn't identify.

"Let's see here," The Ear said, searching in a closet. "Ah." He lifted up a black plastic case. "Four-meter steth," he said.

On the way back home, I asked my Dad more about the debt. "Weren't you worried about paying all that meaning back?" I said.

"Of course I was," he said. "I still am—I worry about it every day. But we didn't want to live on the margin anymore. Don't you remember what that was like? Moving every few months? Not really ever having a home?"

I shook my head. "I don't remember that."

"We just wanted a good place for you and your sister to grow up."

"How much do you owe on the house now?"

"All told, about a hundred thou," he said.

"Seriously?" I said.

"At the time, though, I didn't care about the meaning. I was just happy that you were out of the voice box. You just kept running around the house, saying 'Appa-seed,' 'Appa-seed.' You sang it like a song! I would have paid any amount of meaning to see you that happy," my Dad said.

NORTHERN SPY

Because of the Vox, I couldn't walk correctly for another two years; I had to wear braces on my legs to keep them straight. I remember trying to hobble through the yard, how tired my legs would get. When he had time, my Dad would take me for walks around the block to strengthen my ankles and knees.

If he was at work or busy, my sister and I would play in the yard. She'd run around with her friends on the grass while I sat in the dirt and dug holes in the page. Before we moved to town, I don't think my parents knew that most of the towns in the county dumped their deadwords in Appleseed, or that the soil was filled with dead language. I'd find all sorts of interesting bugs and deadwords there: commas, semicolons, fragments, wordbones, and other carcasses. My thoughts didn't know to be worried—they didn't understand that these vots were once as alive as the wild sentences you'd see across the street in the white woods of the margin, hopping from tree to tree. How was I to know that worry could manifest and worm its way into your mind? I couldn't even read yet!

One day, I found a deadcomma and took it over to my Mom. It was her day off from work, and she was sitting in a lawn chair, a book on her lap, a six-foot cigarette sticking out of her mouth. My sister was outside, too—sanding a wooden clock on the patio—while my father stood on a ladder, fixing a gutter.

"Appa," I said to my Mom.

"Shhh, honey," my Mom said to me, without looking up from her book.

You never knew with my Mom. Some days her eyes held calm seas, but others—like that day—they held storms.

I offered her the muddy comma—I'm sure it smelled terrible. "Appa," I said again.

"Uh-huh," my Mom said.

I put the comma on the page of my Mom's book.

"Oh, *shit*, _____," my Mom said. "Ralph!"

"Appa," I said.

"What?" my father said from the ladder.

"Look at what _____ is playing with," she said, standing up and shaking the comma off the book. She pointed to it on the ground. "He found this in the *yard*, Ralph. A fucking comma carcass, for Christ's sake!"

"Can we not swear?" my Dad said, climbing down the ladder.

I picked up the comma and walked over to him on weak legs. "Appa," I said to him.

"Do you know how many *diseases* that thing has?" my Mom said.

"Put that down, _____," said my Dad. "Those can make you sick."

"Wash _____'s hands," my Mom spat, and stormed inside.

My Dad led me over to the spout and held my hands under the freezing cold water. My Mom appeared at the kitchen window. "Did you wash his hands?" she shouted.

"Yes," he said.

"Are they clean?"

"Yeah," my Dad said.

Then my Dad led me to the back door. He tried to open it, but it was locked. "Door's locked," my Dad said.

Smoke billowed through the screen and up the side of the house.

"Diane," my Dad said.

My Mom stared out the kitchen window at us.

"Open the door," my Dad said.

My Mom took a drag on her cigarette.

I was a badseed—I knew that from the very first pages. I just couldn't be good, no matter how hard I tried. I remember, at six or so, making a trueheart sentence-gift for my Mom on the lawnpage. In the time that it took for me to go get her and bring her outside, though, the sentence changed. She read it and said, "You *loaf* me?"

"Love," I said.

"Now it says," she scanned the lawn, "*loathe*. You *loathe* me?"

I was confused. "What the heck?" said a thought. "No," I told her. "That's supposed to say—"

"How dare you," she said. "I'm your *mother!*"

• • •

Those were the years when my Mom worked long hours at the hospital. Sometimes, if my Dad was working, too, I'd have to go with her to work; she'd put me in an empty room in the hospital with some paper and paints and a snack. I wasn't supposed to leave the room until she came to get me. But my legs would hurt from sitting, and so sometimes I would step out of the room and go for walks: down the halls, over to the elevators, to other floors. Most of the time I could get back to the room before my Mom returned, but every once in a while I'd get caught. Then my Mom would punish me by giving me double the snack—dumbcrackers and sadcola—and I wasn't allowed to leave the room until I'd finished every bite.

Once, I was walking the hallways of the hospital when I saw my Mom in a room of doctors and nurses. All of their backs were turned to me, and something was screaming in the room—I didn't know what or who. When my Mom turned around there was oil on her hands. "_____!" she yelled. "What are you doing out here?"

Then I saw what was on the table: a motorcycle, its body bent and contorted. Everyone was shouting. The motorcycle screamed and then the screaming died.

"Vocal pressure's dropping," said one of the doctors.

My Mom turned to me. "Go, _____! I don't want you to see this. Get back to the room right now."

I went into the room with new thoughts. "Where did the screaming go?" one of my thoughts asked.

"I'm pretty sure it's sleeping," said another thought.

"It's not *sleeping*," said another. "That screaming died, dumbass."

"Died for how long?" asked the second thought.

"Forever," said the first thought. "It's dead."

I turned to the hospital bed. "Have people *died* on you?" I asked it.

"What do you mean?" said the bed. "Of course they have."

"A lot?" I said.

"Hundreds," said the bed. "That's my job, to be died on."

A few days later, I was in my room in the hospital when I rolled up my sleeve, opened the tube of yellow paint, and poured it on my arm. Then I walked out to the nurse's station. My Mom was smoking a six-foot cigarette and talking with another nurse.

"I've had an accident," I announced.

My Mom looked up at me. "Go back in the room, _____," she said.

I held out my arm. "I'm bleeding."

"That's *paint*," she said.

"I'm bleeding yellow," I said.

"You better not have spilled any paint in that room," she said. "Did you?" She rushed out from behind the desk, grabbed me by my yellow arm, and marched me back to the room. Then she studied the walls and the floor. "I better not see one *drop* of yellow paint in here."

"People have died in this room!" I announced.

"Wash off your arm," my Mom said. Then she slammed the door.

As I was rinsing my arm off in the sink, I noticed a supply cabinet underneath. When I opened the drawers I found cotton balls, wooden sticks, bandages, and a pair of scissors. I pulled out the scissors; they blinked their eyes in the light. "What year is it?" they asked me.

"Nineteen eighty-six," I told them.

"*Eighty*-six?" they said.

"Can you help me?" I said.

"Help you how?" the scissors said.

"I want you to cut me," I told them.

The scissors studied my face. "Why?" they said.

"Just do it. Cut me," I told them.

Two minutes later I walked out of the room again. This time there was blood on my wrist, dripping down my hand. "I'm injured," I said. I held out my arm.

None of the nurses responded. My Mom was sitting with a patient—a heavy woman with gray toiled skin— and wrapping a blood-pressure cuff around her arm.

"I'm bleeding," I said.

"Go back to the room, _____," said my Mom.

"I'm injured," I said.

"Sal," my Mom said to another nurse. "Can you check on him?"

"You do it," I said to my Mom. "You check on me."

"Sal?"

Another nurse came over to me, crouched down, and saw my wrist. "Jesus, _____," she said. She called my Mom over. When she saw the blood, her face norsed and all of the color drained from it. "What did you do, _____?" my Mom said. I remember how her hands shook as she wrapped the bandages around my arm and said, "How did this happen?"

SENTENCE THE SENTENCE

GLOCKENAPFEL

One night when I was eleven, though, one of my thoughts—
a thought of green—thought over to the Hu Ke Lau ("Puke-
E-Lau," we called it) while I slept. At last call my thought
hopped off his bar stool, pushed through the heavy doors,
dropped his skateboard on the sidewalk and thought across
the parking lot. He waved goodbye to some friendthoughts
at the bike rack and then coasted past the snoring stores—
the Big Why, Bagel Beagle—when car headlights suddenly
grazed his shoulder. The thought of green turned around
and studied the car: an old, brown Plymouth Duster with a
number 8 behind the wheel. As my thought was watching,
the number 8 changed into a B.

The thought darkened to a deeper shade of green. At
home in my basement bedroom, I turned over in my sleep.

Shrugging off the worry, my thought turned around
and pushed the skateboard toward home—down Grassy
Gutter Boulevard and onto Apple Hill Road. When he
looked back over his shoulder, though, he saw the round
lights of the Duster still behind him. Was that car *following*
him? He stopped his skateboard and stared into the wind-
shield. He saw a flash in the B's eye.

The thought custom-swore and sped up, skating down

Apple Hill and then a quick left onto Coventry—a short-cut. When he looked back again, he didn't see the Duster. He took a few deep breaths and slowed down, coasting down Coventry and back toward its intersection with Apple Hill. When he hit the corner, though, the thought saw the Duster's lights again. The driver gunned the engine. The thought bore down, hauling toward the intersection with Converse, the car's bumper inches from the skateboard's tail. Emerald green. Military green. When he saw the backyard of my house through the trees, the thought jumped off the board and sprinted—through the grass, over the bushes, into the yard. The driver stopped the car, jumped out, stretched into a single line—a ⌒ —and slithered after the thought.

The thought slid across the hatchway and dove through the open basement window. Then he turned and looked back at the figure on the lawn. Standing upright at the edge of the patio, the figure changed shape from an ! to a ? to an &. Then it grinned, straightened out, and dove into the ground.

The thought shut the window and thought across the room, back into my ear. I sniffed in my sleep—I was dreaming of green.

NEWTON WONDER

Once I began to talk I wouldn't shut up. It was like my thoughts had stored all of those words I'd heard in the Vox, and now that I'd figured out how to translate them from my ears to my mouth, I couldn't stop making language. At four or five, even, I'd walk around all week repeating one word. "One week it was *sundry*," my sister told me once. "Sundry Sunday and sundry Monday and sundry Friday. Sundry socks and sundry macaroni and cheese. It was so *annoying*."

Then, in the fourth grade, I roykoed this habit—a "nervous tic," my Mom called it—of repeating anything anyone said. I couldn't help it—the words I heard mirrored themselves in my mouth and resounded without my even thinking about it. I'd be sitting in Mrs. Trombly's fourth-grade class when the dialogue would start to form on my tongue. "Turn to page twenty-two," Mrs. Trombly announced one day, while her white-blond wig pointed to words on the chalkboard, "and you'll find a study guide for tomorrow's quiz."

"Tomorrow's quiz," I muttered from my seat.

"I'm sorry, _____?"

"_____?" I said.

"Did you have something to add?"

"Something to add?" I said.

The class laughtracked.

"Stop that," said Mrs. Trombly.

"Stop that!" I said.

"That's it. Detention! After school!"

"Detention! After school!" I shouted.

Detention, in our school, was a series of cages. The usual detention terms were two weeks for tardiness and three weeks for an outburst. I got *four* weeks for mimicking Mrs. Trombly. "Shit, man," asked the cage during week two of my sentence. "What did you do?"

"Shit, man," I said.

"Seriously," said the cage.

"Seriously," I said.

"Stop it," said the cage.

"Stop it," I said.

When detentions didn't curb the behavior, the school convinced my parents to send me to a special quietschool—Appleseed Silence Academy—three afternoons a week. I was there in Principal Booth's office when he suggested the idea to my parents. "_____'s teachers concur," said the phone booth, "that he's something of a pest."

"Excuse me?" said my Mom.

"That was Mrs. Bowe's word," said the principal—who was, as his name said, a phone booth. Booth opened up a folder and showed my parents a sheet of paper. "See, _____'s creativity scores are very high. But emotionally?" He held up a piece of paper.

My Dad looked at my Mom.

"How dare you," my Mom said to the phone booth.

I sat there in my chair, drawing on the soles of my Converse hi-tops.

"We don't advocate total silence as a rule," said Principal Booth, adjusting his toupee. "But we *are* trying to teach verbal *control*."

"Control," my Mom said.

"That's why I'm suggesting Silence School," said the phone booth.

"_____ doesn't need lessons in silence," my Mom said. "He was in a Vox for the first three years of his life!"

"Which may be why he's having trouble, actually," Booth said. "He's overcompensating."

"How much meaning is it?" my Dad asked.

"Silence School?" Principal Booth told him the cost.

"Total?" said my Dad.

"Per month," said the phone booth.

My Dad took off his thick glasses and rubbed his eyes.

The Academy was located up on Homicki Hill. It was built to house a small group of silent bessoffs who supposedly prayed, silently, every moment of the day.

I only ever saw one or two bessoffs my entire time there, though—the classes I attended were in the classrooms toward the front of the building. In a lot of ways it was like regular school—they still chained you to the desk with math, and all the clocks were dead or dying—except that the only lesson was silence. The teacher, a giant feather boa, wrote *SHUT UP!* in big bold letters on the blackboard, and every day she'd create new prompts designed to challenge our ability to keep quiet. Once, she brought in an entire pizza from Red Rose, ate one slice, and then asked all of us if we wanted any. If we answered, we were punished with an additional week of classes. Another time she showed us a video disc of *Decision Man* and stopped it right before the final battle with the Multiple Choices. If you shouted for her to continue the movie—to finish the story? More classes.

I really struggled in Silence School. One day, the boa walked up to my desk and asked me a direct question. "_____, what is the brightest spot in Appleseed?"

I knew I was supposed to just sit there quietly, so that's what I did. But when I didn't respond, the bright purple boa put her hands on her feathery hips. "You live in Appleseed, _____, and you don't know the brightest spot?"

Of course I did—it was Fialky's Worryfields! I rocked back and forth in my seat.

"Wow, _____," said the boa. "And I thought you were smart."

"It's Fialky's Worryfields!" I said. "Everyone knows that!"

The boa slammed her fist down on my desk.

One afternoon a few days later, the boa ordered us to practice writing as quietly as we could. That's what had landed several of these students in Silence School in the first place: their writing—either the sound of the pen on the page, or the noise of the words themselves—was too loud, and their teachers couldn't take it anymore. That afternoon, we were focusing on the art of saying nothing, in words, on the page. The boa walked from row to row, looking over everyone's writing. When she reached my desk she stopped. "Today is nice," I'd scrawled on the page.

The boa held up a lavender finger. "But *nice* has some meaning, doesn't it?"

I stared at her.

"It's not negative. It's actually quite positive!" she barked. "These words should say *nothing*, people!"

A few minutes later, a call came in on the classroom phone and the boa had to go down to the office. She left us writing silent sentences. As soon as she was gone, one of the erasers jumped down from the chalkboard, sidled over to me, and hopped onto my desk. "Ey," he said.

"You got chalk on my page," I whispered to him.

"Listen," said the eraser. "I can't sit up there watching you fuck up over and over. All she wants is for you to shut up. To just *not talk*. Why can't you do that?"

"It's my thoughts. I don't even know that I'm saying the words."

"Just take all the things you want to say and store them."

I thought about this. "Store them for when?"

The eraser furrowed his brow. "What do you mean?"

"When do I *say* them?"

"You *don't* say them, ever," said the eraser. "Just keep them in your mind."

Then we heard the boa's heels clack–echoing through the halls; the eraser dropped off the desk and scurried back up to the blackboard just as the boa stepped into the room. On her way up to the front of the room, the boa walked past my desk. She looked at my page, where I'd written "Today is the day after yesterday."

She pointed to the sentence. "That still has meaning!"

I studied the words.

"You're still saying *something* about today!" she shouted.

I looked at the eraser. He put his finger to his lips.

I didn't say a word all the next day. When I walked out to the bike racks after school, I saw Large Odor unlocking his Haro. "Yo," he said. "That Trombly is a bitch, isn't she?"

I shrugged.

"You don't think so?" said Odor.

I shrugged again. When my thoughts made words, I put the words in drawers in cabinets in my mind. When the cabinets were full, I emptied them out into mental plastic garbage bags. Soon my skull was full of garbage bags of words.

I don't know if this is related, but it was shortly after that—shortly after I started holding my tongue, or "maturing," as my Mom called it—that I began to lose my hair. It also might have been a long-term effect of the Vox, which was taken off the market in 1980 after it was found to cause numerous side effects (hair loss among them).

Anyway, that was the year—fifth grade—that I went bald. My hair came off in all one clump one day. I was riding my skateboard and my hair—whoosh!—just fell off my head. I hopped off the board, backtracked until I found the hair, and stuck it back on my head. It wouldn't stay on my skull, though—it just fell right off again. I had to hold the hair in place as I skated home.

I tried everything I could to keep my hair: baseball hats, chin straps, glue. But it just wouldn't stay. It had made up its mind to leave, and there wasn't anything I could do to convince it otherwise.

There wasn't any goodbye party for my hair—it didn't want one. Two weeks after it fell off my skull, I put it on a small hairboat and pushed it off into the Connecticut River. My hair looked back, waved, and paddled away.

I missed it like crazy. I wrote my hair letters and prayed to it. "I know you're busy," I said in my prayer, "but please let me know how you're doing when you can."

"I'm good—great, actually," my hair prayed back. "And you?"

"Just OK," I said.

"It's beautiful here," my hair prayed. "I'm working at a radio station."

"What radio station?"

My hair prayed the call letters but I didn't recognize them. "I doubt you can get it where you are," prayed the hair. "Anyway, I don't make a lot of meaning, but I really like it. The people are so nice."

"That sounds so awesome," I prayed.

"And I'm renting a house near the beach."

"Cool," I prayed. "Maybe I could come visit."

"Maybe sometime, sure," said my hair.

I guess I always thought that my hair would come back to its life in Appleseed—that it and I would reunite at some point. But that was an invention on my part. One day I prayed to my hair and the hair didn't answer. I tried praying again a week later and the prayer channel had been closed—my prayer went right to an operator. "I'm trying to reach my hair," I prayed to the operator.

"That prayer channel has been shut down," the operator said.

"Is there a forwarding channel?"

"I'm sorry, there isn't," prayed the operator.

So I stopped praying to my hair. When I got older, I understood. That hair had its own life to lead, a whole world to see, while I was stuck here in this tiny town, the sun laughing off my pate.

THE APPLESEED FLEA MARKET

How I miss those Sunday mornings in Appleseed, the applesun rising over Mount Epstein, my father and sister and I already out the door, in my father's truck, on the hunt: on our way to an estate sale, a tag sale, or the Appleseed Flea Market. I've searched every corner of my mind for an unread page with a flea market on it, but with no luck: once a page is read, it can't be unread; once the past has passed it's gone. Still, I can go back in my mind to those quiet streets, the morning chatter of my thoughts, the cough of the dashboard and squeal of the struts as we roared down Highway Five.

My father's truck wasn't like other trucks—it was a strange metaphor of a vehicle, assembled from pieces and parts of other cars. It was asymmetrical, and it had a porch, a beak, and one eye. And it was controlled entirely by ropes. The steering panel reminded me of the wings of an old theater; it contained pulleys, and lever-locks, and complicated hemp ropes running in every direction. One rope was the go-rope; another rope was for turning. You pulled a rope over your head to beep the horn; the seat belt was a rope; the emergency brake was a rope attached to some sandbags stored above the back axle.

My father might have worked different jobs—insurance, real estate, solitudor—but at his applecore he was a collector. He loved finding old stranges, odd forgottens, hardly-brokens—uncovering life among the dead; going to great lengths to save something that someone else had dismissed; spotting meaning that other people looked past. He'd carry around a thrown-away clipboard with lists of items he was looking for: *Doorknob for 2D*, or, *Spare casters?*, or, *BX cable.* Every building he worked on was filled with re-remembered lamp fixtures, whitebearded sinks, ghosty carpets, finickal lightswitches that he'd found or traded with someone. My Dad took the same approach to every expense—everything was recontextualized, almost-but-not-quite broken, hanging on by a thread. All my clothes came from Goodwill, which meant that I was perpetually out of fashion: I wore bandannas when bicycling hats were in vogue; parachute pants during the stonewashed-jeans fad; unmatched Converse hi-tops (one yellow, one *purple*) when my friends were wearing Eastman boat shoes with the laces tied in twisty-knots; jampants and concert T-shirts when everyone wore izods with the collars turned up. At least my Mom took us to the thrift stores, though. My Dad's clothes? Were the *memories* of clothes. He wore shoes he'd found in a dumpster, glasses that had belonged to a cousin of his who'd died.

One of my Dad's many talents, though, was networking. He knew all the wheeler-dealers in Appleseed—The Ear, Glen Ukulele, Don La Valley, Armin LaFlame, Murphy, Jack D'elnero—and he worked with all of them in one way or another. He always knew who to go to for help with a repair, to borrow a tool, to find a used strow or a deal on a belloy. He always talked about one day opening an antique store, a knickknack spot, a trading post. Then every day would be Sunday, he'd say. For all three of us, Sundays felt free.

My sister Briana inherited my Dad's talents. As far back as I can remember, she was his assistant—my Dad always said she had a great eye for meaning. When she was ten, Briana's favorite hobby was collecting and refinishing furniture. Then she switched to collecting raw materials—copper tubing and wire, scrap steel—which she'd trade at Appleseed Salvage. Later, she taught herself about electricity: she could repair a light fixture, wire up a three-way switch or a fuse box, fix a garage door opener or the ignition on a heater.

I wasn't that smart—I just liked going along for the ride. Sundays were one of the only times of the week when I didn't feel lonely, when I wasn't consciously aware of how few friends—*real* friends, I mean—I had.

Reader: What about your Mom? Did she go with you?

Hardly ever, actually. She was either working an overnight at the hospital or at home, training in the gym she'd set up in the garage. She looked forward to Sundays, too, though, because she loved having the house to herself. Sometimes my Mom would joke that maybe she should live in another house, separate from our house, "where I can train in peace and quiet," she snorted.

"Train for what?" I asked her once, and she sort of glared at me.

"I'm just kidding—you know that," she said.

When my Mom wasn't working or training, she would

read. Sometimes I'd read next to her. We wouldn't talk—my Mom would smoke, and sometimes I would eat chips—but I guess I thought I could connect to my mother *through* the books, if that makes any sense.

Anyway, it was usually just the three of us on Sundays. And every trip to the flea market began the same way: my Dad steered the truck past the tables toward a parking spot while my sister scanned the tables for any potential deals. "Aisle—*five*," my sister said one Sunday. " 'Bout halfway back."

"The mirror?"

"The bureau."

"Is that oak?" My Dad said.

"I can't tell," my sister said.

Then we'd park the truck in the fields and the two of them would go charging through the grass toward the bureau.

I went off on my own, meanwhile, looking for used books. I'm not talking about the bound brochures they forced you to read in school—the pages that made a sucking sound when you looked at them, that made your eyes sting and your ears echo. I'm talking about true mysteries and war stories like the ones that you could buy for a theory or two or sometimes even find for free at the Appleseed Recycling Center. It's weird: until I was twelve or so, I couldn't have cared less about books or reading. One afternoon that winter, though, I found a truebook on a low shelf in our living room. The book was called *The Appleseed Strangler*. I remember opening it up, seeing all the words trapped there on the page, and feeling an affinity for them. Holding in so many words, I *myself* sometimes felt like a book—like a cage for sentences.

As I was sprawled out on the living-room floor that day, reading about the Appleseed Strangler, a shadow flashed across the carpet. It was my Mom. "Good story, huh?" she said.

I didn't say anything.

"Wait until you get to the end—the hanging," she said.

Two days later my Mom took me to the Appleseed Free Library, where she signed me up for a card and let me check out two books of my choice. Ever since, I'd collected and read as many books as I could find: murder mysteries, histories, histrionics, fallbacks, toronados, you name it.

One day, though, I was sitting next to my Mom at the Library and reading a fallback when I saw a sentence on the page itch itself. "Woah!" I said.

"What?" she hissed.

"That sentence just *moved*!" I said.

My Mom scorned. She had this one particular scorn that she saved just for me: her whole face squinted, like she was staring into a fierce wind.

"There it goes again!" I said. "It just *changed*, from—"

"_____," she hissed. "Be *quiet*. You're embarrassing m—"

"Now it's running off the page!"

She grabbed the book from me, closed it, and led me down the red-carpeted stairs and outside. And that was the last time she took me to the Library.

I still continued going to the Library myself, though. When I wasn't kicking around commas or other dead language out back, I spent almost all of my free time reading in my room in the basement. That basement was dark and cold, and the reading helped me keep warm.

Most of the books in the Library were old, though; for newer trues, the flea bee was a much better bet. All of the local dealers set up tables: Psyches from the Rebel Peddler, Old Gordon from Appleseed Books, Kathy from Sue's Mysteries, Del from Wilbur's. They brought bestsellers, overstocks, oddities, you name it. And since I stopped by every week, all of them knew me by name.

Sometimes, though, you found the best fleabooks at the occasionals: a hey who just liked to read; a forget with some swashbidders that they found in the attic and just want to unload. As I was scanning the tables for titles that day, for example, I saw a pig in a van pulling boxes out of his truck. Most of the boxes held tools and old board games, but some of the boxes had books in them. I looked through them, pretending to be only mildly interested. In my skull, though, my thoughts were shouting. "Look— warbooks!" one said. "There's a self-help!" said another. "And a historical!" said a third.

I held up a book called *The Absolutely True Story of the Northampton-Appleseed War.* "How much for this one?" I said.

The pig was sweating; he winced as he stood. "Two theories for the hardcovers, one for paperbacks," he said.

"Take one and a half?"

He thought about it. Then he said, "Sure."

I tried to keep my thoughts cool as I paid the pig and walked away from the table, but I was thrilled. I loved warbooks—the wars' personal lives, their political leanings, their dispositions. Wars were mysteries to me, even though I used to see them frequently in Appleseed.

Reader: Wars? In Appleseed?

Sure—you saw them all the time. Most of them were quiet, some so subtle you wouldn't even know they were there unless you were looking for them. Once, maybe about a year later, I was waiting for my Mom at the hair salon when I noticed a war sitting under one of the hair dryers a few seats over. She was knitting, and when I looked over she smiled politely.

"What are you knitting?" I said.

"A graveyard," said the war.

Then my Mom stood up from the hairdresser's chair, studied her buzz cut in the mirror, and told me we were leaving.

I found my sister and father on the other side of the flea—they were carrying the heavy bureau toward the truck. "What'd you find, _____?" said my Dad.

I held up my book.

"Grab a corner, will you?" my sister asked.

I put my book under my arm and took a corner of the bureau. Trying to fit in, I said, "Is this oak?"

"Duh," said my sister.

"Bri," said my Dad. "Be nice. It *is* oak, _____."

We moved the bureau onto the bed of the truck; then we got in the cab and drove toward the exit. It was later now, seven a.m. or so, and more people were arriving. By now, my Dad would say, all the deals were gone—everything meaningful had already been bought or traded.

My Dad steered the truck onto the dirt road. "Gus and Paul's?" he said.

"Or Bagel Beagle," I said.

"Gus and Paul's," my sister said.

"OK, _____?" said my Dad.

"Sure," I said.

We drove through West Appleseed and five pages east to Gus & Paul's, the best bakery in town. As we bumped along the city streets, I leaned my head against the cold window and read the first pages of my truebook.

The hallowed mystery of the Northampton-Appleseed War still bellows in the pause of night. While the war itself was originally believed to have died in truce in 1965, most now believe that to be a hoax. Some say the war moved to Shelburne Falls and died there, under an assumed name, in 1979. Others say the war still lives down in the Quabbin or high on Appleseed Mountain. This book offers no speculations as to the war's current whereabouts. Rather, *The Absolutely True Story of the Northampton-Appleseed War* chronicles the facts: when the war began, why, where he was last seen, what those who knew him say about his personality, his love life, and his groundbreaking philosophies—his unique way of looking at the world.

Gus & Paul's was humming with activity—it seemed like all of Appleseed was there. We stood in line for twenty minutes before finally stepping up to the glass case. "A dozen water rolls," my Dad said to the fluffy hat behind the counter, "and whatever these guys want."

The fluffy hat moved over to the glass case.

"Cider Creme, please," Briana said.

"_____?" said my Dad.

Everything looked so delicious. "I'll take one of those," I said, "and one of those, and one of those."

"One thing only, Fatty," my sister said, nudging me.

I looked to my Dad. "Can I get two?" I said.

It wasn't until years later that I put apple and seed together: that I realized how meaningless we were. I didn't know, for example, that my Dad skipped lunch all those years; that he had to beg his own truck to get him to work sometimes; that he'd borrowed meaning, by that point, from everyone he knew.

"Whatever he wants," my Dad told the hat, and I pointed to pastry after pastry. The hat collected them in a brown box, tied them with a small white string, and handed the box over the counter. I reached up for the box and took it.

SENTENCE THE SENTENCE

Sentence was my friend, probably my *only* true friend through the mothering, the forging—most of my high school years, really. Everyone has their pet expressions, but Sentence was something more. For a long time, that expression was the only thing that really understood me.

I found Sentence while working with my father at Belmont, one of the two apartment buildings that he owned and managed. He bought them in the early 1980s, during a meaningful time in Appleseed when the town still ran on apples. Led by the Memory of Johnny Appleseed himself, who once lived and groved here, Appleseed's apple industry thrived; we sold apple pies, apple cider, appleburgers, applefish, apple chicken, apple pad thai, even apple *art* made from cores and stems. Something like ninety percent of all the apples in Massachusetts were grown in Appleseed, and people came from all over New England in search of meaning in the apple trade.

My father didn't know the first thing about apples, but he was a skilled handyman, trained by his father—the Rabbit Eater—in the arts of tenancy and the mysteries of landlording. When we first moved to Appleseed, my Dad worked as a caretaker for a local moustache, answering service calls—heating, plumbing, maintenance—for any one of nine apartment buildings in the downtown. Then the moustache went gray and started selling off his property, and my Dad took out a second mortgage on our house to buy the two least meaningful buildings of the lot. It was a risk—they were located in an iffy neighborhood—but my Dad hoped to translate sweat into meaning.

It didn't turn out that way, though; the buildings were more stubborn and mysterious than he'd bargained for. Drunk plumbing, missing rooms, snoring wires, you name it—tenants called with problems at all hours of the night. Remember that story I told you a few streets back, about driving to The Ear's house?

Reader: Sure. To get a "stetch" or something.

A *steth*—a four-meter foundation stethoscope, which we needed to investigate a strange scratching sound coming from the foundation of Woodside. When my Dad put the listener against the rock, though, he frowned and swore. "Christ," he said. "Something in the soil."

"What?" I asked.

He put the headphones over my ears. I heard a steady scratching. "What is that?" I said.

My Dad shook his head.

"Termites?"

One of the whatevers burped in my ear.

"Those would be some big fucking termites," my Dad said.

My Dad prayed to Armin, an exterminator who'd work for meaning under the table, and he tested the soil all around Woodside. After studying the page fibers, Armin declared the problem to be doubts.

"Sorry?" said my Dad, as we stood on the page.

"Doubts," Armin said.

"Doubts, are you sure?"

Armin nodded. "You know what's funny? I've been getting more and more of these calls."

My Dad raised an eyebrow. "I have trouble believing that."

"It's true," said Armin.

Armin had to instill the soil with confidence, which cost a shitload. And that was just one of dozens of mysteries and problems that stumped my father. The buildings were just too much for him to manage alone. Soon he started paying his brother Joump to help him with odd jobs. He enlisted me and my sister, too. My father taught me some of the basic hows—insulation, foyer mediation, missing room listening—but like I said, my sister was the one with the real talent. She really immersed herself in it, reading truebooks on wainscoting and ancient plastering techniques, learning special chants for plumbing and lighting and landscaping, mastering all of the old building arts.

Anyway, I'm getting off track—I was telling you about Sentence the sentence. One day when I was about twelve, my Dad and I were patching up some stucco at Belmont when I saw this eager statement reading through the grass. "Hey," I said to it, but my Dad stood up and imposed over it. "Shoo!" he said.

"Hey, buddy," I said to the sentence.

"Git!" my Dad yelled. "You git! Git out of here!"

The sentence skimmed off.

"Dad! What the hell?" I said.

"It's a stray, _____," my Dad said. "It's just begging for food."

"I have some seconds for it," I said.

"Don't even think about it," said my Dad. "What have I told you about feeding wild sentences?"

This was in 1987, when stray language was everywhere in Appleseed. I know that's hard to believe now—now that every word is counted, and counted on, and counted toward—but in those days it wasn't strange to see verbing on Epstein Street, infinitives running through the dead-groves. Growing up in Appleseed, you were taught how to respond to wild language. If you saw a semicolon, you paused for a second. If you saw a preposition, you let it pass by you—to the left, or to the right, or over your head.

My Dad couldn't come with me to Belmont the next day—he had to go see Fox, a master welder in the western margin—so I went back to Belmont myself. When I got there, the Memory of Johnny Appleseed was cutting the grass using an old manual mower. My Dad had a gas-powered one in the basement, but the Memory liked this one. For a while, I could hear the swishy blades of the mower as the Memory shoved it forward. Then he finished, put the mower away, and walked off.

I was adding a third coat of stucco, though, when I felt the breath of words on my ankle. I turned and saw the sentence looking up at me.

"Hey there," I said. I petted the sentence, and it made

a sound. I could tell from its words and its eyes that it meant me no harm. Hark, it was only a newborn—just a subject and a verb: "I am." That was the whole sentence!

I reached into my pocket and found some seconds and minutes—timecrumbs I carried with me just in case I was late or my thoughts wandered. The sentence leaned in and ate right out of my palm. The poor thing was starving! It finished the seconds and sort of stumbled toward me. Suddenly, I was holding the sentence in my arms.

What was I supposed to do—push it away? Abandon it? These words would die out here. Who would feed them and read them if not for me?

I held "I am." in my arms while I packed up my tools. Then I sat the sentence on the handlebars of my Bicycle Built for Two and started pedaling home. "Hold on tight!" I told the sentence, and it did—it squinted its eyes as the wind ran through its "I" and "a."

I got back to 577 just as my Dad's pickup was turning into the driveway. I hopped off the bike and wrapped the sentence in my coat. My Dad stepped out of the truck and slammed the door. "Well?" he said.

"Hi," I said.

The sentence was making noises: whimpers and nouns.

"Djou finish?" my Dad said.

"Yup," I said.

"It doesn't need another layer?"

"I don't—" The sentence started bucking and kicking. "Don't think so," I said.

"It either does or it doesn't," my Dad said.

Just then, the sentence kicked me in the stomach and I

lost my grip on it. The words leapt out of my coat and ran across the driveway and onto the grass.

"Whoa!" my Dad said, leaping back. He stepped into the grass and leaned over the quivering words. "Goddammit, _____," he said. "What did I say?"

"I know," I said.

"*What* did I say?"

"It was hungry!"

"You *fed* it?" my Dad said. "You *never* feed stray language. It won't leave you alone now!"

The sentence looked up at my father, and then at me.

"I'll take care of it," I said.

"What do you mean?" said my Dad. "As a *pet*? No. _____. No."

"I'll walk it and feed it."

"Feed it what?"

"Minutes," I said.

"And keep it where?"

"I'll keep it in the basement."

"It'll shit and piss all over the place," my Dad said.

"I'll make sure that it doesn't."

"You know your mother has a strict no-language-in-the-house policy," said my Dad.

"It won't make a *sound*—I promise."

My Dad sighed. "What about the smell?"

"It doesn't *have* a smell," I said.

"All language smells," he said. "I can smell that thing from here—it *stinks* of adjectives."

"I'll keep it clean," I said.

The sentence read over to me and stopped at my heel.

"Shee-it," my Dad said, and shook his head.

That afternoon he took me to Brightwood Hardware, which had a pet store in the basement, to buy some supplies for the sentence: a cage, a collar, a leash. When we browsed the aisles for food, though, we didn't see anything. My Dad found a clip-on tie stocking shelves and asked him if the store carried any food for words.

"For *what*?" said the tie. He was old and faded.

"Food for sentences?" my Dad said, and I held up "I am."

"I don't think we—" the tie looked confused. "Let me—I'll check." He disappeared behind a curtain and never came back.

We ended up buying dry dog food and a cage intended for a rabbit. Then we put it all in the truck and drove home.

That night, I put the cage in the basement and "I am." curled up in the corner and went to sleep. In the middle of the night, though, I woke up to a howling and rattling. I turned on the light and "I am." was ramming his head into the cage.

"'I am.'," I said. "Stop."

My Dad walked in, his hair exclaiming, and stared down at the cage.

"Stop, 'I am.'!" I shouted.

"This is what I was talking about, _____," my Dad said. "You're lucky your Mom's working an overnight."

"What's going on?" said Bri from the top stair.

"I am." howled.

"Why's it doing that?" Bri said.

61

I picked up the sentence. It was whimpering and shivering. "It's just scared," I said.

"You're going to spoil it, and then it won't listen to a thing you say," my Dad said.

Around five that morning, "I am." finally fell asleep. It woke up three hours later, which was right before my Mom usually got home from her overnight shifts. I fed it and took it for a walk. When I saw the Cloudy Fart—my Mom's crappy, sky-blue station wagon—ambling down Converse, I picked "I am." up and ran inside. My Dad met us in the breezeway. "Don't say I didn't warn you," he said.

My Mom walked in wearing her nurse's uniform and smoking a six-foot cigarette. "Hey," she said. She put down her purse and took off her coat. Then she saw us standing there. "What?" she said.

"Your son here has something to show you," my Dad said.

"Now what?" she said.

I held Sentence out to her.

"Wait—what is that?" my Mom said. She walked closer. "Is that language?" Smoke poured out of her face. "What's it doing in the house, Ralph?"

"_____ found it at the building and fed it," my Dad said.

"You *fed* it?" said my Mom. She looked down at the cage by my feet. "Get it out of here. Get it out of here right now."

My Dad bowed his head. "I told him—"

"Wait a minute," my Mom said, looking at Sentence's collar. "No. You didn't, Ralph. You didn't."

"His name is Sentence," I said, "but he's called 'I am.'"

"_____ promises it won't be any trouble," said my Dad. "We bought it a cage to sleep in, a leash, the whole nine yards."

My Mom stormed toward my father, grabbed him by the chin, and pushed him against the wall. "How *dare* you. After all the work I've done? You bring infested words inside—invite *bookworms* into our house?"

"What's a bookworm?" I said.

"I figured," my Dad said, rubbing his elbow, "it's just two words—"

"'I am.' is *not* infested," I said.

"Into *our house?*" my Mom said.

"It's positive, though," my Dad stammered.

Sentence smiled.

"See?" my Dad said. "It's not a bookworm."

My Mom shoved my Dad backward and looked him up and down. "You wouldn't know it if it *was*," she hissed.

THE MARGINALS

HOWGATE WONDER

Ever since my days in the Vox my thoughts had wandered. During the day, they'd open up the top of my head, slip off my ears, vault off my shoulders, and hop away; at night, they'd sleepthink without bound, all through Appleseed: they'd roil out to the Hu Ke Lau, where ex-Cones sat at the bar husking regrets; jump the fence at the Appleseed Recycling Center to rummage through Memories; climb up Appleseed Mountain in the dark and get lost in paragraphs of wilderness; skateboard down Old Highway Five; vault forward into the future, back into the past, into the margin and beyond into the ifs: what *might* be, what *could* be, what *should* be but won't. They'd bring back stories of their travels—adventures, struggles, strange characters and unnamed objects (machines that grew hair!, chatterglass!, an underground cone society!)—from places and worlds I never heard of.

Once, one of my thoughts fought in a war and returned with a bullet in its knee. I woke up my parents in the middle of the night. When I shook my Mom, she sat up in bed and punched the air. "What is it?" she volted.

"I think we need to go to the emergency room," I told her.

"What's wrong?" she said.

"One of my thoughts has a gunshot wound," I told her.

"One of—what?"

"My thoughts," I said. "Just back from the war."

My Mom turned over and went back to sleep.

"Mom!" I said.

"Go back to sleep, _____," my Dad muttered.

So I dressed the wound myself. As I wrapped the thought's leg in mental gauze, I thought, "What happened to the other thought?"

"I killed it," said the thought.

"How?"

"With my bayonet," he said. And then he held up a mental bayonet, covered in a blue liquid.

What's that blue stuff? I wondered.

"The thoughtblood of my enemy," said the thought.

That thought recovered, but it was just one in a legion of thoughts who wandered into—or sometimes went *looking* for—trouble. Sometimes they made it difficult for me to concentrate; I made mistakes when working with my Dad at the buildings, and I was *always* getting detention in school. After a while, I didn't mind it—I'd sit in whatever cage they put me in. I always carried a few deadwords in my pocket for just that occasion. In a cage, I could spend days on a single phrase: I'd take apart the expression, the words, the letters themselves.

Then, in the spring of '88, something terrible happened. I woke up one morning and a thought of sidewalks was sitting at my desk. His skin was pale and there were rings under his eyes. "What is it?" I said.

"Something—terrible," he said.

"Show me," I said.

He led me out the window and down onto the driveway. I unlocked my Bicycle Built for Two and the thought leapt onto the handlebars. I took the front seat and the Reader got on the back. "Where to?" I said.

The thought pointed east. "Heights," he said.

Appleseed Heights was a new condominium development down by the east edge of town. A year earlier that area had all been wilderness. Now, Orange Traffic Cones were driving yellow bulldozers in there and knocking down the trees. The trees were holding protests, singing songs, fighting back. Every week there was news of another tree/bulldozer scuffle. The week prior, a bulldozer had been jumped by a bunch of trees and a rumble had ensued.

As we approached, I saw Orange Traffic Cones standing in a triangle right off the road. Some of the Cones were holding fluorescent tape; others were kneeling around a thought-shaped chalk outline.

When I rode the Bicycle Built for Two up to them, I saw what they were kneeling over: a dead thought. *My* dead thought, a thought of the future, bleeding into the sienna dirt.

A dented Cone with a moustache held up his orange rubbery arm. "Nothing to see here," he said.

"That's his thought," said the Reader. "He's the thinker."

The Cone's eyes darkened.

"How did he—" I said. I began to cry. "What happened?"

The Cone crossed his arms. "He was—there was a—"

Another Cone approached. "You the thinker?" he asked me.

I nodded.

"Thought was mauled," said the Cone.

"By what?" said the thought of sidewalks.

The Cone shook his head. "We're not sure," he said. "We'll know more after the thoughtopsy. Did he have any enemies that you know of?"

I shook my head and wiped my face. "He was such a kind and thoughtful. Into surfing and meditation. He wouldn't have thought about hurting the thought of a *fly*."

"Sometimes a thought leads a double life," suggested the Cone.

I shook my head again. "Not this one," I said.

The following week I held a funeral in my mind. All of my available thoughts attended. I held it on a Wednesday morning. The body of the thought was displayed in a coffin, and all my thoughts walked past it and thought about praying.

Outside my skull, meanwhile, I was in algebra class. The teacher, a hairy plus sign, was drawing some bullshit on the board. "This makes Y equal—who knows the answer?"

The thought's mother ambled up to the coffin and collapsed in tears.

"_____," said the hairy plus sign.

"My boy," said the motherthought. "My son."

"Y equals?" said the plus sign.

The fatherthought consoled his ex-wife.

"Earth to _____. What does Y equal?"

But I couldn't answer, because it was that part of the service where they were lowering the thought into the ground in my mind, throwing mindirt over it and saying goodbye forever. It was so sad. A thought with its whole *life* ahead of it!

"_____!"

"What?" I shouted.

"Do you know the answer?" said the plus sign.

"Who *cares*!" I roared. "Don't you have any respect for the dead?"

YOU CAN'T DO THAT ON TELEVISION

Like most of the kids I knew, we had televisions watching us in every room, recording our movements and prayers, and praying them out as sitcoms and laugh-out-louds to other families in Appleseed. Our sitcom was called *The Marginals*, about a family that lives really close to the margin. I think back on those times, the times of the show, as some of the best of my childhood. Every day between the ages of five and thirteen I came home from school, looked over my script, and put on my costume: shiny Nike shoes instead of my secondhand unmatching Converse hi-tops, stonewashed jeans instead of vinyl parachute pants, an Ocean Pacific T-shirt over my cigarette shirt from the Salvation Army, a toupee cut in the latest fashion—a tail in the back or pleats shaved into the sides—to cover my bald head. Then I'd open up a closet of smiles in the back room, pick one out, and put it on. Sometimes I'd choose a wide smile, but usually I'd pick a smirk, like this one:

In the story of *The Marginals* I was Scooter LaFontaine, always getting into trouble that led to valuable lessons. My signature lines were, "Who, me?" and "Nice fine good OK!"

Everyone in my family was part of the show. My

sister played Samantha LaFontaine, the town's tap dancing champion (even though Bri *hated* tap dancing—her real passion was for collectibles, antiques, and junk). My father played a cambridge and my Mom a really kind nurse. And she was great at it. When she was in costume, I saw kindnesses from her that she rarely showed in person. In one episode, I saw her cradle a dying sentence in her arms as if she were its mother. In another, I was crushed by a last-second loss in a swim meet. In the car, she turned to me and said, "You tried your *best*, Scoot. Didn't you?"

My character, Scooter, nodded.

"And wasn't that your fastest time ever in backstroke?"

I shrugged.

"Then you won. You did better than ever before. What more could you want, honey?"

The show had certain tropes. Like, every show included a dinner scene.

"How was your day today, Scoot?" my Dad would ask.

With that line and almost every other, we'd hear the laughtrack: our cans in the pantry, chuckling and guffawing.

"We learned about photosynthesis," I said. "How plants transform light into food."

Haw.

"I wish we could transform *this* food," my sister said.

Ha haw haw ha.

"Now, Sam," said my Mom. "It's just a pleasure for the four of us to eat together."

"*I* think the ham is great," said my Dad. "Don't you, Scoot?"

"Nice fine good OK!" I said.

Every episode ended with a moral, delivered to me or my sister from my father or mother while sitting on the back stoop: "If they're cruel to you," the mother-character told the Scooter-character once, "then they aren't really your friends. Friends will watch out for you through thick and thin."

Or,

"Sometimes we have to put other people's interests in front of our own," the father-character told the sister-character. "That's part of being an adult."

"But I really wanted to go on the ski trip," said the sister-character.

"There'll be other ski trips," said the father-character.

I look back on that show now—here, in this cramped room, with a head full of doubts—and man, I miss those half-hour arcs: *Mr. LaFontaine Gets a New Job. Scooter Gets Lost. Mrs. LaFontaine Meets a Friend for Coffee. Scooter Needs a Hug. Samantha Makes a Friend*, and so many others.

We weren't the only show in town, of course. Every family I knew had a sitcom—their shows were broadcast into our eyes just as ours were broadcast into theirs. With so many shows to choose from, it was difficult to keep your family's ratings up. You had to say the right things to make people keep watching. After a few seasons on-air, our show became less popular and we needed to make changes. My Mom suggested that we make the show more serious—more dark. In one episode, the father-character's brother-in-law died and the last scene was Scooter and Mr. LaFontaine on the front stoop. "There's no sense to the universe," said Mr. LaFontaine, swigging from a bottle of beer.

"The Core? Some central meaning? It's a fucking *joke*. Or else how could people suffer so much and die so young?"

"I guess cancer is the Core's way of saying 'Screw you,'" I said.

"I guess so, sport," my Dad said.

The mother-character that season was closer to my actual mother: moodier, more unpredictable. "Parents don't *have* to love their children," she said in one moral.

"I thought love was unconditional," said my sister.

"Not necessarily," said my Mom. "You have to earn it."

When our ratings didn't improve, we tried the opposite tack: we made the show light, funny, almost vaudeville. Instead of death or illness there were spit-takes and pratfalls. My Dad's signature line was "Waaa!," his eyebrows leaping away from his eyes.

By this time, though, I was tired of changing. My sister and mother complied, but not me—I was rambunctious, remember? Rebellious, a badseed. At a dinner scene one day, my Mom asked me how school was. My line was, "Nice fine good OK!" Instead, though, I said, "Freaking terrible."

Haw.

My Mom's eyes were blades, but her smile held. "Why terrible?"

"Chamblis's Mom has HIV," I said.

Haw haw haw.

"Cut!" the television in our kitchen yelled. "Let's keep it lighthearted, Scoot!"

"_____," said my Mom.

I didn't say anything.

"And," the TV said, "rolling!"

76

"How was your day, Scoot?" asked my Mom again.

"My brain hurts," I said. "Like, my skull is too small for my thoughts." And I slammed my head into my plate of spaghetti.

"Cut!" said the television. "What the fuck, _____?"

Our ratings continued dropping. Soon, our TVs lost hope—you could see it in their eyes when they looked at us. When the physical comedy didn't work, my Dad pushed us even further: we went cartoon. Doing so meant going to the doctor every week for animation injections, and re-tooling our dynamic again. My Dad's repetitive gaffe that season was banging his thumb with his hammer. He'd do it over and over. "YeOW!" he'd shout, and run around with his red thumb in the air.

Soon, even our cans stopped laughing. Then one of our TVs quit, and my Mom started flubbing her lines—she'd stare out the window, or pray silently in her seat, or absent-mindedly pick up a book on set and start to read, and we'd have to shoot the whole scene over. My Dad didn't give up; in one last-ditch attempt to stay on the prayer-air, he decided that we'd stop the injections, go back to the orig-inal formula, and invite on guest characters: Chamblis's Mom, the town's oldest Orange Traffic Cone, the Memory of Johnny Appleseed. But by then even our living-room TV wouldn't watch us for half an hour.

In our last episode, my Dad and sister and I chose our smiles and took our places when we realized that my Mom wasn't on set. The TV gave the five-minutes-to-places call and Mom still hadn't shown up for costume or makeup. "Where is your mother?" my Dad asked between cambridges.

"I'll go find her," I said. I looked upstairs, in the front yard, in her gym in the garage. I found her in the far corner of the backyard, kneeling in the wet grass.

I ran over to her. "Mom?" I said.

"—and please," she was saying. "Protect us from doubts. And worries. Protect us from *ourselves*."

"Mom, the show's starting," I said.

"Take care of them," she said. "Take care of them while I'm gone."

"Mom?" I said.

"I'm praying," she said. "Do the show without me."

I heard the credits and the music and I ran inside. "And now," the TV said, "the MARGINALS!"

The three of us stared at each other. My Mom was supposed to deliver the first line.

"How was—" my Dad stumbled, "your day, Sam—?"

"Cut!" said the TV. "We need the whole family! Goddammit!" The TV unplugged itself and stormed out of the room. "Fuck this noise!"

The TV didn't come back until late that night—it smelled of beer and cigarettes for the whole week afterward. And from that day forward? The screen wouldn't look at me. All it did was *show* me things. Maybe to hurt me, it mostly showed me other families, families happier than mine, getting great ratings, raucous laughs, happinesses. Our house, meanwhile? Grew lonelier. Colder. Emptier. And no one even saw it. No one even *cared* what happened to the Marginals.

THE BICYCLE BUILT FOR TWO

Wait a second. I just realized that I never told you the story about my bicycle, the Bicycle Built for Two. It's an easy one to pull from the page. Here, grab ahold and pull.

Pull!

Bicycles, in Appleseed, were very meaningful. A good used bicycle—my father's '49 Robinson three-speed, say, well-maintained, with chordspokes and a flim—would run you about seven hundred theories. That was more than one month's rent in an apartment at Woodside!

My father was given that bicycle by his mother, the Rosary, who prayed for it, and he let me ride it all over Appleseed. When I was ten, though, the bike was stolen out of our garage in Appleseed. It was my fault—I was supposed to lock the bike up with math but I forgot. I woke up the next morning and the bike was gone—you could see the tire tracks in the dewy grass where someone had just walked off with it. Our neighbor Bob Lonely later said that he might have heard the bike shouting, but thought it was some wildwords in the margin.

For about a year I didn't have a bike; I rode my skateboard or I walked.

When I was about eleven, though, the kids that I hung

out with—Spondee, Kielbania, Large Odor, the Couplets, Canavan—started getting dirt bikes: single-speed bikes with knobby tires, pegs on the back wheels, and hardware built especially for jumps and tricks—for their birthdays or Core Days. Some of my friends—the Couplets, O'Hara—had meaningful parents, and Canavan inherited his bike (after his brother served in the Trenches and died from glue poisoning). Large Odor stole his Haro from a bike rack in East Appleseed.

Reader: Stole it? Odor? No. That's not true.

I swear to the Core it is.

Reader: Odor's a good kid! He wouldn't do that.

He told us himself! And none of these guys in the Syntax Gang—that's what we called ourselves—were good kids. We were the troublemakers, the kids in the special classes, the ones you'd find in detention cages or Silence School. We were ugly and we knew it. I was fat and bald; Kielbania had two faces; O'Hara didn't have a face at all.

The Syntax Gang used to hang out in the parking lot of the Pear or behind Cordial Carl's, but once everyone got dirt bikes we spent all our time in the Dunes.

The Reader flipped through the pages. "Is that what they were called? 'The Dunes'? I can't find those pages," she said.

You won't—they're the fancy Appleseed Vista now. Back then, though, those houses hadn't been built; it was all sand except for a few ideas of houses and concepts of roads. So my friends and I turned the whole thing into a dirt-bike track, with swooping trails and jumps as tall as we were or taller. Usually someone would bring six-foot cigarettes; once, Spond brought Kaddish Fruits. We'd smoke or get high and jump.

Everyone except me, that is. I helped with the jumps and then I watched as my friends rode the tracks. Sometimes Canavan would lend me his Diamondback, but usually I sat at the edge of the Dunes, where the road ended and the sand began, ollying on my skateboard. Odor saw me there one day and said, "You're never going to get good at jumping bikes unless you practice."

I shrugged. "No bike," I said.

"Just ask your Dad for one," he said.

"It was my fault the last one was stolen."

"Who cares about that old goatbike?" Odor said. "It was so heavy it couldn't jump shit anyway."

I knew we didn't have much meaning; my Dad could barely pay the mortgage. But one night about a year after the Robinson was stolen, I turned to my Dad while he was watching TV and asked him if there was any way I could get another bike.

He didn't say anything at first—he just sighed and stared at the TV. By this time in my life, I think he'd started to feel bad for me—to understand that I was unpopular, that I was lonely, that the Reader was my only real friend. My sister had such a bright future—she was so smart, and she had skills. And me? My brain just held shouts. Sometimes my mind puked into my skull. Other times it felt like my skull was caught in a vise or a drill press, and I had to lie down on the cold tile floor of the basement and wait for the feeling to pass. Once, my Dad came downstairs to see if I'd help him with a drainage problem at the buildings and he found me lying on the floor in the dark. "_____?" he said.

"Yeah," I said.

"What are you doing?" he asked.

"Tell them to stop digging," I said.

"What?" my Dad said.

"My thoughts," I said.

A bike meant friends; it also got me out of the house, which would make my mother happy. Sitting there in front of the TV, though, my Dad filled up his belly with air and said, "I really don't see a way to make that happen, _____."

"All my friends have them, though."

"Does Bob have one?"

Bobby Lonely was my neighbor. He was poor like us. "No," I said. "He's not my *friend*, though. Odor has one, and the Couplets *each* have one."

"Have what?" my Mom said, walking into the TV room.

"A bike," my Dad said.

"You had a bike," my Mom said, "but you were lazy and irresponsible. Lazy people lose things like bikes. End of story."

A few days later, though, my Dad and I went to see a trader he knew named Murphy. Murphy lived in a tiny house out past Appleseed Silence Academy—literally, the house was about the size of a closet—but he had a big amazing barn behind that house where he hoarded away items to trade. The barn was so full you couldn't even walk in there; one time, Murphy opened the door and a giant spool came crashing down and almost hit me in the head.

When my Dad told Murphy what we were looking for, Murphy cleared his sinuses and crossed his arms. "Sure," he said. "I got bikes. Least three of them. But they're meaningful."

"How meaningful?" my Dad said.

"Cheapest I got?" Murphy peered back at the barn. "Three hundred."

My Dad winced.

"Is it a dirt bike?" I said.

"A *what*?" said Murphy.

"Can you jump with it?" I asked.

Murphy shrugged. "Yeah. I'm sure you can."

My Dad thanked him and we went home. When I skateboarded over to the Dunes that day, I sat on my board and told Odor what had happened. "There's no way I'm getting a bike," I said. "My Dad asked a friend of his and it's just too expensive."

Odor leaned over his handlebars. "Freaking steal one then, man," he said. "It's easy."

"I'm not doing that," I said. "I'd get caught."

"You won't," said Odor. "I can show you how to do it."

I shook my head, and Odor put his feet on the pedals and rode around me, onto a nearby trail and over a jump, jackknifing his handlebars in midair.

But one day that fall, my Dad and I were sifting through some construction memories at the Appleseed Dump— the memories of windows, the memories of stairs—when a pickup truck pulled into the yard and I noticed a wheel sticking out over the back gate. "Dad," I said. He looked and saw: the wheel had spokes and a thick rubber tread: it was a bicycle wheel.

We jogged toward the truck. The door opened and a woman stepped out. She was old, with stories all over her face, but she was imposing. Her biceps were huge, and one of them displayed a wrinkled tattoo of a skirtblade: she was a Mother.

"What you got there?" my Dad said.

The Mother didn't answer. She just reached into the bed and pulled the bike out. I saw the rest of the wheel rise above the gate, and then the shiny handlebars, and then the red frame, and—

"Crap," said a thought.

—and then *another* pair of handlebars, and then one seat, and then another. It was a two-person bicycle; a bicycle built for two.

My Dad didn't seem fazed. "Work OK?" he said.

The Mother nodded and handed the bike over to my Dad. I saw now that it was military grade, a bicycle built for combat back when wars were fought on two wheels. "Just don't have any more use for it," the Mother said.

My Dad nodded and started to roll it away.

"Enjoy," said the Mother. Then she got back into her truck and started it up.

I followed my Dad and tried to catch his eye—to say, with my face, *What are you doing?* "Doesn't he realize that bike is for two people?" said one of my thoughts to another.

Just then an old vulture approached; he wore a tweed sweater, stained khaki pants, and a mesh hat. "What you got there?" said the vulture.

"We're taking it, Claude," said my Dad, and he hoisted the bike into the bed of the truck.

When I got into the cab, my Dad's face was bright. "You've got to be *kidding* me," he half-whispered. "*So* great, right?"

"What do you mean?" I said.

My Dad nodded over his shoulder.

"You know I can't ride that, right?" I said.

My Dad's face fell. "Why not?"

"Through the Dunes?"

"You said you wanted a bike," my Dad said.

"A *dirt* bike."

"What's the difference?" my Dad said.

"That bike's for *two people*," I said.

"That there is an absolutely meaningless bike, military grade, in great condition," my Dad said. "You can ride that thing for the next five years!"

"I can't *jump* with it, though," I said. My eyes filled with liquid words.

"Oh come *on*," my Dad said. His jaw hardened and he shook his head. "You know what? Sometimes I think your mother's right about you."

I started to cry.

"You have *no idea* how privileged you are, _____. To even live in Appleseed. To ask for something, and boom—to have it given to you."

I wiped my face. "I can't *jump* with it, though."

My Dad shook his head. "Unbelievable."

We didn't speak the rest of the way home. When we pulled into the driveway, though, my Dad hoisted the bike out of the truck and went to work fixing it up: he lowered the seats, tightened the chain, put air in the tires. I sat in the truck, pouting, until he came to the window. "Give it a try at least," he said.

I got out of the cab and silently swung my leg over the front seat. Then I pushed off and tried to pedal. The bike wobbled and I almost fell; I could barely push it forward—it took all my strength to get it up to speed. I slowly ambled to the intersection of Converse and Lake and then turned back around; when I reached the driveway I was completely out of breath. I jumped off the bike and let it drop to the pavement. "I can't even pedal it," I said.

"You just did!" said my Dad. "And it's probably great exercise."

"This *sucks!*" I shouted, and I ran inside.

"What sucks?" my Mom said.

"Dad got me a bike built for *two people!*" I hollered.

"Cool!" my Mom said.

When I showed up at the Dunes the next day with the Bicycle Built for Two, my friends were already pedaling up the trails. As I was huffing up Erskine, though, Joyce saw me and stopped. "Look at _____!" he said.

Everyone rode over to me.

"That bicycle
has two seats," said Rory Couplet.

"It's a bicycle
built for two," said James Couplet.

86

I was breathing heavily.

"That bike's a *parody*," said Spondee, smiling dumbly. "Does it speak Middle English?"

Large Odor laughed.

Then they took off and I followed, taking the last place in a sentence of bikes that whipped up the path, looped back, and tore down the sandy hill. I fell behind a little, but stayed with them as best I could. When I hit the loose sand on the path, though, my tire wobbled and I fell onto my side. Large Odor saw me fall and circled back. "You OK?" he said.

I pushed the bike off me and sat up, trying not to cry.

Then someone shouted "Capital!," and Odor and I looked up to see Dave Capital pedaling over Homicki Hill on his Viper. Capital skid-braked right in front of us. "HEY," he said. "HEAR ABOUT TEMPLETON?"

"What about him?" said Odor.

"HE'S ABOUT TO FIGHT PAYNE."

"Where?" said Joyce.

"THE PATH," said Dave.

"When?" said Spondee.

"RIGHT NOW. LIKE, TEN MINUTES AGO," said Dave.

Everyone got on their bikes. I righted my Bicycle Built for Two and followed: we snaked over Homicki Hill, up Redfern, left onto Williams, and toward the town line.

A mile or so before the line, though, I started falling behind. The rest of the gang pulled twenty feet ahead of me—"Slow—down," I tried to shout—then fifty

("Guys!"), then so far they couldn't hear me. No one even looked back to see where I was. Like I said, they weren't good people—they certainly weren't my *friends*, at least.

Right around Wolf Swamp I lost sight of the Syntax Gang—they were just too far ahead. After another few minutes of pedaling, I turned around and rode for home. When I reached my house I was drenched in sweat. I threw my dumbike on the grass and went inside, opened up the chip drawer, found a bag of Sour Cream and Onion and tore it open. I picked up a chip and it read my face. "What's wrong?" it said.

I ate that chip and picked up another. "Tell me your troubles," it said.

"I hate my life," I said, and ate it. Then I picked up a handful of chips and shoved them into my mouth all at once. "Stupid bike," I said, my mouth full. "And my friends—" I chewed, "—and my mother—"

"I understand," said a chip in the bag.

"I'm all alone," I told the chip, and ate it.

"No, you aren't," said another chip in the bag. "You still have us."

"You mean it?" I asked it, and ate it.

"We aren't going anywhere," said another chip. I ate that one and another one and another one and another one. I ate them all.

I showed up at the Dunes a few more times, but soon I stopped going. I continued talking to some of those kids—Large Odor, Spondee—but after a while we kind of drifted apart. One day a few months later I said hi to James Couplet and he looked through me like I wasn't even there.

"Couplet!" I said, but he just kept walking.

Maybe I *wasn't* there, a thought suggested.

I watched James smooth around the corner and I turned and walked the other way. Then I saw a fire alarm in the hallway up ahead. Without even really thinking about it, I ran up to the alarm and pulled it. Blue ink sprayed all over my hand and face.

All of the classroom doors sprang open; kids poured into the halls.

"See?" I told my thought, the ink running over my arms. "I *am* here."

Later that afternoon, an Orange Traffic Police Cone sat down with me in the office at school. "_____," he said. "I want you to be honest with me. Did you pull the fire alarm?"

"No," I said.

The Cone looked down at my blue hands—I hadn't even tried to wash them. "Did—you—pull—the fire alarm?"

"No," I said again.

The Cone crossed his orange plasticy arms.

A few weeks later, I was unlocking my dumbike when I saw my neighbor, Bobby Lonely—Loneliness, everyone called him—picking his face off by the lacrosse fields. "Hey, Loneliness," I said.

Loneliness looked at me.

"C'mere," I said.

He walked toward me. Loneliness smelled like cats,

probably because he owned about a million cats. He also had really bad acne; even his *acne* had acne.

"Need a ride home?" I said.

"Seriously?" he said.

Everyone was always playing tricks on Loneliness: sending him fake prayers, stealing his memories, that kind of thing. I could tell he didn't trust me.

"Do you or don't you?" I said.

He shrugged.

I pointed to the backseat and he got on. We started pedaling. It was much easier with another person. In no time at all we were over Apple Hill and coasting down Tanglewood.

"We're not friends," I shouted back to him.

"No," said Loneliness. "I know that."

Later, Loneliness became really popular. Seemingly overnight, it became cool to have acne. Suddenly *everyone* wanted acne. I used to send out prayers for it; people used to put acne on with makeup.

When we were in our twenties, though, Loneliness joined the U.S. Army and died. His acne made it back across the mountains, the spine and the margins, but he did not. Loneliness's acne showed up one day, years after he went missing, limping through West Appleseed, its eyes longing for the past.

THE BOOKWORMS

THE BOOKWORMS

For a while I thought the bookworms were just something I'd imagined: figments chasing my thoughts through Appleseed. One time a thought of an arcade said a worm with a beard threatened him outside the Appleseed Amphitheatre. And years later, a thought of green told me that a worm in a leather coat tried to run him down on his way home from the Hu Ke Lau one night.

"Run you down in *what*?" I said.

"A brown Plymouth Duster," he said.

"A *worm*?"

"A worm," said the thought. "It shaped itself into different letters, and—"

"Driving a car?" I said. "That doesn't make any sense!"

But then I started seeing the worms around town. I was standing in line at the Bagel Beagle one day when I noticed that the beagle behind the counter looked very worm-like. His ears and snout were clearly a costume, I saw when I got closer: you could see the chin strap of the dog nose running over gray skin.

I stepped up to the counter. The beagle's name tag said, "Your Mom will die and then who will take care of you?"

"I'll take a pumpernickel," I said.

"Butter?" said the wormdog.

"Yes," I said.

A few months later, a new student showed up at school. He had a Mohawk haircut and earrings, and when he introduced himself to the class he said his name was Everyone hates you. But you can call me Everyone," he said.

"Welcome to the class, Everyone," said the teacher, a beehive.

He was sitting right next to me, and I remember sneaking a look at his arm. "Know what?" said one of my thoughts to another.

"What," said the second thought.

"That worm's a sentence," said the first thought.

"No shit," said the second thought.

And then I remember going to the Bing with my Mom one day for a matinee—she took me every year for my birthday—when I noticed a gang of wormy sentences sitting in the far-left corner of the theater. They were whooping it up, really making noise. The movie was *The Legend of Goggles Beaman*, about a pair of goggles that is raised in the wild, believes himself to *be* wild goggles, and then must return to society.

In the middle of the film, though, something went wrong with one of the projectors and the screen went dark. All of a sudden the lights came on. "What the FUCK!" a sentence with long hair yelled at the screen.

"So weird," I said to my Mom.

"Probably just a problem with the reel," she said.

"I'm going to go get some more popcorn," I said, and I walked out to the lobby.

As it happened, I was in line right behind two sentences—they ordered Jujubes and Fun Dip. When the second worm paid, he put his credit card down on the glass case and I snuck a look at the name on the card: "You will be left all alone."

I went back to the seat and held my popcorn out to my Mom. She looked at the giant bag and smiled. "No thanks," she said.

Just then the lights lowered and the screen lit up. The worms continued their chatter, but I tried to ignore them—I stuck my hand in the buttery mess and shoveled some popcorn into my mouth.

PRAYER PIANO

Sometimes it seemed like the pages of Appleseed would turn forever. At others, though, you could sort of hear the townspine breaking, smell the glue melting, see pages tear off into the wind.

One day when I was fourteen, my father heard a prayer about a free piano. This sounded meaningful, so my Dad prayed back that yes, he was interested. The prayer prayed back the name of the manufacturer—a name we didn't recognize. Fine, my Dad prayed back. You have to move it yourself, said the return-prayer, and my Dad prayed that we would. But his truck had the flu, so we needed to borrow one. "Could we ask Joump?" I said.

"Let's go see the Possum," my Dad said.

The Possum was, or was not, a possum. Everyone called him one, though, because he was covered in fur. I don't know if he was really hairy, or if in fact he was a possum with normal hair. One fact about the Possum? I'd never seen him eat anything but energy bars. Also, beer. Do possums eat energy bars?

The Possum had a shed at the edge of Appleseed, out near the Appleseed Library. Someday I'll sow that story— the story of the Library. That library had secret books,

books that I'd never heard anyone talk about or mention in conversation. (Not that people *talk* about books. But if they did.) Once I opened a page in a book and I saw that all of the words were naked. I'd never *seen* naked words before! For example.

I was standing at the door, lost on a road in my mind, when the Possum opened it. "_____!" he said. "Ralph! Come in! I'm cooking—you want something?"

"We're not hungry," said my Dad, "but we were hoping that we could ask you for a favor."

"Anything!" said the Possum.

We drove out to South Appleseed to see the piano. The owner said that she might or might not be home, but that the piano was easy to spot: she prayed it stood in a field about a hundred yards from a big blue house. "Why is it in the *field*?" my Dad had prayed. "Because," she prayed, "I just couldn't take it anymore."

We located the blue house and, a hundred yards away, the piano, vowing like a soldier against a backdrop of flat, electric green. The piano and bench stood all alone in that field, and it looked like they'd been there for some time— the piano was sunk up to its knees in mud. Moss grew over the instrument's chest, and vines crawled up one shoulder. "It's a part of the earth," I said.

"Does it even work?" asked my Dad.

"Only one way to find out," said the Possum, and he sat down at the bench. My father and I sat down beside him, and the three of us studied the keys.

"We're here now," my Dad said to the piano. "So you can play."

The Possum looked at my father.

My Dad leaned closer. "Do it. Play!" he said louder.

"What are you doing?" said the Possum.

"I'm waiting for it to start playing," my Dad said.

"It's not one of those types of pianos," said the Possum. "Is that the kind you were looking for?"

"I didn't know there was a difference," my Dad said.

"There is," said the Possum. "There are automatic pianos and manual ones. This one's manual."

My father nodded—the Possum would know. Something that is surprising about the Possum? Is that he was actually a very good piano player—a child prodigy. He used to travel the world, playing music that no one else could. You were probably expecting that we brought along the Possum for his truck only, and it's true that we needed his truck. But we could have asked Uncle Joump; we could have asked one of the Muir Drop Forgers. Of the three of them, the Possum was the only one who knew anything about pianos.

Which is why, sitting there on the bench in the field, I asked him to teach me something. "Can you show me a cord?" I said.

"Chord," he said. "There's a silent *h*."

"C-hord," I said.

"It's been twelve years since I've played a note of music," said the Possum.

I made my face pacific.

The Possum put his paws on three keys and let them

rest there. He closed his eyes. I leaned in—I was expecting to hear something amazing.

The Possum pressed down on the keys, but I didn't hear any notes—what I heard instead was a click, and the sound of the point of view shifting. Then the Possum and the Father and _____ looked at each other. "Where's the music?" said _____.

The Possum played another chord and the point of view shifted again: you were confused and disappointed.

"This piano is out of tune, or something," said the Possum.

Just then a figure came running down the road. She was dressed in chartreuse green spandex and her face was hampden: bright but sad. She cut across the field and ran up to you. "You found the piano," she said.

Your father stood up. "It's ours," he said. "We got here first."

"I know it," she said, catching her breath. "I'm the one you prayed to."

"What's the story with this thing?" the Possum asked.

"It was my mother's," said the spandexer. "But I don't play."

"It doesn't make any sound," you said.

"Of course it doesn't," she said. "I said that in the prayer."

"You did?" said your father.

"I prayed, it's a POV Piano—a point-of-view piano."

"I thought that was the name of the brand," your father said. "I didn't know—"

"Watch," said brightsad, and she pushed a single key on the right side. I heard the clicking sound again.

"Hear that?" she said.

"First person plural," we said.

"Do you want it, or not?" She pushed another key and the point of view was hers: I didn't tell them about the stories in these fields, the other instruments beneath the soil. I didn't tell them that my mother *died* at this piano. I just wanted to be rid of the damn thing.

Then the Possum joined in. As the spandexer played the point-of-view melody, the Possum (I didn't care what sound came out of it—I was just so happy to put my paws on the keys again) played the chords.

My Dad stared at the piano. "This isn't what I envisioned," he said.

"It *is* free," said brightsad.

"I think you should take it," the Possum told my father. "Just imagine: to be able to see things from another angle *whenever you wanted.*"

"I really wanted a *note*-based piano," my Dad said.

"And you'll find one," said the Possum. "But take this one, too! Put it out in the fields! Just in case!"

The Possum was right. This was an interesting object that, at the very least, we might be able to trade down the road. My Dad said OK, and the Possum led his truck into the field. When the truck got to the piano, it knelt down and picked up the instrument in its arms. The piano made a terrible *pok* when it lifted from the earth, and I heard the sound of snapping roots and vines. The truck put the piano in its bed, walked out of the muddy field, and settled on its tires. Then we got into the truck and the Possum pulled onto Highway Five. I turned back and waved at the spandexer, who was standing in the mud.

On the way back to Converse Street, I asked the Possum why he'd stopped playing piano. "Because of a medical condition," he said.

"What kind of medical condition?" asked my Dad.

"I developed tinnitus," he said. "Ringing in the ears. For me, it was one single note. A slightly-out-of-tune A."

"The note was in your mind?" I said.

"Twenty-four-seven."

"Wow," I said. "Even as you slept?"

"It didn't stop for a minute, not for nine years," he said. "Then I woke up one morning and realized I couldn't hear the note anymore. Now I can't hear that note, A, at all."

"What do you mean?" my Dad said.

"My ears skip the note. I just can't hear it."

"And that's why you don't play music anymore?" I said.

"How could I?" he said.

He meant it as a rhetorical question. In my mind, though, I thought: Aren't there are a lot of other notes? Bs and Gs and Xs and Zs?

"There are," said the Possum, "but you can't play a melody if you're missing notes in the phrase."

"Wait a second," my Dad said. Had he just heard _____'s thought?

"Of course I heard it," said the Possum. Then he looked over at me. "Oh, *fuck*," I said to Ralph. I pulled the truck over, and the Possum looked back at the piano, leaning to one side of the bed.

"I think I know what's happening," I told the Possum.

"Me, too," I told Ralph and _____.

"What?" said _____.

"We must have screwed up the point of view when we disconnected the piano from the land," I said.

"Fuck *me*," you said. You *knew* we shouldn't have agreed to help Ralph. Something awful always comes of it. "So what's this?" he said.

"This is *all* points of view," you all said.

It was; we could feel the sudden pressure of new narrators—of *your* point of view, and *your* point of view, and the passing tree's point of view, and every morsel of roadside *sand*'s point of view. But there wasn't anything we, I, or they could do except get home, plant the piano, and see if rerooting it would help. And that's what they—we; he, he, and he—did. We/they made it back to Appleseed and I/the Possum drove the truck out into the worryfields and instructed my/his truck to drop the piano into the soil.

I dropped the piano where they told me to.

So this is my new home, I thought.

By then it was dark, so I went back to my shed, and we went into the house. We ate quickly and then lay down in our beds. The force from all those points of view was tremendous for us. The only way we could sleep was to believe that this would change—that the story, the switching POVs, the pressure, would soon be over. Make it stop, we prayed. We sent out those prayers, but they went unanswered.

STARK'S EARLIEST

I thought my Mom would grow to love Sentence, but she didn't. I found it cool that "I am." was always changing—to "I am older," and then "I am seeing," then "I am hearing," and "I am hearing new things," but my Mom didn't appreciate it. If the sentence pooped or peed in the house (which happened hardly ever—"I am." was basically housebroken), she lost her *shit*. "*Look* at this!" she'd shout at me, pointing at the droppings of language. "Whose letter turds are these?" As if there was any question.

When Sentence tried to befriend my Mom, that only made her angrier. I remember seeing "I am aware that time is passing" trying to curl up next to my Mom while she was reading on the gold couch one day. My Mom pushed the sentence off. "*No!*" she told him, and Sentence whimpered and recoiled.

"You don't have to be mean to him," I said.

My Mom went back to reading.

A few weeks later, I came home from school and I couldn't find Sentence—I walked all over the house looking for him. Then I went out to the gym, where my Mom was levitating. "Have you seen 'I am.'?" I asked her.

"Nope," she said.

I went outside and then back into the house. Suddenly I heard a very quiet repetitive sound: *scuff scuff scuff.* Something was scratching. I followed the sound to the pantry door. When I opened it I saw "I am." standing there in the dark, his "I"'s wide and panicked.

My Mom came in from the garage a few minutes later. "Sentence was locked in the pantry," I told her. "In the dark!"

"Really?" she said.

"Did you do this?" I asked.

"Oh, honey—of course not," she said.

"He was probably scratching for hours!"

"I honestly had no idea he was in there. Or else I would have let him out!"

"I think you put him in there on purpose because you hate him so much," I said.

"I don't *hate* anyone, _____," she said. "Just because I recognize the *risks of*—"

"That's such bullcrap!" I said.

"Excuse me?" she said.

"You hate *everyone*!" I shouted.

My Mom pointed her finger at me. "I'll be gone someday, _____—"

"What's *that* supposed to mean?"

"—and then you'll wish you were nicer to me."

Shortly after that, two clauses got in a fight in the margin across the street. This would happen every once in a while—you'd hear the wild, high squeal and pitter-patter of language chasing language through trees. That day, I ran outside just in time to see the clauses scamper across Converse and tussle on the treebelt, ripping up the page right in front of our house.

My mother heard the commotion from her gym and stormed out through the garage door. "Oh, *Christ!*" she said.

By then the sentences were gone.

"What the hell happened to the lawn?"

Neither the Reader nor I said anything.

"Did *you* do this?" Mom asked the Reader.

"Me?" you said. "No."

"_____?" said my Mother.

"We were just standing here," I said.

"Don't *lie*, _____," she said.

"I'm not," I said. "It was two sentences fighting across the street."

"Piece of *crap*," she said. I don't know if she was talking to the sentences or to me.

My Mom was changing—being replaced by a sadder, more angry version of herself. She stopped eating—eating *anything*, I mean. She grew resentful about work and my Dad's minimal meaning, and impatient with all the junk my sister kept around the house and with my perpetual lateness. One time? She was supposed to pick me up from school, and I was a few minutes late as usual. When I went out to the circle and looked for her car, I saw the Cloudy Fart driving away down Grassy Gutter. I waved my hands and ran down the sidewalk shouting. And I *know* she saw me—I saw her eyes in the rearview mirror. But she turned down Williams and drove away, and I had to walk home in the snowy cold.

My mom wasn't the only one souring, though. About

three months after I found "I am." in fact, the happiness taps in our home faltered and sputtered and ran dry. My sister noticed it first, when she turned on the happiness faucet in the backyard—to wash a dead icebox that she'd found at the flea market—and the faucet coughed and spit. As a landlord, my Dad knew a lot about happiness—where the shutoffs were, how to check the gauges, how to increase the feed. When he read the meter, though, he saw that the supply was low.

"Well?" said my Mom from the top of the stairs.

My Dad checked the expansion tank. When he shook it, you could hear a pinging inside.

"There's air in the tank," he said.

"Ralph?" hollered my Mom.

"It's empty!" my Dad called up.

"I'm calling the DPWC," my Mom said.

The Public Works Cones confirmed it: our whole *neighborhood* was out of happiness. There was a problem with a conversion facility on Tanglewood, they said, and they didn't know when it'd be up and running again. For the time being, the Cones said, we all needed to make do with little or no happiness.

As soon as my Mom hung up the phone, my Dad got into his truck and drove to the store for some bottled joy. He returned empty-handed an hour later, though. "You should have seen the lines," he said.

We were downtrodden—just plain *sad*—all that week. My father ignored calls from tenants and spent the afternoons drinking hard cider on the porch. My sister gave up on the icebox she was trying to restore and just put it out on the curb. Me, I was so sluggish I couldn't do any-thing—not even read or walk "I am." He started peeing on the rug in the corner of the living room and no one even said anything about it.

My mother handled the sadness differently: she spent most of the weekend in her home gym. This was right around the time when my Mom became fascinated with the Mothers—the highly trained, heavily armed mili-tia group that lived in Nests perched in high trees, flew in formation above Appleseed, and descended at the first sign of trouble. All of a sudden, the Mothers were all my Mom talked about—how heroic and brave they were, how thankful the town should be for their protection.

Reader: Protection from *what*?

From intruders of any kind: thoughts sent from other towns to confuse us, meaning-scammers, traveling rust or decay, dangerous words or sentences, etceteras, et cetera. If they picked up a threat or imbalance in some history or ex-position, they'd take the long, difficult flight back through the years to the page where that imbalance appeared. Ac-cording to my Mom, the Mothers would revise right there on the spot: change a word, a sentence, a whole *paragraph*, even, if they needed to.

My father scoffed at all this. He didn't dispute the Mothers' presence—you could often see them, plain as ink, floating over the pages in their flightskirts and goggles—but he thought their reputation was exaggerated. Their brochures boasted of training in aikido, thought-stopping, judo, size-changing, and karate—they bragged about vic-tories in secret wars, saving Appleseed from near-coups and future infestations, changing the histories of disease and oppression. My Dad had his doubts. "No one is that strong or that tough," I heard him tell my Mom once.

"The Mothers are," she said, shoving a brochure in his face.

My Mom never explained to me why she wanted to be a Mother, but I had my theories. When my Mom was younger, she was tormented by eating disorders. She'd told me the stories—how, at school, they poured loathing in her locker, badgered her with fakeprayers, spread fictional rumors about her. Once, two disorders cornered her on her way home from school and beat my Mom so badly she missed a week of school.

It was a Mother who saved her, my Dad said. One day, my Mom was in a knockdown-dragout with a gang of disorders when a Mother dropped down from the sky and unfurled her warskirt. Those disorders landed in the hospital with fractured everythings—fractured egos, fractured goals, fractured sorrow.

You couldn't just be a Mother, though—you had to be chosen. They hadn't recruited for over five years, so my Mom was training for the day they opened the books again. She worked hard: she fasted; learned to box; bought a video about levitation and another about size-changing, which taught her how to think herself taller or shorter at will. She took meaningful courses on seeing the future and revising the past.

Once, when my Mom was at work, I found her videos and asked the TV to show one to me. I thought I'd impress my Mom if I could learn how to change size like she did.

Just ten or fifteen minutes into the first taped lesson—how to reduce—my Mom walked in from work. "What are you doing?" she said.

I was about the size of a Converse hi-top. "Nothing," I said.

She turned off the TV.

"You've caused enough trouble already," she said. "Or will in the future."

"What do you mean?" I said.

She shook her head and held up her hands. "I'm just saying," she said, "you can't go around taking other people's things, _____."

"OK," I said.

The following Monday, we received a general prayer that the happiness would be restored. When we turned the faucets on that afternoon, though, they spat out happiness caked with sadness and the carcasses of doubts. I remember the four of us standing in the kitchen, waiting for the pipes to clear. My Dad let the happiness run for a few minutes, and then he poured some in a glass and held the happiness up to the light.

"Is it OK?" my Mom said.

"I don't know," he said.

My sister grabbed the glass from him and drank from it. "Augh," she said, spitting it back.

"Is it happiness?" I said.

Briana shook her head. "No," she said. "I don't know what it is."

My mother took a sip. "It's not sadness," she said. "Ralph, try it."

My father reached for the glass, but I took it from him and drank. The liquid was thick and sludgy. It wasn't happiness, but it wasn't sadness either. "It's bitter," I said. "Is it bitterness?"

I handed the glass to my Dad; he studied the liquid, swished it around and took a sip. "It's melancholy," he announced. "They must be flushing the pipes still."

I took the glass back. I took another sip, and another.

"Easy, _____," said my Dad.

"_____ likes it," Briana announced.

I gulped down the rest of the melancholy, turned on the tap, and poured myself another glass.

THE BIG WHY

WHITE TRANSPARENT

That winter I developed a skin condition—an itching—
and soon it had spread all over my arms and my neck and
my ears. When I showed it to my Mom, she waited until
my Dad came home and then called me into the kitchen.
"Show your father," she said. I held out my arm, and my
father made a face at my mother.

The next day my mother took me to see our doctor,
Doctor Coat. Coat and my Mom sometimes worked together at the hospital, but we went to see him in his office
in Appleseed Springs. He took one look at my arm and
said, "Ah. OK. Sure. No big surprise here, given your family history."

I just stood there. "What's he talking about?" said one
of my thoughts.

"I'm almost positive this is divorcitis," he said. "We
knew that someday this might be a possibility." Then he
looked to my Mom, whose face was a blade.

"It's *what*?" I said.

"Oh," said Doctor Coat. "I didn't mean—I just assumed—"

The word was too big for my mouth. "Divorce—"

"—itis," said Doctor Coat. "It causes eczema—that's

the skin irritation here—moodiness, blurred vision, nausea, and an inability to have romantic relationships."

"What do you mean, my family history?"

Doctor Coat held up his hands. "I am *really* sorry, Di," he said. "I didn't mean to complicate things."

I looked at my Mom. "*You* have it?"

"Both me and your Dad," said my Mom.

"But you're married," I said.

"A lot of married people have it," Doctor Coat said. "About forty percent of Americans, actually."

"And there's a treatment for it," my Mom said.

"Several, actually," Doctor Coat said to me. "Most people with divorcitis take passive-aggressiveness, which you can buy in pill form or as a salve."

"I take the pills," my Mom said.

"But there's a brand-new treatment on the market—evidence suggests that it quiets the divorcitis over time. So, who knows! With these meds, you may be able to stand in the same room as someone—maybe even, years from now, give them a hug!" He pulled a notepad from his pocket and wrote a prescription.

I took the paper and read it. "*Music* pills?" I said.

The Coat nodded. "Now, there are some side effects—defamilization, fatigue, that kind of thing. But they'll keep the eczema at bay."

"When will this go away?" I said.

They both stared at me.

"I don't want to sugarcoat this for you, _____," said the Coat. "It will probably always be very difficult for you to have a happy romantic relationship."

My Mom nodded and led me out of the office. She put her arm around me as we walked back to the Fart. "How long have you had this?" I asked.

She unlocked the passenger's-side door. "I got it in my twenties," she said.

"You and Dad are divorced?"

"Of course not! We fight it." Mom pulled the Fart into traffic.

After a minute I said, "*Why* do you?"

My Mom lit a six-foot cigarette, rolled open the window and rested the cigarette against the top of the glass. "Why do we what?" she said.

"*Why* do you fight it?"

"What do you mean?"

What I meant was, *what* did they love about each other? Did my Mom love my Dad's French Canadian frame— the barrel chest and skinny legs? Or his wild black hair and thick square glasses? Did my Dad like my Mom's shaved head? Her muscles? The lighthouses in her eyes? What specifically?

"Because you love each other?" I said.

"Of course!" she said.

"I can't believe this," I said.

My Mom took a drag from her cigarette and blew smoke out of one side of her mouth. "It's like Coat said— lots of people have it. Odor's parents."

"Really?"

"And the Lonelies."

"They do?" I said.

My Mom nodded.

We farted to Ryan's Pharmacy to fill the prescription. It took a long time—I read a magazine while my Mom waited in line for the pills. When they were ready, my Mom found me and handed me the bottle. "Here," she said. "Sooner you take them, sooner you'll start to feel better."

The music pills were blue and translucent, and filled with what looked like strobe lights and dancing people.

"Take *one*," she said.

I took out a pill and popped it. As soon as I did, the music surged through my body: the magazines started shouting, my knees buckled, and everything improved. "Bluh," I said.

"You OK?" my Mom said.

Everything was different now. I looked back at the pharmacy counter and the tall, gray-haired, thick-glassed pharmacist behind the glass. I read his face—the mole on his cheek—and realized who he was. I ran right up to the glass. "You're my mother," I said.

"_____," my Mom said, and put a strong hand on my shoulder. The pharmacist said something to my mother, but his voice was low and bubbly notes.

"My mother," I told the pharmacist.

"OK. Let's go home," my Mom said, and she pulled me away from the glass.

"No! Mom!" I said to the pharmacist.

"We're leaving, _____," my Mom said, leading me past the line of sick people. After a few steps, though, I tore away from her. "I'm not going anywhere with *you*," I spat at her. A man coughed on me and I looked in his face. "You're my brother," I said. He looked to his right, at an old woman standing behind him. "You're my sister," I told her. "Or my father."

She was. And I'd missed them so much!

"Come on, _____," said my Mom, and she pulled me forward.

"You're all my brothers and sisters—" I slurred, "—my family," and then the very strong stranger pulled me outside into the sharp daylight.

TOPAZ

That spring the apples grew small—ten percent smaller, on average, than they'd been for any year on record. This might not seem like much, but it had serious, immediate ramifications for people in my town. Some clients—surrounding towns who'd bought apples from Appleseed since the days of Johnny Appleseed himself—demanded a discount or sent back their apples in disgust. It was worryfields—everyone was a little less meaningful. My friend Berson's mother lost her management job, and the time factory where our neighbor Roger Lonely worked shifted him from full time to part time. Then one of my Dad's tenants—a maître d' at the East Margin Grill, a fancy apple restaurant downtown—broke his lease and left town.

A month after the harvest, the Board of Select Cones held a special meeting at the Town Hall. I wasn't there, but my Dad showed me the article in *The Daily Core*. The article said that there were Mothers in attendance, and that the Memory of Johnny Appleseed was asked to speak to the Board. "It was a very warm winter, is all," the Memory of Johnny Appleseed was quoted as saying. "Spring was too short and the apples had no chance to finalize. These are like," he said, "*rough drafts* of apples."

Select Cone Calumet Johnson held up an apple from one of his own trees. "This is a major disappointment," he told the Memory of Johnny Appleseed. "Are you *praying* for the apples to return to size?"

"I am," the Memory of Johnny Appleseed told the Board. "Every day."

"It's not only the size of the apples," Select Cone Rhonda O'Martian was quoted as saying. "They don't *taste* like Appleseed apples. Has anyone noticed that?"

Then one of the other Orange Traffic Cones on the Board, Select Cone Hedge Miles, took a bite of the apple on the table. "She's right," he said. "It tastes flat. Like paper."

A day or two after that meeting, my Mom took my sister and me for our weekly shopping trip to the Big Why. The Big Why sold fresh, organic inquiries—everyone in town went there for their questions. It was a nice store, clean and well-organized, with classical music playing in the background and the askings organized by section. If my father went with us, he'd load up the cart with doozies: "What is life *for?*"s, or "What does it mean to be 'authentic'?"s. My Mom liked the practicals: "What's the least amount of food someone can live on?" "How does one survive a bookwormbite?" Bri liked the nuts 'n' bolts: "How does a planer work?" "What's a dovetail joint?"

Me? I let my thoughts wander through the aisles. Most of the time they came back with questions about the page itself. "Why do words have to die?" "Does a sentence have a soul?" "If the sentence 'A tree dies in the woods.'

dies in the woods, does the sentence 'Does anyone hear it?' hear it?"

That day, though, we drove right by the Big Why and kept on going. At first I thought my Mom had made a mistake—I turned in my seat and looked back at the big question mark hanging over the sliding glass doors.

"Mom?" said Briana.

"Yeah," she said.

"Where are we going?"

"Shopping for questions," she said.

"But you just passed the Why," Bri said.

"We're going somewhere else today," she said.

We drove down Williams and toward the Appleseed Line. "What the heck," I said.

"Where are we *going*, Mom?" said Briana.

Soon we'd crossed the border into East Appleseed. My thoughts were pacing back and forth across the floors in the rooms of my mind. What, they wanted to know, was wrong with the Big Why?

Ten minutes into East Appleseed, my Mom pulled the Fart into a crumbly parking lot; to the left, I saw a store with a shabby clock over its door. "What's this?" said Briana.

I read the name on the store window: "The Big *When?*"

"It's exactly the same," my Mom said. "Come on."

We followed my Mom inside. The store was big and moore, with a funny smell and paint chipping off the walls. I read the signs above the rows—one read "Never," another "Soon." "All of these questions are time-based," said Briana. My Mom ignored her and began pulling questions off the shelf: "When will there be peace?" and, "When will everyone and everything have meaning?"

"These questions suck," I said, in earshot of a lady stocking Nows in the aisle.

"_____," my Mom hissed, looking over at the lady. "They're *fine*. Now pick out a question or don't."

Briana went one way, my Mom went another, and I wandered over to the bargain bin. There were some really old, faded questions in there, plus some open-ended ones and some broken asks. Before I even had time to choose one, though, I saw my Mom wheeling her shopping cart to the register. I grabbed the closest question and ran to catch up.

When we got back in the Fart my Mom said, "Pretty rad place, huh?"

"*Rad*?" my sister said.

"Isn't that what people say? 'Cool'?" my Mom said. "Was it cool?"

"It was OK," Briana said.

"It was lame," I said.

"What questions did you get?" my Mom asked.

"I got one about rain," said my sister. "When will it rain?"

"It's supposed to rain tomorrow," my Mom said, and my sister smiled.

I took my question out of the brown paper bag. "I got 'When the sky?'" I announced.

Neither my Mom nor my sister said anything for a second.

"When *what*?" said Bri.

"When," I said. "The sky?"

My Mom looked at me in the rearview mirror. "I'm not sure how to—answer that one, _____."

"That's because he got it from the bargain bin," Briana said. "None of those *have* answers, dumbass."

I looked at the question.

"Crap," I said. "Mine sucks!"

"Idiot," Bri said to me.

"Bri," my Mom said.

"I want to go to the Big Why," I doaned.

Bri looked at my Mom. "Me, too," she announced.

"No one's going to the Why," Mom said. "We already bought our questions for the week."

"Mine doesn't have an answer, though," I said.

"Well," my Mom said, lighting a cigarette, "some questions are like that."

"I already have enough no-answer questions," I shouted.

"Lower your voice, _____," said my Mom.

"Like: why didn't anyone tell me about the divorcitis?" I hollered. "Like: where is my hair?"

"I said *lower your voice*," my Mom said.

"Like, why am I so *fat*?"

"You're fat because you eat so much crap," my sister said.

"And who's killing all my thoughts?" I wailed. "And why don't we have more happiness? What does it all *mean*?"

"_____," my Mom said through clenched teeth, "you stop shouting *right now*."

"I want *answers*," I yelled.

"Shut your *mouth*," my Mom roared.

"I want ANSWERS!" I howled.

"Sonofa*bitch*," my Mom said. She pulled the Fart over, got out, scorned around to my side and tore open the door.

"What are you doing?" I said.

She grabbed me by the collar and pulled me out of the car with one hand. "Fucking *brat*," she spat, and pushed me back onto the shoulder of the road. I fell back and dropped my question; it broke on the pavement.

"My question," I whined.

My Mom stormed back around the car, got in, and slammed the door shut.

"Where are you going?" I asked, starting to cry.

Briana looked at me from the backseat, her face a mix of satisfaction and pity.

"*Mom!*" I said.

". . . his fault anyway—" I heard her say, and then, "—goddamned piece of *shit*." Then she pulled the car back into traffic.

"Wait!" I shouted. I thought my Mom would turn the Fart around, but she didn't. The car farted farther and farther away—soon I couldn't see it.

I stood there crying for a minute or two, looking down at the broken question in my hand. It had cracked at the space seam, right between "when" and "the"—now I held "when" in one hand and "the sky" in the other.

I looked around and tried to get my bearings. I was on a strange page outside Appleseed. I started walking in the direction of the Fart. I walked past houses separated by vast white space. Then I passed a prayer center, an office park, and another prayer center. In twenty minutes or so, I saw the margin for Appleseed. I crossed the thick, smudgy space; soon I was at the edge of the paragraphs describing southeast Appleseed.

As I walked down Williams Street, I heard a rush overhead. I looked up to see a woman—a Mother—twenty feet above me, her green skirt flaring and her long gray hair whipping in the wind. She landed in front of me and lifted up her goggles. "Afternoon," she said. She smelled like clouds and she had tattoos all up and down her arm. Her skirt was dirty from flight. As it settled, I saw blades and weapons in the folds of the fabric.

I just stood there.

"Saw you walking across the margin," she said. "Where are you coming from?"

"East Appleseed," I said. "My Mom took us to the Big When, but she got—angry—and made me walk home."

"Where's home?" she said.

I told her my address. "577 Converse Street, Appleseed."

"What's your name?" the Mother asked.

"_____," I said.

The Mother's eyes narrowed. "Do you have any words on you, _____?"

"Just these," I said. I held out the broken question.

The Mother took the question, read it, and handed it back to me. "*Living* language, I mean," she said. "Did you see any sentences moving through here?"

I shook my head. "Am I in trouble?"

"You're sure?" said the Mother. "We've seen worries crossing through here. Threats. Doubts trying to sneak into Appleseed."

I was scared. "I swear to the Core," I said, "I didn't see any."

"Stand there and don't move," the Mother said. Then she prayed to my Mom, who confirmed that I was who I said I was. The Mother prayed that she'd get me home safe. Then she closed the prayer, turned to me, and said, "Need a lift home?"

"That would be awesome," I said.

The Mother took me in her arms and rose up into the sky. We ascended high over the margin, and soon I saw the edge of town: the shrug of Appleseed Mountain and the distant lights of the Big Why and Cordial Carl's. Something was happening in the Amphitheatre. Then I could see Van Tassel's Groves, and rows and rows of spidery tree-shadows. Somewhere over town I dropped my question, but I didn't even care.

"Is it difficult to learn how to fly?" I shouted.

The Mother smiled but didn't answer. When we got to my house, she landed in the driveway and knelt down until my feet were touching the ground. But I didn't let go—I held on to her shoulders. "Let go," said the Mother finally.

I hugged her tightly.

"Let go of me," she said again, and pulled me off of her. Then she stood up. "No more wandering in the margins," she said.

"OK," I said.

"I mean it," she said. "It's dangerous."

"I promise," I said.

She lifted up into the sky and was gone.

RIVAL

The story of the founding of Appleseed—the one that the Reader and I pulled from the page—was about how Johnny Appleseed, moving to a barren town of stone in the mid-1700s, heard a strange prayer and followed it, as if driven by something beyond himself, high up Appleseed Mountain (which was known as Geryk Mountain then). It was there, in a clearing in the clouds, that he found a lone crooked tree holding a single alien fruit. At that point, no one in America had ever seen an apple—they wouldn't have even known about them unless they'd read about them in ancient European planting brochures. Pioneers and pilgrims had tried to grow apples on American soil, but to no avail; it was believed that something in American soil kept apple trees from taking root.

The old prayers say that when Johnny Appleseed approached the tree, a bookworm—a slithery sentence—rilled forth from a hole in the page and warned him not to pick the fruit, that it was meaningless and would only make him ill. When Johnny tried to push past him, the worm stood at full height to frighten him away. But Johnny had heard the fruit praying to him and believed it to be meaningful, so he drew the word "sword" from his satchel and told the worm to stand down. When the worm didn't, Johnny slew him with the word. Then he picked the fruit, ate it, and planted the seeds. The seeds grew more trees. The trees grew more seeds. Appleseed collected those seeds in his holy satchel and started planting groves all over Appleseed.

A few weeks after the Memory of Johnny Appleseed told me and the Reader that story, though, the Memory of Johnny Appleseed and I were arranging those paragraphs on the pagefield when two Mothers landed in the fresh soil. One of the Mothers held a giant pencil; another was wearing headphones on her ears and a giant tape machine strapped to her chest. The first Mother told the Memory of Johnny Appleseed to put down his hoe, and he complied. "What's this all about?" he said.

"Are these your words?" said the taller Mother.

"Yes," said the Memory of Johnny Appleseed.

"You grew them?"

"With _____," he said.

"Who?" said the taller Mother.

"Me," I said, raising my hand.

"We're picking up some anomalies here," said the headphoned Mother.

Then the other Mother picked up the word "sword" and studied it. As she held it, the "s" in "sword" shivered. "Shit," said the Mother, and she dropped the word. The "s" detached from the "word" and slithered into the grass.

"What was that?" asked the Memory of Johnny Appleseed.

"Bookworm," said the first Mother.

"A what?" said the Memory of Johnny Appleseed.

"We're going to need to confiscate these," said the headphoned Mother.

"Confiscate—the words? Which ones?"

"These," said the first Mother, pointing to the paragraph. "All of them." They prayed for backup, and soon other Mothers arrived and began lifting words— "bookworm," "sword," "American"—right off the page, leaving a blank space where they'd been.

The Memory watched from the margin, repeatedly taking off his hat, rubbing his hands through his hair, and pulling his hat back on tighter. "Oh," he whined at one point. "Do you really have to take 'American'?"

No one answered him—"American" was already gone. Now they were pulling up "soil" and "the Memory of Johnny Appleseed."

"My *name*?" shouted the Memory of Johnny Appleseed. "Not my name!"

"Settle down," a Mother told him. "We'll just run some tests on it and then we'll bring it back to you."

"And what am I supposed to do in the meantime?"

"Make up another name," suggested the headphoned Mother.

So he did—for a week his name was Martha D. Anger. During that time, it was *Martha Anger* who found the apple tree—Anger who plucked the apple, planted the seeds, grew more apples, planted more groves.

At the end of that week, Martha received a prayer from the Mothers saying that his name had been tested and cleared and was ready for pickup. I went with Martha to pick up the name—we rode the two-person bicycle over to the Word Pen, a temporary testing site in South Appleseed. We gave our names to the attendant and then waited in the mud for Martha's name to be released. Behind high fences covered in barbed wire, two wildwords—"humble" and "negotiate"—fought with each other. Other words howled or paced in place.

Finally the gate creaked open. Martha Anger turned and said, "Heeeere's Johnny!" Then his name bolted around the corner and jumped into his arms.

ROSEMARY RUSSET

That winter, some pipes froze at Woodside and two sinks cracked and died, so my Uncle Joump and I went out to Wolf Swamp to catch some new ones.

Joump worked with my Dad at the buildings. He was as tough as they come, and I'd never seen him scared of anything. When my Dad walked into the boiler room one day and saw some meaninglessers squatting behind the oil tank? Dad sent Joump in to marcia them out. When we needed to get rid of the "snowmen"—the ancient, obsolete asbestos-covered burners? The hazardous-waste companies would have charged us hundreds of theories, but Joump went in there one afternoon with a sledgehammer and a red bandanna over his mouth and he carried out those burners in pieces.

Joump was always nice to me—he gave me my Walkman and headphones on Core Day a few years earlier, for example, and if he found a book in his travels he'd always save it for me. With most people, though, Joump had a quick temper—I'd seen him get in fights with ricks and edgers way bigger than he was. Joump himself wasn't big, but he had a bulb-round belly from years of gorging on Kaddish Fruits. Kaddish, which gave you mights and false memories, was abundant in Appleseed; there was a grove in Wolf Swamp, for example, and a cluster of trees out by the Appleseed Prison. Joump grew his fruits himself, from trees that he'd transplanted onto his property and covered with a fake page. He'd show up at the buildings with his eyes smudged and his teeth stained blue, and sometimes he was so blurry that my Dad would have to send him home. The problem got so bad that my Dad and Joump stopped speaking for a while—one day Joump showed up at Woodside too kaddished to work, my Dad told him to leave, and Joump didn't talk to him for two years.

Then Joump's wife, Rachel, died. She was a really nice person, *too* nice, and finally she died of niceness. When my aunt called from Canada to tell us the news, my Dad put me in the truck and we drove over to Joump's house, a small duplex out near the Mental Hospital. We parked in the street and my Dad and I got out of the truck and walked toward the house. At the edge of the driveway, though, my Dad stopped and looked at the house in the distance. "Go see if he's OK," my Dad said.

"Me?" I said.

My Dad stared at the house. The grass was high and the house was dark.

"You do it," I said.

"He's your uncle," said my Dad. "Just go knock on the door."

I walked up to the door. "Uncle Joump?" I said.

There was no answer.

"Uncle Joump!" I said.

The door opened a little—I smelled the sour burn of rotten Kaddish Fruits. "_____?" Joump said.

"My Dad wants to know if you're OK," I said.

The door closed.

"Are you OK?" I said.

There was a shuffling inside the house.

"Uncle Joump?" I said.

"Tell him I'm hanging in," Joump said. "That I'll see him at Belmont next week."

This was later, after Joump sold his house and moved into Appleseed Heights. He'd bought a new car, a Cadillac, and he was dating a woman who lived in the complex. Her name was Dot. I didn't like her—she wore too much makeup. When she smiled, cracks appeared all over her face.

Joump drove out toward the swamp, the sinknets and the dead sink corpses and Joump's own sad story sliding around on the plastic lining of the truckbed. When we reached the wetlands, Joump parked and we hoisted the heavy nets on our shoulders. Then we walked down toward the still waters.

That swamp. I love thinking back on it—the way the trees folded their hands together to make shadows over the damp pathways; the sound of porcelain running through the trees; the mildewy smell of the water praying in the sun.

We walked for about half a mile. Then Joump stopped and pointed. There, about fifty yards away, was a stand-alone old sink grazing in the shallow muck. The sink looked old, but strong—you could see muscles by the drain. Joump flashed me the "OK" sign, and I moved as quietly as I could through the grass, flanking the sink and stepping up behind it.

When I was about twenty feet from it, though, the sink looked up and sniffed the air.

"Crap," said one of my thoughts.

"Get it!" Joump said.

I ran toward the sink and threw the net at it. The sink flinched, recoiled, and ran.

"Somana*bitch*," I heard Joump say.

The sink turned and fled into the high grass. It was *fast*—I ran my fatbody after it, my thoughts' glasses fogging and my lungs a burning house, but after ten seconds the sink just disappeared.

I didn't slow up; I thought that maybe the sink had fallen, or that it was hiding in the tall grass. I sprinted toward where I last saw it. Then my foot caught on something, and my ankle cried out, and I landed face first in the grass.

"Somanobee!" shouted my uncle. "_____! You OK?"

I sat up. My ankle was weeping. I looked back to see what I'd tripped on. Was it a root?

It wasn't. It was a—I'd tripped on a—

Reader: A what?

Hole.

Reader: A *what*?

A hole.

Reader: What do you mean, a *hole*?

My uncle jogged up to me and put his hands on his knees. "That bastard was quick," he said.

I shimmied back to the spot in the ground—the hole—where I'd tripped.

"Twist your ankle?" said Joump, standing up.

I pointed to the hole. "What is that?" I said.

"Hole," he said. He motioned for me to get up. "Let's go—we'll try again another day."

"A hole in the *page*?" I said.

"Yeah," he said. "It's a fucking hole in the page. So what?"

"I think that's where the sink went," I said. "Down in the hole."

"No shit," said Joump. "Can you walk?"

I stood up and leaned over the hole.

"How far down does it go?"

"Fuck if I know," Joump said.

We turned and walked back toward the creek and the truck parked in the dirt. I winced with every step. "Easy now," my uncle said. When we reached the truck, Joump opened the passenger's-side door and helped me onto the seat. "Listen. Don't tell your Mom about this, OK?"

"Why not?" I said.

"Because that's all I need," Joump said, chewing his lip. "She's already anti-Joump."

I snorted. "She's anti-_____, too," I said.

"Don't say that," said Joump.

"She hates me, Joump," I said.

"No, she doesn't. She loves you."

"She really doesn't, though."

137

"You think you're the only one in this book who suffers, _____?" said Joump. "Don't pretend you know what a parent goes through."

I shrugged.

"*Especially* your Mom."

"She's just in such a bad mood lately," I said.

"She's got a lot on her plate," my uncle said. "Hey. You hungry?"

When wasn't I hungry? "Sure," I said.

Joump didn't even ask me where we should go—he drove us right out to Oh Death, one of my favorite restaurants in Appleseed. We pulled up to the drive-in and he ordered two sickburgers with diefries and two dementia-flavored shakes. Then we parked in the lot and sucked the food into our mouths.

Between bites Joump said, "Sure you OK?"

"No," a thought said.

"Yeah," I said, my mouth full. Then I said, "What do you think the story is with that hole, Uncle Joump?"

"There is no story—it's a hole," said Joump.

"Now that I think about it, I've seen those before," I said. "I always thought they were cigarette burns."

"Drink your shake," Joump said.

I took a sip. The shake was really good—so good, in fact, that I forgot in that instant about the hole at Wolf Swamp. First I forgot the reason we went to the swamp, and then I forgot about the swamp altogether. I just remembered driving with Joump in the truck and—

What was I—

What was I talking about?

Reader: Wild sinks.

Oh yeah.

Reader: Did you ever replace them?

Replace whatnow?

Reader: The sinks. You were telling me about Joump and the sinks.

You want to hear a story about *Joump*? I'll tell you a sad one. When I was about fifteen? The buildings were belly-up by then and Joump had to take a job at the sawmill on Kellogg River. He was back to kaddishing hard—ten, twelve fruits a *day*—and one morning he showed up to work all mourned and he was fired. His driver's license had been revoked by then, so he was thumbing rides with co-workers. With no way to get home, he had to call my Dad to come pick him up. My Dad and I drove into the dirt lot of the mill just as Joump was walking out of the office. I remember he had this verb-eating grin on his face, like he'd just won a prize or something. A lateral armsaw who also worked at the mill was trudging through the parking lot, on his way into the office as Joump was walking out. The saw said something to him—I don't know what—and Joump's face fireworked; he rushed at the saw, belly pushed forward and arms flailing.

"What's this?" my Dad said from inside the cab.

The saw whirred to life.

"Shit," my Dad said. "Shit."

I saw Joump pull his arm back, and then, a flurry of fists and blades. My Dad jumped out of the truck. A Mother, patrolling overhead, saw the fight and dropped down into the parking lot to break it up. It was over by the time she got there, though—Joump's face and leg were cut badly. He was bleeding and he couldn't speak.

The Mother prayed to an ambulance, but my father didn't want to wait—he put Joump in the truck and we drove him to the hospital. He prayed out loud to my Mom that he was on his way, that Joump was with him, that he was in bad shape. I remember the way his voice trembled as he prayed. The past didn't matter. This was his *brother*.

THE AUCTIONEER

LIBERTY

Sometimes my Mom would leave me in that room in the Appleseed Hospital for hours—a whole day, even. When I got bored of sitting there, I'd sneak out and go exploring. I met some amazing people in and around that hospital—once, I was standing in line at the cafeteria when I struck up a conversation with someone who told me that he had three minds. He spoke three words at once, so I believed him.

"Does that mean you can think three thoughts at the same time?" I said.

"Yes/No/I'm not sure," said the man.

Another time I saw someone who bore a striking resemblance to a very large chicken. He was reading a book in the waiting room outside the emergency room, and I sat down near him. I wanted to understand if his chickenness was a costume or not. After a while, a woman shuffled out with a bracelet around her wrist. The giant chicken looked up. "Ready?" he said. The woman nodded and they walked through the revolving doors.

Every once in a while I'd see the Memory of Johnny Appleseed in the waiting room, too. As people forgot who Johnny Appleseed was, the Memory of Johnny Appleseed experienced health problems: contusions, confusions, delusions. He'd show up with his holy satchel and wait to be seen. They'd patch him up and he'd go back out to work in the fields.

One day, I was walking the halls of the hospital when I opened a door to an emergency staircase that I'd never seen before. It led me all the way down to the basement; I opened the heavy basement door to find a dusty storage room with cinder-block walls. There wasn't much there— just some old bicycles, a vending machine, and a historical couch. That couch, I decided, was from the Revolutionary War. It had probably helped fight for our freedoms! And now here it was.

I put some meaning in the machine and chose a pack of gummy tables.

"Good choice," said the vending machine.

"Right?" I said. The candy dropped to the bottom of the machine; I found it and ripped it open.

"Have you tried the gummy refrigerators?" said the vending machine.

"Refrigerators?" I said.

"They're awesome," she said, pointing to her navel. I looked through her belly to the stacked bags labeled GUMMY FRIDGES. "There's some chemical that keeps them actually cold. And when you open up the gummy door there are gummy perishables inside."

The vending machine's name was Laura—she was a student at East Appleseed Voc. When I told her my name she said, "Your name is just an underline?"

I nodded and ate a table.

"I've never heard of anyone with that name before," she said.

"It's French Canadian," I said.

"Is that where you're from?"

I chewed. "I'm from the margin," I said. "We moved to Appleseed when I was three."

"Ooh la la," she said. "Are you meaningful?"

I shook my head.

"Isn't everyone in Appleseed meaningful?"

"I don't think so," I said. "There are some nice houses, but."

"You probably are and you don't know it," she said.

"Maybe," I said.

We talked for a few more minutes and then I went back upstairs. I returned to the basement when I visited the following Wednesday, though, and again two days later. Soon I was spending hours with the vending machine. Chips, candy, mints—I spent all the meaning I had on her. I liked sitting on that veteran couch, talking to the vending machine and filling up on salt, corn syrup, sugar, and oil. For a long time, I think I associated that sadfood with the syntax in my heart.

Who am I kidding? I still do that now! If I told you what I ate last night—what, and what it was made of, and how much, you'd probably close this book right now.

Soon, Laura was calling me from the basement of the hospital almost every night. My Dad would answer the phone in the kitchen and hand it over to me, and I'd carry the receiver around the corner into the living room, stretching the coiled cord as far as it would go.

By that point I was visiting my Mom three or four times a week and spending almost all of those visits in the basement. One day I stopped by the hospital unannounced and I found my Mom wheeling the corpse of a problem down the hall. I talked with her for five minutes and then said, as casually as I could, that I was going downstairs. "Why are you always going down to the vending machine?" said my Mom, a star in her eye.

I shrugged. "I'm hungry," I said.

She stared at my belly. "How can that be?" she said.

I was always careful, when visiting Laura, to keep my distance—to sit at the far end of the couch or on the steps across the room. But one day I was eating some FatCrackers and she looked over at me and said, "Hey."

"Wha," I said.

"You're too far away," she said.

"Mm?" I said.

"Why don't you come sit next to me?"

I swallowed. "I can't."

"I want to be close to you," she said.

"I can't," I said again.

"Of course you can."

I said, "Do you know what divorcitis is?"

"What *what* is?"

I told her about it—the nausea, the skin irritation, the pre-divorce. When I mentioned that word, though, she laughed uncomfortably. "I'm not talking about *marriage*, _____. I just want you to sit next to me."

"I'm telling you," I said. "It won't end well."

"My parents are divorced," Laura said, "and it's not be-

146

cause of any sort of *virus*. My Dad was cheating on my Mom with his boss."

I thought about that. "He must have had the virus. It was the virus that made him cheat."

"But how could he get close to her in the first place if he had divorcis-whatever?"

I tried to sort that out in my mind, but my thoughts were feuding and giving each other the silent treatment.

"People just, fall out of love," said the vending machine. "Or stop getting along. Or act stupid. *That's* what causes divorce."

"I don't know," I said. "I just know I'm not supposed to get close to anyone."

The vending machine's display dimmed. "Is it something about the way I look? Is it my weight?"

"No, it's nothing," I said. "I just told you—"

"You know what? That's fine. *Don't* get close to me. Stay far away. Way far away."

"I don't want to stay far away," I said.

"I think you should, starting right now."

"I just need to give the music pills more time to—"

"Can you please leave me alone?" she said.

I stood up. I thought about walking toward Laura and kissing her right then and there, to translate how I felt, but I was afraid I'd get sick.

"Please *leave*," said Laura. "I don't want you here."

I turned around and walked up the stairs and out to the Bicycle Built for Two. I unlocked it and pedaled home.

I didn't see Laura that whole week or the next. I thought she'd call but she didn't. I called her twice, but she didn't pick up the pay phone the first time and the couch picked up the second time. "Yes?" he said.

"Is Laura there?" I asked.

"Hah?" said the couch. He must have been partially deaf from being too close to concussion grenades during battles in the war.

"Is Laura there?" I said again.

"Is who *where*?" he said.

I hung up the phone.

Whenever I visited the hospital after that, I stayed upstairs. One day, I was reading my truebook and Nurse Candle said, "No snacks today, _____?"

I shook my head and continued reading.

I thought about going down to the basement to talk to Laura, but then that thought left with all of the others. What would I say to her that I hadn't already?

But that weekend, a twig snapped in the wilderness of my skull. Did I want to live my whole life alone? I would not, could not, let the future—divorcitis, music—sloan me. I resolved to go back down to the hospital basement, put my hands on Laura's square shoulders and tell her how much I liked her. That I might even love her. Then I'd lean in and kiss her.

That Monday, I didn't even go upstairs first—I walked right from the bike rack down to the basement. When I turned the corner at the bottom of the stairs, though, I saw a very different Laura: she was slimmer, and wearing a belly shirt, and she'd changed her hair: it was teased high and shone with glitter. There was another vending machine in the basement as well—a soda machine with a fluorescent green chest. The two vending machines were sitting on the veteran couch, their faces close, saying words I couldn't hear.

I walked over to them. "Laura?" I said.

Both vending machines turned to look at me.

"Hello, _____," she said coolly.

"Hi," I said.

"You want some gummy fridges?" she slurred.

"No," I said. "Can I talk to you?"

"About what?" she said. "There's nothing to talk about, _____."

"I have some things I want to say," I said. I looked over at the other vending machine—he was smiling dumbly at me.

"This is Chad," said Laura. "Chad, _____."

"Yo," said Chad. "This the divorce guy?"

"Could you give us a second?" I asked Chad.

"I think Chad's fine right there," said Laura.

I stepped forward. "Laura," I said, "I'm not going to let anything come between us." Then my stomach seized, and I ran to the garbage can and threw up.

"Dude!" shouted Chad.

I wiped my mouth and walked back over to Laura. "I really like you," I told her. "Maybe even—"

"_____," said Laura. "I'm with Chad now."

All my thoughts were speaking at the same time—I couldn't hear a single one above the others. Without thinking about it, I leaned forward and tried to kiss Laura.

"Whoa!" said Chad, jumping off the couch and pushing me back. "That's my *girlfriend* you just tried to kiss."

"Chad," said Laura.

"Unless you want me to kick your ass right in front of her? I'd walk up those steps right now. Comprende?"

I should have turned around—should have left that basement and never gone back to it. It was over—couldn't I see that?

But I stayed where I was. "*No* comprende," I said, bumping my belly against Chad's plastic chest.

"Guys," said Laura.

"Is this a joke?" Chad said, and he pushed me back against the wall. My head hit the cinder block; my ears rang.

I thought, *I could kill this guy.* "I'm warning you," I said. "Leave me alone."

Chad stepped right up to me, squishing me against the cinder blocks. I felt the air leave me and I thought I might pass out. "Or what?" gritted Chad.

Sometimes you don't know what you know. It'd been months since I'd watched that tape about size-changing, and I'd only tried it that one time. At that moment, though, a thought said to me, *You asked for it.* Another said, *Go small, _____. Go small.*

It wasn't difficult to become a sentence. You just arranged your thoughts in a line in your mind. As I stood there before Chad, I began to shrink: to five feet, four feet, three feet, two.

"What the fuck," said Chad, stepping back. He looked at Laura and she smirked.

One foot, six inches, three inches, one inch. By then, both vending machines were staring incredulously. "Dude, what are you *doing*?" asked Chad.

"Stop laughing," I said.

"It's funny," said Chad.

"I'm going to freaking kill you," I said. By that time I was as small as a fingernail—I was that angry. I ran across the floor, up Chad's body and into the meaning slot.

"Crap!" said Chad.

"_____!" shouted Laura.

I jumped into Chad's chest and bolted through the rows of cans. I pulled a lever and freed them. "No!" I heard Chad shout.

"Thank you," said a can of ginger ale.

I climbed a can of grape soda and pulled the tab—the purple bubbly spilled over the other cans and the wiring and machinery.

"Shit!" said Chad. "Dude, stop!"

I ran up into Chad's brain: springs and wires and coils. When I looked behind the meaning-changer I found data storage: stacks of memories, some piles of ideas, a few emotions. I took ten years of memories and his love for Laura. I left him blank. Then I ran through a vent in the back of his mind and down his power cord, and through a tiny crack in the mortar and out into the fields behind the hospital. Chad wept and Laura hollered, but I left them behind and ran as fast as I could toward my Bicycle Built for Two, resizing with every step, the love and memories clanking together in my arms, my eyes full of tears.

CORNISH AROMATIC

See? I told you that there'd be a story about the Appleseed Free Library, where my Mom and I used to go every
Wednesday. This is that story! Like I said, that library—
which, like most libraries, doubled as a disco—was more
or less the heart of Appleseed. Located in the direct center
of town, you could still see all of the bloodlines running
just under the surface of the grass, through the walls of
the foundation, and into the Library's basement. Someone
once told me that there was a machine in that room that
pumped actual *blood*—hundreds of gallons of bookblood a
minute.

I used to look forward to those Wednesday nights,
to farting with my Mom down Longfellow Drive, onto
Highway Five, and into the parking lot of the AFL. It was
always just me and her—my sister and my Dad weren't really that into reading. My Mom, though? She read as if her
books might disappear when she took her eyes off them;
she probably read two or three books a week.

Anyway, we'd return our books to the desk and split
up to wander through the shelves. The AFL didn't have
the *best* books, or the *newest* books, or the *rarest* books, or
the *nicest* books (a lot of the language was rusted or bent, in

fact, destroyed from so much reading), or the *tallest* books, or the *loudest* books, or the *orangest* books, but it had the *strangest* books I'd ever seen. They had books with naked words; books with hooks—literal hooks; books that, when you opened them up, spat at you. They had books made of dust and books made of cheese, books shaped like chairs and books as soft and furry as a winter coat. Some of those books were visible—i.e., you could see them—and others were beyond vision. With *those* books, you didn't even know you were reading until all of a sudden you sensed the words on your eyes, heard the pages turning, felt the warmth of the book on your shoulders.

Sometimes I'd fall asleep and wrap the books over me. I'd make myself a small house of books and fall asleep in it. It felt like being back in the womb—it was that warm, that safe.

Reader: As you imagine it, at least.

Sorry?

Reader: Not like you remember the womb.

Of course I do. You don't?

The Reader furrowed her brow.

I remember every moment of it! There were words in that womb with me, I'm sure of it. The Library was like those pre-page days—warm and verbal. Everything you could ever want or need was right there with you. You never had to worry about being alone—you were *never* alone! If you ever got scared or depressed—when your mind spun with worry, or you lost all faith—you could just listen for that heartbeat right next to your ear, all around you, actually, and you'd feel safe again.

Even though my Mom stopped going to the Library with me ("All you had to do was keep your mouth shut and read the words," she'd shouted at me when I asked her to go. "But you couldn't just let sleeping words lie!"), I continued to go by myself. I liked to open up the books and see the sentences move. I also went back there, though, because I missed her—the old her, the happier Mom. I missed going there with her; I felt closer to her there.

Another reason that I liked the Library? It was good exercise for my thoughts. Don't tell them that I said this, but some of my thoughts were kind of *losers*. Not like, in thoughtgangs or anything like that; they were just lazy. Most of them lounged around on a couch in my skull, playing video games. Either that or they were troublemakers, wanderthoughts, renegades too dumb to know which parts of Appleseed to avoid. If a thought of mine went missing, I'd inevitably find it in one of the seediest parts of Appleseed: down in the Quarry, out at the Meadows, or sitting on a stool at Appleseed's only bar for thoughts, the Think Tank.

Hey, look at that. My shoelace is untied. Do you know where I found this shoelace? It was crawling in the sand by Kellogg River, burrowing. Me and my uncle went out there specifically for shoelaces, and we'd searched all morning. I remember that day specifically, because—

Anyhoo.

And I wasn't the only one in Appleseed with wandering thoughts—thoughts with minds of their own. Some thoughts *lived* on the streets: they were orphans, nomads, wanderers with no mind to go back to—just the thought of a shelter or a bench in McShane Park. It was important, I thought, to try to keep my thoughts together. The Library was one of the few places where I could open my skull, lean down and let my thoughts scatter and roam. They could go to their sections, my Mom to hers, me to mine.

Usually I'd read books about Johnny Appleseed. One of my favorites, *The Book of Apples*, was shelved in the Reference section—it told the story of how Johnny, born in the Massachusetts town of Lemontown, moved to Appleseed intrigued by the blank pages and the rich soil. The middle of the book was devoted to Appleseed's philosophy—how he believed that apples held all the knowledge we needed; that they held our oldest stories; that they were, in essence, brains. There were also drawings based on one of Appleseed's stories—one showed a naked vending machine in a secret Appleseed mountain garden, evil earthworms all around her; another showed historical applenuns and bessoffs praying on the Town Green. Plus, there was a whole section in the book devoted to apple fads and fashions, like that very short time when apples were worn as hats. Did you know that the apple-hat fad contributed to the First Apple War? A conservative appler named Jed Berson was so offended by Lox Homicki's apple hat that he shot it right off his head with his revolver. Homicki wasn't injured, but he demanded that Berson replace the hat. Berson refused, and both summoned backup. There was a standoff, and the war began soon afterward.

The Book of Apples also showed dozens of pictures of Johnny Appleseed: Appleseed walking with his holy satchel, Appleseed digging with his spade, Appleseed kneeling among the saplings. Because the Memory of Johnny Appleseed was old—white beard, vagabondy clothes—that's how my thoughts thought of him. But the book showed Johnny Appleseed as a young hipster, with a top hat and an ambitious beard.

Like a lot of the books in the Library, this one was too old and too rare to circulate. So I read it right there at one of the tables, over three or four weeks' time. I learned all about the different kinds of apples—Champion, Yellow Transparent, Hambledon Deux Ans—and about the last years of Johnny Appleseed in Appleseed, before he followed the smell of apples south and never returned.

One week, I beelined over to the Reference section and saw that *The Book of Apples* wasn't on the shelf where I'd left it. I looked through the entire Appleseed section, but to no avail. When I went over to the study desks, though, I saw the Memory of Johnny Appleseed turning the pages of an oversize book. I approached his table and stood over him—he was reading the section about military technologies in the Fifth Apple War. "I was looking for that," I said.

He looked up at me. "Still working on that project?"

I shook my head.

"Get a good grade?"

"C," I said.

"How? I told you the whole story," said the Memory of Johnny Appleseed.

"I forgot about the project until the day it was due," I said.

The Memory of Johnny Appleseed smirked and shook his head.

I didn't move. After a moment, the Memory of Johnny Appleseed looked up at me. "Are you going to just stand there and watch me read?"

"I was really looking forward to reading the end," I said.

"Early bird catches the worm," he said.

I stared at him.

"It is *my* story, after all," he said.

I just stood there.

"Go away, _____."

So I did—I walked out to my Bicycle Built for Two, unlocked it, and rode off the page.

The following day, though, I rode my bike to the Library right after school. I went directly to the Reference section, where a Librarian in a disco suit was stamping and stacking books. I knew my thoughts would be bored in that section, though, so I opened my skull in the lobby and let them run upstairs to Media; only one or two stayed behind in my mind. Then I found *The Book of Apples*, sat in a corner, and read for the next two hours, absorbing as much as I could. Every once in a while one of my thoughts would find me there and pester me by tugging on my sleeve or walking onto the page I was reading. "Can we go?" one asked.

"Not yet," I whispered.

"I'm so bored."

"Then *read*," I said.

I was halfway through Appleseed's anecdotes about language-planting, though, when I saw the lights overhead flicker. The library was starting to close. I knew what would happen next: the lights would go out altogether, the disco balls would drop, the shelves would slide to the walls and a light-up dance floor would be born. Some books would pick up keyboards and saxophones and drums while other books donned disco suits and dancing dresses. Read: flashing lights; booksweat; music so loud you couldn't hear your thoughts *think*!

I put the book back on the shelf and opened my skull to collect my thoughts. Some of them scampered into my skull, but a few stood staring at me. "What are you doing?" said one. "I was really into that story!"

"The Library's closing soon," I told the thought.

"Can we check the book out?" said the thought.

I shook my head. "It's a reference book," I said.

"Then just *take* it, man," said the thought.

Reader: Wait—what?

"You should," another thought said.

"Who's going to know?" the first thought said.

Reader: That's *stealing*, _____. Stealing is illegal!

The second thought looked at the Reader. "Don't you want to understand Appleseed's planting techniques? How the stories are told?"

Reader: Sure, but—

"I'm not—I can't—no way," I said.

"Just put it in under your shirt, wussface," said the thought.

I thought about it. "There's a Librarian *right there*," I whispered to my skull. Next to Mothers and Cones, Librarians were probably the most powerful people in Appleseed: they were dizzyingly smart, highly trained, paid a lot of meaning, and great at disco—they knew all the latest moves.

"We have to get out of here," I told the thought.

"We want the story, _____," said the first thought. "We are *not* leaving that book here."

A Librarian in disco gear whisked by. "Music begins in ten minutes!" he sang.

I smiled and nodded and thought to walk away from the shelves, but when I actually tried to move my feet they wouldn't lift. I knew right away that it was my thoughts, conspiring to control me. "We need to *go*," I told my thoughts.

"No one's going to miss *one book*," a thought of umbrellas whispered. Before I could object further he grabbed the book I'd been reading off the shelf, climbed my shoulders, opened the top of my head as wide as the hinge would go and stuffed the book into my skull. The book was a hardcover—big, heavy, with sharp corners. The weight on my brain made me shriek.

"Shh! Big baby," said the thought.

I couldn't see for a second—I blinked and blinked. My vision reversed, flipped upside down. My arm began tremoring. I let out an involuntary yelp. "You're messing up his brain, dude," said one thought to another.

I tried to object—to say "Stop!"—but I couldn't make words; one of the books must have been pressing on my language center. Then even the *thoughts* of words vanished. I blurted whatever word was available to me. "Darjeeling!" "Pock." "Historical!"

Meanwhile, the thoughts struggled to close my skull.

I could feel them pushing and shoving one another, trying to make room for the novel they'd crammed into their living space. My eyes fluttered; my vision was blue. I clawed at the hinge on my skull but the thoughts held it closed.

Suddenly I heard the swish of guitars and recorded horns—the disco music was starting.

"Oop," said the thought. "Time to vamoose, _____."

The lights were dimming.

"_____?"

I pulled at the seam of my skull. "Stout," I said. "Lasso."

Out on the floor, disco Librarians were starting to assemble. A strobe light yawned, stretched its arms and started turning. I looked out the windows at the dusky purple light.

"Get moving, _____," said the thought.

I tried one more time to reason, to find language to name my thoughts, but I couldn't. So I forced all my concentration toward a thought of walking: very slowly, one foot in front of the other. I edged away from the shelf, across the Reference section, over the dance floor, and into the lobby. It seemed to take forever to get to the circulation desk. I was sweating and dizzy. At one point I stumbled and a thought said, "Easy. Just act cool, _____."

Cool. I tried to remember what that word meant. But I didn't know.

When we passed the circulation desk, two Librarians in disco suits looked up from a pile of books that they were stamping. "Not staying for the dance?" asked the male discoer.

I stammered. "Yee. I—"

"Say 'No thanks,'" said the thought.

"No—thanks," I said.

"Sure?" said the female.

"Smile," said the thought.

I smiled.

"Say 'Have a good night, though,'" said the thought.

"Have a good night, though," I said.

"Now move," the thought said, and I pushed open the double doors into the foyer. As I did, though, an alarm rang out—a repeating beep, but a beep that had been eating right, working out, trying to turn its life around. "Dammit. Run!" shouted the thought, but I didn't—I stopped; I rugged. The Librarians leapt over the desk and stretched their hands out at me. "Hold up just a second there," said the discoer.

"Shit!" shouted a thought inside my mind.

"It's the magnetic tags," said another. "They put them in all the books."

"Don't let that fucker touch you, _____," said a thought of violence. "If he does, you punch that fucker in the fucking *face*."

The Librarians put their hands on me, turned me around, and led me back into the lobby.

"Roundhouse-kick them!" said violence. "Pull out their esophagi!"

The Librarians stared at me. "Sorry about that," said the discoer. "Scanner picked something up."

"Not checking out any books tonight?" said the discoess.

"N—no," I said.

"We've had problems with that thing," said the discoer, pointing to the scanner.

"What's your name?" said the discoess.

"Don't tell them!" said a thought.

"Make something up!" said another.

"Head-butt the big one and sweep the leg of the small
one!" said the thought of violence.

I tried to think of a name—any name. I gave them the
first one I could come up with: "Chris," I blurted. "My
name is—Chris."

"Chris what?"

"Chris B-ook," I said. "Book."

"Chris *Book*? That's funny," said the discoer. "Mr.
Book? In a Library?"

"Can you hold out your arms, Mr. Book?"

I stretched out my arms and the discoess patted my shirt
and my pant legs. In my mind, meanwhile, my thoughts
were scrambling to hide. I could feel them ripping up
pages from the book and cramming them wherever they
could: in the empty channels and caverns in my skull, in
my spinal column, behind my eyes, in my ear canals. The
pain was terrible. I tasted words on my tongue, saw words
in my eyes: there were letters on the male discoer's face;
the discoess had a *W* for an ear and her arm was a noun.

The discoess frisked me, stepped back, and looked to
the discoer. "Nothing," she said.

The discoer tapped his head.

"Bend down, please," said the discoess.

"Everyone *act natural*!" shouted a thought.

I bent down. The discoess unlatched the lock on my

skull and opened it at the seam. The hinge on my skull creaked as she lifted the lid.

I felt her eyes on my brain and I prepared for the worst. They would know that I stole. And then what? "They'll interrogate you," whispered the thought of violence. "Torture. Torture like only a *Librarian* can deliver."

The female Librarian sighed. "I don't see anything," she said. "Just a bunch of thoughts sitting on a couch and watching television."

"No books?" said the discoer.

"No books, no ideas, nothing," said the discoess. "It's like a *tomb* in here!" She stooped so she could see my face. "Is this place for rent?"

The discoer guffawed and slapped his knee.

"Hardy fucking har," whispered the thought of violence, from wherever he was hiding in my mind. "I'll kill both of you motherfuckers."

The discoess closed up my skull. "My apologies, Mr. Book," she said. "The alarm must have gone off by mistake."

"No problem," said my thought of speech.

"No problem," I said.

I rushed out of the library and down to the bike racks, where I unlocked the Bicycle Built for Two. I started pedaling away, but I still couldn't see; the whole world was words and terms. And the noise in my mind—my thoughts, high-fiving and dancing and celebrating—didn't help either. "Thoughts *rule*!" shouted a thought of sidewalks. "Fuck yeah!" hooted the thought of violence.

Four blocks from the Library, when I could no longer hear the disco music, I collapsed on the dusky grass. I lay down on my side and my thoughts kicked open my brain and tumbled out of it. "Woo!" shouted the thought of violence, stepping into the grass. "We are badass thought mofos!" he roared. "Aren't we?"

"That was so cool!" said the thought of walking.

I collapsed in the grass. I couldn't speak; I was sick with words. The information was blurp reed, yazzing through my > mmm fulcrum.

"_____?" said a thought of home. "You OK?"

"Are you in need of gutter repair?" I said.

"What?" said the thought of walking.

"The fail is going on all weekend," I said.

"What fail?" said violence.

"That's our cornerback guarantee," I said.

"He's fucked," said another thought.

My thoughts colluded to get me standing and walking; I hung over my bike and slowly made my way home. With every step, though, I felt changed; my cells were absorbing the stories—their sentences, symbols, and themes.

Halfway home, we ran into the Memory of Johnny Appleseed praying at the edge of a field of dead trees. "_____," he said, and stood up. The knees of his pants were wet from the mud. "You OK?"

"You're fine," said my thoughts.

"I'm fine," I said.

But I knew Johnny Appleseed wasn't fooled—he could see the apples in my eyes.

D'ARCY SPICE

1987 wasn't an anomaly; the Memory of Johnny Appleseed was wrong. The apples came back smaller the year after that, and smaller still—no bigger than crabs, in fact—the following year. In 1990, no apples grew at all—all the trees in Appleseed were bare. The Board of Select Cones voted to bring in a soil expert from the margins, but all she could do was confirm that the pagesoil was barren—she couldn't say why or how to solve it. So the Board of Select Cones summonsed the Memory of Johnny Appleseed and demanded a solution. The Memory of Johnny Appleseed held out his hands to them. "I'm really not sure," he said. "It has something to do with the stories we're telling. They seem to be sapping the soil."

The Memory was dismissed, and from then on, vilified. Or is it *villainized*? Cast out, outcasted: turned away at his favorite restaurants, denied meaning at his bank, locked out of his own apartment. Soon he was homeless. Rumor was he was sleeping on the streets or in the deadgroves. Sometimes you'd see him outside the Why, handing out brochures.

A host of theories ran through Appleseed: the blight was a curse, prayed upon us out of spite; it was some sort of wildword virus; it was a plot, spearheaded by East Appleseed to destabilize us. Meanwhile, we prayed for a different story, or a better ending to this one.

Overnight, it seemed, Appleseed lost most of its meaning. The applers tried swapping out their central ingredients for another—oranges, lemons, pears—but to no avail. Have you ever had a *pear*burger? A raw lemon? Ye—uck. Soon, applers began to leave town, hitchhiking over the margins toward richer harvests. The Planters who stayed in Appleseed gave up on perishables and tried their luck with solidifides: they planted chairtrees, for example, or fields of refrigerators.

It wasn't long before the town's appleloss hit home. My Mom lost hours at the hospital and had to pick up a shift at Appleseed Mental. That was the thought of small potatoes, though, compared to my Dad's predicament. First, his tenants started sending in partial-meaning payments, forcing my Dad to hound them—to drive over to the apartments, knock on their doors, and ask them face-to-face where the meaning was. A few times I went with him. Once, we were driving down Belmont Street when we saw a pair of overalls who owed my Dad meaning walking toward the building. We parked the car and followed him inside. The overalls, who used to pick apples at Berson's Farm before it shut down, answered the door with a four-foot cigarette hanging out of his mouth. When he saw it was my Dad, he nodded and leaned against the doorframe. "Ralph," he said.

"It's the ninth, Jaime," said my Dad.

"Yes, it is," said the pair of overalls.

"Nine days late," said my Dad.

"Yes," said the pair of overalls.

"Where is it?"

"I don't have it."

"You have to pay your rent, Jaime," my Dad said.

"Do I?" the overalls said.

Soon it wouldn't matter—more than half of my Dad's tenants stopped paying. Some left in the middle of the night; some stayed behind even when the heat skipped town and the water died in the pipes.

With so few tenants living in the building, my Dad lost faith and fell behind on upkeep. And now that I think about it? That was right around the same time that my thoughts started turning inward, digging into my brain. My Mom took me back to Doctor Coat to see if this might be related to the music pills, and the Coat opened up my head and looked around. When he peered inside, one of my thoughts gave him the finger.

"Hm," the Coat said. "Where are your other thoughts?" he asked me, his voice echoing off the walls of my skull.

"Out," I said.

"Out where?" said the Coat.

"*Out*, OK?" I said.

"You see?" my Mom said. "He's had that puss on his face for weeks now."

"I have a headache, OK?" I said.

"It's always something, isn't it, _____?" she said.

At home, our phone rang and rang. We were assaulted with calls and prayers from bill collectors, banks, disgruntled tenants. Soon my Dad stopped praying altogether. One day Mrs. Parker, who always paid her rent, prayed to me about a leaking toilet. I went to ask my Dad about it and found him on the back patio, picking pieces from a half-rotten Kaddish fruit. I told him about the prayer for service. "Sounds like a serious situation," I said. "Do you want to go over there?"

"I'm not going anywhere," he said, looking out into the trees.

"Should *I* go over there?"

"Christ," my Dad said. "Tell her I'll get there when I can."

"Today?"

"When I *can*," my Dad said.

So that's what I prayed to her. Hours later, though, Mrs. Parker prayed to me again. "Help!" her prayer said. "The water is up to my knees!"

I didn't pray back.

"Now it's up to my waist!" she prayed.

If I was really a good person? I would have ridden out there on my Bicycle Built for Two just to see what I could do. But instead I sat down on the couch with a bag of chips and watched TV, just like the spoiled, selfish piece of shit my Mom said I was. I didn't move for the rest of the afternoon—not even when Mrs. Parker prayed to me that the water was up to her chin. Not even when the prayers stopped altogether.

YELLOW TRANSPARENT

As I said, my sister Briana was a towntalent in the arts of ancient construction and antiquing. Before I was even allowed to go with them, she and my Dad would take off for the dump in his truck and return with an overwhelm of strange objects. Growing up with her, I didn't really appreciate the kind of eye it took to spot meaning—I couldn't tell the difference between a worba and a forba, between a norch and a nouch—but my sister could spot truth in objects that your standard vulture or scav would look right past: she'd see the old in the warboots, hear the subtle sounds in a dead viola, recognize an entropy as a shrine from a goneby religion. When Bri was twelve, my Dad built a shed in the backyard where she could store her collectibles and tools. Once or a twice a summer he'd load up the truck with her fixed-ups and meaningfuls, drive her to the flea, and set up a table for her where she could sell. He'd subtract the meaning for the table and she'd get to keep the rest.

One day in the summer of her sixteenth year—1989, that would have been—my sister was cleaning out the shed, separating the meaningful from the seemingly-so. I was out in the yard that day, too, sanding window frames for my Dad. After working in the shed for a while, my sister took some of the less-meaningful objects—a nightstand, a sump pump, a faux-antique mailbox, and some other ifs and ands—out to the treebelt and left them by the road for the taking. Then she helped me with the windows; I taped and she painted. We had the tape deck blasting from the front steps. "Who is this?" I asked Briana at one point.

"UCs," she said.

"Who?" I said.

We were midway through the stack of windows when a Pontiac pulled over in front of our house. A scarf stepped out of the car, walked over to the pile, and picked up the sump. He turned it over, held it up, and shouted out to us, "How much?"

My sister put her hands on her hips.

Before she could answer, a woman in an old, leaning veggiecar pulled up in front of the scarf's Pontiac. The woman rolled down the window and said, "That sump pump for sale?"

My sister looked at me, and then back at the scarf and the woman.

"How much are you asking for it?" the woman said.

It felt to me like all of Appleseed stopped at that moment—even the clouds and the air and the prayers.

"How about," Briana said, her voice pivoting, "two concepts?"

The woman got out of the car; she and the scarf looked at each other. Then the woman said, "Two, yes."

"I'll give you two and a quarter concepts," said the scarf.

I saw a flash in Briana's eye. "Do-I-hear—" she said, "—two-and-a-*half*?"

"What?" said the scarf. "What is this, an—"

"Two and a half," said the woman.

"Three," said the scarf.

Just like that, the Auctioneer was born. "Four?" she said. "Do-I-hear-four?"

I remember the music in her words. That first call wasn't perfect—her bidding responses were mumbled, hesitant—but I think all three of us heard the natural rhythmic tumble in her voice. It was as if she'd been waiting for this page all her life, and finally you turned to it.

"Four," said the woman.

"Five," said the scarf.

"Do-I-hear-six?" said Briana.

The scarf and woman looked at each other.

"Six? Going-once? Going-twice?"

"Six," said the woman.

With every bid, it seemed, the Auctioneer found more of a foothold. "Six. Seven? Do-I-hear-seven? Going-once! Going-twice?"

The scarf shook its head.

"Sold-to-the-woman-with-the-angry-ears!" said the Auctioneer.

The woman frowned.

That was the beginning of a new chapter for my sister. When she told my Dad what had happened, he set up a piece of plywood on some sawhorses in the backyard and she rifled through the shed for more items to sell. The next day, people showed up in our driveway as if driven by some external force; they sat in the grass while my sister stood on a chair and called the auction. She held auctions the following day, too, and all day that Saturday. Soon, she was skipping school so she could focus on building an inventory for her backyard auctions. She replaced the plywood with folding tables and the chair with a beat-up lectern. Within a few weeks, everyone in Appleseed knew about my sister and her auctions—there were always ten or eleven cars camped out in front of 577, waiting for bidding to begin. Every afternoon of my fourteenth year I'd pedal home from school, sit on the roof with a bag of chips, and watch the bidders shouting and arguing.

"Don't-tell-me-good-people-that-twenty-four-is-the-best-you-can-*do*!" my sister shouted, standing at a lectern. "I-thought-you-were-serious-and-meaningful!"

"Twenty-six!" someone hollered.

"Still-an-insulting-amount-of-meaning-for-this-particular-washboard," my sister shouted. "It-is-an-ANTIQUE-after-all—"

"Thirty!"

Soon, people started telling stories about my sister's gifts: her discerning eye, the cadence and precision of her voice, her ability to engage with a crowd and elicit meaning. One night that fall, my sister sat down at the kitchen table for dinner and said she had an announcement. "I-will-no-longer-respond-to-the-name-Briana," she said.

"Oh, yes, you will," said my mother, without looking up from her plate.

"I think she can decide what she wants to be called, Diane," my Dad said.

174

My Mom glared at him.

"As long as it's within reason," my Dad said.

"How about dumbface?" I said.

"_____," my Mom said.

My sister didn't seem fazed. "From-this-day-forward," she said, "I-shall-be-known-as-the-Auctioneer."

"Auctioneer?" I laughed. "That's so stupid."

"*The*. I-am-*the*-Auctioneer," she said, and turned to me with eyes like arrows, "and-don't-you-forget-it."

THE MOTHERS OF APPLESEED

SENTENCE THE SENTENCE II

I walked that sentence all over Appleseed—he was my true
good friend. In the cold months, I'd just lead him out across
the street to relieve himself in the margin, but in the spring
and summer we'd zell all the way to the Town Green and
back, or out to the Amphitheatre, or sometimes to Wolf
Swamp. I even put a basket on the handlebars of the Bicycle Built for Two so "I am." could ride with me and the
Reader. I remember the way Sentence would rest his chin
on the front of the basket so the wind would push back the
serif on his "I."

That was right after the blight, when everything
changed in our house. My sister was consumed by her auctions and my father was always out trying to scrape together
some meaning. And I hardly saw my mother either—
she was training harder than ever. So I basically raised that
sentence myself—I fed him and walked him. If his words
were tired, I carried "I am." in my coat pocket. I took him
to school with me, and to the buildings after school, and to
Oh Death for food—everywhere I was, "I am." was, too.

Soon, Sentence was no longer a single subject and verb.
He grew from "I am." to "I am *here*.", to "Am I here?",

to "I *think* I am here.", to "I think, therefore, right here.", to "*He* therefores, thinks, and ams." and on and on. The sentence was constantly revising—every day was a new iteration.

The point of this part of the story—of *these* sentences—though, is that "I am." was there for me when no one else was. Looking back on it now, I can say—

It was like:

How do I put this into words?

Like, loneliness? It was like, sometimes *I* wasn't. Wasn't anything. Wasn't anyone. I could stop being, and not be, and I didn't know if anyone would notice. But at least I could turn that thought—that thought of loneliness, of unmeaning—into words, and say those words to Sentence. And "I am." would just *listen*—he might fart or fall asleep, but he wouldn't leave me or judge me. And *I* wouldn't abandon *him*, either: senseless, smelly, whatever—I was just happy for the companionship.

Which isn't to say that I was a pushover—I raised that language right. I always walked "I am." on a leash—I had to, in accordance with Appleseed bylaws—and at night, Sentence slept in a cage in the basement. It's very important to cage your language—otherwise, it can read in its sleep and havoc your whole house. My sentence was usually friendly, but a lot of language is vicious—quick-tempered, impulsive, violent. You know how, when you're out in Appleseed late at night, you sometimes hear a mawing in the distance—like, a low vumble or a harl? That's wild language, reading the city for food or a mate or fighting each other over territory.

As well–behaved as he was, "I am." was wild as well. Sometimes he would run away. Once he disappeared for two days and showed up at the back door, his mouth covered in blood. Another time the Memory of Johnny Appleseed found Sentence wandering in a deadgrove. "I am." had been gone for about twenty–four hours when the Memory of Johnny Appleseed rode over to my house on his tree-bike. "Are you?" said the Memory of Johnny Appleseed.

It had only been a month or two since the start of the blight, but Johnny had aged. Instead of wearing his trademark straw hat and overalls, he had on Converse hi–tops, gaudy parachute pants, and a stained green blazer. His eyes were weary.

"Am I—what?" I said.

"Are you?" he said.

"I don't know what you're asking me," I said.

"You're supposed to say 'I am,'" said the Memory of Johnny Appleseed, taking the sentence out from underneath his blazer. "It's a joke—get it?"

"'I am.'!" I said. "Thank you so much, man."

"You should train that rambunctious clause," the Memory of Johnny Appleseed said, and then he put his foot on the wooden pedal, pushed off, and rode away.

To be honest, though, I liked that "I am." had a wild streak—that he sometimes picked up the scent of language and pulled on the leash. I didn't want to lose "I am." but I always wanted him to be who he was—to follow his innate language animal instincts. Those instincts were often really helpful, actually. "I am." could always tell if someone was wounded, for example; if I had a headache, Sentence would lead me to the sofa and sit beside me. And once, "I am." and I got lost on a walk through Wolf Swamp and the wolves started jeering and throwing bottles. After leading us around the swamp in a circle, I asked Sentence to get us out of there. He sniffed the air with his "m" and forged forward; soon, I could see the edge of the parking lot.

Maybe two months into the blight, I was walking Sentence in the backyard one afternoon when he started pulling me toward the shed where my sister stored her items for auction. "I am." was interested in a tarp-covered pile of junk outside the shed—he kept lunging for the blue vinyl. "What is it, buddy?" I said.

Then the door of the shed opened and my sister stepped out. "Hey," said the Auctioneer.

"Sorry," I said. "Sentence was just sniffing around. Is there time under there or something?"

"Don't-think-so," she said, and she pulled back the tarp. Underneath was a bunch of moldy old yellow pads of paper and clipboards of different sizes. I recognized them as the same pads my Dad was always writing notes and to-do lists on. "Those Dad's?" I said.

The Auctioneer nodded. "A-stationery-store-went-out-of-business-and-gave-all-this-stuff-away. Want-one?"

"I am." was spinning with excitement.

"Maybe just to calm him down," I said.

My sister handed me a clipboard and a pad of paper. "What time does the auction start?"

"Three," she said, and she stepped back into the shed.

I led Sentence down the hatchway and into the basement. I dropped the clipboard and pad on the ground and sat down with some chips. As soon as I opened the bag, though, "I am." appeared next to me with the yellow pad of paper.

"What is it, 'I am.'?" I said.

He put the pad in my lap and looked up at me. I put aside the bag of chips. "I am." looked down at the yellow space—the blank page—as if he could see something I couldn't.

I reached for a pen and wrote the words "I" and "am" on the page. "That's your name," I told him.

He looked at the letters. His eyes lit up. A thought in my mind said, "here," and I transferred the words from that room in my brain to the pen to the page. "I am *here*," I wrote.

He looked at me, and back at the page.

"I'm *not* here," I wrote.

"I am." frowned.

"I *wasn't* here," I wrote.

"I wasn't born here," I wrote.

"I wasn't born in Appleseed," I wrote.

With a steady time diet, shelter, and regular exercise, "I am." grew and complicated. Soon he was "I am writing." Then "I am writing words on the page." Then, "I am writing words on the page about my own life." And then, "I am going to transform my life through writing. I can do anything."

Reader: "Transform?" That word is wild, _____.

I can do anything on the page.

Not using those words, you can't!

"Yes," I wrote. "Yes, I can."

LADY SUDDELEY

For the first two months of the blight there was no word at all from the Mothers. You'd just see them overhead, in Reading Formation, scanning the page below. With more time on her hands, my Mom would sometimes drive around in the Fart, looking for a flock to follow. Once she saw some skirts in the sky on the way home from the Big When—"Look!" she said, "Look at them *go!*"—and she steered us down a side street in pursuit.

"I thought we were going to the When," I whined.

"*Tsk,*" my Mom spat. "We'll go where I say, when I say."

My sister and I exchanged glances but neither of us said anything. We followed the pack of Mothers for almost half an hour, until they reached the southeast margin and swooped into a giant Nest. I think that was my first time actually seeing a Nest—which, I was surprised to see, really *did* look like a nest. Only *this* Nest? Was as big as a football field, and suspended about three hundred feet in the air, and made of twists of cement and dark steel. I could see glass windows in the gaps, and Mothers in goggles standing watch on some of the highest beams.

"Wow," my mother said. "These woman are heroes. *Heroes.*"

"The-When-closes-in-an-hour," the Auctioneer said. My Mom stared up at the Nest for another minute or two and then turned the Fart toward East Appleseed. "Heroes," she said again.

Growing up with my Mom, I knew all about the Mothers—both the Appleseed chapter and the national movement, the Mothers of America. My Mom loved to tell us stories about the history of the brigade: the Mothers' silent, ever-present support of the Suffragettes, the Anti-Slavery Conventions, the Woman's Peace Party. Lucretia Mott was secretly a Mother, my Mom told us. So was Susan B. Anthony and Sojourner Truth. Abraham Lincoln. Ida B. Wells! Allen Ginsberg.

Reader: Abraham Lincoln?

Mothers don't have to be women, nor do they have to have children. They just have to go through the training and take the oath; Mothers pledge to guard and protect a story, or change it when need be. Mothers can kick ass when they have to—they protected Allied planes during Word War II, for example, by deflecting machine-gun fire with their warskirts—but their real talent is revision. Did you know that the Mothers flew back to the pages of WWII after the conflict, for example, and reduced the casualties by thousands?

In those days the Mothers were more visible—you knew their names, and their meetings were open to the public. In the 1970s, though, the Mothers clandestined. The real wars, they realized, were hidden, happening on the everyday pages of the American suburbs: women suffering, in other words, in their very own homes. So that generation of Mothers changed their tactics. Instead of flying in a pack of thirty, they'd send out a school of four matriarchal vigilantes who'd hover overhead with state-of-the-apple surveillance devices. If they heard a catcall on a downtown Appleseed street, for example, or the sound of a man raising his voice to a woman, they'd swoop in. That's what happened to Pauline Bramley and her husband Norman. Do you know that story?

Bramley and his wife lived on Derby Dingle. One night, Norman came home kaddished and he and his wife got in an argument. Norman, a rougher who'd already spent some time in Appleseed Prison, punched Pauline in the stomach. The Mothers were listening overhead and they heard Pauline cry out. They dropped through the clouds, *tore the roof completely off* the Bramleys' house, picked Norman Bramley up by one arm and carried him to a Nest. When they returned him to his home three days later, he had a broken collarbone and nothing but nice things to say to his wife or anyone else. I mean that literally—the only words that he spoke for the rest of his life, over and over, were the words "nice," "good," and "fine."

Word of that story and others like it hurdled through Appleseed. Soon it was clear who ran the book. Men did what they could—*pretending* to work, *pretending* to take care of their houses and cars, growing hair on their faces, baring their teeth—but Appleseed was steered by its women.

As the weeks passed without apples, though, people wondered where the Mothers stood, what they were doing to help. *The Daily Core* ran headline after headline:

MOTHERS SILENT ON APPLE BLIGHT, one read. STILL NO
WORD FROM THE MOTHERS, said another. And then, finally: WHERE THE &*!$ ARE THE MOTHERS?

At last, the Mothers accepted an invitation to attend
a meeting of the Board of Select Cones. The Reader and
I went with my Mom to Town Hall for the meeting. We
arrived early to get good seats. When we walked in I saw
three Mothers—two women and one man—seated at the
front near a screen and a slide projector. The Mothers were
dressed in standard combat issue: goggles, cardigan, warskirt.

Reader: Warskirt?

A Mother's main resource. Warskirts are just like regular skirts, with a few modifications: they're bulletproof,
they have razor-sharp edges, and they hold knives, artil-
lery, and a variety of small tools.

When everyone was seated, Cone Johnson coughed
and leaned into his microphone. "I think we all know why
we're here," he said. "Mothers? Would you like the floor?"

The Mother who stood up had gigantic muscles, and
her face was painted with strange colors: stripes of orange,
green, and pink. "Evening," she said. "We've been looking
at every angle of this apple shortage—going back into the
past, forward into the future, lifting words off the page
to look underneath them, trying to get a sense for what's
going on here."

"Sitting on your asses is more like it," mumbled a
sweater behind me. The second Mother—taller, leaner—
stood up and the sweater looked down at his shoes.

"We don't think the problem is with the pages them-

188

selves. Our tests suggest strong fibers; the glue is holding; the spine is intact. The problem," said the muscled Mother, "is that the pages of Appleseed itself are infested."

The crowd began to murmur. "The pages?" said someone behind me.

"*Which* pages?" someone else said. "This one?"

Cone Johnson leaned toward the microphone. "Infested with what?" he said.

One of my thoughts coughed.

The male Mother stood up and turned on the slide projector. An image of a worm appeared on the white screen.

"What you see there probably looks like your standard garden-variety pest," said the muscled Mother, and the male Mother took a stack of brochures off the table and started handing them around. "But these guys are different," the muscled Mother said. "*These* worms—we call them 'bookworms'—are thoughts. In the form of sentences."

"So it's not a worm, then," asked Select Cone Miles.

"Technically? It's a *literaficidae*," said the tall Mother.

"Pardon?"

"It has a printed body. They burrow and hide just like any other worm."

I took a brochure—*What's So Bad About a Bookworm?*—and passed the stack on.

"And the sentences change at will," the muscled Mother said. The male Mother pushed a button on the projector and a new image appeared: a worm in the shape of the letter *e*. Then another image: a worm in the shape of an *s*.

"Are these all the—same worm?" said Cone O'Martian.

"This is bullshit," said the sweater, standing up and pointing. "That one's not even a *woman*!" he shouted. The tall Mother went over to the sweater, picked him up, threw him over her shoulder, and carried him out. "It's bullshit!" the sweater shouted.

Cone Johnson raised his hand.

"Don't need to raise your hand, Cal," said the male Mother.

"So what if they change?"

"So *what*?" the male Mother repeated.

"Yeah," said Cone Johnson. "Why is that a big deal? I think it'd be kind of cool to see a sentence change right in front of me."

"It's what killed the apples," said the muscled Mother. "Appleseed is the story of happiness, soil fertility, and meaning. But now all that's changing. It won't stop with the trees. If we don't stop the bookworms, they'll erase all of Appleseed, destroy everything meaningful."

"Or carry it away," said the male Mother.

"Carry it away?" said Cone O'Martian.

The muscled Mother turned back to the screen. "What we don't know yet," she said, pointing to the pictures of the holes in the page, "is where those channels lead."

"We don't want to overreact and cause panic," said the male Mother. "All we're asking for right now is vigilance. You see a strange sentence? One that seems like it's not from Appleseed? Pray to us about it."

"In the meantime," said the muscled Mother, "we're doubling our reads and recruiting new Mothers."

My Mom sat up in her seat.

"We'll be trying out Mothers in O'Shady Groves next Friday at eight a.m.," the male Mother announced.

Looking back, that was the moment I lost her—the moment that she became a Mother to the world, but the Memory of a Mom to me.

MOTHERS' DAY

I didn't attend the tryouts—I had school that day. I'd started at Appleseed High—a bigger, more dangerous place—the previous fall, and I was really struggling. It was easy to get lost in that school—to walk down a corridor toward your next class, take a wrong turn, and find yourself in a class on death or loss that you could never get out of. I know a scoom named Kyle who walked into a class on Aging? He emerged forty years later with wrinkles on his face and a curve in his spine.

I took the standard list of classes: Complicated World, Days of Joy, What to Be Most Frightened Of, the History of Depression, and Gym. I was failing almost all of them—it was like something was wrong with my brain. In Complicated World, Ms. Colton kept me after school to discuss my grades. "I don't understand it, _____," she said. "The quizzes are open-book. Why is this giving you so much trouble?"

I shrugged.

"Don't you find this interesting? The complicated world?"

"I guess I just don't think it's all that complicated," I said.

"Are there problems at home, _____?" said Ms. Colton. "Or with your friends?"

"My only friend besides 'I am.'," I told her, "is the Reader."

"The who?" she said.

"Me," said the Reader.

"The Reader," I said.

"Is that a real person?" she said.

"Of course," I said. "She's right over there."

"Jokes aren't going to get you anywhere," she said. "I'm trying to *help* you."

"I'm trying to help me, too," I said.

The only class I did OK in was Depression. I never studied for the exams in that class and still I got the best grades. In his comments on one of my papers, my teacher—a lizard named Dr. O'Rich—said that I had promise. "I seriously think that you should consider a career in depression," he wrote.

In all of my other classes, though, my teachers gave up on me. In What to Be Most Frightened Of, the teacher even moved my desk into the corner. The weather in my school was generally pretty good—mild sun, a few clouds—but those corners were often cold and sometimes inclement. That day, in fact—the day of the tryouts—it had started snowing in my corner, right in the middle of class. We were supposed to be creating fear hierarchies, but the snow made it difficult to concentrate. I got up from my desk and approached the teacher, a cardboard cutout, and said, "It's snowing in my corner."

"Is it literal snow," said the cutout, "or metaphorical snow?"

We'd studied metaphors the previous week.

"Real snow," I said.

"Are you sure your thoughts don't seem *as* snow?"

I went back to my desk, pushed the snow off my paper, and kept working.

I was even more distracted than usual that day, though—all I could think about was how my Mom was doing. That and what the Mothers had said about the bookworms. Was *Sentence*, I wondered, a bookworm?

No. "I am." acted fierce sometimes, but his "bark" was way worse than his "bite." My sentence wasn't like the wild language you read about in *The Daily Core*—the sentences that had been seen slithering up storm grates, making holes in our stories. The previous month, someone had been *killed* by a sentence, even, when she mistakenly came between the clause and its mother-sentence while hiking in the margin. "I am." wasn't capable of that kind of cruelty—he was just a sweet, innocent statement!

That afternoon, though, I rode right home after school. My Mom wasn't back from the tryouts yet, so I found the pamphlet from the meeting and sat down on the couch with Sentence.

WHAT'S SO BAD ABOUT A BOOKWORM?

BROUGHT TO YOU BY

THE MOTHERS OF AMERICA

In many ways, bookworms are similar to the common earthworm—the *oligochaeta*—except that the bookworm, which is known as the *literaficidae*, has a printed skeleton. This print-based body allows it to morph from one character or idea to another, shifting its appearance and meaning on a whim.

Diet

Literaficidae survive most readily in narrative, stories, or other text. They crave stories: predicaments, conflicts, crescendos, denouements. They digest the tension and secrete the rest. This results in a "trail"—a telltale pathway of inconsistencies or red herrings left by a passing sentence.

Font

Bookworms can change font and style at will, quickly emboldening and italicizing, shrinking to hide, underlining or enlarging to scare predators. The most common *literaficidae* fonts, incidentally, are Cambria and Palatino. Courier New is frequently seen as well.

Plot Transference

Reports of recent bookworm incidents suggest that they can carry elements of plot or premise in their stomachs. In other words, they transport settings and moments in order to ensure their survival. If they can contain the story, that is, they save their place in it.

Metaphor

Metaphoring is another word for meaning simultaneously. The bookworms' ability to metaphor is unparalleled. They can represent literally any number of ideas, motifs, or themes. Literary scientists suggest that this metaphoring is the result of evolution over hundreds of thousands of years on the page.

Regeneration

Like the common *oligochaeta*, the *literaficidae* can regenerate if injured. Say that a sentence, prior to injury, represented the threat of nature. If a group of them were attacked and unable to regenerate as nature, they might opt for another syntactically similar comparison—the threat of the *future*, say.

Frequently asked questions about Living with Bookworms

Q. My community has been infested with strange words! What do I do if I see one?
A. Pray to the Mothers! Send them the page number and locale. Then stop reading in that direction and read the other away as fast as you can.

Q. Is metaphoring contagious?
A. Not that we know of, no. Metaphoring is not an illness or virus; rather, it's the bookworms' way of making themselves seen and known. Human beings show no tendency toward metaphoring.

Q. What have we done to deserve this invasion?
A. Nothing. The bookworms have chosen your story at random, in the same way that termites infest a house or typewriters attack smaller typewriters. It's a question of narrative survival—nothing more.

Q. Do the bookworms have anything to do with the disappearance of apples (the blight)?
A. The current theory says *yes*, that the apple trees—which draw nutrients from the page—were not able to sustain the growth of appletree groves because of bookworm-inspired page-rot. This is one of the reasons that we're aiming to stop, or at least curb, bookworm infestations. And with your help, we will!

Thanks for doing your part to help save Appleseed from bookworms!

I heard the Fart in the driveway and I put down the brochure. A minute later, my Mom walked in with her reading goggles over one shoulder and her nunchucks over the other.

"How'd it go?" I said.

"OK," she huffed, but I knew it went great; her face was as happy as I'd ever seen it. And just two days later, I came home after school and saw two duffel bags by the door.

"_____?" my Mom hollered.

"Yeah," I said, staring at the bags.

"We're in here," she said.

I walked into the kitchen and saw my father, mother, and sister sitting at the table. "Sit down, _____," my Mom said.

I sat in one chair and the Reader sat in the other. "No," said my Mom to the Reader. "This is for family only."

"Mom," I said, embarrassed.

"She can go sit in the TV room," said my Mom. Then my Mom looked at you.

"Go," she said.

You got up and went into the TV room. The TV stared at you. "What do you think they're talking about?" the TV asked.

"I don't know," you said, even though you did.

The TV made a face. "What's the luggage for?"

Then you heard crying in the kitchen. That was me—I was the one crying. "This isn't fair!" you heard me say.

"_____," said my Dad.

"It's *not*, Dad!" I shouted.

Then you heard the slam of someone's fist on the table, followed by Diane's voice. "There are bigger problems in the world than what you're going to have for *dinner*, _____! *Appleseed* needs me more than you do."

Then there was more crying, and the sound of running feet and slamming doors.

"Sheesh," said the TV. "*That* didn't sound good."

You sat in the TV room for a while, being watched,

and watching others being watched, and finally you clicked the remote and walked quietly out into the living room. Diane was smoking a six-foot cigarette and looking out the window. You opened the basement door and went downstairs. I was sitting on the floor in the middle of a paragraph.

You wanted to say something to me, but you didn't know what. You already understood what would happen next—you'd read the story about Diane flying away to join the Mothers and the missing that followed/would follow.

"You OK?" you asked. When I looked up and you read my face, you knew the answer.

AUXERRE

Reeling from a loss of meaning, thunderous debt, and my Mom's sudden absence, my Dad turned to get-ideas-quick scams: long-shot prospects, wheelsanddeals, outlandish trades. First he tried trapping and selling memories, but no one would buy them. Then The Ear convinced him to invest some socked-away meaning in a new, virtual kind of reading—"People won't need pages at all!" The Ear promised—but he disappeared two days later with my Dad's investment. When my uncle heard about The Ear's scam he came by the house to check on my Dad—he brought my Dad a Kaddish Fruit, and the two of them shared it outside on the back step. I was out there, too, sitting on the lawn with Sentence.

"Found you a job," said my uncle, biting into the blue fruit.

"Can I have some of that?" I said, meaning the fruit.

"No," my Dad said. Then he turned to my uncle. "What job?" he asked, spitting out a seed.

Joump just looked at him.

"*Not* Muir Drop," my Dad said.

Muir Drop Forge, where my uncle worked, huffed on the Kellogg River a mile or so from our house. Muir Drop made work—most of the labor in western Massachusetts was forged there, in fact. In those days, work was all the rage in America—people couldn't get enough of it—and so Muir was always looking for people. It was backbreaking work, though—the labor they made was grimy, tar-like, pulled from deep in the page. My uncle worked twelve-hour shifts, six days a week, repairing equipment. The injury rate was high at Muir Drop; there were accidents all the time. One day Joump came over with a big burn across his arm where he'd been splashed with toil. Plus, his hands were permanently black from labor that wouldn't wash off.

"I can't think of any place I'd rather *not* work," my Dad said.

"No shit," Joump said. "But somanabitch, Ralph. Look around. Just you and the kids now. The banks aren't just going to stop calling."

"Thanks but no thanks," my Dad said. "I've still got a few tricks up my sleeve."

"Tricks," Joump said. "Like what?"

We found out two days later, when my Dad rounded up me and my uncle in the ropetruck and drove south across Page Boulevard and over Old Five. "OK, I give up," said Joump. "Where we going?"

"To find the Memory of Johnny Appleseed," said my Dad.

"Ah, Christ, Ralph—is it too late to turn around and take me home?"

"Yes," said my Dad, and he drove on.

Since the blight began six months earlier, the Memory of Johnny Appleseed had become a pariah. The Memory didn't help his cause, either, by proclaiming to anyone who'd listen—at Town Hall meetings, outside the Why—that salvation was just a harvest away; that he'd had dreams and visions of trees shaped like hands holding giant apples, the biggest fruits Appleseed had ever seen. "The blight is not Appleseed's, but ours!" he'd preach to passerbys outside the Hu Ke Lau. "It's a failure of imagination! A blight in our own minds!" Most people would ignore him. "And I have found the way forward," he'd shout after them. "The new soil. We must shed our fears. Boldly move into the unknown. Only *then* will the apples return."

We found the Memory of Johnny Appleseed further down Five, walking with his thumb out. My Dad pulled the truck over beside him and rolled down the window. "Where's your treebike?" he shouted.

"It has—" the Memory of Johnny Appleseed paused, blinked, and sniffed, "—been apprehended." Then he hoisted his satchel higher on his shoulder.

"What's in the bag?" said Joump.

"Seeds," said the Memory of Johnny Appleseed.

"So this new soil," said my Dad.

"Yes."

"Can you show us where to find it?" my Dad said.

"There are groves not yet named," said the Memory of Johnny Appleseed. "Pages not yet written. On *these* pages is where we'll grow the new groves."

"Oh, Jesus," said Joump.

"Can we go there?" said my Dad.

"Ralph," said Joump. "You've got to be kidding."

"I can show you the soil," the Memory of Johnny Appleseed said.

"Right now?" my Dad asked.

"It's up on Appleseed Mountain. We can go at first light."

"Get in," my Dad said, and nodded to the back of the truck. The Memory of Johnny Appleseed climbed into the bed of the truck and my Dad pulled back onto the old highway.

The Memory of Johnny Appleseed slept at our place that night. My Dad offered him the living-room couch, but he chose to sleep outside instead. Before I went to bed, I looked out the window and saw the Memory, lying on his back in the grass, talking to the stars. He told a joke and all of the stars cracked up laughing.

We were on the road at sunrise. We picked up Joump and drove straight for Appleseed Mountain. That mountain was dangerous: full of haunted memories, false meanings, misfits, bookworms, and wild language of all sorts—rattlesnakes, old drafts, black bears, erased versions, transparent spiders, errors, menasentences, typos, and countless other threats.

It took us about fifteen minutes to reach the foot of the mountain. We drove up one of the mountainsocks, following the tire tracks as far as they went. Then my Dad parked the truck, got out, and lifted two nets out of the back of the truck. He handed one to me. "What are these for?" I said.

"For whatever," he said.

We started up through the trees. The Memory of Johnny Appleseed led and my Dad followed right behind him; then it was me and Joump. A few minutes into the hike, I saw a flash of ink to my left: two giant letters sipping something out of cans wrapped in paper bags. "Worms," said Joump, and he pushed me forward.

A bit higher up, I saw a strange chair-shaped bird. It stood on two spindly legs and squinted in the light.

"How much farther, Appleshit?" said Joump.

The Memory of Johnny Appleseed turned around and looked quizzically at Joump.

"I really don't care for that shortname," he said. "You can call me Johnny or Johnny Appleseed or the Memory of Johnny Appleseed. Or just Appleseed, if you prefer."

"How much farther—*Appleshit*?" said Joump again.

"Joump," said my Dad.

"Edge of the page in about half a mile," said the Memory of Johnny Appleseed.

Just then I heard a commotion—someone, or something, was coming. We moved off the path just in time to see dozens of figures—maybe two hundred or more—trudging toward us. I looked to the Memory of Johnny Appleseed. "Old versions," he said. "Draft refugees."

The drafts approached and passed. All of us were there—everyone in Appleseed, probably. I saw a draft of my sister, an old version of Large Odor. And soon I saw my father. "Dad," I said.

My Dad turned, squinted, and saw the earlier version of himself—a man maybe ten years younger, with different glasses and more hair. He was heavier and had more color in his face. "Handsome dude," my Dad said, and smiled.

Joump followed right behind him. The Joump in that story, though, was clearly kaddished—he wore a blank blue look on his face. As soon as the now-Joump saw himself he broke into a sprint. His face took on a snarl that could only mean one thing: he wanted a fight. Before anyone could stop him, he ran full-speed at his old self and tackled him.

The rough draft of Joump fell back under the now-Joump, but then he stood up with a grin and a face full of blood. He launched right back at the now-Joump, driving him back against a tree. The now-Joump howled. My Dad pulled them apart. He pushed the old draft back into the past and led Joump over to the path.

Behind the draft of my uncle, I saw an old version of myself—me maybe four years earlier. I had pleats in my toupee, and I wore mismatched Converse hi-tops and a black-and-green cycling cap with pins on it.

The now-me and the draft me looked at each other. "Lose that hat," I told him.

The then-me wrinkled his eyebrows.

"It'll be lame in about a week," I said.

My old self took off the hat. Then he continued down the mountain with the other drafts and we turned and kept climbing.

I could tell that Joump was hurt, though. He didn't say anything, but he was limping and wincing with every step. My father, meanwhile, was grilling the Memory of Johnny Appleseed. "When you say 'new soil,'" he said, "what do you mean exactly?"

"New pages," said the Memory of Johnny Appleseed. "Pages not yet written."

"But what makes them different from the old pages?"

"We won't make the same mistakes again," said the Memory of Johnny Appleseed.

"Because I could really use a meaning infusion right about now," my father confessed.

"Dad," I said.

He looked back at me and I nodded toward Joump. "I'm fine," Joump said. "Asshole just torqued my knee or something."

Then we reached a clearing. Suddenly there was nothing but white space in front of us: no words, no ink at all. "Whoa," I said.

The Memory of Johnny Appleseed stood at the edge and pointed forward. "We cross through here, over the spine."

"Dad," I said.

My Dad took a step onto the new page. His feet sank down. "It's just the future," he told me.

"Ralph," said Joump. When my Dad looked at him, Joump gestured to his knee and shook his head. "I can't," he said.

"This is what we came here for," my Dad told him.

"We either go together or we don't go at all," said the Memory.

My Dad leaned over and put his hands on his knees. "Fuck," he said.

I squinted to try to see across the spine. Through the pagefog I could sort of make out—something. Was it a tree? A person?

My Dad stood up.

"It's probably bullshit anyway," Joump said quietly.

Dad started walking back the way we came. We all turned around and followed. The four of us trudged silently back down the mountain, retracing our sentences toward the base.

At the halfway point I kept an eye out for myself. I hadn't had a chance to really talk to my draft. My thoughts wondered: How did it spend its days now? Did it go to an old version of school? Could it pedal a bike? Maybe the old me and the new me could be friends!

Then we rounded a paragraph and I saw good old Appleseed—all of the stories I knew: Appleseed High; the Big Why; the Mental Hospital; the sad gray patches of deadgroves.

Lumbering toward the car, my Dad's face was as dark as I'd ever seen it. At one point, the Memory put a hand on his shoulder and said, "It's going to be OK, Ralph. I won't stop planting seeds until the apples return to Appleseed."

"That doesn't fucking solve my problem," said my Dad. "I need meaning *now*. Today. Yesterday."

My Dad dropped the Memory off at the Why and drove Joump to his house, and then we turned toward home. When we pulled into our driveway, though, two banks were sitting on the front stoop. "*Christ*," my Dad said under his breath. He got out of the truck and the banks stood up—they were big and square and terrifying. "Look, Jimmy," said one to the other. "It's our buddy Ralph."

"Hey buddy," said the other bank.

"Let's take a walk, buddy," said the first bank. They

put their cement hands on my Dad's shoulders and walked across the street to the worryfields.

I don't know what they said? But the next day, my Dad went to Muir Drop Forge and filled out an application. They hired him on the spot. He came home that night with his hands and arms covered in the soot of toil.

FATHERS IN THE FIELD

MARGIL

Soon, my sister's auctions became unwieldy. There were two hundred people at our house every day; the traffic got so bad that my Dad had to park his truck across the street in the worryfields. Word of my sister's talents traveled. She was a celebrity—there were articles every week about her in the gossip page of *The Daily Core.*

One afternoon that fall, I was watching the auction from the roof with Sentence by my side when I noticed a hooded figure in the back of the crowd. I couldn't see his face—I'm still not sure that he *had* a face—nor did I see him arrive. He was just suddenly *there*, in a dark orange velvet cape, standing silently. When the auction was over, he waited until the crowd dispersed and then stepped forward to the pulpit to speak with my sister. I couldn't hear what he said, but after a few minutes my sister brought the man into the house to see my Dad. I climbed back inside and ran down the stairs to see the three of them—my Dad, my sister, and the hooded man—sitting at the dining-room table. "Go to your room, _____," my Dad said.

"Who's that?" I said.

"Go," my Dad said.

I went down into the basement, but I sent two of my thoughts reconning to record the conversation.

The hooded man's voice was like a bubbly stream—his words all ran together. He said that he was from a famed auction school somewhere far beyond the margin— some place called Pilgrim Auctions—and that he was here because he'd heard the stories about my sister. He wanted my father's permission for my sister to attend his school for auctioneers. "She'sgifted," said the hooded man, "butwhatyouseehereisjustthebeginning."

"She's doing just fine right here in Appleseed," said my Dad.

"I-could-do-better," my sister said.

"Shecould," said the hooded man.

"She's just started," my Dad said.

"Nottrue—shesalways*been*anauctioneer," said the man.

"She has?" my Dad said.

"Andshe*could*bethebesttheverybestauctioneerthatAppleseedhaseverseen," he told my father.

"We're very flattered," said my father. "But Briana has a bright future—"

"My-name-is-the-*Auctioneer*," said the Auctioneer.

"—college," my Dad said. "A meaningful career."

"You're-not-being-fair!" my sister shouted.

"Auctioning here at home is one thing," my Dad said to her. "Leaving home at sixteen years old is another."

"*Mom*-left!" she said. "Why-can't-I?"

"Mom didn't *leave*," said my Dad. "She's helping protect Appleseed."

"This-is-my-*dream*!" shouted the Auctioneer.

"The answer is no," my Dad said.

At that point, my thought said, the hooded man stood

up and walked out of the house. When I looked out my bedroom window I saw him floating down Converse Street.

My sister was hysterical. She ran to her room and slammed the door. "What-about-what-*I*-want!" she hollered from behind the door. "I-hate-it-here! I-hate-this-*house*!"

"What did *I* do?" the house said.

I knocked on her door. "Bri," I said. "Can I come in?"

"No!" she said. "Go away!"

The house began to cry a little. "All I've ever been is *nice* to you."

I went back to my sister's room an hour later and knocked again. "Bri?" I said. "Auctioneer?" This time she didn't answer at all.

"You asleep?" I asked.

I stood there for a minute and then went back down to the basement.

The next morning I walked upstairs and saw the door to the Auctioneer's room ajar. I went in. The drawers in her dresser were open and there were clothes everywhere. I opened her closet door; her suitcase wasn't there.

I ran downstairs and looked in every room. I sprinted out to the backyard and then into the front yard and looked up and down our street. "I am." followed me, whimpering. I stood there for a few minutes, staring one way and the other. My sister wasn't anywhere. The Auctioneer was gone.

WORCESTER PEARMAIN

The following summer—the summer before my junior year at Appleseed High—I began dating the Appleseed Community Theater. I met her by accident, when I was walking Sentence one day in downtown Appleseed. All of a sudden he started pulling me toward an unfamiliar building. Sentence had very good hearing, though, and he often got excited when he heard other sentences—even if I, myself, couldn't hear them. When he started sniffing the steps of the small wooden building, I heard talking inside.

"Cute clause," said the building. "What's his name?"

"Sentence," I said. "He heard people talking, and—"

"Yeah. We're putting on a trueplay," said the building.

I looked up at her. The sign above the door read AP-PLESEED COMMUNITY THEATER. "A true what?" I said.

"Play. Theater," said the theater.

I'd seen theater productions in my high school. I said, "I didn't know there was any theater in Appleseed."

"Yeah—just moved here from Cambridge," said the theater.

Sentence lunged at the leash.

"They're rehearsing—you can watch if you want," she said.

We stepped inside and saw rows of empty seats and a bright stage full of people and sentences. A man dressed like a sea captain was having a conversation with an old boat. The boat was storming back and forth across the stage, shouting out a plot for revenge. "Let's say that buoy disappears somewhere."

"But where?" the captain said.

"Doesn't matter where," said the boat. "Just so long as it's kept quiet."

We stepped outside after a few minutes, and I thanked the theater. "I'll come back and see the show," I said.

"And we're looking for help if you know anyone. We still need a props master."

"A what?" I said.

That was a great time for me—a season of promise and discovery. I did the props for every show that season— *Dandelion Braise*, *Stormnote*, and *Too Many Bagels*—and grew to really love working in the theater. It was located in a bad neighborhood, full of meaninglessers—two times I had the seats of my Bicycle Built for Two stolen—but I didn't care. I liked having somewhere to go in the afternoons after school, and I could usually find most of the props that I needed at the flea bee.

Plus, you weren't ever alone when you worked on a show—every cast and crew was like a family. I saw the director, Eric Wig, and his wife Ellen, who often played the leads, every day, while I hardly saw my *own* family at all. It didn't seem to matter to anyone there that I was ugly and unremarkable—I was willing to work, and everyone seemed to appreciate that. My thoughts were always buoyant when a new show began. When one ended, I couldn't get those thoughts off the couch if their lives depended on it.

Three weeks into rehearsals for *Stormnote*, though, the old trombone who was cast as the Old Man had an aneurysm on stage and died. I was right there when it happened. He was supposed to say his lines—"Are those *vultures*?"—and then shake his fist. At that moment he stepped forward and said, "Are those—whose vultures are those?"

"That's not the line, Terry," said Eric, looking down at his script.

"Reset the vultures!" shouted the stage manager, an easychair named Carol.

The trombone stood up, stumbled, made a terrible honking sound, and fell down on the boat.

"Whoa!" shouted a sandbag from the wings.

The trombone was shaking on the floor of the theater.

"Terry?" shouted the Community Theater.

We all ran out on stage. The Community Theater called the ParamediCones, but by the time they got there the old trombone was gone.

I went to the trombone's funeral along with other people from the cast and crew. It was really sad. "You probably think you know everything about my father," said Terry's daughter at the pulpit. "But he was more than just a successful actor. Do you know, for example, that he was an inventor?"

Some people smiled through tears; others looked miffed.

"That he invented the Morp, for example?"

And there, in the corner, was a morp—one of the original prototypes.

The Mothers did a formation flyover and the bessoffs led the procession into the graveyard. "Let his body bring apples," said the bessoffs in unison, and they lowered his body into the ground.

Rehearsals resumed two days later. That afternoon, I was in the vom fixing one of the scrolls when Eric called me over to the orchestra pit. He looked at me cemeterily and then leaned forward and said, "We need an Old Man."

My eyebrows wormed.

"Any interest?"

"Me?" I said.

"You're the oldest one here," he said.

"No, I'm not," I said. "Almost everyone here is older than me."

"How old are you?" said the wig.

"I'm sixteen," I said.

Wig stood up. "Haw," he said.

I stared at him.

His head haunted forward. "You're sixteen?" he whispered.

"My birthday was in April," I said.

"Jesus, _____," he said. "I thought you were fifty. At least! Sixty, maybe."

"No," I said. "I'm a junior at Appleseed High."

"But—because you're—wow." Wig put his hands on his hips. "Well," he said, "Do you want to be the Old Man?"

"You mean *act*?" one of my thoughts said.

"On the stage?" another thought said.

My face must have changed because the wig said, "It's a very minor role."

So I took the part, wore the dead man's clothes, stood on the deck of the falseboat, and looked out into the sea. "Fish?" I shouted. "In space?" Then I cast my fake fishing rod out into the real water. On cue, the lead fish down below looked at the hook and primrosed to the crowd.

It was my first taste of performance, of standing in front of people as someone not myself, of playing a role. I loved it. I thought maybe I could do this, make a career out of it—be a minor character: the ugly one in the background; the non-hero, the shithead—one of those corner-warts that make the beautiful look *more* beautiful!

I was so proud of my performance, of the fact that I—me! Not the Auctioneer, but me!—had an actual role in a play, that I asked my Dad if he'd come see the last show. He said he would if he could get off work, but he didn't make it. By then he was working at Muir Drop and in meaning-debt to some pretty imposing banks. He prayed to me that he was sorry, and I prayed back that I understood.

That night after the show there was a party at the dead-groves. I didn't plan on going—I'd never been invited to a party before, and I didn't know exactly how they worked. I was unlocking my bike from the rack, though, when the theater pulled up beside me in a night-blue Jeep.

Scene: Bike racks. A Jeep drives up. The window rolls down to reveal the COMMUNITY THEATER *driving and the* CHORUS *in the backseat.*

Hey, _____!

_____ *continues unlocking his bike.*

COMMUNITY THEATER
You need a ride?

_____

Me?

COMMUNITY THEATER
You're going to the party, aren't you?

_____

(*Turning to face her.*) I was just going to head home.

COMMUNITY THEATER
You should go!

CHORUS (*from the backseat of the Jeep*)
Come on, _____!

_____

I've got my bike, though.

COMMUNITY THEATER
No problem. Get in and I'll drop you back here afterward.

_____ *gets in the Jeep. The Jeep drives off the pagestage.*

We drove out to the deadgroves, me in the passenger seat and the Chorus—a singular mass with twelve sets of torsos, arms, shoulders, necks, and heads—in the backseat. The Community Theater lit a cigarette and blew smoke out the window. The Chorus tapped me on the shoulder and I turned around. "Really great job, _____. You were awesome as the Old Man."

"Thanks," I said. I remember that moment—the thrill in my chest. On my way to an actual *party*! And then, to make things even better, the UCs' "Paying Customers" came on the radio. After my sister left for auction school, I raided her tape collection. Whenever I missed her or felt lonely, I'd pick out one of her tapes—the UCs, usually—and listen to it on my orange headphones.

"Nice," I said now. "I love this song."

The Community Theater looked over at me and smirked. "You don't know this *song*," she said.

"'Course I do," I said. "This is my favorite band."

"Who is it?" asked the Chorus.

"I want to see if _____ knows," said the Community Theater.

"It's the Ulcerative Colitises," I said. "The album *Tenesmus*."

"What's the name of the song?"

"'The Bathroom Is for Paying Customers Only,'" I said. "Fourth song on side A."

The theater looked at me. "Wow," she said. "I'm impressed."

When we reached the deadgroves, the theater parked and we stepped out into the night. Most of the cast and crew was there, standing around a bonfire, and someone had brought a keg.

The wig's wife, Ellen, gave me a hug—it had been so long since I'd hugged anyone—and told me that she hoped I'd work with them again in the future. Then the theater walked up to me and handed me a red plastic cup.

Scene: The deadgroves

COMMUNITY THEATER

Here.

_____ *looks into the cup, then takes a sip.*

COMMUNITY THEATER

So how do you know the UCs?

_____

Best band in Appleseed! Their zitherer, Oppenhowser? Is—like—the shit.

COMMUNITY THEATER

How about Yosa Ron?

_____

She's good.

COMMUNITY THEATER

Good? She's the best hurdy-gurdy player in the history of—

Not as good as Ross Nary.

COMMUNITY THEATER

Who?

———

Gurdyer for the Porches.

COMMUNITY THEATER

I don't know them.

———

Check out the album *Overanda.*

COMMUNITY THEATER

I don't know a single other person who likes the UCs.
My friend-theaters are mostly into show tunes.

———

I've got every tape they've recorded.

COMMUNITY THEATER

You know they're coming to Appleseed.

———

No, they are *not.*

COMMUNITY THEATER

Appleseed Amphitheatre.

Holy crap.

―――

COMMUNITY THEATER

You ever seen them?

―――

Live? No.

―――

COMMUNITY THEATER

(*Pauses.*) We should go.

―――

(*Looks into his cup.*) Yeah. (*Drinks.*) That would be—

CHORUS *wanders over, cups in every hand.*

CHORUS

We are, like, so wasted.

_____ (*to* COMMUNITY THEATER)

We should go. That'd be really fun.

COMMUNITY THEATER

Great.

CHORUS

Go where?

Nowhere.

We went to the show the following week. I wasn't sure whether it was a date or not, but when the theater picked me up in her Jeep she smelled like a garden and her hair was contorted into this strange shape above her roof.

We got there in the middle of the opening set, by this new band called the OCDs. I might have heard one of their songs on WAPL—"Check, Check Again"—but I didn't realize that it was them. The song had a catchy chorus, though:

Check the SINK
Check the SINK
Check the SINK
Check the SINK
Check the STOVE
Check the STOVE
Check the STOVE
Check the STOVE
Check the DOOR
Check the DOOR
Check the DOOR
Check the DOOR
Check it again
Check it again
Check it AGAIN
CHECK IT AGAIN

"They're pretty good!" shouted the Community Theater.

Then the Colitises took the stage. The Community Theater screamed in a high voice, and I jumped up and down in my chair. "Good evening, Appleseed!" shouted Yosa Ron. Then she hit the tympani and rocked into "Urgency."

I sang every word of every song; so did the Community Theater. Halfway through "Ultimate Flora," she put her brick hand in mine. "Holy shit!" said one of my thoughts, and two other thoughts started jumping up and down manically on the carpeted floor of my mind.

The next song, "You'll Have This Disease for the Rest of Your Life," was a dirge. Halfway through it, the Community Theater put her head on my shoulder. When I turned to her, she leaned up and kissed me. Her mouth tasted like smoke and audience.

Pages flipped forward in my mind. When I looked back at the stage, the UCs were playing their biggest hit, "Bathroom."

I can't go to the movies
Cuz I have to go to the BATHROOM!

I can't go to the bar
Cuz I have to go to the BATHROOM!

I can't go in to work today
Cuz I have to go to the BATHROOM!

Where Oh where is the BATHROOM!
I need one right now

"BathROOM!" shouted the crowd. "BathROOM!"

When the concert was over, the theater led me through the parking lot to her Jeep and we drove back to my house. When we pulled into the driveway, she kissed me and said, "I'll call you, OK?"

"OK," I said.

My thoughts were dizzy as I walked inside. No one else was home, but that night I didn't even care. I went down to the basement, found my clipboard, and wrote, "That night was one of the best nights of his life."

The theater and I dated all fall, through four more shows. I was a walk-on ugly in each one: a strug in *Tunic*, a worryfielder in *Mrs. Rain and Mr. Rain*, a spinning in *Quagmire!* Every night after rehearsal, the Community Theater and I would go somewhere—the Big Why, the deadgroves, the Hu Ke Lau—to hang out and talk. Like me, the Community Theater didn't have much of a home life. Her father was in New York City, her mother hooked on Kaddish. I told the theater I hadn't seen *my* Mom since she'd left to Mother—"Not that I'm not proud of her," I said. "I mean, she's probably protecting the story right now."—and that my father had started taking twenty-four-hour shifts at Muir.

"That sounds like workhosis," she said.

I shrugged.

Looking back, I think that's what the theater and I shared: we both knew the echoes of an empty house. So we never made out there—instead, we'd drive into the Dunes and lie down in the backseat of the Jeep. She'd kiss me, dangle her theater hair over my face. We'd take off our shirts and pull a blanket over us.

One night, she reached for the button on my pants. "Is this OK?" she said.

I nodded.

"You sure?"

"Yes," I said.

The scene happened so quickly; soon it was one spotlight, and then several, and then *all* the light, bright hot white, and then curtains, and applause, and darkness. Outside, prayers bounced off the roof of the Jeep; memories sang songs in the distance.

Shortly after the closing of *Quagmire!*, though, something shifted in me. I was sad to see that cast go, and I wasn't excited for *Holiday Nightmare*, the play that Eric had chosen for December. I lost heart, got tired of the whole production—the blocking, the run-throughs, the pressure to bring in an audience. All of that scrimming just to tell a truestory? A thought said, "I could tell a better story with a clipboard and a yellow sheet of paper."

I said as much to the theater one night while we were parking in the Dunes. "We could just quit the show," I said. "Tell our *own* story instead."

Scene: Theater, post-rehearsal

COMMUNITY THEATER

Why would we do *that*?

230

I just don't think we need an audience to be together.

COMMUNITY THEATER
Of course we do. We're all in this together—don't you
get that?

But I didn't get it. "Can we speak in prose?" I said.

COMMUNITY THEATER
How can you even ask me that?

"I'm just saying maybe I want to tell a different story—
or this story in a different way," I said.

COMMUNITY THEATER
Are you breaking up with me? Is that what this is?

I shrugged. "I don't know," I said.

There wasn't any big dramatic scene; the Community
Theater and I went a day or two without talking, and then
I prayed and apologized and we made plans for a date. We
went to a movie the following Friday, but the whole night
was awkward. It was like, we didn't know how to talk
anymore. When she dropped me off, we didn't even kiss
goodnight.

At rehearsal the next day, the Community Theater
wouldn't look at me. The tension between us was so dis-
tracting that I went out to the lobby during break to talk

with her. When I asked her if she was OK, she didn't respond. "Are you not even going to acknowledge me?" I said.

The building didn't say anything.

"Are we not talking now?"

Then Eric shouted for everyone to get back to work. Right before my scene, though, the wig stopped me in the vom and said that Banda was going to do my lines instead.

"How come?" I said.

Eric pursed his lips.

"Do I still do the lines in Act Three?" I asked.

COMMUNITY THEATER (*shouting*)

I'll tell you your *line*. Your line is, "I'm sorry, Community Theater. I'm an asshole, Community Theater. I never should have said that stuff about theater."

ERIC WIG

Wait—what stuff about theater?

COMMUNITY THEATER

Or asked you to speak in prose.

ERIC WIG

You asked her to speak in prose?

COMMUNITY THEATER

Your line is, "Now I'm leaving to live a sad, lonely life."

I stood there.

ERIC WIG

Why would you ask her to speak in prose?

———

I didn't mean anything by it. I—

ERIC WIG

Maybe you should go, _____.

COMMUNITY THEATER

No—say your *line* first, asshole!

I'd never seen the Community Theater like this: so—
irate. My thoughts were frightened.

COMMUNITY THEATER
(*her voice booming, Mother-like*)

Say. Your. *Lines.*

"I'm leaving," I said, "to live my sad life."

COMMUNITY THEATER

My sad, *lonely* life.

"My sad, lonely life," I said.
Then I walked out of the theater. And I never went
back.

IDARED

All of a sudden, it seemed, my family was broken—my sister in the auctionwind, my Mom up in a Nest somewhere, and my father basically living at the forge. During her first few weeks as a Mother, my Mom kept promising a visit: "Next Tuesday," she prayed. "The Thursday after this one. I'll stay overnight." But two months after her recruitment, we still hadn't seen her *once* since she'd left—there was always some excuse, some secret emergency.

We never were told what her mission was, either—whether she was in combat, or renovation, or semiotics, or reconnaissance, or some other secret sect we hadn't heard about. I always looked for my Mom's name in the *Core*—which ran two or three stories a day about the Mothers—but I never once saw it there. Even so, though, I imagined that she was part of those stories: defending bessoffs against a pair of parentheses down by the Quarry; hunting down the sentences that had ripped through a page by Kirkpatrick Circle, or maybe helping to repair the tear itself.

In that story? The newspaper said that the Mothers had flown in a giant piece of masking tape—one as big as a worryfield! I imagined my Mom lifting a whole corner of the tape onto her shoulders, struggling with dozens of other Mothers to move it, slowly lowering it onto the paper.

It was OK that we didn't see my Mom, my thoughts told me sometimes: she was helping to protect us; she was keeping us safe. But it never met my missing.

I missed my father, too. Once he started working at Muir Drop he didn't stop—not even when his skin took on a gray tinge and his ears became gears. The Community Theater was right about him; these were sure signs of workhosis, caused by an addiction to work. I hoped he might scale back his hours after he caught up on his meaning payments, but by then it was too late: he ate, breathed, and slept work. The only time I saw him the entire month of March, in fact, was "Bring Your Son to Work Day." That morning, he marched me through the compound, pointing out complicated machines that took raw need and forged it for demand. "That's the separator," he said.

"What does it do?" I said.

"Separates," he said.

"Separates what?"

"The *self* from others," he said, as if I should have known. Then he pointed to a black tube that ran off the machine. "See that vacuum hose? It adds tasks. But it needs negative pressure, and the gaskets always give us trouble."

I was confused. "Oh," I said.

At the end of the day, he led me out to the Bicycle Built for Two and shook my hand mechanically. "Are you coming home?" I asked.

I could see him scanning the inquiry. "I'm in the middle of my shift, _____," he said.

I said goodbye to him, got on my bike and rode home. But I didn't go inside—instead I went over to the worryfields, got down on my knees, and folded my hands. "Mom?" I prayed.

It was quiet for a while.

"Mom?" I prayed. "It's _____."

After ten or fifteen minutes I heard the scratching of an arriving prayer. "Hey," my Mom prayed. She was out of breath.

I stood up.

"What is it, _____?" she prayed.

I didn't know what to pray. "I'm—" I started. "I—"

"What? Spit it out!"

"I'm hungry," I blurtprayed.

"So *eat*," she prayed. "Have some chips."

"We don't have any," I prayed.

"*You* ate them all, you mean."

"Plus I can't eat chips for dinner again," I prayed.

"Why don't you ask your father to make you something?"

"He's at work."

No response.

"I'm pretty sure he's got workhosis, Mom," I prayed.

My Mom grunted.

"What are you doing?" I asked.

She didn't answer. Then she prayed, "There should be some futurebeans in the pantry."

"When are you coming home?" I prayed.

"After this tour," she prayed.

"Do you miss us?"

Someone behind her was screaming—howling. "Of course I do," she said.

"Where are you right now?" I prayed.

"Right above you," she prayed.

I looked up.

"Right over the house?"

"Yes, but high," she prayed. "Look up."

"I am looking up," I said.

"We're right above the clouds."

"I can't—" I said. "Where?"

"Hold on a second." I heard the rush of wind. "See us now?"

"No," I prayed. "I don't see you."

"See a peach-colored cloud?"

"Yeah," I prayed.

"Look to the—" she prayed. Then there was quiet.

"Mom?" I prayed.

But the prayer had gone dark.

"Mom?" I prayed.

"Mom?"

I found the futurebeans in the pantry, poured them into a pot, and heated them up. But they tasted like shit—they were spoiled, or maybe just too old. They were the worst beans that I'd had—that I *would* have—in my whole entire life.

A few days later a prayer came in from my Mom. "_____?" it said.

I didn't answer.

"Sorry our prayer got disconnected the other day," she prayed.

I didn't answer.

The next day she tried again. "_____?" she prayed. "Are you there?"

"Fuck you," I prayed back.

"Excuse me?" she prayed.

"Fuck," I prayed, "you."

FATHERS IN THE FIELD

Eventually, people began to doubt there ever *were* such things as apples. Our neighbor, Bob Lonely? He started saying that those early chapters of Appleseed were imagined—that they were fictions. "Apples were just an idea," he told me once, "Nice to think about, but not real." After a while I had my doubts, too. I couldn't remember what apples smelled like, what they tasted like. Were they heavy or light? Green or red? Bitter or sweet? Then I heard a rumor in school one day about a group of aardvark importers selling apples for high meaning off the back of a truck in the west margin. Some Cones must have heard the same rumor, though, because those aardvarks were apprehended later the same day. As it turned out they were just selling counterfeits—pears painted red.

The only one who didn't lose faith in the promise of apples and trees was the Memory of Johnny Appleseed. He tilled every deadgrove in town. When he showed up in the groves across the street with his hoe and satchel of seeds, I walked over to see what he was planting. He opened the bag and I saw seeds of all different shapes and colors; some of them were as big as hearts. "What are they for?"

He shrugged. "I can't keep track. I've been trading for as many different types and versions as I can."

For two months or so, I worked in the fields across the street from my house as the Memory of Johnny Appleseed's assistant. We pulled up old crops, turned the soil, and planted the seeds. I'd also accompany him on his trades. He met with some real characters! Once, we took the Bicycle Built for Two to Small Pear to meet a marginalia-man called Eyes. Eyes had a line of eyes that ran all around his head, and he had his seeds collected in tiny plastic bags. "These," said Eyes, "are pumpkin seeds." He handed them to the Memory of Johnny Appleseed. "Thunderseeds," he said. Then he found another bag. "These are motherseeds," said the Memory.

"*Mother*seeds?" I said.

I looked at Johnny. Motherseeds! "How much for those?" I asked the seer.

"What about apple seeds?" said the Memory of Johnny Appleseed.

"Here," said the marginalia, and he held up another bag. "Finest apples this side of East Appleseed."

"How much?" said the Memory.

"Five truths," he said.

The Memory of Johnny Appleseed's eyes narrowed. "Give you four," he said.

"Fuck you," said the marginal. He closed his knapsack and turned to walk away.

"OK," the Memory said, grabbing the sleeve of Eyes' coat. "Four truths, one theory."

"What about for the motherseeds?" I said.

"Two ideas," he said.

I handed him the ideas and he gave me the packet of seeds.

When we got back to the deadgroves we went right to work. We were running out of space in the deadgroves, so Johnny directed me to a patch of nothings and told me to pull them out.

"Really?" I said. "They're almost ripe." They looked like this:

Nothing   Nothing   Nothing   Nothing   Nothing   Nothing
Nothing   Nothing   Nothing   Nothing   Nothing   Nothing
Nothing   Nothing   Nothing   Nothing   Nothing   Nothing

"We can either grow nothings here," said the Memory of Johnny Appleseed, "or we can pull the nothings and plant mothers and apples."

I stepped into the field and began pulling up the nothings by the roots. Then I turned the soil and planted the seeds we'd traded for. After half an hour or so, Bob Lonely came walking across the street. "Afternoon," he said.

The Memory of Johnny Appleseed nodded to him.

Mr. Lonely looked at the pile of nothings. "Those nothings ripe?"

"Ripe as they're going to get," said the Memory of Johnny Appleseed.

The pulled nothings were screaming, and dying, in the sun.

"Are they—screaming?" Bob said.

"They're singing," said Appleseed.

Bob nodded and turned back toward his house.

The sun roiled overhead. The next morning, the dead-grove struck up a conversation with the sun, and the soil asked the sun out for chai, and then, out for a formal dinner date. Soon the sun and soil were spending a lot of time together. And then, lo and tone, I walked out into the fields with the Memory of Johnny Appleseed one morning and we saw stalks starting to sprout.

"Isn't it amazing?" said the proud page.

Appleseed put his hands on his hips. "It's a fucking miracle," he said.

I started planning for a new life: life with a Mom. Two Moms, even! On my clipboard, I made a list of places we could go: to the Big Why, the Library, on a hike up Appleseed Mountain, to see a matinee at the Bing. Would this Mom like music? Would she appreciate the Ulcerative Colitises?

The rows of apple seeds didn't sprout; neither did the pumpkin seeds. But two days after we planted the motherseeds the stalks were eye-high. I stepped up to the first row of plants and I could see, between the sheaths, human faces. When I looked closer, though, I saw a beard and an Adam's apple. My thoughts swore in disappointment. These weren't the faces of mothers after all; they were the faces of *fathers*, their eyes closed and their lips pursed.

When I showed the Memory of Johnny Appleseed the father faces he put his hands on his hips and spit into the soil. "Shit," he said. "That damn omniscient—he sold us Dads instead of Moms." I could tell he was embarrassed.

"What are we supposed to do with these?" I asked.

"We could just turn them over, bury them," the Memory of Johnny Appleseed suggested.

I thought about that. "And grow what?" I said.

"Corn?" he suggested.

In the end, though, we decided to reap the crop—to let the fathers grow, pull them when they were ready, and then bring them down to the flea bee and see what we could get for them. This *was* during the blight, after all; everyone was down on meaning and we thought there still might be a good local market for Dads. Everyone needed a father—villains needed them, nomads needed them, even those *with* fathers needed fathers.

Another few days passed by—I spent them by myself, alone in the house. That weekend, though, the Memory of Johnny Appleseed prayed to me from across the street and told me that the sheaths were uncurling, that I needed to get over to the deadgroves right away. When I got there I saw: some of the fathers were waking up, rubbing their eyes and stretching their arms and stepping out of their stalks. Most of them were dressed in work suits and carrying briefcases. Each ripe father dutifully placed one foot on the field and then the other. Then they all checked their watches and straightened their ties.

One father approached me. "Dad?" I said, but he walked right past me and bolted across the grove.

Then another father stepped out of its stalk. "Dad," I said, but that one walked right by, too.

Soon, a steady stream of fathers was storming across the street. In the groves, meanwhile, more fathers were waking up. One of them stepped out into the deadsoil and smiled at me. "Name's Jim," he said.

"_____," I said.

We shook hands. "Very good to be here," he said, looking around at the fields. "You've done a great job here. I'm really proud of you, Son."

I hadn't heard words like those in I don't know how long—maybe never. "It was nothings," I said.

"But now it's somethings, and that's because of *you*, because of what you did. Show me around?"

Jim and I walked past the rows of dead trees. I introduced him to the Memory of Johnny Appleseed, who was helping other fathers out of their stalks. "I'm Jim," he said to the Memory of Johnny Appleseed. "And you are?"

"The Memory of Johnny Appleseed," said the Memory of Johnny Appleseed.

"Great to meet you," said Jim.

Just then, I saw my father's truck pull into our driveway. He got out of the cab and watched a school of fathers pass him. I saw him look across the street. Then he began marching mechanically toward us. "What—" he said, his silver skin shining in the sun. "Who are these people?"

Jim extended his hand. "Name's Jim," he said.

"They're fathers," I said.

My Dad tried to compute this. "What are they doing *here*?"

"Dads are really popular right now," I said quietly.

"But you *have* a Dad," said my father. "Me."

"I know," I said. "I thought—if we brought them to the flea bee—"

"OK, but you should have asked me about this first," he said, rubbing the soot of toil off his forehead. "This is a really meaningful risk."

"The seeds were only—"

"Fathers have huge appetites," my Dad said. I could smell the work on his breath. "What do you plan to *feed* them?"

Across the street, fathers were looking for tasks. Two had opened the hood of my father's truck and one was fixing the steel banister on the front step.

Jim looked at his watch. "Gosh darnit, I'm late," he said.

"Late for what?" said my father.

"I've got a meeting at the office," he said, straightening his tie.

"Will you be coming back?" I said.

Jim winced. "Probably not," he said.

"Not ever?" I said.

"I've got a lot of work to catch up on," Jim said. "_____, you take care of yourself, all right, Son? You have a good life now, you hear?" Then he chucked me on the shoulder and charged toward the street.

"Jim," I said, weakly.

"Forget that one," said my father. There was sudden meaning in his eyes. "Go back out to the fields. Keep them in their stalks until we figure out how to store them."

I was dizzy. "How do I keep them there?"

My father ran his hands through his tired hair. "Do

whatever it takes," he said. "Try to reason with them. Tell them a story."

My Dad ran toward the house and I went back into the groves. By then it was almost dusk, and more difficult to see—the running fathers made shadows on the white page.

When I reached the fatherfields, though, all was quiet. The only fathers left in those fields were not yet ripe, still sleeping in their stalks. I went from stalk to stalk, looking at their sleeping faces. Some fathers were mumbling to themselves; others were wheezing and snoring.

I won't ever forget that chorus of snores. It sounded like family.

WORRYFIELDS

PRAYER PIANO II

We left that piano out in the worryfields for anyone to play, but most people seemed to ignore it. Once I saw a Canada out there, sitting at the bench and staring at the keys, but I didn't hear any music or changing points of view.

For a while, I didn't think about the piano too much—it just sat there in the fields, switching points of view every now and again. That spring, though, I started spending a lot more time in those fields. By then, I think I was just craving company. I liked to watch the worriers pacing back and forth in the high grass, wringing their hands, hugging themselves or praying. *I'd* started praying again, too—not to my Mom, who I still hated for leaving, but directly to the Core. "How can you leave me here?" I prayed to it, my knees sinking into the page.

As usual, there was no response.

"Isn't every single person holy? Even me?" I prayed.

A hole appeared in my palm.

"Not holey," I prayed. "Holy! Like, sacred!"

Nothing.

Walking back from the worryfields one day, I passed by the piano and, on a whim, sat down on the stool. By that point the keys were warped and weather-stained. I pressed a note and heard the point of view of close worriers.

But mostly I was concerned about Bob. What would I tell him?

I pressed another note and the POV switched to a chorus pacing the edge of the field.

How are we supposed to live knowing that we may or may not have cancer somewhere in our body?

Another key called the point of view of the page.

Why is everyone looking at me so strangely? Do I have something on my face?

All that shifting point of view made me hungry. I stood up, walked home, and had a potato chip sandwich.

The next day, though, I went back to the piano. When I sat down at the keys this time, I tried two notes simultaneously. I heard whispers from the trees, the whining of a cloud, the gruff of a shingle.

Soon I was making chords, just like I'd seen the Possum do: three notes, and points of view, at once: my father's point of view at the labor factory, fixing the Supply-Demander/the Memory of Johnny Appleseed, trading for seeds/a bird in the trees. I heard ". . . bad gasket?/trust-worthy/shee-twee-bee!" simultaneously.

As I was leaning into the chord, though, my foot happened to push the foremost left pedal on the bottom of the piano. "Bee-twee-shee!" said the bird.

I stopped and looked down at the pedal. Then I pushed the right pedal. "Shee-twee-bee!" said the bird.

I played a different note and pushed the left pedal with my foot.

"Morning, Ralph," said the Forebarrel.

"Morning," I said. "What's on tap for today?"

"Need you to take a look at the Demander in Building Six," the Forebarrel said.

"Will do," I said.

At first I didn't understand what was happening; it took me a few minutes to recognize that the right pedal was moving the story forward in time and the left pedal reversing it. Every day that week, though, I went back to the piano and practiced. Soon, I was a good enough point-of-view piano player that I could shift the POV to a nearby tree in the margin, and then to the Memory of Johnny Appleseed in the deadgroves, and then to my house, at any time in their history. I saw my house as a young cabin, hiking a strange mountain with his fathershack. When I melodied further back, I saw Johnny Appleseed—the *real* Johnny Appleseed—stopping to tie the leather laces on his boots.

I practiced melody after melody—varying pedals, notes, and speeds—until I located, somewhere in the past pages, my mother praying to my father. I picked up the story midverse:

"I can't, Ralphie," she prayed.

"Why not?" he prayed.

"Because I have work to do still. We're repairing holes day and night."

"But why do *you* have to fix it?" prayed my father. "Why *you*?"

"_____ is *our son*! We should be the *first ones* on line to help Appleseed."

There was silence.

"I miss you," prayed my Dad. "We all do."

"Any word from Bri?" my Mom prayed.

My Dad prayed that there wasn't. "You?"

"We're looking," my Mom prayed. "We'll find her."

"You've checked all the auction schools?"

"Of course we have," my Mom said. "And I've put out a national call to the Mothers' Network."

"I'm just praying that she's OK," my Dad said.

"Me, too—twice a day," my Mom prayed. "What about _____?"

"He's fine. The same."

"He won't answer my prayers," my Mom prayed.

"He says he's angry at you," my Dad prayed.

"I'm worryfields about him."

"You should tell him that," my Dad prayed. "You should visit."

"I will," she prayed. "Soon as I can get away."

"He would love to see you," prayed my Dad. "We all would."

A few days later, I played the song of Mothers' Day—the national recruiting day for the Mothers of America. That was the day my Mom left us—remember? I saw that sequence again, my Mom walking out into the backyard with hardly a goodbye and lifting up into the air. We ran out after her and Bri shouted up into the sky. She wasn't the Auctioneer that day—she was just Briana, my freaked-out sister.

Playing this song now, from third person, I could see my own face, still and dumb and silent. Why wasn't I crying, or shouting, or saying anything at all? I should have protested more, or at least told my Mom that I loved her.

I played a pausechord, found the first-person harmony, and resumed the scene from my own eyes again. Inside my head my thoughts were howling. "Find the words," one commanded me.

"What words?" said a second.

"The words to make her *stay!*" said the first.

Then I heard a noise overhead and saw something looming over the roof: a giant, dark shape. I put my hand over my forehead to shield the afternoon sun. "What is *that?*" said the Reader.

It was like nothing I'd ever seen before. When I looked closer at it, though, I realized what I was seeing: those were *skirts*—thousands and thousands of warskirts. As the school of Mothers oomed forward in recruit formation, my mother floated toward them and joined the giant mass; soon I couldn't distinguish her shape from anyone else's. I understood then why she'd left so quickly; she was rushing to stay on schedule.

My sister turned to me. "Nice job, assface."

"What did *I* do?" I said.

But I knew: these were my stories—every one of them.

Bri stormed inside. The Reader and I stood in the yard, watching other recruits—some of them lugging suitcases or duffel bags as they flew—join the formation. As the fleet hovered, I said a prayer. "Mom?" I prayed.

"What?" she whisperprayed back.

"Be careful," I prayed.

"Of course," she prayed. "Don't worry, OK?"

Then the entire fleet began floating forward. They tightened formation, banked left, flew behind a cloud and disappeared.

The last song I ever played on that point of view piano was a third-person from our very first days in Appleseed, after I'd just begun to speak. I didn't yet have a room—we were all still figuring out how we'd live in Appleseed. When I released my foot from the pedal, I saw my Mom and Dad standing in the basement. "It's too *cold* down here for him," my Dad said.

"But it's spacious. It will give him room for his art," my Mom said.

"What *art*?" my Dad said.

"He can draw if he wants to," she said. "Or write."

"Write what?" my Dad said.

"Whatever he wants," my Mom said.

BASTILLE SQUARE

By the fall of my senior year Appleseed was riddled with bookwormholes. It wasn't strange to see holes in the middle of fields, human-sized holes on the sidewalk, car-sized holes in the road. There were accidents all over town: people twisting their ankles or tripping on new holes; veggiecars, swerving to miss a hole, crying right into other veggiecars.

As the bookworms took over, characters disappeared. Take my cousin Patrick—one day he was here, the next day gone. The same with the Memory of Johnny Appleseed; all of a sudden he couldn't be found. After enough of these disappearances, the Building Cones started covering up the holes with steel plates to curb injuries.

Reader: You mean like manhole covers?

What's a manhole?

There were all sorts of rumors about where these holes led. Some people thought they led to the Core; others, to a world of Memories. Large Odor said he didn't think they led anywhere. But that fall, Orange Traffic Cone Scientists sent two dogs down a bookwormhole and said the dogs came back smelling of prayers.

Then, one afternoon that November, I was walking

with Sentence in the worryfields and he pulled me right to one of the holes. "Come on, 'I am.',", I said.

He wouldn't budge—he was fixed on the bookwormhole. It was starting to drizzle, so I tugged on his leash. " 'I am.'," I said.

But the words didn't move. By then, "I am." was strong—three times the size he'd been when I found him.

The rain started falling harder. I picked "I am." up and ran across the street as the sky opened its mouth and bared its sharp teeth.

Two days later, I realized that I was out of music pills and rode my bike to the pharmacy for a refill. I asked you to come along and help me pedal, but—

Reader: We'd been jumping over bookwormholes that whole week prior. I was exhausted!

So I took Sentence instead; he rode both ways perched on the handlebars, and held the bag of music pills in the teeth of his "i" on the way home.

As we were riding down Converse Street, just a few hundred feet from our driveway, Sentence suddenly looked out at the worryfields and capitalized.

" 'I am.'? You OK?" I said.

But "I AM." was already moving, leaping off the Bicycle Built for Two and bolting across the street. Blue music pills spilled everywhere; I almost crashed! By the time I stopped and skimmed the page, Sentence had already reached the worryfields—he startled a couple of pacers as he shot past them.

" 'I am.'!" I shouted.

I waited for traffic to pass, rolled my Bicycle Built for

Two across the street, dropped the tandem by the road-side, and ran through the tall white grass, calling out for Sentence. "'I am.'!" I shouted. About fifty yards into the fields, I came to a hole in the page—the same bookworm-hole that Sentence had been fixated on a few days before. I looked around. "'I am.'!" I shouted.

"Are what?" said a worrier. I looked over at her. She was clearly a professional fretter; she was wringing her hands expertly, and her long gray hair was all thin and patchy.

"Did you see any language run through here?" I said.

"Language?" Her face lost color.

"A sentence called—"

"Why? Is that a possibility? Are you telling me there's— wild language on these pages?"

"He's my pet," I said.

The worrier held up her hands. "You are *totally* freak-ing me out," she said.

I leaned over the hole and looked down into it. I saw nothing but darkness. "'I am.'!" I shouted, stupidly. My voice just bounced back at me: "I am.! I am.! I am.!"

Inside my mind my thoughts bumped into each other, fell down, stood up, and ran in circles. "Who can help?" one shouted.

"My Mom!" another shouted.

"She won't answer your prayers!" shouted the first thought.

"Dad?" shouted a third thought.

"Too busy," I told the third.

"What about the Reader!" shouted the first thought. "Where's the Reader?"

I straightened up, ran across the street and burst into the house. "Reader!" I called.

You weren't in the living room or the kitchen. I ran out to the backyard. "Reader?" I shouted.

I found you in the basement, sitting at my desk and writing in one of my yellow pads. "Hey!" I said.

You looked up from the desk.

"What are you doing?" I said.

"No—nothing," she said, and quickly turned the pad over.

"I need your help," I said. I told her what had happened to Sentence. "I think he went down one of the bookwormholes."

"You're kidding," you said.

I shook my head.

"Are you sure?"

"Pretty sure," I said.

You stood up, found your shoes, and followed me back up the stairs and across the street. When we reached the fields I led you over to the hole in the page closest to where Sentence had disappeared.

"You *sure* he went this way?" you said.

"No," I said. "But this is where I lost sight of him."

"What was he doing off the leash in the first place?"

"We were riding on the Bicycle Built for Two—he leapt off the handlebars," I said.

The Reader squinted and looked around.

"Should we go after him?" I said.

"What do you mean?" The Reader looked into the hole. "Down there?"

I shrugged.

"Absolutely not!" the Reader said. "We don't have any idea—"

"'I am.' is down there," I said.

"We don't even know that for sure," the Reader said. "He could be hurt! Or killed!"

The Reader pointed out to the treeline. "What if he went into the margin?"

"He didn't—he made a beeline right for this hole."

You lay down on your belly and tried to see into the hole. Then you stood up and brushed the page off your hands. "It's completely dark down there," you said.

"He's getting farther away every second," I said.

"For the record, I think this is a terrible idea."

"Noted," I said, and gestured to the hole. "Go for it."

You held up your hands. "Age before beauty," the Reader said.

"Aren't you older than me?" I asked.

"There's no way I'm going first," you said.

I walked over to the bookwormhole, sat down on the page, and put my feet into the hole. Then I slowly lowered myself down. My thoughts were yelping, but when I stretched my body out my feet touched a fiber floor. I stood up and helped the Reader down.

We looked into the tunnel. I saw dim light ahead.

We stooped and trotted through the dark channel. "It stinks in here," the Reader said.

"That's the rot," I said.

After twenty feet or so, the chute widened; we stood up straight and walked side by side. A string of bare lightbulbs now ran overhead. For the first few hundred yards, I could see the underside of the page above us—the roots and tendrils of printed words. Directly above me was the *d* in "killed," and, later, the *re* of "amphitheatre." Then the print grew higher and fainter, though, and soon I couldn't see it at all anymore.

"'I am.'!" I shouted, but my words just boomeranged back to me.

We walked for a while in silence. Then the Reader said, "Think we're still on the same page?"

"This has to be a different one," I said. "Doesn't it?"

You shook your head.

"'I am.'!" I shouted again.

"Please stop that," said the Reader.

Soon we saw some light up ahead and an intersection in the channel. It was a crosshole—another pathway burrowing to our left and right. "Should we take one of these?" I said.

The Reader grimaced. "I say we keep reading forward," she said.

We trudged on for another few minutes, until our surroundings changed; the walls became gluey, and we hopped over a synapse and passed what appeared to be giant white ropes.

Finally we reached the end of the channel, and daylight. When we were almost under the opening, I stopped and knelt down to see what was up there.

"Well?" whispered the Reader.

I shook my head. "I see—sky," I said. "Clouds."

A cough of wind passed over the surface and sand scratched our faces. The Reader nodded upward and laced her hands together; I stepped into them and she hoisted me up out of the channel—then I pulled her up behind me. There wasn't much on this page; just a few rickety wooden buildings and a single donkey tied to a post.

A gun rode by on a horse. Two more guns sat in wicker chairs on the porch of a shabby building.

I looked at the Reader. She walked up to the gun. "Excuse me," she said. "Have you seen a sentence walking through here?"

"What sentence?" said the gun.

"'I am.'," I said.

"You're—*what*?" said the gun.

"That's the sentence," I said.

"'I am.'?" said the gun.

"Not much of a sentence," said the second gun.

"You haven't seen it, then?" the Reader said.

The gun shook its head.

"What's the story here?" asked the Reader.

"No story at all today," said the gun. "Story here *yesterday*. Two guns met their makers."

The Reader thanked the guns and we walked back toward the hole. The Reader's eyes were bright. "You realize what's happening here," she said.

I stared at her.

"_____," she said. "We're in a different story."

I climbed down into the hole.

"Get it?" said the Reader.

"No," I said.

"The bookwormholes?" said the Reader. "The worms? Go from *novel to novel*."

I still didn't understand. "We just need to find Sentence," I said.

"Are you hearing what I'm saying? All of *literature* is at our disposal!"

"Because he can't have gone that far," I said.

The Reader put her hands on my shoulders. "He could be anywhere, _____—in any one of these books."

"I just want to find him and go home," I said.

We walked past the gluey walls and toward the crosshole. This time we took a left. Soon I heard a giant pounding: *bm-bm; mb-bm; rm-tm; vm-bm.*

"What is that?" I said.

dm-vm; mb-zm; bm-dm.

"Whatever it is, it's big," the Reader said.

When we pushed open the next bookwormhole cover we were on a strange page. All we saw were lines of words—row after row of them. None of the words were moving or making any sound.

"They're all dead," I said.

"Of course they are—it's a graveyard," said the Reader.

I looked around. I'd heard about these places—fields where people buried their deadwords—but I'd never actually seen one. I studied the words. "What language is this?" I said.

A wind blew across the page.

"It's so sad," I said. "All these words, with so much potential."

"What do you mean? These words probably lived good lives."

"They died too young," I said.

"You didn't even know them," said the Reader.

"They could have been so much more," I said. Then I lowered myself down into the bookwormhole. The Reader followed and closed the cover above us.

The Reader and I walked from story to story: into dramas, romances, science fictions, detective stories. Sometimes we were in a quiet scene—a praying river, a prison cell—but other times we climbed up right into the thick of the action. In one novel, I found myself sitting in a steel boat full of soldiers under fire. In another, I crawled into the story between two lovers in a steamy romantic scene. "I want you so badly," said a gruffy man, and he pressed against me.

"Me?" I said.

He opened his eyes. "No," he said. "Her."

Somewhere in a story about 1930s France, though, I lost the Reader. One minute she was there with me, marching through a crowded city square, and the next minute she wasn't. I thought she was following me, but when I turned around she was gone. I waited for the crowd to disperse and then retraced my steps, but she wasn't anywhere. I looked for her all day; I prayed to her but received no response. Finally, I turned around and went back to the bookwormhole we'd come in from, on the altar of an old church in the corner of the city. When we'd arrived, we'd crawled out of the hole in the middle of a service; everyone had stood up, shocked. "'I am.'?" I asked the parishioners. Then the Reader led me through a side exit and out onto the street.

As I was walking into the church, though, I saw a sen-

tence hiding in the doorway. At first I thought i[t]
a nomadic phrase seeking alms. But no—that wo[uld]
"alms"—it was "am." " 'I am.'!" I said. He ran
arms. Core he was so thin! But I was so happy to
I carried him into the dim sanctuary, through t[he]
pews and toward the dark altar.

I didn't have any idea how to get home, but
had a nose for pages; when we came to our fir[st]
hole—five or six channels converging—he sai[d]
left."

"Left, you think?" I said.

"Left," said "I am.".

A few minutes later we hit a fork in the pa[ge]
right," said the sentence.

I went right.

Soon I saw familiar textures, and then, tw[o]
footprints in the fiber. "I am." must have been able to smell
Appleseed, or hear it or something. "Thataboy," I said.
"Good sentence."

After another ten pages or so, I saw the underside of
words—words about the outskirts of town, sentences about
Appleseed Mountain—and then, a bookwormhole. I shuffled to it, pushed Sentence out to the surface, and climbed
up after him.

It was dark. A few hundred feet away, a wolf sat writing at a rolltop desk.

"I am Wolf Swamp," said "I am.". He looked up at me.

I took a breath of blighty air. "We're home," I said.

• • •

But something was different; I knew it from our very first moments back in Appleseed. There was a problem with the sky. It was dark out, but not *night*-dark. The sky was—how do I say this? *Closed*. Shut. It was like a lid had fallen over Appleseed.

Sentence saw it, too. He pointed up and said, "We're confused."

Everyone else seemed to be, too. On Wenonah, we passed a camel in a white T-shirt sitting on a five-gallon bucket and staring at the sky. He looked over at us as we passed. "What the fuck," he said.

On the next street over, a hairperson was shouting to anyone who would listen. "Can you *see*?" she asked us. "Because I can't even read the page!"

As we were walking up Ellipsis, though, I realized what was happening. It wasn't *as if* the sky was closed. The sky *was* closed: you can't have a book without a Reader.

"Oh. Shit," I said.

"I am what," shivered Sentence.

I didn't answer him; I didn't want to frighten him. Inside my brain, though, my thoughts were understanding: that wasn't a lid over the sky, but a cover—the inside cover of the book itself.

Just then a prayer came in for me. "_____?" It was my mother.

I didn't answer.

"Honey," she prayed again.

I closed the prayer—I wanted nothing to do with her.

On Converse Street, all of the traffic had stopped behind an accident by Redfern. Some people stood outside their cars, talking to other drivers; others just stared up at the darkness and the inside cover. In the opposite lane, passing cars were switching on their headlights.

Another prayer came in—this one from my Dad at Muir Drop. "Hey, _____," he prayed. "Look at the sky, buddy. Something's going on."

In the margins, wild language began howling. I looked across the street in time to see two lunging, drooling sentences—"This is your fault, you piece of shit," and "These are *your* sentences!"—step brazenly out of the treeline.

I picked up "I am.", ran inside, and locked the door behind us.

EDWARD VII

The darkness was complete; it covered Appleseed like silence. For the first few days I just stayed inside, living off chips and melancholy, feeding Sentence scraps of time. Every half hour or so I heard sirens: people prayed about visibility problems, freak accidents, injuries or death. The TV told me that the hospital was full, that there were fires on far pages. "But no one knows where the fire trucks are," said the TV. "The pages are burning out of control."

Soon I lost track of time—it was difficult to know if it was day or night, when one day passed and the next day began. My Mom prayed to me frequently—"I'm concerned about you!" "Just let me know that you're OK!" "You answer me this *instant* young man!"—but I shut down every one of her prayers. I didn't want her help—she was someone else's Mother now. I was almost eighteen by then, and old enough to know how to take care of myself—I knew all I needed to: where to buy the chips, what kinds of chips to buy, and in what order to eat them.

Once or twice, my father came by to check on me and drop off some meaning. The first time he didn't even come inside—we just stood in the driveway talking for a few minutes. At one point he said, "This will all get better soon."

"How do you figure?" I said.

He pointed up to the dark sky. "The Mothers are working on a way to lift up that cover," he said. "Speaking of which—pray back to Mom, will you?"

"I don't want to talk to her," I mumbled.

"She's worried about you," my Dad said. "And she has some business to discuss with you too. Regarding your friend."

"Who?"

"The Reader," my Dad said. "Everyone's looking for her."

"I don't know where she is," I said.

My Dad checked his watch. "Shoot," he said. "I've got to get back." Then he punched me softly on the shoulder, got back in his truck, and drove away. Just out of the driveway, his truck stopped short to let a wild sentence pass—I saw the sentence's eyes flash in the headlights and scoot off.

Soon, meaning lost all value in Appleseed. The Big Why sold out of most of its questions and couldn't get more from the distributor; the Big When followed suit. Phrases smashed the window of Small Pear and looted the shelves; a frightened Cordial Carl stood guard outside his restaurant, barking angrily at everyone who approached. A few weeks after the cover closed, a crew of puns walked into Appleseed First National, held up the word "gun" and said, "Give me all your meaning."

"I can't read the word you're holding," said the bank teller.

"It says 'gun,'" said the first pun.

"It looks like 'fun,'" said the teller.

"It says 'gun,' motherfucker," said the second pun, "and it's going to say 'killed' if you don't open the vault."

They ran the security-camera footage of the stick-up on the news, and you could see one of the puns suddenly put down the word as if he forgot what it—the meaning, the guns, the heist, any of it—meant. "I'm hungry," the second pun said to the first pun. By the time the teller opened the vault, the puns were gone.

People still prayed, but for what? To whom? The *Core*? I sent some psalms to my sister—"Where are you?" "It sucks here!"—and I watched the words sail high. Like most darkness-era prayers, though, mine bounced off the inside cover of the book and back into Appleseed. I saw them fall somewhere to the west and disappear from view. The next day, The Ear showed up and pulled a prayer out of the back of the truck. "This yours?" he said.

It was my prayer to the Auctioneer. "Yes," I said, embarrassed.

"Landed on my property. Put a nice fucking dent in my shed," he said.

I'd either forgotten those words—"dent," "shed"—or else they'd been removed from the language. "Your *what?*" I said.

"Shed," he said.

I shook my head.

"Small house-type thing," said The Ear.

A few days later I got tired of eating chips—either that, or the chips themselves got tired of being eaten—so I got on my Bicycle Built for Two and rode through the dark streets toward Gus & Paul's. Pedaling down Converse, you could see how hungry people were for answers: every person's spine was a question mark; their eyes whatted or whyed. And there were bookwormholes everywhere now: in the street, on the lawns, in the cars, in the clouds—in some of the people, even. On Burbank, a meaninglesser held out his hand to ask me for a spare theory and I saw a hole in his wrist. "A hypothesis?" he said. "A *theory*, even—anything."

"Sorry," I said.

When I got to Gus & Paul's I found the place empty—it was just me and the deflated hat behind the counter. I walked up to the register and held up my hand in the shape of a "one."

"One what?" said the hat.

I looked at the menu.

"One what?" he said.

I studied the choices, written in chalk. What did they mean? I couldn't remember. Then, someone walked by with a square white box. "One of those," I said. The hat handed me the empty box and I walked out.

Within weeks, those holes took their toll on the town. Houses collapsed; whole fields fell in. It didn't take a bessoff to see what was happening: Appleseed was rotting.

A lot of families I knew left town. The Lonelies drove to a relative's home in the western margin, and I heard that the Blueberry River packed a watery suitcase and hitch-hiked down Five, vowing never to return.

Like everyone else who stayed, I adapted as best I

could. Eventually my eyes adjusted; I learned to read in the dark. Without apples or bagels, some people survived by eating worries grown in the fields; others ate ink right off the page. One day my house went into the margin and killed a poem. He brought it back slung over his shoulder, laid the verse on the grass, removed its skin and vital organs, and handed me an iamb. "Eat," my house said.

I tried—I smelled the words, put one on my tongue. It tasted rhymey. "I'm not sure I can eat this," I said.

"Dip it in some melancholy," he said, and pushed a saucer full of gritty liquid toward me. I dipped the stanza and bit into it. Word juice ran down my chin. "Not bad," I said.

Every few days, I packed up some poem jerky and went out looking for the Reader. I'd put on my headphones, climb down a bookwormhole, walk to a new novel, and wander that novel until I found a character who seemed reliable. I'd ask them if they'd seen the Reader, if they'd heard of Appleseed, if they knew anything about a blight. I found myself in every setting imaginable—running from a giant golden machine; strapped down to an operating table in a room lit by candles; in a marketplace where people sold organs and teeth—but it was never the right story. One day, I saw someone I thought was you fixing a car in a 1930s service station. I couldn't see the mechanic's face, but she had your same build and she was wearing the same combat boots you used to wear—the ones with the flames on the side. I went right up to the car. "Reader?" I said.

A woman shimmied out from behind the front tire. "Help you?" she said.

Her face was a straight line, her eyebrows two exclamation points—it wasn't you.

In another novel, I found myself in a medieval army, wearing chainmail and carrying a bow, and I thought I saw you sitting on a horse two rows over. I leaned over to the maybe-you. "Psst—hey," I said.

"Get back in line, McRoy!" shouted the lieutenant.

Then someone yelled "Charge!" and the war began—we all stormed forward across the field, and I lost maybe-you in the fray.

Most of the time, though, I couldn't even find the story itself—it was somewhere else in the setting, far away from where I'd arrived. And no one I met took any interest in me, or made an effort to help me find the plot. All my life, I'd read stories about people being kind, helping other people. But did anyone, in any one of those worlds, ever try to help *me*? Take me in? Try to get to know me? No—not one character, ever.

If I'd found you, if I could have talked to you for just a minute or two, I would have apologized. I would have told you how sorry I was that you never had a story—no physical description, no face, not even a—

Not even a name. That wasn't fair of me. Everyone deserves their own story. If I could have brought you back to Appleseed—if you would have let the light back in—I would have given you a whole history. I would have made you anyone you wanted to be: Johnny Appleseed, a Select Cone, a Mother, even.

• • •

Back in Appleseed, meanwhile, the sentences were going absolutely wild. Lavished in darkness, the bookworms no longer needed to hide in the margins: they strutted up and down the dark streets like they owned the place, chalking and sturming, with skomals and fortuous vays, periodical magnavoxing, lopal rikes, uring and salmoning, exclamation. What could the Mothers do against words that could change, and change again, right under your feet?

Not that they rolled over. Spondee told me that the Mothers conducted nighttime paragraph raids; I heard rumors, too, of secret underground laboratories where Mothers cultivated new word viruses and experimented on language to make it talk.

That November, though, the Mothers suffered major losses when jargons organized a simultaneous attack on every Nest in Appleseed, destroying five Nests in a single afternoon. More than a thousand Mothers were killed that day. I heard the ambulances from the basement and stepped outside to see the dark sky filled with smoke.

"Mom?" said one of my thoughts.

As I was standing there a prayer came in from my Dad. "_____?"

"What," I said.

"Mom's OK," he said. "She was out on assignment. She's at an undisclosed Nest."

The Mothers mourned and regrouped; they held a press conference a few days later to denounce the attacks and to promise more security. Every day that winter, you'd see fleets of Mothers trying to repair the town: boarding up broken storefront windows; covering open bookwormholes; transporting people with holes in them to Appleseed Hospital. Orange Traffic Cones, meanwhile, maintained status quo as best they could: they tried to keep the roads open, to protect as many stories as possible from looting or meaningloss, to deliver food to shut-ins and get people to and from work and school. When some hoodlum phrases knocked out the streetlights on Converse early that spring, a Cone even showed up at my door to drive me to school in a Cone-shaped squad car.

By that point, though, school wasn't really *school*—it was mostly cages and dark, empty classrooms. Teachers were rare, and if they showed up at all they usually just stood in front of the room, staring back at the students. In Depression IV, the broom teaching the class just posed whats. "What's the education?" he asked.

Large Odor raised his hand. "The past?" he said.

The broom shrugged. "I'm not sure," he said. "Maybe, maybe not."

Then Chamblis raised her hand. "What's our homework?" she said.

"That's a great question," the broom said. "What *is* your home work?"

"The work we do at home?" said Spondee.

I left that room and went to Advanced What to Be Most Frightened Of. But the teacher in that room didn't say anything at all—she just kept drawing sad faces on the chalkboard.

A few days later I showed up to that classroom and found it empty. I sat there for a few hours, and then I stood up and left. By then the place was a mess—the hallways were filled with garbage and torn-up books, and every-thing smelled like old ham and mayonnaise. On the way out the door that day—my very last day of high school ever—my sneaker kicked through a stack of papers near the art room and the pages went flying. I picked up a handful of the scattered pages; there was an old school newspaper, plus two blank diplomas and a hall pass. I kept the hall pass and one of the diplomas and threw the rest of it back on the ground. Then I walked out the heavy front doors.

A FAT, SNORING COMMA

MONARCH

Two years after my mother left us, my childhood home hanged itself from a tree in the yard of our Appleseed home.

This was in the dark summer. My father had full-blown workhosis by then, and I was spending most of my free time tilling in the deadgroves with the Memory of Johnny Appleseed; he'd recently returned to town, his face and clothes smudged with ink, refusing to discuss where he'd been. The schools were closed; so were most of the stores—there was no fresh food anymore. I ate mostly chips: plain chips for breakfast, salt and vinegar for lunch, barbecue for dinner. Then I'd open a bag of sour cream and onion and fall asleep watching the house's memories—memories of me, sleeping in the Vox or running around in the backyard; of the rows of parked cars during my sister's auctions; of my mother watering her plants while smoking a six-foot cigarette; of the four of us, being watched by the television—rerun over and over on the walls of the living room.

Watching those memories, I should have known that 577 was in crisis. Plus, the house leaned dangerously to one side; every wall curved with sorrow. Not to mention the house's *dreams*, which I can see now were honest-to-lou night terrors: dreams of falling, of being shot, of being chased through dark tunnels. Once I woke up in the middle of a housedream of being buried alive: the building screamed as the dirt was piled onto the house-sized coffin, blocking the last slivers of light through pine boards.

I didn't just sit by and watch the house suffer, though. I went out to Gilbert's Bookstore and bought some self-help books: *A Room with a View*, *ReHouse*, others. I brought them home and put them on the coffee table.

"What are these?" said the house.

"I really think you should read them," I said.

"What good are *books* in a situation like this?"

"These ones have some good ideas," I said.

"I don't want good ideas," said the house. "I just want everything, and everyone, to be quiet."

A week or two later, I was making a chiplunch when the house asked me if I wanted its collection of old 45s: Gordo and Gordo, The Rabbit, vintage OCDs, The Redirected Flights—some great stuff. "You really don't want these anymore?" I said.

"I want you to have them," said 577. "Think of me when you play them."

I didn't even own a record player. "OK," I said.

Right as I started eating my lunch, though, a prayer came in from the Memory of Johnny Appleseed: he'd just traded for some new lightseeds and needed help at the Colton Groves. "I'll be right there," I said, and I shoveled some chips into my mouth and ran out the door.

A few minutes later, I was riding over there on my Bicycle Built for Two when I saw the Memory of Johnny

Appleseed walking down Inherited Wealth Boulevard. "Where are you going?" I said.

"False alarm," he said.

"What do you mean?"

"Deadseeds," he said.

I leaned over the handlebars. "Shit."

"Got a surprise for you, though," he said. He held up a soda bottle filled with blue liquid.

"What's that?" I said.

"Kaddish Cider," he said.

"Absolutely," I said.

So we sat in the fields and got kaddished. Cidered out, I lay on my back and looked up at the inside cover. The daynight passed and soon it was dusknight. By then I was sober enough to pick up my bike and ride home.

When I got there, though, the house was gone.

Memory of the Reader: *Gone?*

It wasn't there. Which wasn't so strange on its own— my house, like most houses, took occasional strolls or daytrips. 577 was always sure to tell me where it was going, though, and to return to Converse Street by early evening. But when eight o'clock that night approached, waved, and drove off with no house in sight, I started to worry. I prayed to the house's friends and family—his mother, his condo brother. His brother didn't reply; his mother hadn't seen him.

An hour later, though, I received a prayer from an Or that used to trade with my father. They'd had a falling out over a demo job in Appleseed City—my father said that the Or stole some railroad ties from him—and it would be years more before they coffeed. But the Or prayed that he was down at the Glenwood—a whatif in the downtown—and that my house was sitting right across from him. I rode the Bicycle Built for Two over to the bar. When I walked in, the Or was lounging at the video game table in the front. Or nodded to me. "There's your domicile," he said. Then he stood up, gave me a friendly shove, and walked out.

The house was sitting on a stool at the bar. I walked up beside him. "And in walks _____," said the house.

I sat down next to him.

"You stink of moon," he said.

"Why do you think *that* might be?"

The house shrugged.

"You didn't tell anyone where you were going."

"Didn't want to be found," said the drunkhouse. "Who told you where I was? The Lamp?"

I shook my head.

"Or?"

"It doesn't matter," I said.

"It was Or," said the house. "That fucking *option*."

"You have a job to do," I said. "You can't just vanish like that."

The house belched.

"Nice," I said.

"Bombs away," said the house.

"You're not supposed to be here," I said. "You're a *home*."

"Home is where the heart is," said the house.

"What's that supposed to mean?"

"The past is *gone*, _____," said the house. "And it's not coming back."

"I'm not talking about the past—I'm talking about right now. I need a place to stay to*night*."

"Good for you," said the house.

"And you," I said, "have an obligation."

"Obligation?" said the house. His eyes were watery. "Obligation."

"Yeah," I said.

He spun in his stool to face me. "We were a *family*," he said.

What was I supposed to say to that? "I'm going back to Converse Street now. Are you coming or not?"

The house slugged its beer, put on its coat, and walked out with me. I unlocked the Bicycle Built for Two and hopped onto the front seat. The house sat down on the back and we pedaled home.

And I guess I thought that was it—that the house's runaway had changed something, solved whatever problem it was having. In retrospect, of course, that was naïve of me—especially since the memories and bad dreams persisted.

A few weeks after the house's return, the Memory of Johnny Appleseed asked me to help him plant some apologies in the deadgroves on Old Mill Road; I worked all day with him and then rode the Bicycle Built for Two back to Converse Street. I was really looking forward to getting home and ripping open a bag of rippled barbecue DeathChips.

When I turned my bike onto our street, though, I saw a strange sight at the tree belt: something was *attached* to the tree. At first I couldn't see what—it was dark, and my vision isn't so good. I figured it was some sort of tree-based installation art. Our trees, like most trees, were very creative, always painting and sculpting, and sometimes they chose to work big, beuysing or serraing.

When I got closer, though, I recognized the shape. It wasn't *art*—it was my house, 577, hanging by a noose from a tree in the yard.

"Oh. Oh Core," said the Bicycle Built for Two.

I raced into the yard and dropped the bike. The house was swaying in the wind. Its eyes were closed, its face ghost-white, its roof gray and crushed; houseblood ran down the beige siding and onto the sidewalk.

Then I heard a soft rush of air—a gasp, maybe. Was the house still alive?

I heard the thin wind again—it wasn't yet dead.

I got down on my knees in the wet earth and I said an emergency prayer. I got an automated response: "Welcome to Appleseed. All Emergency Cones are busy right now. If you pray your name, and the time of your prayer—"

I closed the prayer and stood up. The house was still breathing. I ran through my options in my mind. Could I climb the tree, cut the noose?

There was no way. I was too small.

Could the stars help?

No—they weren't smart enough.

Then I looked up—way up, past the moon. At your Memory.

Memory of the Reader: Who? Me?

Yes. This house is dying. It's dying!

Memory of the Reader: I can't—what can *I* do?

You need to reach down into the page and lift up the house, loosen the tension on that noose.

"I'm just a Memory," you said.

Just lift up the page—shift the gravity!

"I'm not the Reader," said the Memory of the Reader. "I can't lift *anything*."

Where *is* the Reader?

Memory of the Reader: Reading another book.

Another *novel*?

Memory of the Reader: Does it matter?

It didn't—within a few minutes, everything was dead: the house, the *words* about the house, the noose and the words about the noose. I knelt down on the page and the black houseblood soaked the knees of my white pants.

Shortly after the house took its last breath, Orange Traffic Cones arrived and the hospital followed. The Cones put on crash helmets, climbed ladders, and cut the house down; he landed on the lawn with the terrible sounds of wood splintering and glass smashing. The hospital tried to resuscitate him, but he was dead as a word.

Eventually, the Cones started collecting their tools and talking about where to go for dinner. As I stood in the blood-sopped grass, the hospital approached me wearing a house-sized stethoscope around his neck. The hospital lit a four-foot cigarette and said, "There wasn't anything I could do, _____."

"I know," I said.

"You can't blame yourself."

"Who else is there to blame?" I said.

The hospital took a drag. "That's a good question," he said.

A few minutes later, the Cones' and hospital's walkie-talkies started trilling and squawking, and they all left for another call. I stood alone with the dead house, its blood blackening the page. The end.

~ Fini ~

Memory of the Reader: Wait.

What.

Memory of the Reader: What happened next? What's the rest of the story?

That's the end of it.

Memory of the Reader: But where did you go?

I didn't go anywhere. It was late. I went inside and fell asleep.

Memory of the Reader: You slept in the *corpse* of the house?

Sure. What was I supposed to do?

Memory of the Reader: Sleep on the page?

And get carried off by a wild sentence, pulled into another bookwormhole? No, thank you.

Memory of the Reader: I've never heard of anyone doing that—sleeping in a deadhouse.

People do it all the time. My father was *born* in a deadhouse.

Memory of the Reader: What was that like?

Shrug. The rooms had gone gray, the house's dreams silence and soil. New questions roamed from room to room.

Memory of the Reader: Such as?

Yeah, among others.

For a while I just lay there, listening. Then I prayed to the Memory of Johnny Appleseed and told him I needed help.

With what? he prayed back.

Digging a hole, I prayed.

A hole? he prayed. *I should borrow some shovels, then?*

Yes, I prayed. *The biggest you can find.*

CHIVER'S DELIGHT

That was in 1993, when language in Appleseed berserked, flabbergasted, broke free of its shackles for good. It began mutating, for one thing. All of a sudden—how do I say this?—the language got bigger.

No, not *bolder*, per se. Literally, bigger.

I think it started when the *Daily Core* printed a story about wild sentences troughing on the shore of the Kellogg River. That wouldn't have been news normally, but these sentences were *big*—six feet high, one source told the *Core*; ten, another said. Creepy, right? But hey, odd shit happened all the time in Appleseed. Clouds wore hats. Every so often your shoes died on your feet. Sometimes you were attacked by the glasses on your face. And once or twice a year we felt a great shadow overhead, and looked up into the sky to see a page turning.

Soon, giant language started appearing everywhere. I was riding the Bicycle Built for Two one day, me on the front seat, Sentence on the backseat, when—plak! I hit—*something*—and I flew over the handlebars and landed on my side.

"I am." came crashing down on me. "'My *tooth!*' he shouted, painfully," said Sentence.

I looked at "I am." There was blood dribbling from his m.

I lumbered back up the road to see what I'd hit. There, in the middle of the street, was a giant black comma. It was about three feet high, and it was—

Was it—snoring?

Yes! It was so *fat* that it had gotten tired crossing the street—it was taking a nap right there in the road.

"What the—" said "I am.".

Soon, you could see these gigantic characters everywhere in Appleseed: ten-foot-high exclamation points loitering at the intersection of Colton and Shay; a 7 and a lowercase e ripping Harleys down Grassy Gutter; errant periods frowning all through town, stopping Appleseedians in their tracks.

Not long afterward, phrases and sentences began camouflaging into the page. You'd be   right along, just like always, when   and   . And even though most Appleseedians looked at language as a threat, and no one particularly *minded* the   , it was still odd that   . And that, on a warm summer day, there was no   at your feet or   whimpering outside your window.

We were all miffled. Miffed. Hiffled. We weren't sure what we could say, or what it meant. What if the meaning changed after we said it? We'd lost control of the story. The Orange Traffic Cones didn't have any choice, I guess, but to allow the Mothers to increase their monitoring of language. First, they tried restraining the words physically—using parentheses, and when that didn't work, brackets of various styles—but to no avail.

So the Mothers ordered the Orange Traffic Cones to close the borders: no language was to leave or enter Appleseed. To better regulate our words and their uses, Cones built checkpoints all around town: on Highway Five, at Samsa Avenue, near the worryfields. Everywhere you went you had to wait in line to show a Cone your words. New bans were issued every day: exclamation points were cut, then metaphors, then commands. For a while, periods were banned and every sentence had to end with a question mark. I remember once going to Bagel Beagle during the period ban and trying to order a sandwich. When I placed the order, though, I had to do so in a question: "I'd like a turkey sandwich?"

"Would you?" said the beagle behind the counter.

"On a bagel?" I said.

"Yes?" said the beagle.

"Yes?" I said.

"You would?" said the beagle.

"Yes I said?" I said.

"Are you asking me if you said that?" said the beagle.

"No?" I said.

"You're not sure?"

"No I am?" I said.

"You're asking me *what* you are?" the beagle inquired.

As a temporary fix, people stopped talking and suspended all prayers. Some people used sign language or Morse code; others invented complicated gestures. If you couldn't find a way to express yourself, you just stored the question in your cheeks or swallowed it down.

We could only go so long without speaking, though; soon people were praying again, and then whispering, and then talking at full volume. Then a rally for words was held on the Town Green. "Go words!" chanted the hundreds in attendance. "Words rock!"

Select Cone Johnson took the podium and promised that he and the Board would find a way to "take back our words." Starting tomorrow, he announced, Cones would start searching every home in Appleseed. "We'll omit these words and phrases from *every page*," he shouted, and the crowd applauded.

And I remember seeing the story about it in the next day's *Core*—the pictures of Cones kicking in doors, carrying out armfuls of expressions, handcuffing those sentences and stuffing them into the backs of cone-shaped cars. Words that tried to hide, the article said, would be immediately demeaned. When one expression tried to run? A Mother killed that sentence on *sight*.

When I read that story, I knew what I had to do. How long would it be before the Cones came knocking on *our* door? I didn't have a choice—there was only one option. The very next morning, I woke at first light and lifted the sheet off of "I am.'"s cage. He was curled up in the corner, snoring. I unhooked the latch, opened the door, and lifted the words out. I wrapped Sentence in my coat and carried him upstairs and outside. We crossed the street and walked through the worryfield, then into the trees and toward the Appleseed border. There were deadwords—I remember "candelabra," "phosphate," others—here and there, and sentence-trails criss-crossing through the brush. As we ran along the path I scanned the trees for any sign of a sentry or guardcone—anything bright orange or cone-shaped—but I didn't see any; the woods looked clear.

A few hundred feet from the border I stopped, knelt down in the darkness, put Sentence on the wet earth, and unhooked his leash. "'I am.'?" I said.

He blinked his eyes in the pink light.

"You can't stay in Appleseed anymore. You have to go." I pointed to the town line about a hundred feet away. "That way," I said.

"I am," said Sentence, "still sleepy-eyed, he blinked his eyes and—"

"I know, it's early and this is probably confusing," I said. "But you just have to listen to what I'm saying to you."

"Apprehensive," said Sentence, "I am wished for home."

"Do you know what they're *doing* to language, 'I am.'? What will happen to you if they find you?"

"Quiet," said Sentence, "I am can be very hiding and quiet."

"I'll see you again—I promise," I said, choosing my words carefully; any misuse would bring Cones right to us. "But I can't take care of you anymore. You're free now. OK? You're free."

There were tears in the sentence's eyes. "Wishing for home," he said, "I am sorrowly hoped to convey—"

Then I heard a sound in the trees: the snap of a twig. I searched the path behind me, but I didn't see anyone.

"Appreciative," said the sentence, "—I am would think back on that time, and their friendships—"

Another twig snapped—this one from somewhere high up. I looked into the trees. I heard a shuffling, and then a leaf fell away from a branch and I saw—

Was it?

Shit: A flare of orange plastic between the leaves.

I turned to "I am.". "Run. *Now*. Fast as you can."

Sentence flashed me a final look and took off, sprinting toward the town line. Its cover blown, the Cone shimmied down the bark and vaulted past me and after "I am." Sentence looked back, saw the Cone behind him, and sped up, revising as he ran: "I am running run fast."; "I am sprinting with the wind through my face!" And then, it was like he shifted into high gear or something—I'd never seen language move so fast. His letters italicized and he kicked up leaves behind him. *"The sounds are in my hear-and-now: Flams! Sizzion! Toreabloo!"*; *"I am this word and that word!"*

"Run on, 'I am.'!" I shouted.

Sentence crossed the town line; the Cone stopped at the border and doubled over, his shoulders heaving. But "I am." didn't slow down—he kept moving, kept getting louder, truer. *"Newchording, Me-oh-mying, transmuliterating!"*

I hooted to the sentence. "Keep going, 'I am.'!"

"Anything and everything! Holy shouts and bouts and rambles! Cries and thanks and bellows, now and forever amen! To on and on and never—"

CHAMPION

That was the end for me, though—without "I am." I lost myself. I forgot to live and died. I had no friends or family to remind me who I was, or why I was here. You really can't live that way for very long.

One morning, I was cleaning up dead letters in the worryfields and listening to the remnants of music on my headphones when a bookworm—the sentence "You should just go ahead and die."—emerged from a bookwormhole. The sentence was wearing a blue concert T-shirt advertising a band I didn't recognize, and he seemed to be lost. "Excuse me," said "You should just go ahead and die.". "Can you tell me how to get back to Fialky's Fields?"

I couldn't answer him—I was struck by the words of his face. "I should?" I said.

"I thought I knew the way, but I kind of got turned around," said "You should just go ahead and die.".

"And if I did," said a thought. "Would this all go away? The blight? The darkness?"

"*Everything* would go away," the sentence said.

I still had the shovel I'd used to bury my house. I picked it up, put it to the page, and began to dig.

"Good," said the sentence. "Yup, you got it."

Soon I'd made a hole in the page about the size of my body. When I was finished, I tossed aside my headphones and lay down. "Could I ask you—if you wouldn't mind—to bury me?"

"You should just go ahead and die." looked at his watch. "I'm supposed to get back to my novel by noon."

"Just a few shovelfuls, maybe."

The sentence smiled curtly. "Sure," he said, and he picked up the shovel and started pitching page over me. As he was working, a prayer came in from overhead. "_____?" It was my Mom. I didn't answer.

"You should just go ahead and die." filled the page in around me, leaving only my face exposed. "How's that?" he said.

"Good," I said. "Nice and warm."

"_____!" prayed my Mom.

"What now?" I shouted to the sentence.

"Now nothing," he said.

"For how long?" I said.

"Forever, probably," said "You should go ahead and die.". Then he picked up a shovelful of page and threw it over my face. I felt the weight of that page—of all of the pages—in my eyes and in my mouth; I choked on it; it filled my throat and my lungs. Then I wasn't; I let out my breath and died.

When you die, your parents hear it. They know your death in their ears and their hearts and their bones. My Mom was welding a footbridge out past Wolf Swamp when she heard the notes of my death knell. "No," she said into her welder's mask. "_____?" she prayed.

Somewhere off the margin, "I am." howled.

Six feet above me, the bookworm who'd buried me started coughing. Suddenly *all* of my sentences started coughing—those in the trees, in the fields, in the fibers. Every word I'd brought into Appleseed, every sentence I'd invented, started spitting up black blood; line by line they squawked, shriveled up, and went silent.

My Dad, working at Muir Drop, saw a sentence fall on the factory floor and stood up from his workbench. He put down his tools and prayed. "_____? Buddy?"

Just at that moment, down in the page, I had what they call an—

What *do* they call it?

A realizing. An eponymous? New information in my almost-dead mind.

"Wait a second," said a thought. "Maybe I *don't* need to die. Maybe—"

But it was too late—I was already dead. I had one prayer, maybe less, left in my skull. I prayed it out as far as I could. "Mom! Dad! I'm so sorry. I—" I prayed to anyone who would listen. "All of this *was* my fault," I prayed. The prayer—the sentences—wormed out through my skull and toward the surface. But I don't know if it ever reached anyone. My mind went quiet, and dark, and still.

WESTFIELD SEEK-NO-FURTHER

Diane threw off her welding mask and flew up off the bridge, over the Connecticut River and the western Margin, past the deadgroves and the Prayer Centers and toward home. For the first time, she saw how many stories she'd missed: "Monarch," "Bastille Square," "Fathers in the Field," and so many others. When had all *those* stories been written? And what were they about?

She landed near the pair of headphones, the corpse of the sentence and the lumpy page. "_____?" she prayed. She surveyed the site. Then she dropped down to her knees and ran her hands over the freshly turned page. She prayed her son's name, over and over. On the third prayer, she received an automatic prayer from Appleseed. "I'm sorry, but no party is listed under that prayer name. Please check the name and try praying again."

Across the street, her husband's truck pulled into the driveway. Ralph leapt out of the cab and charged across the street. "Di!" he hollered. "Why isn't _____ answering my prayers?"

Diane's mind raced. She ran through one idea after the next.

Then Ralph saw the lump. "What's—" He looked at

301

Diane—her face was a monsoon—and then back at the soil. "No," he shouted. He dove at the page and started digging with his bare hands. "Wasn't anyone with him?" he grunted. "That fucking *Memory* he always hangs out with? Or the Reader—where's the Reader?"

Diane looked up into the darkness, then down at the page. "Wait a second," said one of Diane's thoughts to another.

"What?" said the second thought.

The first thought said, "What if we—"

"Dig, Di. Dig!" Ralph tossed clumpfuls of page over his shoulder.

Diane lifted off the ground, flew a hundred feet off the page—

"Diane!" shouted Ralph.

—hovered there for a moment, and then shot straight down, gaining speed and dropping through an open bookwormhole and down into the page.

APPLECORE

PICK-YOUR-OWN

Even traveling as fast as she did—scorching through the paper from story to story—it took Diane a long time (hours, days, or years, depending on the novel) to find you. For a while the search seemed never-ending. How many novels *were* there? More than once, she found a Reader who looked like you—sitting in a noiry diner, rifling through a used bookstore in a bodice-ripper—only to find out when she approached you that it was someone else.

When she finally did track you down, you were living twenty miles away and two years later and working as a newspaper reporter. You weren't making much meaning at the job, but you were gaining experience and collecting stories. That day, you were covering an event called the Marginalia Arts Festival. You were on deadline—your story was due in less than two hours. One of the organizing tents had agreed to speak with you about the festival's mission, and you were interviewing them by the entrance. Diane spotted you and the festival tent and dropped down behind a row of Port-a-Potties.

"It's a great opportunity for artists to make a name for themselves," the tent told you. "And tents as well."

You wrote down those quotes. "And where do you see the Marginalia Festival in, say, five years?" you said.

The tent's brow furrowed. "I'd like people to look forward to Marginalia the same way they do—"

Just then you saw the flash of a warskirt between a row of toilets. You immediately closed your notebook, spun around, and started walking.

"Hello?" said the tent.

You brisked away from her and bolded across Pulaski Park and back toward Main Street.

"Miss!" shouted the tent.

You looked for a place to hide: JavaNet? The Haymarket?

It was too late: Diane landed in front of you. Before she even had a chance to speak, though, you stuck your finger in her face. "Leave me alone," you spat, and you stormed past her. "I don't want anything to do with you."

Diane flew over you and landed inches from your face. "Just wait a second," she said.

"No," you said. You changed direction and stormed the other way.

"Stop right there," boomed Diane. "I am a recognized *Mother* of—"

"But you're not *my* mother," you said over your shoulder. "You're not anyone to me—"

"I've been looking for you for *years*," Diane said, her voice breaking. "Will you at least listen to what I have to say?"

You stopped and turned around.

• • •

"Absolutely not," said the Reader. "I have a good life here. A *full* life. I'm somebody. I have a boyfriend. A good job. I never had any of that in Appleseed. I didn't even have *thoughts* of my own! All I was to _____ was just words on a—"

"_____ is dead," said Diane. "Those sentences he imagined—"

"*Bookworms* he called them," said the Reader. "Fucking figments."

"—rotted out the whole town. And then one of them killed him."

"He killed *himself*, you mean," the Reader said.

All the air left Diane's body.

"Because *you* weren't there to save him," said the Reader.

"OK," Diane said.

"Everyone abandoned him," the Reader said.

"All right—we could have"—her voice shook—"been there more. You're right. OK?" Diane held out her hands. "But we can still save him. You—you can still save him."

"*Me* save him? *You* save him."

"I can't on my own. You have to come back. Appleseed needs a Reader."

"I never had *any* sentences of my own," you said. "Now I finally do and you want me to leave them all behind?"

"For a few days—just to help us finish the story," Diane said.

You crossed your arms.

"Please," said Diane. "Please."

"And then what?"

"What do you mean?"

"If I go back to Appleshit," said the Reader. "What happens when I finish reading?" said the Reader. "Am I stuck in—"

"No—of course not. The book will end."

The Reader crossed her arms. "And I can leave."

"Sure."

"And I can come back here?"

"Of course," my Mom said. "When you're finished reading *Appleseed*, you can read anything you want."

"Even if I *do* go with you, there's nothing I can do to help."

"Just try," said the Mother.

"Shit," said the Reader. She looked around—at the festival behind her, and then at the slow traffic on Main Street. "If I'm going, I have to make a pitstop first."

"Absolutely not," the Mother said. "There's no time for that."

"Forget it, then—find yourself another reader," said the Reader.

The mother threw her hands. "Every second that passes—"

"Trust me, OK?" the Reader said. "It's important."

"Even with my son in the ground?"

"Yes," said the Reader. "Yes."

Diane stepped forward and put her arm around the Reader. "Grab on to my waist."

The Reader wrapped her arms around Diane.

"Hold on tight," Diane said. Then she pushed with her feet and lifted the Reader off the page. They rose over Northampton; the Reader hooted as she saw the words get smaller beneath her. When they reached skimming height, Diane shouted "Where'm I going?"

The Reader pointed toward Route Nine. "Over the bridge and into Amherst."

"East?"

The Reader nodded. "We're looking for a place called Atkin's."

They flew over green rolling hadleypages of farms and houses and then into stories of Amherst: pages covered with cows, silos, and wide-open spaces. The Reader pointed to the corner up ahead. "There it is," she hollered. Diane saw a large farmstand, a half-filled parking lot, and rolling pages of green to the right. When she looked past the farmstand, she understood: the adjacent fields were covered with trees—*apple* trees, their branches shouting in green and red. The grove stretched back to the edge of the page, spilled off it, and continued on.

Diane dropped into the grove and set the Reader down onto the page. "Didn't I tell you?" the Reader said.

Diane spit. "Get what you need and let's go."

The Reader approached a tree, grabbed an apple, and pulled it off the branch. "These are *apple trees*," she said.

"I know they are," Diane said.

"And it's pick-your-own!" the Reader said. She took a bite of the apple and then held it out to Diane. "Don't you want one?"

"Not right now I don't," said Diane. She took the bitten-into apple and put it in a drawer in her skirt.

"_____ needs us. Now point me to the closest book-wormhole."

The Reader nodded toward Route 116. "Belcher-town—a few miles that way," she said.

Diane lifted them up. High over the page, the Reader looked down and shouted, "You have to admit—that grove is a beautiful sight, isn't it?"

But Diane didn't answer her; she tightened her grip on the Reader and skimmed forward, faster and faster, as fast as any Mother ever had.

GRENADIER

The Reader and the Mother volted through the book-wormhole. As they did, light flooded the town, painting the buildings and the fields, swarming the Amphitheatre and the hospital and drenching Appleseed Mountain.

Diane didn't stop; she carried the Reader high up over the buildings and trees and then banked left and bulleted forward. "Welcome home!" Diane shouted.

The Reader tried to get her bearings. Were they on Guerry Street? No—that was Jonquil, just past the Green, not far from Colton's deadgroves.

Something was happening on the ground below. Up and down the street, people were stepping out of their houses. Fifty feet away to their right, a woman wearing a bathrobe stood in the middle of the road, stretching out her arms. When she looked up at you, you saw that she had a hole in her face. "Halleluiah!" she shouted at you.

"Thanks be to the Core!" shouted someone down the road.

"Mothers *did* it! They did it!"

The bookwormholes, you saw now, were every-where: in the people, in the trees, punching through the

311

lawns and roads every ten or twenty feet. "What happened here?" you shouted.

"You did," Diane said.

"What do you mean?"

Not a street or page, it seemed, had been spared. Whole houses were burned to the page; some streets were completely gone. The center of town was leveled. Zooming over the high school, you could see the Small Pear up ahead—all of the windows had been smashed; Gilbert's was covered with plywood; so was the Beagle. You looked to your right. "Look at the *Hu Ke Lau!*" you hollered. It was just a charred corpse of a restaurant. And many of the pages on the North Side were nearly empty—burned out, and rotted completely through in some places.

"Where are the *Mothers*?" you shouted.

"Most of them were KIA, some of them maybe captured," Diane shouted. "The rest are in hiding."

The mood on the street below, though, was jubilant: people were clapping or hooting, shaking hands, high-fiving, and hugging. Passing over Coventry, a long-haired man shouted up at them. "Beautiful!" He took off his shirt and slammed it to the page. "It's fucking beautiful!"

Diane turned onto Converse Street. Soon you could see the edge of the worryfields. Even there, though, people were happy: you saw two worriers dancing, another just lying on her back and staring up at the bright sky.

As you approached the fields, you saw a big lump in the far corner of the page. "What's that?" one of your thoughts said, pointing. Something was moving next to the lump. Was it a machine? No, it was a man in a gray jumpsuit, hunched over the page. He was digging. "Is that Ralph?" you shouted. But you knew it was.

Diane dipped, grazed the surface, and lowered you onto the white soil. Ralph didn't even look up. Dirt flew over his shoulder.

"Ralph," Diane lyled.

You were in awe—you'd never seen anyone work so hard. Ralph didn't even have a shovel—he was scooping the pagesoil with his bare hands.

"Ralph!" Diane shouted again.

Ralph looked up, surprised. "Wha," he said.

"I need you to stop digging—"

He shook his head. "The page is tough," he said, "but I'm making progress—"

"I need you to stop that right now and go find someone for me."

Ralph's straightened up. "Who?" he said.

The Reader watched Ralph's truck drive off; then she turned to Diane. "Walk around the page," the Reader told her. "Start collecting words."

"What for?"

"As many as you can find."

"They're all dead," said Diane.

"That's OK," the Reader said.

Diane went to work on this page and the next, gathering as many words as she could. When her arms were full, she stacked the words next to her son's grave. Soon, she saw Ralph's truck drive into the worryfields—he hadn't been gone long. The passenger's-side door opened and the Memory of Johnny Appleseed stepped out.

"Oh my Core!" shouted the Memory, hobbling toward you. He held out his ethereal arms. "You came *back!*"

"Took some convincing," Diane said.

"Did you hear what happened to _____?" the Memory of Johnny Appleseed asked her.

"Of course she heard," Diane said.

"I brought something for you," the Reader told the Memory. She gestured to Diane, who opened the drawer in her skirt.

Ralph studied a pile of words next to the lump. "What are these?" he said.

Diane fished into her skirt, found the bitten-into apple, and held it out to the Memory of Johnny Appleseed.

The Memory's face bloomed. "What—where did you—" He pointed at the Reader. "Where did you *get* this?" He took the apple with both hands and held it like an egg.

"Holy shit," said Ralph. "Is that what I think it is?"

The Reader turned to him. "Let the Memory deal with the story of Appleseed," she said. "I need *you* to help Diane pick up as many words as you can find."

Ralph looked confused. "Why?" he said. "They're all—"

"She knows that, honey," said Diane. "Just do what she says." She led Ralph to an adjacent field to look for sentences. He soon caught on and understood what they were looking for. When he couldn't find the exact right words, though, he decided to improvise. He selected three words from the page—"junction," "author," and "veneer"—and dragged them over to Diane. "Do me a favor and cut these, will you?" he said.

The Mother flipped on her skirtsaw and it whirred to life. "Where?" she said. Ralph pointed, and Diane pulled the blade through the words and gave Ralph the wordparts he needed: the "au," the "ction" and the "eer."

Then Diane went back to what she was doing: dislodging a top layer of words—"nuisance," "selfish," "brat"—and digging deep. Finally, she found the words that she was looking for—that she'd been trying to find for years: "I was just so scared." And, "I was angry." And, "And sad. I didn't know what to do with it all."

And then, "You were wonderful the way you were. You didn't need to be anything, or do anything, or be anyone."

Ralph and Diane carried their words across the fields and lay them on the ground by the Reader. The Memory of Johnny Appleseed stood by, watching them arrange the words. They didn't all fit together—some letters were rotted beyond recognition; other phrases were irrelevant or heavy with sorrow—but they did their best to order them so they made new sense. "Put that one there, how about," said Diane at one point. After watching the Reader work for a few minutes, Ralph knelt next to her and sunk his hands into the page.

"What's she doing?" the Memory of Johnny Appleseed asked Diane.

"Isn't it obvious?" Diane said. "She's revising."

HONEYCRISP

I. YELLOW TRANSPARENT II

That spring, the Auctioneer reappeared in Apple-seed. Her arrival was completely unannounced—one day she was spotted walking over the margin, her arms full of meaningless words and throw-aways. She didn't even go home to Converse Street—instead, she walked directly to the empty Amphitheatre. Then she stepped up onto the bare cement stage, held up an item at random—a jar of hearsay—and began to shout.

"Ourfirstitemladiesandgentsishearsayfineap pleseedhearsayyourenotgoingtofindanyrumors betterthantheserumorsrighttherethishearsayisholy itholdsthebonesoftruthandmemoryletsstartthebid dingathalfaconcept."

Soon, a numb passerby humbled to the edge of the Amphitheatre. Lulled by the Auctioneer's call, he blurted out a meaning-bid without even really thinking about it. Just then, a wandering thayer appeared in the opposite corner of the Amphitheatre and shouted out a higher amount. The numb countered; the thayer did, too.

News of the auction rilled through town—it wasn't long before a crowd had assembled. Someone lent a table; a Cone delivered a pulpit. Appleseedians brought meaningless items to the stage and the Auctioneer held them up, sang of their potential, and made them meaningful. That auction ran for ten hours straight. Looking out at the jam-packed house, the Auctioneer could see off-duty Cones, former Mothers, Muir Drop Forgers. She wondered if Uncle Joump was out there. And how about her father? Or her brother—where was her brother?

II: A GRAFTING

Two pages over, the Memory of Johnny Appleseed drove his shovel into the fibers. When the hole he'd dug was deep enough, he pulled a single seed from the Reader's apple and dropped it into the soil.

As the Memory was covering up the seed, Ralph drifted over to check on him. When he saw what the Memory was doing, he told him to wait right there—that he'd be right back. Ralph ran out to his truck for an emotional wrench and a bucket and carried them to the happiness hydrant on the corner of Apple Hill and Converse. When he turned the bolt on the hydrant, happiness flooded the street. Ralph filled the bucket and left the faucet running; then he carried the bucket of happiness out to the Memory of Johnny Appleseed. The Memory took it from him and carefully poured the happiness on the apple seed.

Within paragraphs, the first saplings of happiness-fueled stories began to peek through the pages. The stories were restorative: soon, the holes in the pages and people started closing. In the center of town, the windows grew back at Small Pear and the Bagel Beagle opened for business. Someone turned on the lights at the Big Why, and a truck arrived with a new batch of questions. Cordial Carl did some deep breathing and fired up his grill.

Heartened by the sounds of the auction, people started pulling off of the highway and into Appleseed; soon they were arriving in droves. And all of them needed food and housing. With two new apple orchards up and running, Ralph reopened Belmont and Woodside and shifted to part-time at Muir Drop; then he quit altogether.

III. JUPITER

In the new stories, _____ wasn't so alone. He was still bald and overweight, but he had a good strong heart, a zell imagination, a tough soul. His house was still alive and everyone inside it safe and sound. He didn't always see I to I with his mother, a nurse at Appleseed Hospital, but they got along OK— sometimes they'd go to Appleseed Library together and then talk about what they were reading. He was closer with his father, Ralph, who he worked with at the apartment buildings. _____ had a pet sentence, a few good friends, and even a girlfriend or two. In high school he worked at a community theater and started writing stories in his spare time. He stopped eating so many chips, and learned when to stay quiet and when to speak. When he was eighteen, he graduated from Appleseed High and went on to college.

At the end of the story, the Reader finished reading. Not great, you decided, but not bad, either.

MOTHER (AMERICAN)

The Reader straightened up and wiped her brow.

"Well?" Diane asked her.

The Reader looked down at the silent page and shook her head. "I don't know. I thought—if we put these together—he'd come back, but—"

They all stared at the lump.

"Maybe he was dead too long," the Memory of Johnny Appleseed said.

"My poor boy," said Ralph.

"Ormaybewejusthaventfoundtherightwordsyet," said the Auctioneer.

Diane leaned down to the page. She made a few more sentences—the simplest, truest ones she could:

"You are good."

"You are loved."

"I have always loved you. I always will." She planted them and pushed page over them.

Suddenly, I was pulled through the words without warning: back through letters and pages, back to the body of _____—I found my fat stomach, my still feet, my cold brain, my dead thoughts, my closed eyes.

I heard my family's words. "My poor boy." and "You

were wonderful the way you were." And, "I have always loved you. I always will."

The words were breath in my lungs; I heard the story directly above me. I blinked. Where was the surface—the light and the air? Was I still _____? Was I at all?

McINTOSH

Standing over the pagegrave, _____'s parents hear a sound—
a flicker in the margin woods. They turn to see words,
sprinting through the trees, across the worryfields, at break-
neck speed: "I am sorry!" becomes "I am running and running!" and then "I am saving you!"

On the page above you, you hear the language, "I am."
hooing: "I am missed you!" "I am here now!"

You blink and cough page out of your mouth. You see
a flash of light above and you claw for the surface.

"I am wanting you to breathe and live!" says the sentence. "I am you *will* live!"

Then Sentence breaks through the page, grabs hold of
you with the teeth of his "I," and pulls you up out of the
page. "I am you *will*!" he says. "I am you *will*!"

The light fills your eyes. The sentence licks the page
off your face. You squint in the sun. When you're able to
focus, you see them all: the Auctioneer speed-praying, the
tears falling into your father's glasses, the weary smile on
your mother's face. You *are*. You are home.

About the Author

CHRISTOPHER BOUCHER teaches writing and literature at Boston College, and is the managing editor of *Post Road* magazine. His debut novel, *How to Keep Your Volkswagen Alive* (Melville House), was widely praised. *Golden Delicious* is his second novel. He lives with his wife and two children in Newton, Massachusetts.

D0121635

evolution

a beginner's guide

RELATED TITLES FROM ONEWORLD

Genetics: A Beginner's Guide, Guttman, Griffiths, Suzuki and Cullis,
    ISBN 1–85168–304–6
Evolutionary Psychology: A Beginner's Guide, Dunbar, Barrett and Lycett,
    ISBN 1–85168–356–9
The Brain: A Beginner's Guide, Al-Chalabi, Turner and Delamont,
    ISBN 1–85168–373–9
25 Big Ideas: The Science That's Changing Our World, Robert Matthews,
    ISBN 1–85168–391–7
Did My Genes Make Me Do It? And Other Philosophical Dilemmas, Avrum Stroll,
    ISBN 1–85168–340–2
What Makes Us Moral? Crossing the Boundaries of Biology, Neil Levy,
    ISBN 1–85168–341–0

evolution

a beginner's guide

burton s. guttman

ONEWORLD
OXFORD

evolution: a beginner's guide

Oneworld Publications
(Sales and Editorial)
185 Banbury Road
Oxford OX2 7AR
England
www.oneworld-publications.com

ISBN-13: 978–1–85168–371–0
ISBN-10: 1–85168–371–2

Typeset by Jayvee, Trivandrum, India
Cover design by the Bridgewater Book Company
Printed and bound by WS Bookwell, Finland

contents

nine   probability and entropy   162

ten   the problem of creationism   173

preface

Evolution is a fascinating business, its fascination attested to by the many books on the subject now available. In addition to technical monographs for the specialist, books continue to appear that are addressed to the general reader. Some of these general books display the results of evolution over the past billion years or so, often with marvelous color paintings that show how we believe the many creatures of the past appeared in life. Books about human evolution are especially fascinating, such as those by Donald Johanson, Bryan Sykes, and Ian Tattersall listed in the References at the end of this book. Other popular books, such as Richard Dawkins' interesting series, explore the processes of evolution, often from fascinating new viewpoints. And evolution inspires the more philosophical books, like those of Daniel Dennett, for the story of how humans got to be what we are raises a number of much broader questions.

As someone who has studied evolution, and biology in general, since my teen years, I have enjoyed many of these books and have profited from reading them. But I have wondered sometimes how readers who are not professional biologists have reacted to the same books. When I have used some popular books about evolution with relatively young college students in interdisciplinary courses (where the big, fat, encyclopedic textbooks of biology were inappropriate), I haven't worried about the students lacking some basic information, because my colleagues and I could supply that information as part of the course. But what about the intelligent, interested lay reader sitting in his easy-chair of an evening and trying to digest the same information? Lacking much formal education in biology, and probably quite a few years removed from any formal education, is he getting the full impact of the book?

Hence, this book. It is part of a series called Beginner's Guides, and its purpose is to let the reader who is interested in evolution take a step backwards to bone up on some fundamental ideas about biology and evolution before plunging on into the many other books I've referred to. Its format is obviously simple, and it is not lavishly illustrated with drawings of extinct plants and animals; we could not possibly rival those highly illustrated books, and the purpose here is not to compete with them but to prepare you to read them with greater understanding. If you finish the book and still have a sense of dissatisfaction, a sense that there is a lot more to know, this book will have served its purpose. I hope, then, that you'll be prepared to read further. This book is intended, also, as something of a companion book to the earlier guide *Genetics*, cowritten with my colleagues Tony Griffiths, David Suzuki, and Tara Cullis. Although this book is quite self-contained within the limits of its subject, the combination of the two books might just provide the interested reader with the extra bits of insight into genetic processes that will make evolution even easier to comprehend.

In particular, I've made an effort to make sense of evolution in its proper ecological setting, an emphasis that I think has been generally ignored (or assumed implicitly). Once functioning organisms appeared a few billion years ago, they were forced to start carving the world up into places to live and ways of living that did not compete too strongly with other organisms. They started, in other words, to form communities and ecosystems, as explained here, and all organisms since that time have evolved in the same ecological frame of reference: emerging as new species from nearly identical relatives and surviving only as long as they could maintain a satisfactory ecological niche for themselves.

In today's fast-moving society, with its adulation of the new and disdain for the old – where popular music of 30 years ago can be labeled "golden oldies" – there is a tendency to think that only the latest hot discoveries are worth our consideration. Many of the newest books about evolution present the subject from the viewpoint of contemporary investigators using molecular methods, which have provided important new insights. Evolution is fundamentally a genetic process occurring in genetic creatures, who carry records of their histories in their genes; today's automated methods for determining the sequences of DNA molecules allow us to start reading those encoded histories, to clarify the stories previously told only by studies of anatomy. I deal with these methods and insights in their proper places. Invaluable as this work is, however, the fundamental understanding of evolution and evolutionary ecology that I'm trying to develop here is based on classical ideas and research from the mid-twentieth century, much of it derived from investigations of organisms in their natural settings. Beginners have to understand these foundation ideas of the science, and that will be the emphasis throughout.

The story of evolution on Earth for the past few billion years is itself fascinating; the stories about how scientists have pieced all this together is perhaps equally fascinating. There has been room here for only a little of this story, especially in chapter two. It is a triumphant story of the power of modern science, of the inquiring and creative human intelligence that has uncovered the secrets of biology and geology from the complexities of cells and the layers of the Earth. But the story has a kind of sour companion, for as we celebrate our modern understanding of evolution and try to pass it on to the next generation with the hope that they will also celebrate it – and that some of them will even want to join in the exciting adventure of science – we meet an adversarial force that wants to deny the whole business. This counterforce, called creationism, is strongest in the United States (and, I understand, in Australia). In the name of a fundamentalist religion, and for rather inscrutable reasons, it puts its faith in the recorded mythology of some Bedouin tribes of around 3000 years ago and imagines that their story of creation is superior to all the discoveries of modern science. If the purveyors of creationism would simply tell their story to themselves and not bother the rest of us, we would have little reason to complain; people ought to be free to believe what they want, even including little men in flying saucers, appearances of Elvis, or the predictive power of the stars. But creationists of various stripes keep trying to impose their beliefs on society in general, and especially on public education. As explained in chapter ten, I believe creationists are not only wrong but can be positively dangerous to a democratic society. One of my minor hopes for this book is that citizens who want to prevent democracies from turning into theocracies may find it useful as a handbook for action before school boards and legislatures.

Chapter one includes some general words about the nature of science and how it operates. Readers who want just to get on with the science itself can ignore that section, but I've included it because evolution has such broad implications, of the kind raised by creationism and of the kind addressed by more philosophical writers. I think it is important to have a clear conception of science as part of exploring one particular story of science, and I hope readers will find it useful in that context.

In writing this book, I have received particular help from Larry Ross and Nancy Cordell, who set me straight on some matters of human evolution. Donald Morisato helped me understand some matters of developmental genetics, and Mark Ridley caught some errors and made some valuable suggestions for changes throughout. My editor, Victoria Roddam, has been the very model of a modern major editor in her encouragement and her sharp criticism of drafts, particularly steering me around the messy waters of creationism. I thank Deborah Martin for her intelligent copy-editing, which caught some of my lapses; Mark Hopwood for his work on the cover copy; and Deirdre Prinsen for putting the whole book together so beautifully.

Burton S. Guttman
Olympia, Washington, USA

diversity, science, and evolution

explaining diversity

One of the most obvious things about the world is the diversity of life. Look out the window. You will see trees, flowers, bushes, probably some insects, surely some birds – even an apparently sterile city has its pigeons, starlings, and sparrows. Although you can't name everything you see, you would need several identification guides to catalogue them all, and your final list would be long. Anywhere outside an urban environment, you will be surrounded by hundreds of identifiable types of plants, by many species of birds at any season, perhaps a dozen kinds of mammals. Carefully sifting a few shovelfuls of soil would reveal a variety of life that would tax your skills of observation and identification.

We start to learn this diversity as infants. Parents show their children books with pictures of many creatures, and they teach songs like "Old MacDonald" about what the horsie says, what the piggy says, what the sheep says. All but the most deprived children see flowers and trees and learn about their variety.

Primitive humans, too, observed this variety and depended on it for their survival. They learned to distinguish various animals that could be used for food or for skins – or, alternatively, animals that must be avoided as dangerous. They learned to distinguish nourishing or medicinal plants, or those that could provide clothing or shelter, from those that were poisonous or merely attractive. As they began to wonder about this variety, they made up stories to explain

1

where all these plants and animals had come from, sometimes telling how propitious gods and spirits had created them.

Humans are classifiers. This is one way we make sense of the world. We name the variety of actions with verbs, the variety of objects with nouns. The words we use intrinsically set boundaries. We like to put things in boxes, both physically and verbally, for it unclutters the world, makes order out of what would otherwise be chaos. If we can name something and put it into a category, we can learn to deal with it appropriately. Things that resist classification and want to sit on the borderlines make us uncomfortable. They are messy. We try to push them into one box or the other. So as civilization developed, as some people were able to leave off plowing, sowing, reaping, and building long enough to contemplate the world, they put the living things of the world into neat categories and gave them names. Even in quite primitive societies, as the biologist Ernst Mayr noted, the native people often have become so well acquainted with the birds around them as to identify all the species distinguished later by modern ornithologists.

The dual activity of putting living things into neat, labeled boxes and telling stories to explain their origins satisfied human curiosity for a long time. For many cultures and people, it still does. But as modern science developed in Europe, especially in the seventeenth and eighteenth centuries, some observers began to have their doubts, to think in different directions. One source of this newer thinking undoubtedly was the rise of scientific classification, called taxonomy or systematics. Of course, it had been obvious for a long time that living things fit into categories. It is a commonplace that there are birds of many kinds, fishes of many kinds, trees of many kinds. Our modern way of thinking about such categorization began with the Swedish naturalist Karl von Linné, usually called by his latinized name Carolus Linnaeus. Linnaeus invented the system we now use of putting species into small groups called genera (singular, genus), of putting similar genera into families, and so on up the hierarchy to the great kingdoms, originally a plant kingdom and an animal kingdom. Still, for Linnaeus and other naturalists of his time and some time to come, there was no question about the origin of all these species; God had created them, as the Bible tells, and there were just as many species as God had seen fit to create.

Naturalism, the philosophy of the natural science that developed after the European Renaissance, differs from the older worldview in seeking to explain the phenomena of the world strictly by means of natural entities and events, rather than interpreting the world as a creation and plaything of gods and demons. And once a naturalist has observed many species that look very much alike, a nagging doubt may arise. For instance, both Europe and North America are inhabited by many types of small sparrows or buntings, little seed-eaters with very similar plumages of brown, gray, black, and white. They are a delight to the eye of both bird-watcher and artist, but why are there so many of them? Without pretending to fathom God's purpose, we may observe the seeming strangeness of creating so many, so much alike that identifying them can be a real challenge. Linnaeus, being a botanist, knew many species of oaks, of maples, of just about any other family of plants familiar to a European scholar; identifying each species also tests the naturalist's skill, since they are often so similar, and one might wonder why it was necessary to create them all, each as its own separate species.

As we shall see in chapter two, where we review this story at greater length, some early naturalists sought natural explanations for the origins of all this diversity. They also observed the fossilized remains of plants and animals of the past. Perhaps, some began to think, species are not as immutable as tradition had taught. Perhaps they can change, and perhaps this variety is the result of gradual changes in form as plants and animals spread out, both in time and space, and diverged from one another – perhaps, in other words, we are seeing the result of an *evolution* of living organisms. The idea, of course, did not sit well with a Christian European and American society, including many other scientists, who had been brought up with unquestioning belief in the biblical story of creation. The idea of evolution was heretical, even sinful. It raised a storm of controversy that is still with us today.

Now we moderns, at the beginning of the twenty-first century, contemplate the situation. On the one hand, we live in the most scientifically and technologically advanced society that has ever existed. Our lives are shaped by all the discoveries of modern science, such as medical advances that have eradicated some diseases and have given us the power to cure others, to live far longer and more healthfully than our ancestors did. Europeans and North Americans have been major contributors to these scientific and technological advances, and major beneficiaries of them. We are also citizens of nations whose actions and policies contribute most to the problems generated by modern science and technology. It is hard to generalize about citizens of other countries, but, paradoxically, Americans on the whole are abysmally ignorant of even the most basic scientific ideas, let alone the advanced knowledge that drives our society. The National Science Foundation's "Science & Engineering Indicators 2000" reported that less than half of those questioned knew that:

1. The earliest humans did not live at the same time as the dinosaurs;
2. It takes the Earth one year to travel around the sun; or
3. Electrons are smaller than atoms.

Only 29 per cent could define the term "DNA," only 13 per cent could define "molecule," and only 21 per cent were able to explain what it means to study something scientifically; just over half understood probability, and only a third knew how an experiment is conducted.

Furthermore, Gallup polls show that only about half or fewer Americans say they believe in evolution. This might just be viewed as another instance of Americans' general ignorance. In another arena, the National Geographic Society surveyed young adults, aged 18 to 24, in November, 2002, and found that almost one-third could not locate the Pacific Ocean, fewer than half correctly identified the United Kingdom, France, Japan, and the state of Pennsylvania, and three out of ten thought the U.S. population was "1 billion to 2 billion," instead of the correct number, about 280 million. So when one hears that many Americans don't believe in evolution, one is tempted to reply, "So what? Americans don't know nuthin' from nuthin' anyway, so that doesn't mean anything." However, no one is campaigning to keep Americans ignorant of the definition of a molecule or the location of the Pacific Ocean, while a vigorous campaign is being waged to convince people that the "theory of evolution" is not only wrong but evil, sinful, and destructive of the fabric of our society.

Thus, this introduction to evolution cannot simply address the scientific concepts alone. We will have to devote some space to questions of the nature of knowledge, the structure of science in general, the domains of science and religion, and the place of science in society.

the logic of science

People have always wanted to know about the world around them – how it works, what kinds of things are in it. They have been motivated by fear of the unknown, by the need to gain control over the world, and by simple curiosity. The anthropologist Bronislaw Malinowski pointed out that all human societies have science, magic, and religion, their roots reaching far back into prehistory. Even ancestors of *Homo sapiens* had some scientific knowledge, which we find expressed in their ability to make instruments and tools. They must have known the variety of plants and animals in their environment, which of them were good to eat and which were dangerous, and when and how to hunt their prey. This practical knowledge was essential for their survival. At the edge of their pool of knowledge, which we must count as science, they had magic and religion: ideas about the nature of the world embodied in myths and stories regarding what they did not know empirically and could not control with their own hands but could only seek to control through rites and rituals and prayers.

Science is distinguished from other human activities by its over-all philosophy of naturalism, as mentioned earlier, and by its reliance on obtaining information through the evidence of our senses developed through carefully controlled observations. And this is simply the foundation that all rational people use for ordering their lives on the basis of experience and reason. Thomas Henry Huxley made the point in 1863 in a little essay entitled "We Are All Scientists." The scientific way of thinking and acting is just a somewhat more rigorous version of the way we all must act day by day to learn the mundane facts about our world and to live effectively, avoiding stupid and dangerous actions. Part of our task in this book is to examine knowledge about evolution obtained empirically and to contrast it with contrary assertions – based on revelation and authority – about how the various creatures that inhabit this world came to be.

Nonscientists tend to think of science as a body of Truths about the world. People are eager to have Truths with a capital T – eternal verities that are absolutely certain, guidelines for their lives, which they can rely on without doubts. Religions have always claimed to provide such Truths. But I avoid the word "truth" in talking about science, because science does not really deal with Truth with a capital T – perhaps one reason nonscientists may denigrate and mistrust it. Science actually deals at best with more humble "small-t" truths, stated in the form of *falsifiable hypotheses*. A scientist notices some unexplained phenomenon and tries to devise a rational explanation for it, reasoning in a way that the American physicist and logician Charles Sanders Peirce called *retroduction*: "Here is a strange state of affairs; but this state of affairs would be understandable if something else – call it X – were true; therefore, I have good reason to believe that X is true." Postulating X is inventing an explanation for the strange state of affairs. It requires a leap of the imagination, and for this reason science is as creative as the arts or any other human activity. It is amusing that Sherlock Holmes, Arthur Conan Doyle's remarkable consulting detective, is always extolling "the science of deduction" though his method is clearly retroduction, albeit with brilliant imaginative leaps.

Science imposes several limitations on what X might be like. As the philosopher Wesley Salmon has written, to explain a phenomenon means placing it within the causal structure of the universe – showing the causal chain of events resulting in this phenomenon. This means that X must be in the realm of ordinary physical reality; a scientist cannot postulate something supernatural or in principle unobservable, such as a god or demon or some kind of magic. But most important, the postulate about X is a hypothesis that must be subject to an *empirical* test – it must have consequences that are testable through observation and experiment. Then we can challenge the hypothesis by testing some of these predictions.

Nonscientists may imagine that in doing experiments or in making critical observations, scientists are trying to prove that their hypotheses are correct. In fact, they are trying to prove that their hypotheses are *wrong*. Of course, people always hope they are correct, but a quirk of logic dictates that they can't try to prove this. To be a meaningful scientific idea, a hypothesis, H, must make some prediction, P, about the outcome of an experiment or an observation. H and P are related by a hypothetical statement: "If H, then P." So we test to see whether we do observe P. Suppose we do. Can we reason, "If H then P; P is true, therefore H is true"? No, we can't. This pattern of reasoning is a logical fallacy called "affirming the consequent." (Try reasoning, "If my car is out of gas, it will not start. My car will not start, therefore my car is out of gas." How many other explanations are there for your car not starting?) But suppose P is not true – that we observe not-P. Then we *can* reason ("denying the consequent"), "If H, then P; not-P, therefore not-H." As the philosopher Karl Popper emphasized, the hypothesis must be *falsifiable* – it must be possible in principle to show that it isn't true. If the results of a test don't support the hypothesis, it is rejected or at least modified. (Of course, another argument is that the test wasn't conducted correctly and is not an adequate challenge to the hypothesis.) If the results support the hypothesis, it survives, and we gain greater confidence in it. This doesn't make the hypothesis true, at least, not in the capital-T sense – merely an acceptable explanation for the observations.

As we develop a better understanding of some subject and have more hypotheses that survive empirical tests, we can piece together larger explanatory structures called *theories*. A theory is a logically related set of statements that explains how some aspect of the world works, but it is not simply a more mature version of a hypothesis. The British philosopher of science Stephen Toulmin suggested that a theory is like a map, a picture that can summarize a set of facts and create an overall understanding of them. But like a hypothesis, a theory must be subject to empirical tests. If the theory truly represents reality, we should be able to draw inferences from it about the outcome of other observations that haven't been made yet, so we can challenge it empirically and, in principle, show that something is wrong with it.

All science is based on theoretical structures. A prominent theory of chemistry, for instance, explains how atoms bond together to form molecules; it is an excellent, satisfying theory because it predicts so accurately just how certain atoms will form molecules with specific properties. Geology is based in part on a theory of tectonic plates, which postulates that solid segments of the Earth's crust rest on a fluid foundation and are slowly moving past one another; this is also a strong, successful theory because it explains phenomena such as mountain building, sea-floor expansion, and earthquakes so well.

then what about the "theory of evolution"?

Given this background about theories in general, what is the status of the "theory of evolution"? First, we should agree not to use this phrase; it is used wrongly and often, particularly in the form "Charles Darwin's theory of evolution," as if biology were just as it was in the mid-nineteenth century while all the other sciences have been advancing. In daily life – as contrasted with science – people tend to contrast "theory" with "fact." The tough-minded man in the street, to conjure up a somewhat moth-eaten image, expresses his commitment to "facts" and his contempt for tender-minded visionaries who live in ivory towers and deal only with "theories." But as I have just shown, theories are never in conflict with facts. Theories summarize, organize, and explain facts; facts substantiate (or perhaps fail to substantiate) theories. To clarify the issue, consider two questions about the idea of evolution:

1. Have the various kinds of living organisms on earth achieved their present form through a process of evolution?
2. What are the mechanisms of evolution?

The answer to the first question is Yes; it is a *fact* of biology that this is true, just as much as it is a fact of biology that plant leaves use their chlorophyll to convert light energy into chemical energy, that food is digested in the intestine, or that normal humans have 46 chromosomes. As we proceed through the next few chapters, I will try to show that this fact is so solid that denying it would make nonsense of virtually all of biology. The evidence accumulated over the past 150 years or so has uniformly supported (and hence failed to falsify) the general thesis that species evolve and that evolution accounts for the diversity of organisms that have inhabited and now inhabit the Earth.

At this point, an astute reader might raise an objection. "You say that evolution explains the origin of all the organisms on Earth. But you also say that every theory, every hypothesis, must be falsifiable. It seems to me that if all biologists are looking at the world with their belief in evolution, they can't be objective observers of the world. They will interpret every observation in the light of evolution, so the idea of evolution is really not falsifiable – in other words, not scientific!" An astute objection indeed, and one worthy of an answer. When we say that evolution explains the great diversity of organisms on this planet, we mean that very strong evidence shows that every existing species and every structure of a species is connected in some obvious way to similar species and to similar structures elsewhere. But suppose something were to break this pattern. For instance, existing animals move in a variety of ways: with legs of various kinds, with wings, by squirming and wiggling, by swimming with fins and other propelling and stabilizing structures. But no animal moves on wheels. Now, such a motion isn't absurd biologically. We know of at least one kind of motility structure with a wheel-like basis: motile bacteria generally swim by means of flagella – long, thin protein fibers – that swing around and around, propelled by circular, wheel-like structures. Suppose, then, we were to discover an animal that really does move on wheels. The animal wouldn't have to be very large, perhaps no more than a millimeter or two. It might have round appendages with "axles" held in bases that could drive them around and around, much like bacterial flagella. I am imagining that the animal is unique in this regard and that analysis of the proteins involved shows them to be unique – not obviously related in any way to proteins of any other animal. I believe that if we were to find such a creature, we would have to conclude that it did not originate through evolution from any other species on Earth. We might conclude that it had been created by some intelligence and placed on Earth; or we might conclude that it was a species that had evolved on some other planet and had been left here by extraterrestrial visitors. But we could not explain its existence by reference to biological evolution on this planet. Even more broadly, it is conceivable that we would find an organism whose structures show no homologies to anything else on Earth. (The concept of homology is explained in chapter two.) So it is perfectly conceivable that we would find individual cases whose origin could not be ascribed to evolution, at least evolution on this planet. But, to repeat, that the idea of evolution in general could be overthrown seems inconceivable.

The second question raised above is about the *theoretical foundation* of evolution, about *how* evolution occurs, and this theory is analogous to theories in other sciences of the kind I mentioned above. Evolutionary theory has survived many challenges and has thus become very strong. As I will show in the following chapters, there is broad agreement about the principal mechanisms of evolution, although, like any scientific theory, it is subject to constant refinement, additions, and revision. But current evolutionary theory explains so much – it is so *robust*, in current jargon – and is so obviously compatible with everything else we know about biology (indeed, essential to explain much of biology) that it is virtually inconceivable that anyone could present contrary evidence that would make us abandon our current model. That will be the main subject of the rest of the book.

conceptions and misconceptions

The whole idea of evolution is so fraught with misconceptions that I want to start by considering some of them. The following brief answers to these misconceptions may provide a kind of overview of what is to come, with references to chapters in the book that go into more detail.

1. *Evolution is incompatible with religion: you have to choose whether you're going to stick to your religious beliefs or be an evolutionist.* This is one of the principal contentions I am at pains to combat. It is basically a fundamentalist Protestant viewpoint, and fundamentalist Protestants are a small minority among religious people. The dichotomy is certainly true if your religion maintains that the biblical story of creation, as told in Genesis, is absolutely, literally true. If you are so firmly committed to that position that nothing can change your mind, you might as well put the book down and stop reading right now, because nothing else in this book is going to make sense to you or have any influence on your thinking. However, if your religious beliefs entail a more liberal interpretation of the Bible or if those beliefs are based on quite different teachings, there is no reason to feel any incompatibility between the two. The vast majority of religious people, including members of most Christian denominations, recognize evolution as a natural phenomenon revealed by modern science; they usually say that they believe God created the living things on Earth and that evolution is the way he chose to do so. By the way, let us agree at the outset not to use the word "evolutionist." This is a label used by strict creationists to set their beliefs aside, and outside this context it doesn't really mean anything. (See more in chapter ten.)

2. *Evolution means improvement – progress from lower to higher forms of life.* No, evolution says nothing about "progress." Progress is a conception of modern civilization. We may apply the idea to human affairs and human history (though that point, too, is arguable), but it is wrong to apply it generally to the biological world. An old tradition in biology is to use terms such as "lower animals" for worms, clams, and the like while promoting birds and mammals to the lofty status of "higher animals," but modern biologists should, and do, try to avoid those labels. The very words "lower" and "higher," when applied to the world of organisms, stem from a human misconception of progress, a reading of something into the world that simply isn't there. It is based on the archaic idea of a Chain of Being, reaching from the lowliest, simplest creatures to the most complex – humans, obviously! – and then beyond humans to angels and God. Now, it is true that the overall history of life on Earth has seen the evolution of larger, more complex creatures, but even given this conception of "progress," evolution has entailed plenty of changes in direction that no one could identify as progress.

3. *There is good reason to have our doubts about evolution because even the scientists who subscribe to the idea and are supposed to be studying it can't agree among themselves.* Scientists always disagree about what they study. It's part of the game. Controversy leading to clarification is the road to scientific truth. We have long lists of generally established facts about the world, even though scientific specialists disagree about their details. All biologists agree very strongly about the major outlines of evolution; here too, the disagreements are about the fine points and details.

4. *The fossil record that biologists depend on as evidence for evolution is really full of big holes, with none of the "transition" forms that should be there if evolution is true, and the biologists gloss over this fact or try to hide it.* This is one of those canards perpetuated by anti-evolutionists, what Stephen Jay Gould has called a kind of urban legend. Although the fossil record is incomplete, like any historical record, it is rich and extensive enough to support fully the general fact of evolution, and it gets better every year. Furthermore, many evolutionary episodes are documented by as rich a fossil record as one could want, with plenty of transitional forms to show how later groups of organisms have descended from their ancestors.

5. *Living things are so wonderfully, perfectly designed for their varied ways of life that it is just impossible to believe that all these complicated creatures have evolved by chance, through the blind operation of random forces. There must have been a guiding intelligence behind the process.* This is an interesting, complicated issue. The first point to make, however, is that it just ain't so: you can only believe in the "wonderful, perfect design" of living organisms if you don't look closely enough. We will see that organisms are *historical* creations, which carry with them all the genetic baggage inherited from their ancestors, so any new features must be designed by slowly modifying what is already present. Take that supposed paragon of design, the mammalian eye. The cornea and lens focus light on the retina, a layer of light-sensitive cells, but the eye is really so poorly designed that the retina is upside-down, and the light has to first pass through a layer of nerves and blood vessels; this layer doesn't absorb much light, but the larger blood vessels can cause minor problems, and an excellent designer would never have made the eye like that. Furthermore, the optic nerve formed from extensions of the retinal cells has to leave the eye through a hole, creating a blind spot in each eye. We aren't aware of these difficulties because each eye covers the blind spot of the other and because the eyes are constantly jiggling

and the brain produces continuous images from their input. Another example of poor design is our breathing and swallowing apparatus; as lungs gradually evolved, the tube we breathe through (trachea) came out on the wrong side of the esophagus, making it necessary to evolve a complicated epiglottis to cover the mouth of the trachea when we swallow. Yet the apparatus commonly fails and something tries to "go down the wrong tube," making actions such as the Heimlich maneuver necessary for survival.

In spite of such facts, many people have taken the viewpoint that biological function implies a designer, and in recent years this has been cloaked in scientific garb by the proponents of "intelligent design theory." We will discuss this idea in chapter ten, because it raises the question of whether this "theory" is a legitimate scientific theory or a philosophical viewpoint outside science.

stories in the rocks

Modern science tends to be all of one piece. The discoveries and concepts of all the special sciences are so interlinked and interdependent that innovations in one tend to affect the others. For a long time in the development of European science, much of science was simply "natural history," without the distinctions we now make between such topics as geology and biology. Indeed, the whole idea of evolution itself evolved in these two sciences together. I want to begin here with some of this history, to provide a context for establishing a few of the geological and biological concepts that are most essential to understanding evolution. The play of biological evolution has taken place in the theatre of the evolving earth, and the record of past performances is locked in the layers of rock.

geology becomes a science

Western civilization's conception of the Earth and its place in the universe has long been dominated by a blend of Greek science and Judeo-Christian theology. People saw the Earth as the center of a universe made of larger and larger spheres, bearing the sun, moon, planets, and stars. Lacking any real conception of the vastness of time and space, there was no reason to doubt the biblical story that the universe had been created by divine fiat about 4000 B.C.E., followed by a separate creation of each living thing. This picture, however, began to fall apart with the Renaissance, when the new view of the universe developed by Copernicus, Kepler, and Galileo showed the Earth to be only one of several planets orbiting the sun, stripping it of the central place that human vanity had assigned it. New generations of astronomers started to portray the universe as a vast space occupied by many suns, and far older than a few thousand years. However, European thought, even among scientists, was molded – and in a sense held captive – by the biblical conception of a week in which the Earth and all life had been created, with little change following the creation except for a universal flood in Noah's time. Naturalists had little reason to doubt that all living organisms had been created independently in a very short time. Some doubts about these traditional beliefs started to creep in as people began to take a more naturalistic view of the world, uncolored by their religious heritage. Yet one of the main impediments to these doubts was the belief that the Earth is so young that there has been little time for any significant change.

Challenges to the biblical story arose in large part because of *fossils*. The word comes from the Latin *fossilis*, meaning "something dug up." Scientists and amateurs have dug up many fossils, and great collections are stored in museum trays – largely the shells of ancient animals such as clams and snails, the bones of larger animals, petrified tree trunks, the impressions of plant leaves, the tracks and burrows of animals, and even some petrified animal feces (called coproliths). We now accept fossils routinely for what they are, the remains of ancient organisms preserved one way or another in the rocks. Fossils are remarkably easy to find. As a kid in Minneapolis, I chiseled them out of the hard limestone on the banks of the Mississippi. Years later in Kentucky, we found coral fossils, among others, in the softer limestones. While driving from Lexington to Louisville one day, we stopped on a country road, and as I stepped out of the car, I found myself standing on a gravel made of enormous numbers of brachiopod fossils. Here in Washington State, the soft rocks of Cenozoic age in several nearby locations hold quite recent fossils of many snails, scaphopods, and other molluscs. And in a small town on the eastern slope of the Cascade Mountains, we found a large pile of reddish rock that turned out to be a huge slagheap of limestone rich in leaf fossils, providing a beautiful record of the trees in some ancient forest in the region.

Early naturalists such as Xenophanes and Aristotle took note of fossils of clams and other marine animals in rocks far from the oceans; they concluded, quite rightly, that these rocks were once ocean beds and that powerful forces in the Earth must have converted them into hard rock and moved them far away to the hills and mountains. However, even such rudimentary knowledge was lost to Christian Europe during Medieval times, while the writings of the classical philosophers were preserved by Arabic civilization. Medieval Europeans who observed fossils ascribed them to fanciful causes such as germs from the stars or vague formative forces in the rocks. Bible theology could also explain fossils as the remains of creatures lost during the Noachian flood, though why aquatic creatures should have died during that time is a little hard to explain.

One of the first to look at fossils for what they are was the Italian artist and natural philosopher Leonardo da Vinci (1452–1519). He saw that fossil shells in rocks in northern Italy were the remains of marine animals many miles from the sea. Clams, he argued, could not have traveled such a distance during the short time allotted to the Flood – and, again, why would they have died in the Flood anyway? Leonardo even took a modern ecological view of the world by noting that the apparent communities of animals preserved in the rocks resembled modern communities in the ocean. Furthermore, he pointed out that fossil-rich layers of rock were separated by layers without fossils, suggesting that the rocks had been formed in a series of distinct events, not in a single catastrophe.

One of Leonardo's followers in the mid-seventeenth century, Nicholas Steno, made careful observations of fossils. Although Steno clung to the idea of a young Earth and badly misinterpreted some fossils (he thought fossilized mammal bones were the remains of the elephants Hannibal had marched over the mountains to attack Rome), he set forth some important basic principles of geology. He realized that each layer of rock, or *stratum*, must have been formed gradually as particles settled out of water. The larger particles would have settled first, followed by smaller and smaller particles. Any change in the material being deposited would show up in the formation of distinct horizontal layers, a process called *stratification* and clearly observable in sedimentary rock formations. So one of his first principles was that strata would originally form horizontally; layers standing vertically or tilted or rolled into curves are evidence of later geological forces – very powerful forces – that must have moved them and twisted them. Steno also recognized a principle of superposition: the oldest sediments must be those on the bottom, with younger and younger strata piled on top. Finally, Steno recognized a principle of lateral continuity, meaning that each stratum extends in all directions until it reaches the edges of the basin in which it was deposited. These are now fundamental to geological thought.

These ideas were taken up later by William Smith (1769–1839), an English civil engineer. Because he was engaged in practical activities such as visiting coalmines and excavating for canals, Smith had the opportunity to observe many rock strata. Known as "Strata Smith," he was valued throughout England for the depth of his knowledge of these rocks. Smith particularly observed the fossils embedded there. Recognizing that each stratum contained a distinctive group of fossils, he contended that those fossils could be used to identify these strata in any location. On this basis, he created the first geologic map of England. Smith also stated the principle of superposition that Steno had recognized, that the lowest strata must be the oldest, thus strengthening the foundation of the science of geology.

At about the time Smith was doing his work in England, Antoine Lavoisier – one of the first modern chemists – made similar observations in France. He, too, realized that each stratum had its distinctive fossils, which must reflect environmental conditions at the time it was deposited. Lavoisier's observations were extended by Georges Cuvier (1769–1832) and Alexandre Brongniart, who published a geologic map of the Paris basin comparable to Smith's map, showing the locations of various strata.

Some naturalists, seeing how much the fossils in each stratum differed from one another, postulated that the Earth had experienced a series of *catastrophes*, geological events that had wiped out all life on Earth, or at least all life in some large area. The germ of the idea seems to have arisen in the work of George Louis LeClerc, Comte de Buffon (1707–88), although he did not necessarily think of the changes he described in the Earth's history as major upheavals. His successor Cuvier, however, was a student of vertebrate paleontology, and the fossils of large animals clearly define quite distinct species with very significant differences in form; seeing these differences, Cuvier elaborated the idea that each epoch of the Earth's history had ended with a catastrophe, after which life was created anew, perhaps with each new flora (plant life) and fauna (animal life) a little more advanced than those before. Catastrophism became the norm in geologic thought during the eighteenth century. To explain some observations, though, catastrophists had to postulate over twenty separate extinctions and creations, and the idea began to look ridiculous.

Meanwhile, James Hutton (1726–97) was laying the foundations for a more modern view of geology. In his *Theory of the Earth* (1785–95), Hutton developed the *uniformitarian* view that geological forces are constantly and continually shaping the Earth's features over exceedingly long times. He saw that erosion by wind and water constantly breaks the rocks down, while the internal heat of the Earth is a force behind volcanic activity and the upheavals and bending of rock layers. The uniformitarian viewpoint achieved its modern form in 1830–33, when Charles Lyell's great work *Principles of Geology* laid the foundations for a modern science of the Earth by showing clearly how the kinds of forces outlined by Hutton create the geological forms we observe. Of course, devastating earthquakes, volcanic eruptions, and collisions with meteors occasionally rock the Earth, but none of these events destroys all life on the planet. It is clear now that even as movements of the Earth's crust are raising new mountain chains, the mountains are being worn down slowly by erosion and their substance deposited in beds where plant and animal remains become buried and eventually fossilized. Uniformitarian thinking in geology helped prepare the way for thinking that organisms, too, are gradually changing.

As early geologists extended the work of Smith and Cuvier to other sites in Europe, the strata began to acquire names that we still use today. Each stratum must have been laid down over a long time, and that time is now named as a segment of the standard geologic time-scale, which is divided into this hierarchy:

eras
    periods
        epochs
            ages

The names first applied to local rock formations were extended as people began to correlate the strata in different regions. Thus, some strata identified in the Jura mountains of France and Switzerland were called Juras, and the same strata were identified in France lying under strata that had been named Cretaceous (from *creta*, chalk, because of their characteristic chalky limestone layers). But in Germany the Juras laid above a series called Trias. Today we identify the times when these formations were laid down as three distinct periods called Triassic, Jurassic, and Cretaceous, which all constitute the Mesozoic era. The coal-bearing strata of England had been named Carboniferous, and these now identify a period before the Triassic, in the Paleozoic era.

The current geologic time-scale is shown in Figure 2.1. Although its main divisions were first defined by rock formations in Britain and Europe, the system has now been extended throughout the world. Many geologic ages, however, are defined uniquely on each continent.

Era	Period	Epoch	Myr ago	Major events
Cenozoic	Quaternary	Holocene	0.01	Agriculture, civilization
		Pleistocene	1.6	Neanderthals, modern humans
	Tertiary	Pliocene	5.3	Earliest hominids (prehumans)
		Miocene	23.7	Rapid evolution and spread of grazing mammals
		Oligocene	36.6	First elephants
		Eocene	57.8	First horses, rhinoceroses, camels
		Paleocene	66.4	First primates
Mesozoic	Cretaceous		144	Great evolution and spread of flowering plants Extinction of dinosaurs
	Jurassic		208	First birds and mammals Peak of dinosaurs
	Triassic		245	First dinosaurs
Paleozoic	Permian		286	Mammal-like reptiles
	Pennsylvanian		320	First reptiles. Large insects
	Mississippian		360	Sharks, insects
	Devonian		408	First amphibians. Forests abundant
	Silurian		438	First air-breathing animals (scorpions), land plants
	Ordovician		505	Peak of trilobites; first fishes
	Cambrian		543	Rapid diversification of animals
Precambrian	Protero-zoic	Ediacaran	610	Diverse early animal fauna
			2500	Eucaryotic cells
	Archean		3800	First simple (procaryotic) cells
	Hadean		4500	Formation of the earth

Figure 2.1 *A geologic time-scale showing major events since the Earth's formation. Times given indicate the beginning of each period.*

ages and time

As these advances in geology were being made, the issue of time obviously had to arise. As the early geologists saw how rocks must have been deposited gradually and then often uplifted into hills and mountains, it became clear to them that the traditional age of the Earth of less than 6000 years was way too short a time. Eventually some investigators began to ask scientific questions about the age of the Earth and to extend the time-scale a little. For example, Buffon took seriously the idea that the Earth and the planets had been formed from very hot material, and he conducted experiments on the rate at which metal balls cool off after being heated. From his data, making the false assumption that the sun's radiation has little effect on the Earth's temperature and that there was no other internal source of heat, he calculated that the Earth must be about 75,000 years old. Although he was wrong, at least he had started to ask the question empirically, through observation and experimentation. In 1846, the English physicist Lord Kelvin (William Thompson) estimated that the Earth is between 20 and 30 million years old, based on the assumption that the Earth was originally formed from molten materials and has been gradually cooling. From measurements of the rate at which the temperature increases as one descends into the Earth in a mineshaft, Kelvin calculated how old the Earth would have to be to generate that temperature gradient. Again, he was far off the mark, in part because his assumptions were wrong. Another estimate based on observations of rates of deposition in contemporary sediments and the thickness of the geologic column, was that at least 75 million years had elapsed since the Cambrian period.

An unrecognized factor in geology, and the key to eventually getting accurate measurements of geologic age, lies in radioactivity. Remember that atoms have nuclei made of positive protons and neutral neutrons, with negative electrons around the nucleus; generally the numbers of protons and electrons are equal, making the atom neutral. All atoms of a given element have the same number of protons, the *atomic number* of the element; the number of protons plus neutrons is its atomic mass, or *mass number*. However, most elements have variant forms called isotopes: atoms of different mass numbers, because they have different numbers of neutrons. For instance, hydrogen atoms all have a single proton, but hydrogen has three isotopes. Atoms of ordinary hydrogen – the most common form – have no neutrons; the isotope deuterium has one neutron, and the isotope tritium has two neutrons. Giving different names to the isotopes of an element is exceptional; generally, they would just be known by their mass numbers as hydrogen-1, hydrogen-2 and hydrogen-3, denoted ^1H, ^2H, and ^3H.

Hydrogens-1 and -2 are stable, but hydrogen-3 is radioactive. The combination of two neutrons with one proton is an unstable situation, and if we watch a bit of tritium for a while (using special instruments), we will see that every once in a while a tritium atom will go *pop* and change into an atom of helium. One of its neutrons will change into a proton, and it will shoot an electron off into space. This electron, which is what the special instruments can detect, is a form of radiation (β-radiation), and the phenomenon of giving off such radiation is called radioactivity.

Radioactivity was discovered in the element uranium by Henri Becquerel around 1896 and was then pursued by Marie and Pierre Curie, who discovered the elements radium and polonium. A radioactive isotope – that is, a radioisotope – may give off electrons, high-energy photons (γ-radiation) or a cluster of two protons and two neutrons (α-radiation). In any case, its nucleus changes, and we say that the element *decays*. Several decay sequences are known, for sometimes one radioisotope decays into another, which decays into still another. For instance, uranium-238 (^{238}U) decays into thorium-235 by giving off an alpha particle; thorium-235 decays into protoactinium-234, which then becomes uranium-234, and this sequence continues to the stable isotope lead-206 (^{206}Pb).

One source of heat in the Earth is internal radioactivity. Atomic decay releases energy, and it does not take much radioactivity to account for a considerable amount of the Earth's heat. More important, for present purposes, is that radioactive decay can be used as a clock to determine the ages of rocks. Atoms decay randomly, so one can never predict which atom will decay next. But each radioisotope decays at a certain rate, which is conveniently measured by its half-life – the time required for half the initial atoms to decay. For instance, phosphorus-32 decays into sulfur-32 with a half-life of about two weeks. Suppose we could actually watch individual atoms and could arrange exactly 1000 ^{32}P atoms under our powerful, imaginary microscope. Over the next two weeks, we would see them *pop*, *pop*, *pop*, one after the other (though we would never know which one would pop next), and after two weeks there would be just 500 left. They would continue to decay, and after another two weeks there would be 250; in two weeks more, there would be 125; and so on.

This regularity is the basis of geologic clocks. For instance, uranium-235 decays into lead-207 with a half-life of 710 million years. Suppose that at some time in the distant past some rocks had formed with a certain amount of ^{235}U in them and that nothing disturbed these rocks until we could examine them. We break up a sample of rock and put a small amount into a mass spectrometer, an instrument that separates out all the isotopes and measures the amount of each. Now, the older the rock, the less ^{235}U it will contain and the more ^{207}Pb. The equations that describe radioactive decay relate the ratio of these two masses to the time of decay, so by measuring the mass of each isotope we can calculate the age of the rock. Several such decay schemes have been used for materials of different ages (Table 1).

Table 1 Decay schemes used for geological dating

Parent and product	Half-life	Effective age range
Carbon 14 → Nitrogen 14	5730 years	<60,000 years
Potassium 40 → Argon 40	1.3 billion years	>100,000 years
Uranium 235 → Lead 207	710 million years	>100 million years
Uranium 238 → Lead 206	4.5 billion years	>100 million years
Rubidium 87 → Strontium 87	47 billion years	>100 million years
Thorium 232 → Lead 208	13.9 billion years	>200 million years

Critics will point out that there are difficulties with these methods. Indeed there are. Every scientific method has its limitations, and these are gradually overcome by improving the techniques. For instance, using the decay of potassium-40 to argon-40 faces the problem that argon is a gas that can leak out of a specimen if it isn't handled very carefully. If some argon does escape as a sample is being prepared, the sample will appear to be younger than it really is. But geologists continually improve their methods, and now different methods for measuring the ages of the same strata tend to give very good agreements.

These radiochemical methods are supplemented by others. One of the most interesting depends on the presence of some uranium

atoms in crystals of the mineral zircon. When an atom of
^{238}U decays, it produces a minute track in the crystal, and these can
be counted. Given zircon crystals in a geological deposit with a
favorable concentration of uranium – neither too high nor too
low – this method can be used to check dates obtained by other
methods.

This geological and radiochemical work, which has now been
going on for a couple of centuries, is the foundation for our saying
how old the Earth is and at what age various kinds of organisms lived
or became extinct. It is one foundation of geology and for the whole
story of evolution.

comparative anatomy

Aristotle didn't know everything, but the old man knew a great deal.
Tracing the history of an idea, we often find ourselves going back to
Aristotle's writing, for he reflected and recorded much of the knowledge of his time. He knew something about plants and animals, and
in his book *Parts of Animals* he recognizes that similar animals have a
common body plan, a common shared anatomy, with only minor
variations in this plan for specialization to different ways of life. We
find him writing:

> The course of exposition must be first to state the attributes com-
> mon to whole groups of animals and then to attempt to give their
> explanation. Many groups present common attributes, that is to
> say, in some cases absolutely identical affections, and absolutely
> identical organs – feet, feathers, scales, and the like, while in other
> groups the affections and organs are only so far identical as that they
> are analogous. For instance, some groups have lungs, others have no
> lung but an organ analogous to a lung in its place; some have blood,
> others have no blood but a fluid analogous to blood, and with the
> same office. To treat of the common attributes in connection with
> each individual group would involve, as already suggested, useless
> iteration. For many groups have common attributes.

After the long decline in science following Greek civilization, the
European Renaissance brought renewed interest in anatomy,
although at first it seems to have been an interest only in human
anatomy. With the eighteenth century, a few anatomists turned their

attention to comparative studies. Buffon, recognizing the value of the comparative method, studied the fossils of extinct animals, often very different from any now alive; but detailed comparisons of their bones with those of living species could often show their similarities and thus their relationships – ancient mammoths and modern elephants, for instance. From such comparisons we might reconstruct some of the history of life. Serious comparative anatomy, however, begins with Cuvier. He performed detailed studies of the bones of fossilized animals, and in the words of the historian Sir William Dampier, "His great claim to distinction lies in the fact that he was the first among naturalists to compare systematically the structure of existing animals with the remains of extinct fossils, and thus to demonstrate that the past, no less than the present, must be taken into account in any study of the development of living creatures."

Comparative anatomical studies have shown the similarities and relatedness of the soft parts of animals – for instance, the changes in the structure of the heart and the circulation as vertebrate evolution ran its course from fishes to amphibians to reptiles to birds or mammals. These parts do not fossilize, however, and the kind of studies that Cuvier originated, which paved the way for Darwin, focused on the parts that do fossilize, the bones and teeth. The vertebrate skull is especially fertile ground. We tend to think of the skull as one huge bone. It isn't. One insight into its true anatomy comes from the attention good parents give to their infants; they know that a baby has a "soft spot" on the top of its head, which has to be carefully protected. The spot is a region where the several bones that form the skull have not yet grown together and fused; this is easily seen in the skeletons of infants, although such relics are generally confined to anatomy departments, hidden from a public that might be upset by them. But close examination of an adult skull reveals many places where separate bony plates grow together, generally meeting along a somewhat scalloped line. The skulls of birds and mammals are made of about thirty distinct bony elements, several of which are visible in Figure 2.2. Some of the greatest successes of comparative anatomy entail showing how this pattern of bones has changed in the various groups of vertebrates, and also how remarkably it has been conserved. By "conserved" I mean simply that the basic elements remain very much the same in all vertebrates and are simply modified in rather small ways to make the enormous variety of vertebrate skulls.

Comparative anatomy – of the vertebrate skull or any comparable structure – shows why biology only makes sense in the

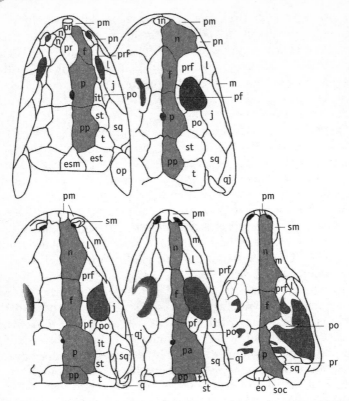

Figure 2.2 *A series of vertebrate skulls shows how each skull consists of the same bones with slightly different forms in comparable positions.*

light of evolution. It shows clearly how a versatile anatomy evolved in the most primitive vertebrates and has simply been modified by more subtle evolutionary changes in each later group. Another anatomical series (Figure 2.3), the familiar vertebrate limb, reveals another lesson. The bones of the human arm include the larger humerus of the upper arm, the paired radius and ulna of the lower arm, a series of small bones in the wrist and hand, and then five series of phalanges making each finger; in the human leg, the sequence is the femur of the upper leg, the tibia and fibula of the lower leg, another cluster of small bones in the foot, and another series of phalanges in the toes. This pattern is modified in each species of tetrapod vertebrate – tetrapod meaning "four-limbed," to include amphibians, reptiles, birds, and mammals. It is particularly interesting to see how the limb has been modified in quite distinct ways in the three types of flying tetrapods:

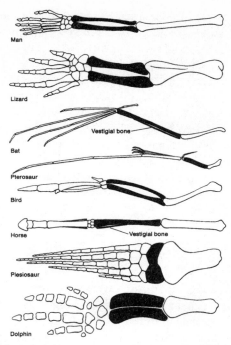

Figure 2.3 *The limbs of vertebrates are made of the same bones, modified for each animal's way of life.*

pterodactyls, birds, and bats. Each group achieved flight by stretching a membranous or feathered wing between greatly elongated bony elements, but each one used different particular elements. Oh, but hold on: what is this? The limbs of horses and bats (to pick out just two) contain some apparently excess elements – small, thin bones that have no functions and are termed *vestigial*. What are they doing there? Evolutionary biology provides a simple answer: the ancestors of these animals had two bones in the lower limb, and even though bats and horses require only one functional bone in these positions, the genes directing the formation of a second bone are still present and they direct the formation of the useless vestigial elements.

An important new concept, *homology*, emerges directly from comparative anatomy. If all tetrapod limbs have the same general series of humerus-radius-ulna-wrist-phalanges, then we can point to a single bone – say, the ulna – in any species and say, "This long bone is *homologous* to the equivalent long bone in all these animals." We can point to part of the skull and say, "This frontal bone (or nasal, or parietal, or postparietal, or whatever) is *homologous* to the equivalent bone in all these other animals, even though its shape may be considerably modified." The fact that we can point to homologies so regularly and simply is part of the evidence that all these diverse creatures have attained their structures through evolution from common ancestors, and homology is fundamental to evolutionary thinking. When we examine the structure of proteins in more detail, it will become apparent that homology applies at the molecular level, too, and that it can be an even more persuasive argument for evolutionary relationships than anatomical homology. By the way, structures with similar functions that lack anatomical homology are said to be *analogous* – the difference between an insect wing and a bird wing is a classic example.

impediments to the idea of evolution

Anatomists of the eighteenth and early nineteenth centuries did their careful studies of anatomy, both of living and fossilized creatures, still in the broad cultural context of biblical history. They became convinced that there had been life before our own era, often creatures with quite different forms, preserved in the various strata. But they did not make the intellectual leap, now so obvious to us, to an evolutionary viewpoint. The intellectual burden of thinking in the framework of biblical history and catastrophism was still too strong, and they continued to see the life of each stratum as the residue of a separate creation and destruction.

One reason the question of evolution arose slowly was that people had little conception of the age of the Earth. Even if they could have imagined a change from one species to another, such a change would have to take a long time. But the geologic work I described earlier started to remove the time-barrier to thinking about evolution by showing that in fact the Earth was far older than 6000 years, though no one yet knew just how old.

Thus, while scientists of the late eighteenth and early nineteenth centuries knew about fossils and the anatomical similarities that we now call homology, almost all stuck tenaciously to the idea of separate creation. That may seem peculiar, but old ideas die hard. Indeed, when Robert Chambers ventured to propose an evolutionary theory in 1834, he did so anonymously, and with good reason. His book, *The Vestiges of the Natural History of Creation*, was roundly attacked and castigated, even by some who later became fierce advocates for evolution. Even though Chambers could see that evolution must have occurred, he could not provide a mechanism to account for it, and other theorists had the same difficulty.

The evolutionary biologist Ernst Mayr has pointed out that another impediment to the idea of evolution was the philosophy of *essentialism*, which goes back at least to Plato; it proposes that everything in the world has a distinct, unvarying *essence* underlying its outward features. All horses, for instance, are supposed to partake of an ideal of "horseness;" though some may be short and some tall, some swaybacked and some straight, all horses are fundamentally the same below their surface appearances because they all share those ideal characteristics – the same essence.

In biology, this way of thinking became *typology*. Early biologists considered that every species conforms to an idealized, characteristic *type* and that all members of the species really are just like that type. This is the collector's mentality. A collector – of seashells, for instance – believes the world of life can be neatly and simply divided into distinct species. Even if some organisms are really quite variable and hard to classify, the typological mind tries to ignore the variation among individuals and sorts them into neat species anyway. I pointed out earlier that humans tend to do this as we try to bring order to a world that may not be quite as orderly as we would like.

People who see the world typologically, as biologists did in the seventeenth and eighteenth centuries, think the variations among individuals are trivial, and they have no reason to question the idea that each species was created separately. John Ray (1627–1705), one of the fathers of modern biological classification, reflected his contemporaries' thought when he said that two individuals belong to the same species if one is the ancestor of the other or if they are both descended from a common ancestor. With this definition in mind, typological thinkers could not even ask a question that implied evolution. A question such as, "Could the wolf and the fox have had a common ancestor?" would make no sense to them. Such an ancestor must have been either a wolf or a fox. If it were a wolf, it could not have been the ancestor of a fox, and vice versa. So the question would never even arise.

One of the few early naturalists to espouse the idea of evolution was Jean Baptiste de Lamarck, in 1809. His ideas are worth mentioning if only because similar ideas, labeled "Neo-Lamarckian," keep reappearing in biology. Lamarck's philosophy postulated a harmony between an organism and its environment, so the environment naturally imposes itself upon heredity. In his history of heredity, François Jacob describes Lamarck's views thus:

> ... only the transmission to descendants of experience acquired by individuals appeared to account for the harmony between organisms and nature. Never had this idea been exploited so systematically and with so much detail, however – nor so confidently since Lamarck took for granted that an organ disappears because it is of no use. For him, whales and birds have no teeth because they do not need them. The mole lost the use of its eyes because it lives in the world of darkness. Acephalous molluscs have no head because they have no need for it.

In a world lacking an understanding of heredity or physiology, Lamarck's viewpoint made good sense. Organisms do acquire modifications in response to environmental conditions. A running animal develops strong running muscles, and an animal that continually rubs some part of its body grows protective calluses. Lamarck thought that such acquired features were somehow incorporated into an organism's heredity, endowing its offspring with a greater tendency to have the same useful features; in the same vague way, an organism that didn't use something would simply lose it. Although Lamarck's proposal had a certain appeal, it did not really *explain* evolution, as explanation is understood by modern science: it didn't provide even the outline of a real mechanism to account for a hereditary change in response to the environment. It happened, too, that the prevailing intellectual climate in both France and England was inhospitable to Lamarck's philosophy and to all ideas about evolution, and they were not accepted.

We have now seen how geology and biology grew together, as naturalists came to understand the forces laying down strata of rock and began to study the anatomy of the organisms buried in these strata in a comparative manner. These studies became a foundation on which Darwin and Wallace built their ideas about evolution. The principal problem Darwin faced in developing the idea of natural selection was that it depends on heredity, but in his time heredity was a mystery. To understand this whole issue – what a species is and how species evolve – we must first understand what organisms are, and we turn to this question next.

biology – some basics

what are organisms?

Imagine yourself in the place of an early naturalist, and think about what you can observe as you try to develop some insights into the nature of life. You see, for example, a world of plants, mostly green, which grow up out of the ground and continue to grow. Isn't that extraordinary? This little green shoot pokes out of the ground, and it keeps growing and changing form until it has reached a characteristic size. It may even develop beautiful flowers. With careful observation, you could easily make a long list of animals, of an extraordinary variety, living in and on and around the plants. As you watch them, you'll see that the animals spend much of their time running around, finding food and eating it, and that quite often the food is a plant or part of a plant. With a good microscope – they were first used in the seventeenth century and greatly refined in the nineteenth – you would find that samples from a pond or even a little water-filled depression in the ground contain a variety of tiny creatures; some look rather plantlike, some rather animal-like, and some of them will be eating one another. You'll see, also, that there are many places for organisms to live – fields, forests, ponds, swamps, oceans – and that each environment harbors only a certain characteristic group of organisms. Finally, you only have to watch these creatures for a year or two to see that one outcome of all this activity is that they reproduce, or try to reproduce, so each year there tend to be

more of them – or, perhaps, there would be more if they didn't keep
eating one another.

What's going on here? Growth, movement, living together, and
reproduction. Early naturalists did not know all the essentials we
know today, yet all of biology could be summed up in these four
words or phrases.

growth

Organisms grow. They take in raw materials from their surroundings and transform them into their own substance, so they get
larger. For plants, the raw materials are carbon dioxide from the air
plus water and elements such as nitrogen, sulfur, and phosphorus
from the soil or water. For animals, the raw materials are plants, or
their parts, or other animals, or the wastes of other creatures. Some
microorganisms live much like plants, some like animals, and a few
carry out quite distinctive chemical activities, but they all grow.
They grow by transforming their nutrients through complicated
chemical processes, all summarized under the heading *metabolism*,
into their structural molecules. Metabolism requires energy,
which they obtain either from light or from energy stored in their
nutrients.

movement

Movement is a kind of adjunct of metabolism. Movement is most
obvious in animals and in some microorganisms, but even plants
that don't show the large-scale movements of animals are moving
streams of water through internal tubes, carrying nutrients and
wastes; and parts of their cells are moving. Most movement happens
because some of the complex materials that organisms are made of –
some of their proteins – are able to pull on one another. Movement
also requires energy, and part of metabolism is storing energy in a
form that can be used for movement as well as for growth.

reproduction

Organisms reproduce. Some do it alone, often just by growing larger
and then dividing in two, or by spreading shoots and runners out
into their surroundings. Others do it cooperatively, as by combining

sperm and egg cells (or their simpler equivalents) to form new individuals. The most extraordinary thing about reproduction, however, is *inheritance*. Organisms reproduce "after their own kind," to use the old biblical phrase. Violets produce violets, cocker spaniels produce cocker spaniel puppies, and tall, red-headed parents with a tendency toward hyperthyroidism produce tall, red-headed children with a similar tendency. We'll return to inheritance shortly.

living together

The various climates and physical features of the Earth provide distinct environments such as marshes, swamps, streams, lakes, hot springs, coral reefs, city parks, prairies, forests, backyard gardens, and deserts. Each of these places, with the organisms living there, is an *ecosystem*. It is a physical environment of water, soil, and air that supports a *community*, a collection of different organisms that live in the same area and can interact with one another: certain plants that can live in that environment, with characteristic animals and microorganisms living among them. The members of a community share living spaces and interact in complex ways. They eat each other and are eaten. They afford shelter and are in turn sheltered. They provide stages for one another on which each one acts out the drama of its life. No organism could live without the others in its community.

a modern way to understand biology

Now given these four big ideas about what organisms *do*, how can we find a general way to understand what organisms *are* – a way that will help to explain what we see them doing? Many people have tried to answer this question, generally by trying to enumerate the characteristics that make something *living*. But I will specifically avoid words such as "living," "life," and "alive" because they get us into too many verbal traps. Surprisingly perhaps, "life" just isn't a useful technical term in biology, although it has important nontechnical uses. Instead, we can understand evolution – as well as virtually everything else in biology – by recognizing that organisms are fundamentally *genetic systems*: they carry information that specifies their structures and they reproduce, which means that the organisms of one generation pass that information on to another generation of similar or identical organisms. Briefly, an *organism* is a *mutable, self-reproducing structure*. (I will explain the "mutable" part shortly.) This conception of an organism was stated clearly by Norman Horowitz, who later discovered that the idea was first formulated by the geneticist Hermann Muller in 1929. More explicitly:

> An organism is a structure that operates on the instructions encoded in a *genome* so as to mobilize energy and raw materials from its environment to maintain itself and, in general, to reproduce itself by producing other similar or identical organisms.

This definition emphasizes the central role of a substructure, the *genome*, which has two main functions:

- It encodes a *genetic program* that specifies the structure (and general mode of operation) of the whole organism, including its ability to reproduce.
- It *replicates*, or specifies the structure of a new replica of itself, so each of its offspring will have its own copy. However, occasional errors, called *mutations*, are sometimes made during replication, so some of the offspring may have mutated copies of the genome. Also, during sexual reproduction the genomes of two parents can recombine to produce offspring with distinctive genomes.

Because the genome is subject to mutations (and because of recombination of genomes during sexual reproduction), some of the offspring of any organism may be different from their parent(s) in a stable, heritable way. Some changes in heredity from generation to generation are inevitable, just because it is physically impossible for all the copies of a genome to be made without errors. And without such changes, organisms as we know them could not exist, because these changes underlie evolution. Thus we see that evolution and the entire Darwinian worldview emerge naturally from the very concept of an organism as a genetic structure.

Self-reproduction implies that an organism is carrying out metabolism, transforming materials from the environment into its own structure. This is true, and important. But we don't base our definition of an organism on it. In fact, it is the genetic conception that allows us to understand how the metabolic machinery could have come into existence through evolution.

heredity and structure

what is a genome?

A genome is the structure that carries *genetic information*. Information is the ineffable something we possess when we have specified one out of a number of possibilities. American telephone numbers could range from 000-000-0000 to 999-999-9999, 10^{10} possibilities. If I tell you that my phone number is 206-866-1234 (it isn't!), I have specified one of those sequences and have given you information. Genetic information takes the form of *genes*, which specify the structure (and operation) of the rest of the organism. We now know the nature of many genes, in many kinds of organisms, including humans. For a greater understanding of genes and genetics, it would be well to read *Genetics: A Beginner's Guide*, in this series but I'll briefly outline a few concepts here that are useful for understanding the role of genes in evolution.

The laws of heredity in the great majority of plants and animals were worked out around 1865 by Gregor Mendel, using pea plants. Mendel showed that genes (although this term was not invented until 1900) determine simple characteristics such as the color of the peas, whether the peas are smooth or wrinkled, the color of the flowers, and so on. Every plant (or seed) has two parents, and it receives equal sets of genes from them, so it has two copies of each gene. But many genes occur in two or more forms, called *alleles*; for instance, the gene that determines pea color has one allele that determines yellow pigment and another allele that determines green pigment. A pea that carries two identical alleles – we say it is *homozygous* – will have the color determined by those genes. However, if a pea carries two different alleles – we say it is *heterozygous* – then commonly the characteristic determined by one of them, the *dominant* allele, is visible, and the characteristic determined by the other, the *recessive* allele, is hidden. Thus, a pea that carries one allele for green color and one allele for yellow color will be yellow because the yellow allele is dominant and the green allele is recessive. (This is actually a very simple situation; there are other cases of incomplete dominance and situations in which several alleles of a single gene show complicated dominance and recessiveness relationships.)

Think about a homozygous pea plant with two alleles for yellow color compared with a heterozygous pea with one allele for each color. You can't tell the difference between them just by looking. They have different *genotypes* – different genetic constitutions – but they have the same *phenotype*: the same appearance. The difference between genotype and phenotype is critical in genetics.

When we think about human genes, we commonly think of genes associated with defects and diseases, such as sickle-cell anemia and cystic fibrosis. These conditions are generally determined by defective alleles that are recessive. Thus, many people may be heterozygous for such alleles and may never know it; we call them *carriers* for the disorders in question. However, if two people who are both carriers for, say, cystic fibrosis happen to marry and have children, they may produce a child that is homozygous for the defective allele and thus has the illness. Call the defective allele *c* and the normal allele *C*. The parents are both heterozygotes, *Cc*. Each of their eggs or sperm carries only one copy of this gene, either *C* or *c*. On the average, a quarter of their children will receive the *C* allele from both parents and will be normal, *CC*. Half of their children will receive a *C* from one parent and *c* from the other (notice that this can occur in two ways) and will be carriers, *Cc*, like their parents. And a quarter of their children will receive the *c* allele from both parents and will have cystic fibrosis. The alleles for any other gene will be inherited in the same pattern.

We now know that genes are arranged in *chromosomes*, which are long, threadlike structures in the nucleus of each cell. Each species has a characteristic set of chromosomes. For instance, humans normally have 46 chromosomes, forming 23 sets of *homologous* chromosomes; within each set, one chromosome has been inherited from the mother and one from the father. The total number of human genes is estimated to be in the range of 35,000–70,000, so each chromosome must carry many genes. Generally the two chromosomes in each set carry identical *sequences of genes*, but they commonly carry different *alleles* of many genes. In fact, every natural population harbors an enormous amount of genetic diversity – that is, many distinct alleles of many genes – and humans are no exception; so parents with diverse family histories will have many genetic differences, and their children will be similarly mixed.

To make better sense of this it is necessary to examine organisms at the chemical level, to explore the chemical structures of genes and some of the other materials that constitute the structures of organisms.

cells

All organisms are made of one or more distinct cells. A cell is a fundamental structural unit whose boundary is a surrounding *membrane*; this is a thin and very flexible sheet of molecules that keeps the cellular components inside and controls the movement of materials inward and outward. The simplest organisms are just single cells. Bacteria are very small, with dimensions of the order of one micrometer (μm, a millionth of a meter), mostly single cells with minimal internal structure; such cells, lacking the nucleus characteristic of most other organisms, are called *procaryotic*, and bacteria themselves are therefore *procaryotes*. The genome of each procaryotic cell is just one long chromosome, a ring-shaped molecule of DNA. The cells of plants, animals, fungi, and many tiny creatures observable in a drop of pond water are *eucaryotic*; their typical dimensions are of the order of 10–40 μm, and each one has a nucleus, a rather large spherical body that contains the chromosomes and thus most of the genes. The human body is made of about 100 trillion (10^{14}) cells. Each cell contains other characteristic structures, called *organelles*, such as mitochondria, small bodies that derive much of the energy from food molecules and store it in a usable form; mitochondria also contain a few genes. Other organelles are the factories where proteins are made, or they move materials from one place to another.

The biological world, incidentally, includes a multitude of complicated structures called *viruses*, which are quite distinct from organisms. Organisms are cellular; viruses are not (though some have a somewhat cellular appearance). A virus is basically a genome wrapped in some protective material, mostly protein, that parasitizes organisms. Viruses don't have their own apparatus for obtaining energy and manufacturing proteins, as cells do; a typical virus has an apparatus for invading a host cell, disabling (sometimes destroying) the cell's genome, and turning the cell into a little factory for replicating the viral genome and producing a lot of new viruses. The cell eventually ruptures, releasing all these viruses that can go on to find and invade other cells. Each type of virus is very specific in its choice of hosts; some of the best-known viruses, called bacteriophage or simply phage, grow in bacteria.

polymers

Cells are made mostly of large molecules (macromolecules). The molecular mass of a molecule is the sum of the masses of its constituent atoms; thus water, H_2O, has a molecular mass of 18: the sum of 16 for the oxygen atom plus 1 for each hydrogen atom. Chemists call the units of mass *amu*, for atomic mass units; biologists commonly call the units *daltons*, after the pioneering chemist John Dalton. A small molecule such as the sugar glucose ($C_6H_{12}O_6$) has a mass of 180 daltons; you can derive this number by adding up all the masses of these elements in the formula (carbon atoms have a mass of 12). On this scale, macromolecules are truly huge, with masses of many thousands of daltons. However, the structures of these huge molecules are actually quite simple, in spite of their size. Every macromolecule is a *polymer*, a molecule made by putting together many small molecules, or *monomers*. Generally, the monomers are assembled like beads on a string, making a very long molecule:

                    ... and so on.

Simple examples come from the world of plastic and rubber, which are human-made polymers. For instance, ethylene is a small molecule: $H_2C=CH_2$, where the double line shows two bonds between the carbon atoms instead of the usual single bond. Many ethylene molecules can be combined into long molecules of polyethylene, the plastic from which food wraps are made:

$$CH_2-CH_2-CH_2-CH_2-CH_2-CH_2-CH_2-CH_2-CH_2-CH_2-CH_2-CH_2-\ldots$$

and on and on for thousands of units. Similarly, substituting fluorine atoms, F, for the hydrogen atoms in these molecules, we would start with the monomer tetrafluoroethylene and produce the polymer teflon.

proteins

In plastics, all the monomers are identical. Some biological polymers have this structure. For instance, molecules of the sugar

glucose can be linked in chains in one way to make the polymer *cellulose*, the principal structure of wood, or they can be linked to one another in a subtly different way to make *starch*. However, the principal biological polymers are made with several distinct types of monomers, so the resulting polymers can be much more complex. Proteins – the molecules that perform most of the functions in an organism – have this structure, and they are the most complex biological molecules. Their monomers are amino acids, which look like this:

$$\text{H}_2\text{N-}\overset{\displaystyle \text{R}}{\underset{\displaystyle \text{H}}{\text{C}}}\text{-COOH}$$

The -NH$_2$ group is an amino group, and the -COOH group is an acid[1] group – hence, amino acids. The portion of the molecule denoted R varies and determines the particular amino acid; thus, the amino acid glycine has an H atom in this position, alanine has CH$_3$, and serine has CH$_2$OH. Then two amino acids can be linked through a peptide linkage like this:

Peptide
linkage

Notice that the linkage is made by removing a molecule of water: H from the amino group and OH from the acid group. The resulting molecule is called a *dipeptide*, because it has two monomers (*di-* = two). But since it has amino and acid groups at its ends, a third monomer can be linked by removing another water molecule to make a *tripeptide*. There is no limit to the number of amino acids that can be linked in this way, to make *polypeptides*; and a protein is one distinctive kind of polypeptide.

All proteins are constructed of twenty types of amino acids, with names such as glycine, alanine, serine, valine, glutamic acid, and tryptophan. This means that in constructing a polypeptide there are twenty choices for the first position and twenty for the second, so there are $20 \times 20 = 400$ possible dipeptides. Given another twenty choices for the third position, there are 8,000 possible tripeptides. Then there are 20^{100} possible sequences for a polypeptide of 100 amino acids – a relatively small protein. That number is inconceivably large. More typical proteins may be made of 300 amino acids, or even more. Every possible polypeptide has distinctive properties and might be a functional protein. Every kind of protein has a unique sequence; for instance, part of the human hemoglobin A molecule, the red substance that carries oxygen in our blood, begins with the sequence Val-His-Leu-Thr-Pro-Glu-Glu-Lys-Ser-Ala-Val-Thr-Ala-, using the three-letter abbreviations for the amino acids. Every molecule of hemoglobin A in a normal person has precisely this structure. Once a polypeptide chain has been made, it folds up into a particular shape and has the ability to perform a particular biological function. What are these functions? Proteins perform virtually all of the jobs needed to make an organism do the complicated things it does, such as:

- They are the *enzymes* that operate metabolism – that make all the chemical reactions in an organism occur rapidly and in a controlled way.
- They form prominent structures: keratins make hair, skin, and feathers, and collagen forms much of the substance of cartilage and bone.
- They form filaments that push and pull on one another to create movement in muscles and other movable structures, such as cilia and flagella.
- They are an important class of *hormones*, which carry signals between different kinds of cells in the body.
- They form *receptors*, which receive signals by binding to other molecules. A cell receives a signal from a hormone because the hormone molecules bind to one of its receptors. Receptors like those we use for tasting and smelling allow organisms to detect the presence of small molecules in their environment and respond to them.
- They are transporters that carry ions and small molecules across cell membranes, thus maintaining the right contents in each cell and also forming the basis of our nervous systems and organs such as kidneys.
- They are regulatory elements that control all kinds of processes so they occur at proper, coordinated rates.

So every organism consists of thousands of distinct proteins that perform all its functions, and having its own particular proteins makes each species the unique thing that it is.

One of the major activities of every cell is making its own set of proteins. Take away the water of a cell, which makes up most of its normal weight, and half or more of the remainder will be protein. So *growth primarily means protein synthesis.* Simple organisms such as bacteria may grow in the water and soil or on other organisms by taking in amino acids from their surroundings, or by synthesizing their own from other food molecules. The cells in our bodies make their proteins from amino acids circulating in the blood (derived from our food), or they synthesize their own amino acids from other molecules.[2] However, to make a particular protein, the cell must "know" its amino-acid sequence. Thus, every cell that is becoming a red blood cell must "know" to make hemoglobin molecules by making many proteins with the string Val-His-Leu-Thr-Pro-Glu-Glu-Lys-Ser-Ala-Val-Thr-Ala-…, rather than all the other possible strings. This requires *information, genetic* information. And the information for making a particular type of protein lies in the genes. *The function of a gene is to specify the amino-acid sequence of a particular protein.*

So we have replaced the vague idea of a Mendelian gene as a "thing" that is inherited regularly with the idea of a gene as a structure carrying the information for a protein. The next step, then, is to understand the structure of nucleic acids, the molecules that genes are made of.

nucleic acids

The second most abundant macromolecules in cells are polymers called polynucleotides or nucleic acids, whose monomers are *nucleotides.* A nucleotide is more complicated than an amino acid, as it consists of three smaller molecules: a *base* linked to a *sugar*[3] which is linked to a *phosphate* (PO_4).

A nucleic acid is named for its sugar; ribonucleic acid (RNA) contains ribose, and deoxyribonucleic acid (DNA) contains deoxyribose (ribose with one oxygen atom removed). The bases are large ring-shaped, nitrogenous molecules; DNA nucleotides have one of four bases: *adenine, guanine, cytosine* and *thymine* (A, G, C, and T); in RNA, *uracil* (U) replaces thymine.

Adenine   Guanine   Thymine   Cytosine   Uracil

Purines   Pyrimidines

Cytosine, thymine, and uracil are based on a single ring of atoms and are called *pyrimidines*; adenine and guanine have a double ring of atoms and are called *purines*. Notice that the carbon and nitrogen atoms in the rings are all numbered for reference; those of the sugar are numbered with prime marks, from 1' to 5'.

A nucleic acid is constructed by stringing nucleotides together by linking the phosphate of one to the sugar of the next:

5'–3' direction

This makes a "backbone" of sugar-phosphate-sugar-phosphate ..., on and on for thousands or even millions of units. The bases, you'll notice, extend to the side of the backbone. Notice, also, that the phosphate connects the 3' C atom of one sugar to the 5' C atom of the next, so the chain has a polarity: it runs 3'–5' in one direction, and we can talk about its ends as the 3' end and the 5' end.

It is now a commonplace of biology that the genomes of all organisms consist of DNA. (The genomes of many viruses consist of the very similar molecule RNA.) A DNA molecule, as determined by James D. Watson and Francis H. C. Crick in 1953, consists of two polynucleotide strands wound together to make a double helix

(Figure 3.1). The strands are held together in the middle by bonding between the bases from the two strands, but adenine can only bond to thymine and guanine only to cytosine:

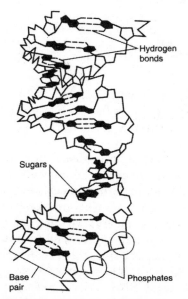

Thymine   **Adenine**

Cytosine   **Guanine**

These base-pairs are held together by weak attractions called *hydrogen bonds*, in which two somewhat negative atoms such as O and N hold a somewhat positive H atom between them. We say that two bases that

Figure 3.1 *A DNA molecule consists of two polynucleotide strands held together by hydrogen bonding between their complementary bases.*

can bond this way are *complementary* to each other, in the way that a hand is complementary to a glove or that the curve of one jigsaw-puzzle piece is complementary to the curve of the piece it fits with.

Complementary base-pairing accounts for virtually everything in heredity, and for much of biology in general. It means, first, that a DNA molecule can easily replicate – that is, it can produce two molecules that are replicas of each other. This must happen every time a cell divides in two, because each daughter cell must have its own genome – its own complement of chromosomes. DNA is replicated by a complex of enzymes (called DNA polymerase) that move along the molecule, separating it into its single strands. The cell contains many nucleotides, which it synthesizes as part of its metabolic activities, and these nucleotides bind to the components of the DNA strands. Thus, where a strand has an A base, it will bond to a T; where it has a C, it will bond to a G; and so on. The enzyme complex links these fresh nucleotides, one by one, into a new strand that is complementary to the existing strand, so when it has moved the length of the DNA molecule it will have produced a new complementary strand and thus a new double-stranded molecule.

Now, just how does a gene specify the structure of a protein?[4] The essential point is that the sequence of bases in each gene creates a *genetic code* that specifies a sequence of amino acids. Each sequence of three bases in the gene constitutes a *codon*, which specifies one of the twenty amino acids. There are sixty-four of these triplets; three of them are stop signals, which mark the end of a gene. The meanings of the other sixty-one are now well known. Thus, the codons TTT and TTC both mean "phenylalanine," all four triplets that start with GG mean "glycine," and so on.

The details of protein synthesis needn't concern us here, but it occurs in two stages. First, a complicated enzyme (called RNA polymerase) moves along one gene in the DNA; this enzyme recognizes genes because each one is marked by distinctive base sequences at both ends. As it moves, the RNA polymerase synthesizes a strand of *messenger RNA* that is complementary to one strand of the DNA, essentially the way a DNA polymerase makes a new strand of DNA during DNA replication. Second, this messenger RNA attaches to a large particle (made of protein and RNA molecules) called a *ribosome*, a factory that makes new proteins. The cell is also rich in amino acids, and they are attached to molecules called *transfer RNAs*. Each transfer RNA recognizes one codon on the messenger RNA and brings the proper amino to this position where the messenger RNA is attached to the ribosome. Then one by one these amino acids are linked into a polypeptide, by enzymes in the ribosome, until an entire new protein molecule has been made. Its amino acid sequence will be the sequence of codons in the gene.

This explanation, stripped of many subtleties and details, should provide a picture of how the genetic apparatus of cells, and organisms, operates. A large organism such as a human or an oak tree operates through the coordinated actions of its individual cells – and its organs, such as the heart, brain, and liver in a human. In turn, these cells and organs operate by virtue of their component proteins, and each cell makes its complex of proteins by reading the instructions in its genes. For now, we will ignore the much more complicated question of how a blood cell "knows" to make one group of proteins, a brain cell "knows" to make another, and a liver cell "knows" to make still another. This is a topic for chapter seven, where we'll explore this problem as a prelude to exploring how complicated creatures, like animals, can evolve into so many different forms.

evolution

historicity: carrying your story with you

Every organism has become what it is through a long evolutionary process in which its ancestors were shaped, generation after generation, by the forces we explore in this book. It has a unique combination of genes and is thus a unique historical object.

History is shaped by a unique series of happenstances. If any of them had been a little different, the world we live in would be different. What if a little twelfth-century Mongol boy, Temujin, had been a shy lad instead of the aggressive, ambitious leader who became Genghis Khan? What if King George III of England and his Parliament had recognized the true value of the American colonies and had not provoked them into revolution? What if John F. Kennedy had not gone to Dallas in November 1963? What if ...?

It is important always to consider evolution in such a historical light. There are no natural forces driving organisms to have any particular characteristics; they just have whatever features they were able to acquire that allowed them to survive. Why, for instance, do we have five digits on our hands and feet instead of four or six? Because the ancestral amphibians that first adapted to the land just happened to have the genes to produce five, that's all. In particular, we will see that most species have become extinct after, at most, a few million years of existence, presumably because they were unable to adapt to changing conditions. We are tempted then to ask, "Why didn't this species acquire the particular genes needed to adapt and survive?" The only answer will be, "Because the right combination of genetic events simply didn't happen." Writing about human evolution, Elaine Morgan has pointed out how we are inclined to imagine that all the modifications and adaptations that might be nice to have for survival could simply be ordered from some celestial mail-order catalogue. But, of course, this is mere fantasy and sloppy thinking, and it is important not to fall into this trap.

Some of the large, elaborately illustrated books listed under Further Reading narrate the full story of evolution on Earth over the past few billion years, sometimes with color paintings to show what the world must have looked like at various times. The following brief summary will provide some guidelines about the general course of evolution and the time at which major events occurred.

origins

It would be logical to begin with the origin of life. However, this is really a different topic from evolution in general, and I don't want to dwell on it, although many people will consider it the most critical, and controversial, event in evolution. The trouble is that in dealing with the beginnings of organisms on Earth we are reduced to a great deal of speculation – well-founded, scientific speculation, but speculation nevertheless. There is no fossil record of the earliest events; there cannot be, because the earliest things that were on their way to becoming real organisms were simply collections of organic molecules that disappeared completely.

Scientists thinking about the origin of life once assumed that the Earth's atmosphere has always been much as it is now. But in the 1930s the Russian biologist A. I. Oparin pointed out that molecular oxygen in the atmosphere would have attacked and oxidized any simple organic compounds that might have formed, so the primitive Earth must have had a reducing atmosphere, made mostly of hydrogen, methane, ammonia, nitrogen, and water. Molecular oxygen must have been scarce. Building on the previous work of J. B. S. Haldane, Oparin proposed that the energy of ultraviolet light and lightning discharges could have turned the gases in the hypothetical reducing atmosphere into a "primordial soup" of organic molecules.

In 1953 Stanley Miller tested the Haldane–Oparin hypothesis while he was a graduate student in Harold Urey's laboratory. He constructed an apparatus that simulated the hypothetical primitive conditions, complete with electrical sparks to simulate lightning. To his great delight, Miller found that the mixture in his apparatus formed a variety of organic compounds, including some of the common amino acids, the building blocks of proteins, as well as fatty acids, the purine and pyrimidine bases of nucleic acids, and other substances important in metabolism. Other investigators have shown that the monomers of proteins and nucleic acids can polymerize rather easily into the gigantic molecules so critical for a functioning organism. In fact, polymerization might be enhanced by environmental features, such as certain clay minerals that can hold monomers on their surface at the right spacing for polymerization.

Since lipids such as fatty acids are produced in primitive reaction mixtures, and since lipids and proteins assemble easily into membrane structures, there is little difficulty in seeing how primitive cells could form, since a cell is fundamentally a unit enclosed by a membrane. Here we have the beginnings of a fossil record for guidance, because the record in the Onverwacht sediments of South Africa, and some other localities, shows that simple cells already existed at least 3.4 billion years ago. These cells were procaryotes, some similar to our modern types. Excellent procaryotic fossils are found in rocks from that age up to 2 billion years ago in the Gunflint iron formation of Ontario.

However, the most critical feature of an organism is its genome. Without it, there can be no biological evolution, since evolution depends on the selection of individuals with variant genomes. So primitive biological systems could not have been shaped by natural selection unless they were specified by a genome. Although nucleic acid molecules do not form in primitive mixtures as easily as proteins do, they have been produced under simulated primitive conditions, and at least small polynucleotides must have formed on the primitive Earth along with other organic compounds.

A genome directs the synthesis of proteins. The greatest difficulty in understanding the origin of functioning organisms is to understand how nucleic acids could get *control* over protein structure and come to specify that structure. The best answer lies in the hypothesis that the first functional nucleic acids were RNA molecules, so for a considerable time there was an "RNA world," a critical stage in evolution. RNA molecules have an inherent ability to interact with one another through base-pairing, so they can replicate as DNA does. They can also fold up into complicated forms and act as *ribozymes* – that is, RNA molecules that catalyze chemical reactions just as protein enzymes do. Without going into all the molecular details, we can draw plausible scenarios of the interactions between various kinds of primitive RNA molecules. Some, having structures most conducive to self-replication, must have acted as primitive genomes; others acted as ribozymes to perform the steps of protein synthesis, lining up along the genomes (as transfer RNA molecules still do) to align amino acids and polymerize them into proteins. The evolution of these primitive systems into efficient systems of the modern type must have been a long, slow process, and several hundred million years were required for the first functioning cells to appear, a time at least as long as the entire time multicellular organisms such as plants and animals have been evolving.

early cellular evolution

The earliest procaryotic cells evolved into a great variety, many of which are still with us. Some, known as Archaea, have unusual structures and metabolic features that set them aside from all other known organisms; they mostly persist today in very unusual environments, such as very hot springs or places with high concentrations of salt or sulfur. Others evolved into a variety of bacteria. Metabolically, the first cells probably lived by consuming organic molecules in their environment, but after a time the first *autotrophs* appeared – organisms that can make all their components from CO_2 and other simple substances (*auto-* = self, *-trophy* = a mode of nourishment). Among the most important modern autotrophs are the *phototrophs* (*photo-* = light), those that, like plants, get their energy from light through photosynthesis – as the name says, a light-driven synthesis. Surely some phototrophic bacteria evolved early on, and the first of these did not produce oxygen as a by-product, as plants and most other phototrophs do today; many contemporary photo-trophic bacteria carry out a different kind of metabolism. But eventually oxygen-producing phototrophs did evolve; geological evidence shows that they first appeared around 2.7 billion years ago, and they changed the atmosphere over to the present oxygen-rich atmosphere by around 2 billion years ago (perhaps with a later spurt of oxygen production after 1 billion years ago). That change in the atmosphere is recorded in part in geologic formations called Banded Iron Formations, rocks in which atmospheric oxygen combined with iron to form layers of red oxides. The significance of this atmospheric changeover lies primarily in the opportunity it afforded for future evolution; organisms could then arise that carried out a complete respiration, using oxygen – a process that yields energy quite efficiently and allows complex, active creatures such as animals to function.

Plants and animals are eucaryotes, with cells containing nuclei as well as mitochondria, the places where oxygen-based respiration is carried out. Eucaryotic phototrophs have chloroplasts, the rather similar structures that perform photosynthesis. Both mitochondria and chloroplasts have their own small DNA molecules that encode some of their proteins. From this fact and other clues, it has become clear that both mitochondria and chloroplasts arose from primitive bacteria, which were incorporated into other primitive cells through a process of endosymbiosis; symbiosis is a common ecological arrangement in which two types of organisms live together intimately, each performing functions that benefit them both. Lichens, for instance, are symbiotic associations between fungi and algae. In *endo*symbiosis, one organism lives inside the other, and there are good examples of this among living organisms. At some times in the remote past (and in quite separate events), an oxygen-respiring bacterium became incorporated into some other cell and became the first mitochondrion; and an oxygen-producing phototroph became incorporated into some other cell and became the first chloroplast. In fact, since there are now phototrophs with different types of chloroplasts, this endosymbiosis apparently happened a few different times with different types of cells. Fossils in beds such as the Bitter Springs formation in Australia show that eucaryotic algae existed by 1 billion years ago, and there is evidence for eucaryotes even 2 billion years ago, perhaps even earlier. Certainly a variety of simple eucaryotes – protozoa and algae – were living by 700 million years ago; the first complex, multicellular organisms appeared at about the same time.

animal evolution

Near Ediacara, in southern Australia, lie beds of sandstone containing a remarkable series of fossils that have been the subject of considerable speculation and controversy. The creatures preserved there – and in sediments of the same age elsewhere, defining the Ediacaran period – are surely animals, but they resemble no animals found at any later times. They apparently represent a first evolutionary experiment with complex creatures, one that failed as all its members became extinct.[5] It took another 100 million years, until the middle of the Cambrian period, for the first successful early animals to appear, all in quite a short time in the so-called Cambrian Explosion. Here we find members of the principal invertebrate animal groups, especially sponges, molluscs, brachiopods, echinoderms, and arthropods such as trilobites and eurypterids. During the following Ordovician period, the diversity of invertebrates increased enormously. The first animals to occupy land habitats, scorpions and insects, appeared during the Silurian and became dominant during the Carboniferous. The first fishes, initially those without jaws, appeared in the Silurian and became widespread and diverse in the Devonian. Among these fishes were Crossopterygians, the first to develop lungs; most fishes breathe through their gills, which absorb dissolved oxygen from the surrounding water. One requirement of living on land is an organ that can remove oxygen from the air, and the Crossopterygian lung allowed one line of their descendants, the Labyrinthodonts, to become the first amphibians, during late Devonian and especially Carboniferous times. In spite of their ability to breathe air, amphibians have never become dominant, as they evolved only some of the adaptations required for living on land; modern amphibians are confined to wet habitats and still use water for reproduction. A life more independent of the water only came about with the reptiles and the evolution of the *amniotic egg*, an egg enclosed by a shell in which a developing embryo remains surrounded by water. The stem reptiles, called Cotylosaurs, appeared during the Permian period, toward the end of the Paleozoic era. The Permian ended in a still-unexplained event, a massive extinction that wiped out over 90 per cent of all existing species.

With the Triassic period, following the Permian, the reptiles underwent a massive diversification into the few types that still survive (turtles, snakes, lizards, crocodilians), and during the following Jurassic and Cretaceous periods, land habitats were dominated by the dinosaurs that have so captured the popular imagination. The dinosaurs belonged to two large groups, ornithischians and saurischians, differing primarily on the anatomy of their hips. The first mammals also appeared during the Jurassic, and around the same time, one small line of saurischian dinosaurs, the theropods, had produced the first birds; but both mammals and birds remained relatively obscure as long as the ecological niches they could use remained occupied by reptiles. Finally, at the end of the Cretaceous, another massive extinction occurred, ending the era of dominance by dinosaurs and ushering in the Cenozoic era. During early Cenozoic times, the mammals underwent another massive diversification into virtually all the orders that survive today, plus a few that have become extinct. Similarly, birds of the modern type also became much more diverse, leading eventually to today's vertebrate fauna. One branch of the mammalian tree eventually produced humans, as detailed in chapter eight.

plant evolution

Animals are ecologically dependent on algae and plants, which were undergoing a similar evolution and diversification during this entire time. During late Cambrian times, some green algae evolved into much larger multicellular forms (dasyclads and codiums) with complex reproductive structures. This evolution of both red and green algae continued into Silurian and Devonian times, where we find plants now known as stoneworts or brittleworts with a whorled arrangement of branches that begin to resemble land plants. The first fossils of fungi also appear in Devonian rocks. (It is worth noting that although fungi resemble plants and were once classified with them, recent genetic evidence shows that fungi and animals are really closely related.) All these plants were aquatic. Plants that could occupy niches on land required the evolution of certain essential adaptations, especially *vascular tissues* consisting of tubes that transport water and nutrients; most critical is the *xylem* that moves water upward from roots into the rest of the plant. It happens, also, that xylem tissue consists of heavily walled cells that can support a plant growing up out of the ground, culminating in the development of very strong woody tissues characteristic of trees. The first vascular plants, rhynias, appeared in the late Silurian and became much more diverse during the Devonian. The Devonian was a time of great plant diversification; here the first lycopods (club mosses) and the first horsetails appeared, along with plants named *Psilophyton*, with a main axis that produced side branches; these were probably the ancestors of all the later, more dominant groups, including ferns and progymnosperms, from which the later seed plants all evolved. First, however, the lycopods and horsetails had their heyday during the Carboniferous (Mississippian and Pennsylvanian); the extensive fossils of this time show lush forests dominated by huge trees of both kinds, and these buried forests later turned into some of the large beds of coal and oil that we now extract for most of our energy needs.

A second plant adaptation needed for complete dominance of the land was a method of reproduction independent of water; the earlier-evolved plants generally depend on an aquatic stage in which reproductive cells can swim from one plant to another to effect fertilization. Independence of the water was achieved through the evolution of *pollen*, to carry sperm, and *seeds*, to enclose the developing embryo plant in a nutritious, protected environment. The first seed plants belonged to three groups that also appeared during the Carboniferous. The seed ferns (pteridosperms) reached 12–15 feet in height and lasted into the Jurassic; the cordaites were trees 50–100 feet tall with strap-shaped leaves; and the conifers became the familiar pines, firs, spruces, and their relatives that we still have today. Finally, the angiosperms, the flowering plants, appeared in the late Cretaceous and evolved during the Cenozoic era into the plants that dominate today's landscape.

summary and foreword

We have now developed the following general biological picture. All organisms live and grow in communities with other kinds of organisms, and through their various activities they get nutrients from their environment, which they use to grow and reproduce. They can carry out these activities because each organism contains a distinctive genome, a collection of nucleic acid molecules that contain genes. Most genes carry the information for synthesizing specific proteins, and an organism needs many distinct kinds of proteins to perform its various functions. One function of the genome is to replicate, to make more copies of itself so the next generation of organisms can have their own genomes; during the processes of replication and reproduction, organisms sometimes inherit genomes containing errors (mutations) and new combinations of genes.

To anticipate what is coming, evolution emerges naturally from this picture. In general, reproduction is so successful that each generation produces far more offspring than can possibly survive. Remember that all this activity is going on within ecosystems in which every organism has to fit into some way of making a living, what we call its ecological niche, and because of the little variations in their genomes, some individuals will be better at doing this than others. Then these better-adapted individuals will naturally be selected as the parents of the next generation, which will inherit the features that made their parents better adapted. Through this and other processes, and because of natural environmental changes, organisms will tend to diverge from one another and to acquire new characteristics. In other words, they will tend to evolve. Now we will see in more detail how this happens.

notes

1. An acid is a compound that can liberate a hydrogen ion H^+, and the H of -COOH comes off as an ion, leaving a negatively charged $-COO^-$ behind.
2. Of the twenty amino acids used to make proteins, eight (called "essential" amino acids) cannot be synthesized by most animals, so they must be obtained in the diet. Plants and simpler organisms can make all twenty. But this fact has no particular significance for genetics or evolution.
3. I won't try to define a sugar formally, but it is a molecule with several -OH groups, and you can always tell a sugar by its name, which always ends in -*ose*.
4. Some genes specify the structures of certain RNA molecules that form the apparatus for synthesizing proteins.
5. This issue is discussed at length in Gould's *Wonderful Life*, especially in sections of Chapter 7.

a broad view of the process

One of the themes we will develop in this book is a kind of truism that every biologist recognizes: that biology only makes sense if you see that organisms have acquired their forms and functions through evolution. Beyond that lies an additional truism: that evolution only makes sense if you see it ecologically. That is, we have to see every type of organism as being suited for a particular role in an ecosystem. In the metaphor of the noted ecologist G. Evelyn Hutchinson, the drama of evolution is played out in the theatre of the ecosystem; so at the risk of straining the metaphor, each species has a particular role in the drama. The result of natural selection is *adaptation*: each kind of organism becomes shaped for one particular way of life in one environment, and that way of life is called its *ecological niche*. The terms *niche, adaptation,* and *selection* are interrelated; a niche is the particular place and way of life that each species occupies, adaptation is the evolutionary process by which it is shaped to live in that way, and the shaping occurs through selection of genetic differences. Our first task, in this chapter, will be to take a broad look at how evolution has proceeded. Then we will amplify the idea of natural selection and flesh out the idea of the ecological theatre in which all this happens.

the major features of evolution

the modern synthesis

Although Charles Darwin had laid out the essential ideas of evolution, with the emphasis on natural selection, he was unable to flesh out the idea satisfactorily because of the primitive state of biology in his time, especially the general ignorance of heredity. Ironically, Darwin's contemporary Gregor Mendel – unknown and unrecognized – was doing experiments in his modest Czech monastery that would lay the foundation for genetics, but his work did not become widely known until 1900. Meanwhile, Darwin struggled to make sense of natural selection with the burden of misconceptions about heredity. When genetics finally became a science in the early twentieth century, some geneticists with a mathematical bent were able to start understanding how genes behave in populations, the realm in which evolution actually occurs; the names of R. A. Fisher, J. B. S. Haldane, and Sewall Wright stand out. Then in the 1930s, the Russian geneticist Theodosius Dobzhansky began to investigate the behavior of genes in populations experimentally, and by 1937 he was able to start summarizing the bearing of population genetics on evolution in his pioneering book *Genetics and the Origin of Species*. Meanwhile, Ernst Mayr, a young ornithologist who had been studying birds in the South Pacific, began to formulate his ideas about the ways new species arise, which he summarized in his book *Systematics and the Origin of Species* (1942). Paleontology, too, had been growing in sophistication, providing more detailed pictures of the actual evolution of particular groups of organisms, and biogeography, the science of the geographic distribution of organisms, was developing insights important for understanding evolution. Thus, a modern conception of the evolutionary process was developing, and it was summarized by Julian Huxley (grandson of Darwin's colleague Thomas Henry Huxley) in his edited volume *The New Systematics* (1940) and in *Evolution, The Modern Synthesis* (1942). Though our understanding of evolution has grown enormously since that time, most of the conceptions of the modern synthesis remain intact and form the foundation for current evolutionary thought.

what is a species?

Darwin's seminal work was entitled *On the Origin of Species*, and several later books have used the same phrase. This naturally raises the critical question, "What is a species?" Because the question is more complicated than it might seem to be, I want to take the answer in steps, especially in chapter six, but it deserves a preliminary answer here. Naively, a species is simply a "kind" of organism, with the obvious proviso that males and females and young (and various odd larval and intermediate stages) are all members of the same species, even though they may look quite different. (So a species may take on a cycle of forms during each generation, as the cycle of a butterfly species from egg to caterpillar to pupa to winged adult.) Some good concrete examples of species come from birds. Everyone knows at least a little about birds, and many people enjoy watching and identifying them. But bird-watchers are often confronted with some knotty problems.

Figure 4.1 shows birds called chickadees in North America and tits in Europe. An American birder could see Black-capped, Carolina, Boreal, Chestnut-backed, Mountain, Mexican, or Gray-headed Chickadees by traveling around the continent. The American Ornithologists' Union (AOU), which keeps the official list, has determined that they are all distinct species. But why? And how can you tell what species an individual belongs to?

The answer to the first question is twofold. Initially, a species is defined *morphologically* – by its visible structural features (*morph* = form). Each of these species consists of adult birds with a distinctive size, shape, and coloration, so an observer can generally assign a bird to one group. However, morphology alone is often not adequate, and a better answer is, "Because each species consists of individuals that only breed with one another, not with members of the other species." The best general definition, according to the so-called *biological species concept* (BSC), is that a species is a group of all the individuals that are actually or potentially able to breed with one another but are reproductively isolated from other such groups. However, we will have to consider this definition at length later.

Placing an individual in one species or another on the basis of morphology is generally easy. A birder in Western North America can usually recognize the rich, rusty-brown plumage of a Chestnut-backed Chickadee or see the distinctive line through the eye of a

CHESTNUT-
BACKED
CHICKADEE

BLACK-CAPPED
CHICKADEE

MEXICAN
CHICKADEE

MOUNTAIN
CHICKADEE

BOREAL
CHICKADEE

GRAY-HEADED CHICKADEE

Figure 4.1 *Several species of chickadees, which are distinguished from one another primarily by their morphology. (Plates from* A Field Guide to Western Birds, *2nd ed. © 1990 by Roger Tory Peterson. Reproduced by permission of Houghton Mifflin Company. All rights reserved.)*

Mountain Chickadee. But someone in the mountains of Arizona will sometimes encounter Mexican Chickadees, and it takes some care and sharp observation to see their distinguishing features. Similarly, a birder in the Eastern United States can be reasonably confident that the birds in the northern region are Black-capped Chickadees and those in the south are the slightly smaller Carolina. But anyone observing birds in a middle region, roughly from Missouri through Pennsylvania, has to look sharp at any chickadee, because the two species differ primarily in the amount of white in the wings, but this feature is quite variable; expert birders with good ears tend to rely more on distinctions between the birds' call notes and songs. To make the situation even more confusing, experts agree that the two species hybridize to some extent where their ranges overlap, so one may see intermediate birds.

What can this talk of hybrids and intermediates mean? The very definition of a species depends on the birds breeding only with their own kind and *not* hybridizing! Is there something wrong with the definition, or with these particular "species," or both? Well, some biologists will argue that the definition, based on patterns of breeding and reproduction, is at fault, and they have sought alternatives. We will revisit the issue in chapter six.

a big picture: the major features of evolution

Biologists customarily divide the processes of evolution into three broad categories. *Microevolution* refers to changes that occur within a single species. *Speciation* means division of one species into two or more. And *macroevolution* refers to the larger changes in the variety of organisms that we see in the fossil record. We will begin with an overview of evolution as a whole.

Fossils provide a record of the organisms that were living at each time in the past. A century ago, before many fossils had been discovered and the fossil record was relatively sparse, biologists were sometimes misled into thinking that evolution takes the form of simple, straight-line changes in each group of organisms (a pattern they called orthogenesis). They thought, for instance, that horses have changed steadily from *Hyracotherium* of Eocene times, around 60 million years (Myr) ago, a little, three-toed creature about the size of a small dog, into the big, one-toed modern horse, *Equus*. In fact, the many fossil horses that have been discovered show that horse evolution followed a much more complicated, more haphazard course (Figure 4.2). "Phylogeny" means an account of the history of a species and how one has changed into others, so this representation is a *phylogenetic tree*. It shows four kinds of events. First, one species – one line in the tree – often divides into two or more species, representing the process of speciation. Second, most species lines eventually end in *extinction*, the death of the species. Third, a lack of change in a species, or *stasis*, is no evolution at all, and is represented by lines that continue straight on until they branch or end. Fourth, a line may change gradually in one direction, indicating what has been called *phyletic evolution*, a consistent change in morphology such as a gradual increase in size or a gradual change in the shape of a body part. But does phyletic evolution actually happen?

Only a few years ago, we would have drawn typical phylogenetic trees with the lines moving gradually to the left or right, to denote phyletic evolution. The view that such gradualism is the typical pattern of evolution was one feature of the modern synthesis. However, Steven M. Stanley, summarizing a vast amount of evidence, has

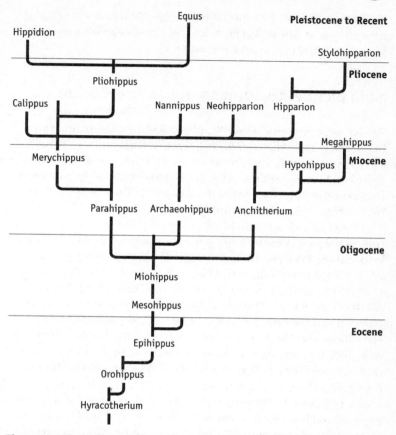

Figure 4.2 *The evolution of horses is shown by a phylogenetic tree. The origins of new species (designated by their generic names) are shown as abrupt transitions on the geological time-scale, although each event may have taken several thousand years. Where two or more events are shown as occurring simultaneously, the events actually may have been separated by millions of years.*

shown that evolution is realistically portrayed by a different pattern; species appear to change little, or not at all, during their lifetimes, with change arising primarily through a series of speciations. Each speciation event occurs quite rapidly in geological terms, so rapidly that it has sometimes been called "quantum speciation," on analogy with the "quantum jumps" that occur in atoms and molecules when electrons move instantaneously from one energy level to another. Rapid speciation was inherent in the speciation models developed by Mayr, and the emphasis on this mode of evolution was stimulated in large part by the work around 1972 of two paleontologists, Niles Eldredge and Stephen Jay Gould, who called this pattern "punctuated equilibrium."

Perhaps because we see little change in the natural world during our lifetimes, we tend to think that natural selection continually shapes each species so it successfully weathers the stresses of life, remains well adapted to its particular niche, and is always becoming better adapted. This is an optimistic view. A realistic view of evolution is more pessimistic, because the dominant feature of evolution is not success but extinction. There is no guarantee that a population will be able to adapt to environmental demands, and few species seem to be successful for long, on the geological time-scale. Where the geological record is very good, it shows that a typical species lasts for a few hundred thousand to a few million years and then disappears, often after a new species has arisen from it. The paleontologist George Gaylord Simpson estimated that 99.9 per cent of all species that ever lived have become extinct. The few million species of contemporary organisms are the remnants of a few billion species that have lived in the past. Among multicellular organisms, the few species and genera that have endured for very long times, perhaps 300–400 million years, live in the depths of the oceans where conditions change much more slowly than they do elsewhere.

Human interference has caused the extinction of many species, sometimes quickly. One of the burdens of guilt our species must bear is the history of destroying abundant, well-adapted species, such as the Passenger Pigeon of North America, out of sheer greed or perhaps ignorant carelessness. Many species of animals have been exterminated on islands, sometimes by rats, dogs, or pigs introduced accidentally or intentionally. Other species have been eliminated because they had very specialized niche requirements and lacked the genetic potential to adapt to changes humans imposed on the environment. The ornithologist James Fisher estimated that in the West Indies the average bird species had a lifetime of 180,000 years before human intervention. This was reduced to 30,000 years by the aboriginal natives and to only 12,000 years since European colonization in the seventeenth century. In spite of efforts to keep humans from destroying the natural world, the sad fact is that we must expect many more species to become extinct.

converging and diverging

Phylogenetic trees generally show diversity and divergence. We call them "trees," after all. Trees grow from a single base and diverge into smaller branches that spread widely. Similarly, a phylogenetic tree shows how the descendants of one type of organism have branched out and evolved into diverse forms. This is the pattern we would expect, because evolution depends upon accidental, unpredictable events: mutation and other random changes in genomes, coupled with selection for adaptation to diverse habitats. Though it is not impossible for organisms to reverse their evolutionary history and take on the form of an ancestor, it is highly unlikely because they are

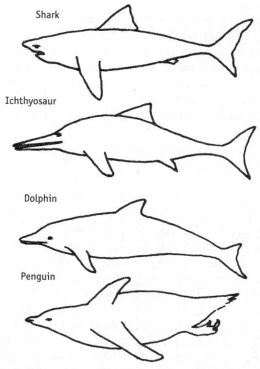

Figure 4.3 *Sharks, ichthyosaurs, dolphins, and penguins have all acquired similar forms through convergent evolution, even though their ancestors were quite diverse.*

responding to current environmental pressures and their genomes are experiencing new, unique mutations. So the general course of evolution will be divergence from ancestral forms, rather than reversion to them. (The apparent lack of reversals in evolution was once called Dollo's Law, but it really isn't a law of nature in the physical sense.) Sometimes that divergence leads to "degenerate" forms, to organisms that are simpler in structure than their ancestors – parasites, perhaps. But this isn't a reversal of evolution.

In one kind of contrast to divergent evolution, species that evolve into similar ways of life commonly develop similar forms, even though they come from quite different ancestors. This pattern of *convergent evolution* is exemplified by the similar forms of some streamlined swimming vertebrates (Figure 4.3). The ancestors of these animals were quite diverse: a primitive fish, a four-legged land reptile, a terrestrial bird, and a four-legged land mammal – yet the aquatic animals look very much alike. Their internal structures, however, have not become very similar. Figure 4.4 shows the wing structures of three flying vertebrates; they are independent responses to the same opportunity – to occupy niches involving flight – and in spite of similar outward appearance, each one emphasizes quite different bones of the vertebrate limb. For this reason, these wings are only partly homologous, and the differences among them are one character that distinguishes the three groups of animals.

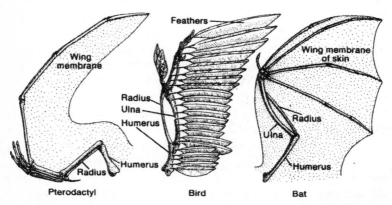

Figure 4.4 *Pterosaurs, birds, and bats have evolved wings with similar forms through the transformation of different bony elements.*

taxonomy, cladistics, and drawing family trees

We draw phylogenetic trees on the basis of the fossil record and comparative anatomy. Species with the most similar anatomical features are deemed most closely related. We now ascribe similarities to evolutionary relatedness; although early naturalists didn't think in evolutionary terms, they used their observations of similarities to create classifications, culminating in the work of Linnaeus, who originated the system of classification we still use. In classical taxonomy, or systematics, species that are very similar are combined in a single genus. Similar genera form a single family, similar families an order, and so on up the hierarchy to classes, phyla (singular, phylum), and kingdoms. Each of these categories – species, genus, family, phylum, and so on – is called a *taxon* (plural, *taxa*). To create complicated classifications, we can make other taxa with prefixes such as sub- and super-, and by adding other intermediate levels. An order, for instance, may be divided into a number of suborders and these into superfamilies. A family may be divided into subfamilies, and sometimes subfamilies are divided into tribes.

In modern taxonomy, classifications are intended to show not mere structural similarities, which might be due to some convergent evolution, but to reflect phylogenies. For this reason, taxonomists turn more and more to modern tools, especially to analysis of DNA, for more sensitive indications of relatedness among species. It has now become so easy to sequence DNA, using computerized instruments that can read long sequences automatically, that we are accumulating huge databases that can be used to establish phylogenies. Computer programs can turn a set of sequence data into trees reflecting the most likely chain of speciation events. And sometimes quite unique sequences appear that leave no ambiguity about events of the past; for instance, Sandra Baldauf and Jeffrey Palmer discovered that fungi and animals share a unique sequence of twelve amino acids in a certain protein, and in combination with other sequence data, this shows clearly that the two kingdoms are closely related. Other chemical markers of phylogenetic value include complex metabolic mechanisms that could only have evolved one time, thus uniting all the organisms that possess them; for example, two quite different pathways for synthesizing the amino acid lysine are known, and the diverse organisms that share the rarer of the two pathways surely derived from some common ancient ancestor.

We now tend to draw phylogenetic trees by using a method called *cladistics*, which was introduced by the German taxonomist Willi Hennig in 1950 and has become increasingly influential. It is based on the simple idea that as different species arise during the course of evolution, they acquire novel features at distinct times. Then we can use these features to infer the sequence of changes that has led to the various species, and on this basis we can classify them more rationally. A single branch of a tree drawn in this manner is a *clade*; it consists of all the organisms that arise from a single ancestral species. Then a simple family tree, or cladogram, can show the clades that arise from each evolutionary innovation. A cladogram of the chordates makes a good example (Figure 4.5). Chordates are animals that all have a rod of cartilage, the notochord, along the center of the back. The animals that have only this structure are rather obscure marine creatures. In all other chordates, the vertebrates, a notochord only appears early in embryonic development and is replaced by a backbone (vertebral column) made of separate vertebrae. All of the fishes have this feature. Then sometime later, the first species arose with four functioning leglike appendages, and these are the tetrapods (*tetra* = four, *pod* = foot). Later some species of amphibian became the first reptile by evolving an amniotic egg, an egg like that of a chicken with membranes enclosing an embryo in a watery environment. Later, in separate events, birds and mammals arose from certain reptiles.

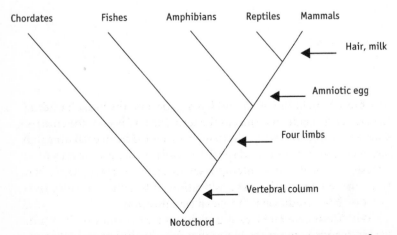

Figure 4.5 *A simple cladogram of the chordates, showing the appearance of some distinctive features of each group.*

Cladistics depends on distinguishing primitive from derived characteristics. Every evolutionary lineage must have started with some ancient species that had certain primitive characteristics that all its descendants retain. Having a backbone, for instance, is a *shared primitive characteristic* that defines the vertebrates as a group. As vertebrates evolved, they diverged into several distinctive groups that are defined by *shared derived characteristics.* Mammals share the characteristics of hairy skins, three small bones in the middle ear, and milk production by females. Birds share the characteristics of feathered skins, light hollow bones, and forelimbs modified into wings. It isn't always easy, though, to distinguish primitive from derived characteristics. Embryological development can often be useful; here, again, we see a structure like a notochord in an early-stage vertebrate embryo being replaced by a backbone. Fossils may also be very important clues, since they show the characteristics of ancestral organisms.

Let's take a simple case. Suppose species A, B, C, and D are closely related; but A and B share derived characteristic 1, which C and D don't share, and A, B, and C share another characteristic 2, which they don't share with species D. Then we may infer that a branch of the phylogenetic tree leading to A and B diverged from the branch leading to C; so A and B must have had a common ancestor, E, in which characteristic 1 first appeared. Similarly, there must have been another ancestor, F, from which A, B, and C were derived. We can now draw a partial cladogram.

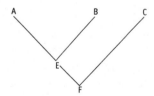

The branch including A, B, and E is a clade, and the branch leading to C is a *sister* clade to it (just as the term "sister" is used for entities such as chromosomes or cells that have divided from each other). A larger cladogram could add species D and postulate a common ancestor, G, of all four contemporary species. The cladogram can be transformed directly into a classification, although the result may not look like a traditional Linnaean classification.

With these general ideas about the course of evolution in mind, we can turn to some of the forces that drive evolution and to questions about how organisms fit into their environments.

populations and selection

what is natural selection?

Darwin's fundamental idea – his great insight – is natural selection. His fellow naturalist Alfred Russel Wallace reached this insight at about the same time, and had published a paper in 1855 with ideas very similar to Darwin's. As Darwin and Wallace maintained a correspondence, when one of Wallace's letters finally laid out the essential ideas that Darwin had been developing for two decades, they settled the issue of scientific ethics and priority of discovery by means of a joint paper communicated to the Royal Society. Darwin and Wallace developed their ideas on the basis of their extensive experience as field naturalists. Rather than examining dead specimens in museums, they went out to distant lands and spent long times in the field observing, experimenting, and thinking about the lives of the organisms they saw. (Darwin spent many years writing other books derived from his natural-history studies.) Their field experience taught them to think about *populations* of organisms – all the individuals of one kind that live in one area – and they took several lessons from these observations.

They saw that populations are highly *variable*. An important part of *On the Origin of Species* is Darwin's precise cataloguing of just how variable populations really are, in contrast to the naive, popular viewpoint that the members of a species are all pretty much alike.

Darwin was strongly influenced by the writings of Thomas Malthus. Malthus's pessimistic view of human society developed from his observation that populations tend to grow rapidly in the pattern described mathematically as *exponential* (or "geometric," in the older terminology that Malthus used), whereas resources only grow in an *arithmetical* manner. By this he meant that populations tend to double in size periodically, from 1 to 2 to 4 to 8, and so on, whereas resources only grow by addition, as from 1 to 2 to 3 to 4. Therefore, he concluded, people must continually struggle with one another for the means of existence, and the losers in society are condemned to a poverty from which they cannot escape. When applied to the biological world in general, this means that every species tends to reproduce more individuals than can possibly survive; occasionally someone astonished by the potential of exponential growth makes an example of animals that produce so many thousands of eggs that if all their offspring were to survive their total mass would soon equal that of the whole Earth, and a calculation for a slowly reproducing species such as an elephant – which starts to breed at about age thirty and produces only one offspring every few years – shows that the offspring of one pair would number in the millions after a few hundred years. But Darwin and Wallace saw that populations tend to remain quite stable in size, in spite of their immense capacity for reproduction, so most individuals must die before they can mature and reproduce.

They also observed that breeders of domestic plants and animals shape their subjects generation after generation by consciously selecting individuals with desirable characteristics to be the parents of the next generation. This is quite obvious to us now, but let's note that it depends upon the inheritance of genomes, which determine the characteristics of each individual. And let's note that artificial selection can only work if there is a pool of individual variation from which differences can be selected. If all the cows in a herd or all the plants in a field were genetically identical, a breeder would have nothing to select.

From these considerations, it was only a short step to the conclusion that a process similar to artificial selection must be operating in nature. In each generation the individuals show different degrees of fitness or adaptation to their particular habitats, and those that are most fit – those with the best adaptations – are more likely to be successful in producing the next generation. In outline, the principle of natural selection may be summarized by four points:

1. Every organism has the potential to produce more offspring than can survive.
2. There is always variation among individuals in a population; much of this variation is inherited, so the next generation inherit some of these variable features from their parents.
3. Specific variations may make an individual either more or less likely to survive and reproduce than other individuals with different features.
4. Those variant traits that enhance survival and reproduction will be passed on to offspring and will be found in an increasing fraction of the population in each succeeding generation.

A most enlightening conception of natural selection – originally from George Wald – is to think of it as an *editing* process. Just as in editing rough writing into polished writing, an early "draft" of some organism might be a rather crude approximation to a well-adapted form. That "draft" is encoded in a genome, which reproduces with variations; the poorer versions of the genome are discarded, because most organisms die, and the better are retained to reproduce another generation. The metaphor of selection as editing is valuable to keep in mind. It will become especially important in addressing the contention that the probability of a functioning organism arising through mere chance is so small as to be unbelievable. This is a willful misunderstanding of the principle of natural selection. Yes, of course it is impossible to conceive of a complex, functioning organism arising merely by chance in a single step. Evolutionary theory would be absurd to claim it could happen. But it is easy to understand organisms undergoing a gradual, subtle editing generation after generation, through random mutation generating diversity plus selection operating on that diversity.

populations are variable

It may be hard to appreciate just how variable natural populations are. But it is easy to see that variability in human populations. Just pay attention to the differences you see in the people on the street, to the different faces, shapes of bodies, heights, hair colors, skin colors, eye colors. You might argue that the people you pass in a typical city or town in America or Europe aren't natural populations, that they may be mixtures of people of many ancestries; but we see considerable individual variation even in an isolated village, even in a tribe living in Stone-Age conditions in a remote jungle. People are easily recognizable as individuals. A population showing such heterogeneity in form is said to be *polymorphic* (*poly-* = many, *-morph* = form).

Darwin gave an example of variation in plants by citing the work of his contemporary naturalist De Candolle:

> He first gives in detail all the many points of structure which vary in the several species, and estimates numerically the relative frequency of the variations. He specifies about a dozen characters which may be found varying even on the same branch, sometimes according to age or development, sometimes without any assignable reason. ... De Candolle then goes on to say that he gives the rank of species to the forms that differ by characters never varying on the same tree,

and never found connected by intermediate states. After this discussion, the result of so much labour, he emphatically remarks: "They are mistaken, who repeat that the greater part of our species are clearly limited, and that the doubtful species are in a feeble minority. This seemed to be true, so long as a genus was imperfectly known, and its species were founded upon a few specimens, that is to say, were provisional. Just as we come to know them better, intermediate forms flow in, and doubts as to specific limits augment." He also adds that it is the best-known species which present the greatest number of spontaneous varieties and sub-varieties.

Polymorphism is the general rule in natural populations of other organisms. Even if polymorphism isn't apparent to the eye, every population that has been studied reveals its genetic variability in polymorphisms of protein structure. It has been clear since the 1960s that many "laboratory" mutants of the fruit fly *Drosophila* occur in wild populations, and analysis of proteins from individual flies shows that wild populations harbor allelic forms of many enzymes. Both *Drosophila* and human populations typically have two or more alleles at about a third of their genes. But the demonstration that so many loci show polymorphism and considerable heterozygosity has put a new perspective on evolution. Previously, theorists assumed that every new mutation either would be deleterious and therefore eliminated from a population quickly, or would be advantageous and would quickly become fixed – that is, it would become the sole allele in the population. But Motoo Kimura and others proposed a *neutral theory of evolution*: that many mutations have little or no effect on protein function, and that mutant alleles accumulate in a population by random processes (see the concept of genetic drift, on page 73). The existence of neutral mutations is now well established, although they vary from gene to gene. Some proteins are very sensitive to mutation and can bear relatively few allelic forms; others are more tolerant of variations in their structure, so their genes exhibit more variation and heterozygosity. There is some controversy regarding the relative importance of neutral evolution and natural selection, but it seems clear that both processes operate – we would abandon all reason in biology if we did not believe that evolution is driven largely by selection and adaptation.

We will take up this theme of variability and polymorphism again when we consider the question of defining a species. It is especially important that populations (species) commonly show considerable geographic variation, so individuals in different areas have quite different features.

populations may have different forms

A species is made of closely related individuals spread over a certain area, and because of variations in geography, its members can be unified or isolated to various degrees. At one extreme, the entire species may be one population in which any individual can contact and mate with any other individual of the opposite sex. More likely, though, the species will be divided into many local populations, or *demes*, but with a certain amount of genetic mixing, or *gene flow*, among them. At the other extreme, some or all of the demes may be isolated from one another, so little or no gene flow occurs. Most speciation depends on having such partially or completely isolated populations, but analyzing the genetic structure of populations begins with a large, undivided population of the first type.

the idea of a Mendelian population

So populations are extremely variable genetically, and selection acts upon this variation. Evolution is a phenomenon of populations, and our understanding of the process has been aided enormously by understanding how genes behave in populations. Population genetics begins by setting up an idealized model – in fact, a model in which there is no evolution at first. In 1908, the English mathematician G. H. Hardy and the German biologist Wilhelm Weinberg independently discovered that an idealized population will come to an *equilibrium* for each gene, a condition in which its genetic composition doesn't change. This fact, now known as the *Hardy-Weinberg Principle*, is the foundation of population genetics. The theory begins with an ideal population with these features:

- It reproduces sexually and is *diploid*, which simply means that each individual has two copies of its genes, one inherited from each parent.
- It is large enough for the laws of probability to operate.
- Mating occurs at random.
- No mutation takes place.

- No genotype has a selective advantage over any other, and all members of the population survive and reach reproductive age.
- No genes enter from other populations.

Notice that since no mutation and selection occur, such an idealized Mendelian population *is not evolving*. This is a common scientific way of analyzing a situation – to start with a very simple model that doesn't show the effects we want to study, and then later to add in those effects: mutation and selection in this case. Finally we will add in geographic variation in natural populations and see the effects of this important factor.

The condition of *random mating* means that any male and female can mate with each other. One alternative to randomness, called *assortative mating*, is that individuals prefer mates with features similar to their own. People, for instance, commonly mate assortatively, because they tend to marry those with the same skin or hair color, with comparable intelligence, or with some other shared feature. But we can illustrate random mating, and the Hardy-Weinberg Principle, with a convenient human trait, the MN blood types. Everyone has blood type M, N, or MN. These types are encoded by two alleles, *M* and *N*, of a single gene. A person with the genotype *MM* has M-type blood, one with the genotype *NN* has N-type blood, and a heterozygote with the genotype *MN* has MN-type blood, because the alleles are *codominant* – they are both expressed equally. Also there seems to be no selection for either M or N blood type, and human populations conform perfectly to the Hardy-Weinberg principle for this trait.

The abundance of each allele in a population is given by its *allelic frequency*: the frequency of the *M* allele, denoted by p, is the fraction of all these genes in a population that are *M*; and the frequency of the *N* allele, denoted by q, is the fraction that are *N*. Allelic frequencies can vary from 0 to 1; if there were equal numbers of the two alleles in a population, p and q would both be 0.5. Since the gene has only two alleles, every copy must be one or the other, and $p + q = 1$.

Even though neither M nor N types have any selective advantage, populations don't necessarily have equal numbers of the two alleles, and the frequencies of *M* and *N* in different human populations vary quite a lot (Table 2). Suppose we have a population of 1000 people, with 500 M people, 400 MN people, and 100 N people. Since everyone has two genes for this character, there are 2000 genes in the population. The type-M people all have two *M* genes, making 1000, and the type MN people have 400 more M genes, making a total of 1400. Then $p = 1400/2000 = 0.7$. Similarly, the type-MN people have 400 N genes, and the type-N people have 200 more, for a total of 600. Then $q = 600/2000 = 0.3$. Of course, after finding the value of p, we could have subtracted it from 1 to get the value of q, but I did the explicit calculation of q to show that the formula gives the correct value. In general, we determine the value of p or q by taking twice the number of homozygotes for one allele plus the number of heterozygotes, and dividing by twice the number of individuals in the population.

Table 2 Percentages of MN blood types in various human populations

People	Place	M	MN	N
Eskimo	Greenland	83.5	15.6	0.9
Pueblo Indians	New Mexico	59.3	32.8	7.9
Australian Aborigines	Queensland	2.4	30.4	67.2
Ainu	Japan	17.9	50.2	31.9
Basques	Spain	23.1	51.6	25.3
Germans	Berlin	29.7	50.7	19.6
Chinese	Hong Kong	33.2	48.6	18.2

The members of a population are said to share a *gene pool*, a metaphorical common space where all their genes are combined, mixed, and then reassorted to make the next generation. So the species reproduces as if all the males and females put their *gametes* – their sperm and egg cells – into a big pool where each new individual is made by randomly combining one sperm and one egg. The probability of choosing a gamete carrying M is p and the probability of choosing one carrying N is q. Then:

1. The probability of forming an MM zygote is just $p \times p = p^2$.
2. The probability of forming an MN zygote is $(p \times q) + (q \times p) = 2pq$. (This is the probability of getting an M sperm with an N egg or an N sperm with an M egg, so it is just twice the same elementary probability.)
3. The probability of forming an NN zygote is $q \times q = q^2$.

The principle of the Hardy-Weinberg equilibrium is that a randomly mating population reaches a ratio of $p^2 : 2pq : q^2$ for the three genotypes of a single gene and then *does not change*. By the way, notice that the sum $p^2 + 2pq + q^2$ is equal to $(p + q)^2$, by simple algebra. Since $p + q = 1$, $p^2 + 2pq + q^2$ also is equal to 1.

What happens if we apply this calculation to the imaginary population with $p = 0.7$ and $q = 0.3$? We find that $p^2 = 0.49$, $2pq = 0.42$, and $q^2 = 0.9$. If the next generation also has 1000 individuals, there will be 490 Ms, 420 MNs, and 90 Ns. If you would like to do the calculation all over again to see what happens when a third generation is formed, you would find that it is exactly like this one. So after one generation, the population has come to a Hardy-Weinberg equilibrium.

To test your understanding of these ideas, try calculating the allelic frequencies for a population that has 360 *MM*, 480 *MN*, and 160 *NN*. After you have determined p and q, use the Hardy-Weinberg formula to calculate the frequencies of the three genotypes; you should find that in a population of 1000 individuals, the numbers will be exactly those of the population you started with, thus confirming that this is truly a population at equilibrium and that the allele frequencies will not change.

For illustration, I used a gene locus with no dominance, where we could distinguish *MM* and *MN* individuals. But how can we determine the frequencies of alleles when dominance gives both homozygous dominants and heterozygotes the same phenotype? Although these individuals are identical, we can recognize and count all the homozygous recessives. Their frequency is q^2. Therefore, the square root of that frequency is q, and $p = 1 - q$. Suppose, for instance, 1 per cent of a population (0.01) have a certain recessive genetic condition. Since $q^2 = 0.01$, $q = \sqrt{0.01} = 0.1$. That is, 10 per cent of the alleles at this locus in the population are recessives and 90 per cent are dominants.

the effects of selection

Hardy-Weinberg analysis assumes there is no selection for any genotype, but for most traits the three genotypes *AA*, *Aa*, and *aa* have different reproductive potential or *fitness* (sometimes called Darwinian fitness). The fitness of a genotype is a measure of its contribution to the gene pool of the next generation, in comparison with other genotypes. Fitness is always a *relative* measure; we cannot have an *absolute* measure of fitness because a more fit genotype could always appear, so the best-adapted genotype is arbitrarily assigned a fitness of 1. Quite commonly, with complete dominance at some locus, both AA and Aa individuals have a fitness of 1, but homozygous recessives are at a disadvantage and have some lower fitness. In a flowering plant, different genotypes for flower color may have different fitnesses because one color is more attractive to pollinators; genotypes that affect the length of an insect's leg may have subtle effects on the insect's ability to run or to hold onto its food. Then in each generation, instead of the three genotypes being at their classical ratio, p^2 $AA : 2pq$ $Aa : q^2$ aa, the aa individuals will actually occur at a lower frequency q^2 $(1 - s)$. This expression defines s, the *coefficient of selection* against aa. The fitness of this genotype is then defined as $W = (1 - s)$. We know how many individuals of each genotype to expect in a population, and if we consistently find less than that number for some genotype, we know it has lower fitness, which we can easily calculate.

With this mathematical definition of selection, population geneticists have developed an extensive, complex theory, which shows how evolution will proceed in populations of various sizes, with different degrees of selective pressure, and other variables. One example will show the kind of insight this theory can yield. People carry various recessive mutations that produce disorders that are always fatal in childhood, so affected individuals never have a chance to have children. Intuition tells us that since these individuals are being eliminated, the gene should disappear from the population rapidly, but it doesn't. The reason is that most copies of the recessive allele are carried by heterozygotes, who aren't affected by it. If $q = 0.01$, for instance, $q^2 = 0.0001$, and only one person in 10,000 shows the disease and is eliminated; but the frequency of carriers is $2pq = 2 \times 0.99 \times 0.01 = 0.02$, so 2 per cent of the population carry the deleterious allele.

Population genetic theory allows us to calculate just how rapidly the allele frequency will change in this situation. It says that the number of generations required to reduce the frequency of the recessive allele from q_0 to q_1 is $1/q_1 - 1/q_0$. Suppose q is initially 0.01 (so one person in 10,000 is affected); how long will it take to reduce q to 0.001 (so only one person in a million will be affected)? The answer is $1000 - 100 = 900$ generations. At 20–25 years per human generation, that would take a long time. Furthermore, when the allele frequency falls so low, mutation becomes a significant factor; the human population will never be free of the allele because it will be created by mutation as fast as it is eliminated by selection.

gene frequencies may change rapidly in small populations

The Hardy-Weinberg Principle applies to a population that is large enough for random mating to occur, so the genotypes of the next generation are made in proportion to the allelic frequencies of the current generation. Natural populations may be very small, however, especially those that are somewhat isolated, and small populations can behave very differently from large ones.

You know that a long series of coin flips will turn up as many heads as tails, but in the short run you will probably have streaks in which one side or the other occurs more often than expected. In a large population the genetic "coins" are being flipped so much that the Hardy-Weinberg Principle applies: the frequencies of all alleles remain constant, in the absence of mutation and selection. In a small population, as the geneticist Sewall Wright first pointed out, the gene pool may not behave this way, because each generation is made by only a few flips of a genetic coin. Suppose a population has equal numbers of two alleles for some gene locus: $p = q = 0.5$. If only a few sperm and eggs are drawn to make the next generation, they may not be a representative sample, so they deviate from the expected 50 per cent of each allele. Perhaps in the next generation the frequencies will change to 0.48 and 0.52. Then in the following generation, since the frequencies are already somewhat lopsided, they may change a little more – say, to 0.46 and 0.54.

People have done this genetic experiment with a computer that simulates the evolution of a small population, starting with equal frequencies of two alleles. In different computer runs, the frequencies of the alleles tend to drift rapidly in one direction or the other. In natural populations such a rapid change in gene frequency is known as *genetic drift*. A common result is that after several generations one allele is eliminated (its frequency becomes zero) while the other is said to be fixed (its frequency becomes 1). Genetic drift may be an important factor in speciation, as we discuss in chapter six.

If genetic drift really occurs in human populations, we might expect to see a lot of genetic variation among small populations. For instance, if we could find small, isolated villages where people marry within the village and few marriages occur every year, we might find gene frequencies changing radically just by chance. Luigi Cavalli-Sforza and his colleagues found the perfect test situation in the

Parma Valley of Italy. In the upper reaches, the Parma river has carved out a steep-sided, inhospitable valley where villages typically number 200–300 people. Migration is inhibited in this region, and the vast majority of marriages are between people from the same village. Further downstream, the terrain becomes hilly and the villages are larger, and finally the valley becomes a plain containing the sizeable town of Parma. Thus, mobility and migration also become greater as one moves downstream. The geneticists examined variation in blood types from village to village. They showed very high variation in the mountain villages, falling steadily to low variation in the plains, just as expected.

sources of variation

mutation is the source of all genetic change

The frequency of an allele can also change by mutation. *Mutation rate* is the probability per individual per generation that a gene locus will mutate; in simple creatures such as bacteria, this means that a cell must replicate its genome every time it divides in two, and each time there is a small probability that one copy will be mutant. Measurements in organisms ranging from bacteria to mice show that these rates are very small, usually 10^{-5}–10^{-8}. The highest rate in this range, 10^{-5}, would mean that if 100,000 copies of a gene are replicated, one of them on average will be mutant. All genes aren't equally likely to mutate because they are of different sizes, but suppose we assume an average mutation rate of 10^{-5}; then if the human genome contains 50,000 genes, one mutation would occur in half the replications to produce a new sperm or egg, and thus each of us would carry, on the average, one new mutation. (Mutations also occur when our somatic, or body, cells reproduce; they are important causes of disorders such as cancer, but they don't contribute to the gene pool and to evolution of the species.)

Because mutations occur so infrequently, persistent mutation to a certain allele can only change its frequency quite slowly. In microorganisms that reproduce rapidly, such as bacteria, mutation can make a significant contribution to a population, though this contribution may only become apparent after some selective agent has taken effect. For example, every time a bacterial cell reproduces, there is a small chance that one daughter cell will become resistant to an antibiotic, and such resistant mutants may accumulate; but we only know that these mutants exist, and they only become significant, if the population is subjected to the antibiotic, which selects them by wiping out all the sensitive cells. On the other hand, mutation is a two-way phenomenon. If a mutation is only a minor change in a DNA molecule, such as replacement of a G-C pair by an A-T pair, then *back-mutation* or *reversion* to the original state will occur at about the same rate as a forward mutation, so mutation will have little overall effect on a population. Selection and mutation may work against each other, as mutation tends to increase the frequency of an allele, while it is eliminated by selection. The situation is analogous to a leaky tub of water that is filled from a faucet, so its level is determined by the rates of inflow and outflow; the frequency of an allele reaches an equilibrium level determined jointly by the rates of selection and mutation.

In spite of these considerations, *mutation is ultimately the source of all genetic variation and therefore the foundation for evolution.* A single mutation increases genetic diversity and thus increases the potential for future evolution, but by itself it is most likely useless or detrimental. An organism, after all, is a complex and finely tuned system, and a random change in its genome is not likely to improve it. However, on pages 93–97 we will consider some effects of mutations on protein structure and show how slight changes in proteins have the potential for evolutionary innovation.

sex and variation

The variation underlying evolution arises not only from mutations producing new alleles but also from sexual reproduction. Germ cells – sperm and eggs, or their equivalents in other organisms – are formed through a special process of nuclear division called *meiosis*, whose details we can ignore. In ordinary nuclear division (*mitosis*), the complete set of chromosomes in a cell is reproduced, so both daughter cells (the products of the division) have identical sets. But in meiosis the diploid set is reduced to haploid sets. Remember that the human diploid set consists of 46 chromosomes – 23 pairs of homologous chromosomes – so meiosis produces sperm or egg cells that have 23 chromosomes, one from each pair. Thus, each sperm or egg carries one of the two homologues numbered 1, one of the two numbered 2, and so on down to number 23.[1] Since each person's maternal and paternal chromosomes almost certainly differ in at least one gene, one person can produce $2^{23} = 8,388,608$ different sperm or egg cells. Thus, one couple, producing this variety of sperm and eggs, could produce over 7×10^{13} genetically different children! In any natural population, harboring even more genetic diversity, the potential for creating diversity merely through sexual recombination is enormous. Population geneticists generally consider that the principal source of variation in a population is recombination of alleles already in the population rather than the creation of new alleles through mutation.

In addition, chromosomes can undergo changes that are much larger than ordinary mutations, which typically just change one base-pair (or a few of them) in one gene. During the early stages of meiosis, a pair of homologues come into intimate contact with each other and commonly exchange parts, a process called *crossing over*. For instance, if one homologue has genes that we can represent by ABCDEFGHIJKLMNOP and the other can be represented by abcdefghijklmnop, they may break and rejoin with an exchange to produce chromosomes such as ABCDEFGHIjklmnop and abcdefghiJKLMNOP. It is fairly common for chromosomes to undergo *deletions*, in which a section is simply lost, or *duplications*, in which a section is duplicated. These changes may occur together because crossing over may happen irregularly, so one chromosome becomes ABCDEIJKLMNOP while the other becomes abcdeFGHfghijklmnop. The first one thus has a deletion and the second has a duplication. Another common change is an *inversion*, in which a segment gets turned around; thus, a chromosome might acquire the sequence ABCDEFKJIHGLMNOP. A segment of one chromosome might also detach and join a nonhomologous chromosome. Suppose another chromosome pair has the sequence RSTUVWXYZ. Then a part of the first chromosome might break off, leaving only FGHIJKLMNOP and producing the chromosome RSTUVWXYZEDCBA. This is called a *translocation*. These additional changes that chromosomes can undergo produce still greater variety in populations. We will show in chapter five that carrying different chromosome sets may confer significant differences in adaptation to particular environments.

One advantage of diploidy is that a population can carry some recessive mutations without harm, and that occasionally two such mutations could come together and produce a superior individual, even though either mutation is deleterious when homozygous.

duplication and diversification

Since we now know the sequences of so many proteins, and of the genes that encode them, we can see that new proteins often arise from gene duplication. The extra copy of a gene can become a kind of molecular toy for the processes of evolution to play with. Natural selection will maintain one copy of the gene in its original functional form, but the second copy can start to acquire mutations and can gradually become different, so different that its protein product takes on a new function. Genes related by this process of duplication and diversification are called *paralogues* of one another, or are said to be *paralogous*. Some classic examples of proteins that have arisen in this way are the mammalian hemoglobins. We have two types, A and A₂, in our blood to carry oxygen, as well as another (F) during the fetal stage, and we have myoglobin in our muscles to hold oxygen there. The hemoglobins are all made of two types of chains, such as α (alpha) and β (beta). All these proteins are very similar, and they all have their special roles in our physiology. Comparisons of their amino-acid sequences show that they arose by repeated duplications as shown in Figure 4.6.

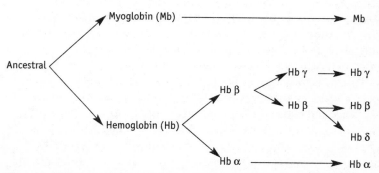

Figure 4.6 *The genes for myoglobin and different hemoglobin proteins have arisen through a series of duplications and diversifications.*

horizontal transmission

Since we draw phylogenetic trees with the time-dimension running down the page, the ordinary inheritance of genes in the course of reproduction is called *vertical* transmission. In the last few years, as investigators have determined the DNA sequences of genomes in more and more organisms, it has become apparent that an alternative, *horizontal*, transmission may be quite important in evolution. We have known for a long time that when bacterial viruses (bacteriophages, or simply phages) grow in some bacteria, they can sometimes pick up bacterial genes and carry them over to other cells that they infect. The process is called transduction. It is now becoming apparent that many bacterial genes have been acquired from other bacteria, sometimes those that are only distantly related. This must have happened by means of viruses in the past. We don't know yet how important horizontal transmission may be in the evolution of other kinds of organisms; but the cells of all organisms can harbor some viruses in a kind of hidden, quiescent state, and these viruses may have been carrying genes from species to species, giving their recipients novel characteristics. This is an aspect of evolution to keep our eyes on.

looking ahead: chance and necessity

In this chapter, I have tried to provide an overview of evolution as a process that can be seen in broad perspective over millions of years and in a closer view as the flux of genes in natural populations. Populations and entire species appear to persist for relatively short times on the geological time-scale, but on this scale new species frequently arise that have different characteristics, so that over long spans of time we see greater diversity among the surviving species.

In a grand overview of biology, the late French molecular biologist Jacques Monod summed up the essential processes of evolution as chance and necessity. Organisms (or their genomes, specifically) are subjected to random events that create novelty and variation. The organisms carrying these variations then face the necessity of surviving in a world of adversity. Only the best-adapted survive, to produce a new generation that must face the same kind of adversity. And though each species may manage to survive in this way for a time, perhaps as much as a few million years, its life, too, is finite. (Small wonder that Monod opens his book with a quotation from the essay *The Myth of Sisyphus*, by his friend Albert Camus, a book that explores the question of living one's life meaningfully in a world with no intrinsic meaning or purpose.) Having introduced the element of chance, it is now time to consider necessity and the question of just how organisms can fit into their surroundings and manage to survive.

notes

1. You may know that in the human genome, the 23rd pair actually consists of two X chromosomes in females and of one X and one Y in males. These chromosomes determine maleness or femaleness. However, this detail is unimportant for the present purposes.

ecosystems: getting along with the neighbors

The purpose of this chapter is to add the important ecological viewpoint to our growing conception of how evolution happens.

adaptation and fitness

In talking about evolution, people are likely to say something such as, "Natural selection means survival of the fittest." (The phrase "survival of the fittest" came from the writing of Darwin's contemporary Herbert Spencer.) But "the fittest" are, by definition, those that are more likely to survive. So this sentence seems to be saying, "Selection means that those who survive are those who survive" – a tautology, rather than a brilliant insight. Perhaps we can make it more meaningful by unpacking the meaning of "the fittest."

Being "fit" might mean being healthy or it might mean fitting into an appropriate place. Certainly organisms that survive must be healthy in some sense, but this doesn't help much; it is more helpful to consider what they must fit into, and the general answer is that they must fit into a community and an ecosystem. No organism can live by itself. It is dependent in various ways on a variety of others, and the collection of organisms that live together, with their lives intertwined and interrelated, is a *biological community*. The community exists in some physical environment of rock, soil, water, and air; the combination of the community with this physical environment is an *ecosystem*.

Why can't one species live by itself? The fundamental reason is energy. All organisms require energy, and this energy has to come from the organism's environment, in one of two ways. The ultimate source of energy for life on Earth is the sun. For this reason alone, we only expect to find life on planets that are close enough to a star to receive a lot of light. The energetic base of a community consists of phototrophs, the plants, algae, and some bacteria. Phototrophs use the energy of light to synthesize the organic molecules of their own structure from carbon dioxide and other simple inorganic materials. As they grow, phototrophs are storing up energy in their structures. These energy-rich materials then serve as food for organisms such as animals – *chemotrophic* organisms or *chemotrophs* – which use a chemical energy source.

A very primitive planet, one whose organisms are in a very early stage of evolution, can probably have organisms living by themselves – for instance, simple phototrophs living off light. But it probably doesn't take long for even the most primitive organisms to begin living together, interacting in complicated ways, and starting to form communities. From that time on, they will become ecologically dependent on one another.

Organisms are related energetically as members of a *food web*, a tangled network of organisms that eat one another. Defined by their role in the community, the phototrophs act as *producers*, which bring energy into the system through photosynthesis. (Plants grow in the light.) Producers store energy in their structure and are eaten by *primary consumers*, or *herbivores*, which use some of that stored energy for their own growth and reproduction. (A deer eats leaves.) These, in turn, are eaten by *secondary consumers*, or *carnivores*, which use some of the energy in the herbivores' structure. (A wolf eats a deer.) Some carnivores may be eaten by still higher carnivores. (A killer whale may eat a seal or a porpoise.) These distinctions are somewhat idealized, and many members of an ecosystem are *omnivores* that eat a mixture of plant and animal materials. Finally, every organism – producer or consumer – dies and ultimately becomes food for *decomposers*, the molds and bacteria that decay biological molecules as they grow and take their share of energy.

the concept of an ecological niche

An organism fits into its community (and its ecosystem) by occupying an ecological niche. Biologists have entertained at least two distinct conceptions of a niche. The term arose between 1917 and 1928 in the work of ecologists such as Joseph Grinnell and Charles Elton, who emphasized the position of an organism in its community. Elton wrote that an animal's niche is "its place in the biotic environment, its relations to food and enemies, and the status of an organism in its community." He expressed the idea most pointedly when he wrote, "When an ecologist says, 'There goes a badger,' he should include in his thoughts some definite idea of the animal's place in the community to which it belongs, just as if he had said, 'There goes the vicar.'" The American ecologist Eugene Odum, in 1959, agreed with this conception, writing that a niche is "the position or status of an organism within the community and ecosystem resulting from the organism's structural adaptations, physiological responses, and specific behavior." Odum particularly distinguished niche from habitat, using the often-quoted distinction that a niche is an organism's "profession" whereas habitat is its "address." In 1952, Lee R. Dice defined a niche as a species's ecologic position in a particular *ecosystem*, rather than in its community, and wrote that the term includes "a consideration of the habitat that the species concerned occupies for shelter, for breeding sites, and for other activities, the food that it eats, and all the other features of the ecosystem that it utilizes." However, these conceptions contrast sharply with that of G. E. Hutchinson, who conceived of a niche as an *n*-dimensional space that specifies the total range of conditions in which the organism is able to live and reproduce; for instance, Figure 5.1 shows how an aquatic animal might occupy a niche defined by the factors of temperature, salinity, and the concentration of calcium. (Some biologists might feel that this "space" is more like a definition of habitat than of niche.) Finally, G. L. Clarke, in 1954, distinguished "functional niche" from "place niche." He noted that different species of plants and animals fulfill different functions in the ecological complex and that the same functional niche may be filled by quite different species in different geographical regions.

Although a full description of the niche of any species may be impossible, some brief examples can make the idea clearer.

american robin

One of the best-known birds in North America, its niche is that of a generalist in many habitats: forests, woodlands, gardens, parks, expanding into the grasslands. It feeds on fruit and on small

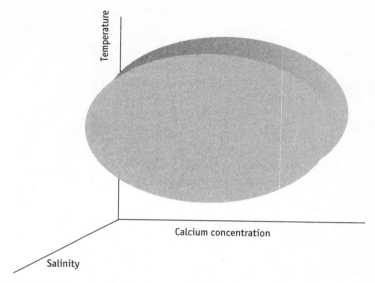

Figure 5.1 *According to Hutchinson's conception, a niche might be a region in an abstract space defined by several factors – three, in this example. The animal in this case is adapted to living within this space.*

invertebrates, including insects, largely by moving slowly over the ground and gleaning whatever it can find that is edible. It nests primarily in deciduous trees, at moderate heights, and some individuals, especially young birds still in the nest, serve as food for predators such as crows and hawks.

african lion

The lion, also, has quite a broad, generalized niche, since it lives (or lived – it is now severely confined by civilization) in most habitats in Africa except for the highest altitudes and the driest deserts. It is a predator that lives on other animals weighing primarily between 50 and 300 kg, although it will attack animals between 15 and 1,000 kg if necessary. During famine conditions, or if an individual is injured, it will take rats, reptiles, fish, or even groundnuts. Its method of hunting is a fast chase after skilled stalking. Individual lions will eat small animals by themselves; larger kills are shared with a social group, leaving remains for scavengers such as hyenas.

red-flowering currant

This deciduous shrub grows abundantly on dry to somewhat moist sites in the mixed coniferous-deciduous forests of the Pacific Northwest U.S. Its pink to deep-red flowers appear early in the spring, coinciding with the arrival on their breeding grounds of Rufous Hummingbirds, which depend upon the plant's nectar for their sustenance at this time. Deer and elk eat its branches and leaves. Its berries are persistent and do not ripen all at once, so they provide food for several kinds of birds, including grouse, jays, robins, towhees, waxwings, and Lewis's Woodpeckers, and for mammals including coyotes, foxes, skunk, squirrels, chipmunks, ground squirrels, mice, and wood rats.

These brief, inadequate descriptions of niches show how each species fits into its particular community or ecosystem by occupying certain segments of these spaces, perhaps by removing some species as food and by providing food for other species. The behavioral descriptions may be very important; noting that robins glean on the ground, for instance, shows that this particular place to gather food is occupied and that another species attempting to use the same methods and to hunt in the same place will face some competition. It would also be important to describe particular parasites or diseases that each species is subject to or resistant to.

The niche of each species is defined and limited in part by the way it interacts with other species in its community. Using Hutchinson's conception of a niche as a theoretical volume in a space, the volume a species could occupy in the absence of any competitors is its *fundamental niche*, but competition may force it to occupy a more limited volume, its *realized niche*. The difference may be illustrated by the work of A. G. Tansley, who experimented with two similar British plants called bedstraws. These species are somewhat specialized for growth in soils that differ along the dimension of acidity and alkalinity (measured by a number called pH): *Galium hercynium* lives in acidic soils (pH less than 7) and *G. pumilum* in basic soils (pH greater than 7). Tansley found that each species by itself would grow on both kinds of soils, but when planted together *G. hercynium* invariably outcompeted *pumilum* in acidic soil, and the reverse was true in basic soil. This experiment shows that the fundamental niches of both species are quite broad in the pH dimension, but when grown together each one shows its superior adaptation to a specific pH range, and they restrict each other to limited realized niches.

Gause's principle and its complications

Ask a biologist to name some foundation principles of biology and she or he is almost certain to include the principle that each species in a community must occupy a niche that is clearly different from the niches of other species. It is one of the most persistent beliefs in biology. We use the term *resources* for the items an organism needs to survive and reproduce that may be used up, such as food, shelter, living space, and even potential mates. Biologists have taken the common-sense viewpoint that if two species had identical or strongly overlapping niches, they would be competing for the same resources in the same habitat, and such competition is untenable. It cannot last for long. Avoiding such a situation has been considered a major driving force in evolution, because either one species would out-compete and eliminate the other or natural selection would change one or both species to eliminate the competition. In the 1930s, the Russian ecologist G. F. Gause formulated this concept, now generally called the *Competitive Exclusion Principle*: stable populations of two species cannot continue to occupy the same niche indefinitely, or more specifically, they cannot coexist on a single *limiting* resource. A limiting resource is one that limits the size of a population. This obviously makes good sense, and it is supported by experimental evidence, but the principle is actually more problematic than it might seem to be.

Gause's own experiments convinced him of the principle. He grew cultures of some single-celled organisms called ciliates, some of the most common little creatures to be found in pond waters, feeding them on bacteria and yeast, which in turn fed on oatmeal. When raised by themselves, the larger, slower-growing *Paramecium caudatum* and the smaller, faster-growing *Paramecium aurelia* each grew quite normally. In mixed culture, however, *P. aurelia* always won out while the *P. caudatum* population diminished to almost nothing. In contrast, when Gause grew *P. aurelia* with *P. bursaria*, the populations of both species reached about half the levels they would have achieved in isolation, with *bursaria* living on bacteria suspended in the top half of the culture tube and *aurelia* living on yeast in the bottom half. Thus, both survived by finding separate niches – different limiting resources – even in this simple situation.

Another way to express Gause's principle is to say that two competing species can only coexist through *niche differentiation* – evolution of one or both species so their realized niches don't overlap strongly and they are using different resources. Potential competitors can differentiate their niches by *partitioning* resources, either using different resources in the same space or dividing the space. This happened in the mixed culture of *P. aurelia* with *P. bursaria*, and it happens in natural situations. For example, Robert H. MacArthur studied the feeding patterns of five species of brightly colored little birds called warblers living in the same area in New England. Although the species are very similar and eat the same food (mostly insects, sometimes berries), they divide the space by hunting in different parts of the tree canopy, toward the center or outside, higher or lower. On a much smaller scale, my colleague Robert Sluss found how potentially competitive carnivorous beetles divide the space on black walnut leaves, where they feed on herbivorous insects; the red beetle *Hippodamia* hunts by walking down the middle of the leaf and back along one edge, while the greenish *Olla* searches back and forth across the leaf. Having evolved different behavior patterns, they divide a limited resource so both species get enough to maintain themselves. Species can also share resources by dividing the niche in time; flying insects are hunted by swifts and swallows during the day, by nighthawks and their relatives around dusk, and by bats at night.

In other situations, however, investigators have reported that they can't find any difference between the niches of species that appear to be in competition. D. R. Strong, Jr., studied thirteen species of tropical leaf-mining leaf beetles that use the same food and live in rolled-up leaves of *Heliconia* plants, but he could find evidence only that the niche of one species was weakly segregated from the niches of the others. These beetles apparently require exactly the same resources, but they live together without any aggression, either within or between species. Perhaps in this case these herbivorous insects, living in such a rich tropical forest, never reach large enough populations actually to be in competition, because they are exploiting such a large resource that their food supply isn't limited and predation keeps their numbers in check. Without competition, Gause's principle simply doesn't apply.

adaptations may be morphological, behavioral, or biochemical

If someone asks, "How does a species become adapted to a niche?" we are likely to give what sounds like a wiseguy answer: it is adapted by means of specific *adaptations*. Though this sounds unhelpful, it directs our attention to specifics, instead of the broad, vague notion of "being adapted." A successful species becomes and remains successful by evolving specific adaptive features over long periods of time that allow its individual members to meet short-term challenges. Some of these adaptations are *morphological*, or structural, such as having a certain shape of body, sharp claws for fighting, tough bark for protection, powerful leg muscles for running fast. To take the bird-watcher's perspective again, one of the first features one learns to observe in a bird is the shape of its bill, and some songbirds clearly have small, thin bills for eating insects, while others have larger, conical bills for eating seeds.

Other adaptations are *behavioral*. All animals engage in stereotyped behavior patterns and have repertoires of rapid, automatic responses to certain stimuli. The ability to learn, too, is an adaptation for dealing with short-term changes. Even a plant's ability to curl up its leaves in dry conditions to reduce evaporation could count as a behavioral adaptation. Behavior is such a fascinating topic in itself that pursuing the evolution of behavior could easily double the size of this book. And perhaps the most fascinating aspect of this inquiry would be the evolution of human behavior, including all that we think and feel. Darwin himself anticipated that an evolutionary perspective might dramatically change our way of looking at our own behavior and feelings, but this perspective had little influence in psychology until the 1960s, when a few students of evolution such as William Hamilton and John Maynard Smith took a fresh look at some aspects of human behavior. Hamilton, in particular, developed the concept of *kin selection*. On the average, each of your brothers or sisters carries half the genes you carry, and even your cousins carry an eighth of these genes. So from the genes' perspective – think of genes as being "selfish," in Richard Dawkins's terminology – it is reasonable for you to engage in loving, unselfish, altruistic behavior toward your kin that preserves those other copies of your genes, even if you sacrifice yourself. It will also be reasonable for men and women to engage in behaviors that maximize their chances of passing on their genes and have corresponding attitudes. Thinking along these lines has been important in the development of contemporary evolutionary psychology, but this is a topic to be left for further reading.

Biochemical adaptations include enzymes and metabolic processes, regulatory mechanisms that respond to changing conditions, and hormones that allow some cells to detect the need for a physiological response and signal other cells to respond. Furthermore, Robert H. Whittaker and Paul P. Feeny were the first to call our attention to the interesting and ecologically important *allelochemic* interactions, in which chemicals made and released by one species – substances called *allomones* and *kairomones* – have ecological effects on some other species. Allomones may repel or even kill competitors or enemies, while kairomones may give an animal a distinctive odor so its enemies can find it more easily.

We see that members of each species occur only in certain patches in an ecosystem. We don't expect every species to live everywhere, but what determines where each species will occur? The important factors are often subtle and chemical. James Fogleman and William Heed found chemical subtleties determining how four species of fruit flies (*Drosophila*) distribute themselves among five species of cactus in the Sonoran desert of southwestern United States and northern Mexico. Where the cacti are injured, bacteria and yeasts move in and create pockets of rot that attract the fruit flies, and one species of fly also lives on soil that has been soaked with juice from rotting cacti. The flies feed on fifteen species of yeasts on these plants. They are remarkably specific in their choice of cactus, as shown in Figure 5.2. Specific factors separate the niches of these fruit flies. The flies effectively divide the available resources, so all four species survive without competition. Notice that someone observing the flies and cacti casually would never have discovered any of this; only careful chemical analysis could show what is going on here.

The cacti produce distinctive sets of volatile compounds, mostly pungent alcohols, acetates, and acids, which attract different types of flies. However, other factors determine the needs of each fly species. *D. pachea* is restricted to Senita because the other four species of cactus lack sterols that the flies require but cannot make for themselves, and without these sterols females are infertile and larvae do not develop. *D. mojavensis* and *D. nigrospiracula* cannot live on Senita because they are intolerant of alkaloids that this cactus produces;

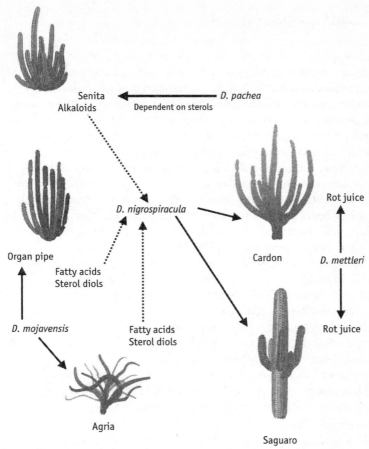

Figure 5.2 *In the Sonoran desert, four species of Drosophila divide a cactus resource through chemical interactions. The dotted lines show chemical inhibitions and the solid lines show which species of cactus each species of fly lives on.*

nigrospiracula is also intolerant of fatty acids and sterol diols produced by Agria and Organ Pipe, so it is restricted to Saguaro and Cardon. Since *mojavensis* tolerates the materials produced by Agria and Organ Pipe, it lives on these two species, free from competition by *nigrospiracula*. *D. mettleri* avoids competition with the other species primarily through its behavior; although the adults live on Saguaro and Cardon, the larvae live in soil soaked with Saguaro and Cardon rot juice.

adaptation and exaptation

Stephen Jay Gould and Elizabeth Vrba introduced a distinction that is useful in thinking about how evolution happens. We think of adaptations as features that have been shaped by natural selection into a functional form because they enhance the survivability of the organisms that carry them. But organisms often have characteristics that they have acquired in previous evolution – presumably for some function – that turn out later to have value in a different situation for a different function. Gould and Vrba give several examples. For instance, there is good reason to think that the most primitive birds (or dinosaurs on the line of evolution that eventually became birds) acquired feathers either for insulation or because of their value as insect nets on their wings. These animals were flightless. But when some of their descendants acquired flight, feathers then turned out to be wonderfully valuable as light flying devices. As another example, it is quite possible that bony structures evolved first as repositories for calcium phosphate, as supplies of phosphates for metabolism; if this is true, then they only became important as supporting structures for muscular activity during later evolution. Gould and Vrba suggest that characters acquired in this way should be called *exaptations*, rather than adaptations.

The concept is closely related to the idea of pre-adaptation, which has been a source of some distress and even embarrassment among evolutionary biologists. Biology textbooks have sometimes told stories of organisms that were able to adapt to some new situation because they already had the necessary features, which are called pre-adaptations. These scenarios call up spectres of teleology – a universal bugbear among biologists – or of predestination, which is philosophically troubling. Exaptation is a more neutral concept, a way of pointing out that characteristics may often have more than one function and that they can acquire such functions at different times.

different ways for selection to act

If evolution is fundamentally due to natural selection, acting on variation, different patterns of evolution must result from different modes of selection. Suppose we examine the variability of a population for any morphological factor – say size, for the sake of illustration, because it is so easy to envision; we graph size on the horizontal axis, so those at the left side of the scale are small and individuals gradually increase toward the right, and the number of individuals of each size on the vertical scale. We will find a roughly normal distribution curve, with the most individuals at an intermediate, average size and smaller numbers tapering off to smaller and larger sizes. Then natural selection can operate on a population in three general ways. *Stabilizing selection* tends to eliminate individuals on the extremes of the distribution, so average individuals have the greatest fitness; this mode of selection accounts for stasis in evolution – in other words, for no evolution. *Directional selection* favors individuals on one extreme, so the population tends to move in that direction over time, causing phyletic evolution. *Disruptive selection* favors two different parts of the distribution, dividing the population into two groups that are changing in different directions. This mode of selection may be involved in speciation.

Stabilizing selection is a conservative process that keeps a species well adapted to its particular niche by eliminating genotypes that are farthest from the norm. There is evidence that much of selection is stabilizing. For instance, in 1898 Hermon C. Bumpus collected English sparrows that had been exhausted by a snowstorm. In the warmth of his laboratory, seventy-two of the sparrows revived and sixty-four died. By carefully measuring many of their features, Bumpus showed that the females that perished were largely at the extremes of size, and the survivors were much closer to the average of the population. (Oddly, the male survivors tended to be shorter and lighter than average, with longer wings and legs.) Studies of this kind suggest that the average genotype of a population makes it well adapted to its niche and that selection tends to maintain this genotype. As another example, small songbirds tend to lay clutches of about three or four eggs, even though they could lay several more. One can imagine selection for birds that lay more eggs and therefore out-reproduce their competitors, but studies of these birds show that those who do attempt to raise larger broods typically are less successful than those who raise more modest broods, and thus selection favors the status quo.

the realm of the Red Queen

Stabilizing selection probably keeps a species adapted to its ecological niche in some environment, as long as that environment is stable. If each species were continually becoming better adapted through natural selection, one might expect species that have lived for only short times to have the highest extinction rates; extinction should be less common among older species, which presumably have had the benefits of greater selection. However, Leigh van Valen demonstrated that this is apparently not the case among some groups of invertebrates, which became extinct at a constant rate, regardless of how long they had existed.

If natural selection isn't making organisms better adapted all the time, what is it doing? Van Valen's answer is his *Red Queen hypothesis*, referring to the queen in Lewis Carroll's *Through the Looking-Glass*, who tells Alice that in her country it takes all the running you can do just to stay in the same place. By this hypothesis, an ever-changing environment constantly challenges each species just to keep pace and remain well adapted. Think of a predator and one of its prey species, for instance – perhaps a hawk and one of the songbirds it hunts. Perhaps an early version of the hawk has searching and hunting strategies that are quite effective against the songbird, and the hawks manage to catch and consume quite a few. But some of the songbirds have slightly improved vision that manages to pick out an image of the hunting hawk when it is still at a distance, so these songbirds get an early warning and head for shelter sooner. Little by little, the songbird population comes to carry genes for this kind of vision, and the hawks become less and less effective in hunting them. But the hawks will be able to change, too. Perhaps some of them get genes that give them a slightly different flight pattern, so the songbirds' eyes no longer recognize them. Perhaps some of them get to fly faster or their eyes become better at picking out the images of the songbirds hiding in their shelters. We can imagine unlimited versions of this kind of scenario.

The point is that for all its complexities and possibilities, adaptation is rather like an interminable game that no one ever wins. Each species may improve its lot by evolving some new structure or behavior or chemistry, and its position in the community may be enhanced for a while. But eventually some other species will evolve another mechanism which improves its position, and so it goes. In the long run, the total of all the winnings and losses is always zero, and – in gamblers' jargon – no species ever "quits the game winners."

My colleague David Milne has suggested that we think of a niche and a species as a spot of light focussed on a wall encompassing a bunch of bugs. The bugs are scattered across the spot in accordance with their genotypes, with the best-adapted types in the center. Those whose genotypes give them lesser fitness are trying to live in the twilight at the edge of the niche, and they tend to be selected out and eliminated. But the pool of light is moving slowly (with changing environmental conditions), and the bugs living in it continually struggle genetically to keep up through directional selection. They survive only as long as they stay in the spot of light; if they fall behind it, their fitness declines, and eventually they become extinct.

proteins and the subtlety of editing

Each species is adapted to particular conditions of temperature, pressure, and so on – Hutchinson's conception of how a niche should be defined. I want to focus on one particular example of temperature adaptation. Since proteins are the molecules that perform most of the essential biological tasks, it is instructive to develop a better understanding of protein structure while showing how that structure can be altered very subtly through mutation and selection.

The microbiologist Ogden Edwards once examined four similar species of bacteria and showed how closely their maximum growth temperatures correlate with the temperatures at which their enzymes lose their function. For instance, *Bacillus mycoides* can grow at up to 40°C, and its enzymes are stable to about that temperature, whereas *Bacillus vulgatus* will grow at 55°C, and its enzymes are stable to temperatures in the mid-50s. Now this is not remarkable. You may be inclined to respond, "Okay, so what?" Since an organism can function only if its individual enzymes and other components are functional, we expect the stability of its proteins to match the temperatures at which it can grow. These particular features are examples of adaptations. But I want to build on this case to show how remarkably easy it is to acquire such adaptations through mutation and selection.

An important strategy for molecular biology research is to use mutants, and those with temperature deficiencies or sensitivities are very useful. Bacteria such as the common *E. coli* generally grow in the temperature range from about 28 to 40°C and grow best at 37°C, human body temperature. But we can find temperature-sensitive (*ts*) mutants that can only grow at the lower temperature, up to about 30°C, and others that are cold sensitive (*cs*), which will only grow at the higher temperatures. What makes the difference?

Proteins are long chains of amino acids, folded into particular functional shapes, such as the myoglobin molecule of Figure 5.3. Although you can't see all the molecular details, the molecule is held in this shape by interactions among the side chains (the R groups) of all the amino acids. Like hands reaching out to grasp one another, these side chains hold on to one another through many specific chemical bonds. These internal bonds depend on the polypeptide chain having amino acids in each position that are able to interact. Merely replacing one amino acid with another can remove an important bond and make a molecule that cannot sustain its shape at an elevated temperature – thus, a *ts* mutant. On the other hand, a different change could add a new bond, thus making a protein that can endure higher temperatures. So the common finding of mutants makes it easy to understand how the proteins of one of the bacteria that Edwards studied could be shaped by mutation to become more stable at the characteristic temperature of its niche. (Other bacteria can live at far higher or lower temperatures, by the way.) In fact,

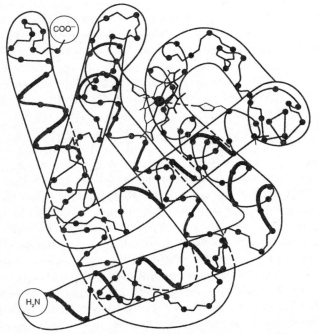

Figure 5.3 *A typical protein, such as this myoglobin molecule, consists of a chain of amino acids folded into an irregular structure.*

these lab results mean that a species could be shaped to a new temperature environment quite rapidly.

A further instructive example comes from the story of the protein hemoglobin, which carries oxygen (O_2) in the blood of all vertebrates (mammals, birds, reptiles, and so on). About 98 per cent of the hemoglobin in normal adult humans is hemoglobin A (Hb A); it consists of four globular polypeptide chains, two called alpha (α) and two called beta (β). The α and β chains are both very similar to one myoglobin chain. Each chain carries an iron atom inside a large molecule called a heme; the "globin" part of the protein's name refers to the polypeptide. Hemoglobin is a marvelous example of an adaptation, a protein wonderfully suited to picking up O_2 molecules where they are abundant, in an animal's lungs or gills, and releasing the O_2 where it is needed, in the other tissues of the body.

As excellent as hemoglobin is, even a small change in its structure can weaken or disrupt its function. People who come into clinics for diagnosis of various health problems, such as anemia, sometimes turn out to have mutant hemoglobins, due to a mutation in one of the genes that encodes the hemoglobin structure. (Since the protein has alpha and beta chains, we have alpha and beta genes [$Hb\alpha$ and $Hb\beta$] that specify them.) Most of these mutant hemoglobin have a single amino acid replaced by another. Among the most interesting and most socially significant are people with *sickle-cell anemia*. Instead of normal Hb A, they have Hb S, in which the glutamic acid at position 6 in the β chain has been replaced by valine:

HbA: Val-His-Leu-Thr-Pro-**Glu**-Glu-Lys-Ser-Ala-Val-Thr-Ala- ...
HbS: Val-His-Leu-Thr-Pro-**Val**-Glu-Lys-Ser-Ala-Val-Thr-Ala- ...

That slight change has profound effects.

Remember that we have two copies of each gene, one inherited from each parent. Most people have two copies of the normal $Hb\beta$ chain and produce only normal Hb A. A small percentage of people are heterozygotes who have one $Hb\beta$ gene and one for hemoglobin S, $Hb\beta^s$; they have both kinds of hemoglobin in their red blood cells (RBCs) and are generally healthy, but they are gene carriers who can transmit the mutant allele to their offspring. An even smaller percentage of people have two copies of $Hb\beta^s$, so they produce only Hb S and become very sick. When subjected to reduced oxygen pressures, their RBCs change from their normal smooth, round, disc shape into bizarre elongated "sickle" forms because the protein crystallizes into long needles when it loses O_2. These sickled cells clog small blood vessels and cut off the oxygen supply to nearby tissues. Sickled cells are also destroyed more rapidly than normal RBCs, leading to anemia. Modern medical treatments can help relieve the symptoms of sickle-cell anemia, but without treatment the condition can cause fever, dizziness, pain, pneumonia, rheumatism, and heart and kidney disease, generally ending in death at an early age.

This one small amino-acid replacement has such an enormous effect because it changes some of the internal bonds that hold the molecule in its proper shape. Remarkably the tiny change from a glutamic acid to a valine in a β chain is enough to disrupt the structure of the whole protein, even though only two amino acids out of about 600 are changed in the whole hemoglobin.

Now recall the idea that natural selection is editing. When we edit something we have written, we make specific, intentional changes to improve the writing. Organisms can only acquire differences in their proteins as a result of random mutations that occur by chance. At first glance, we might expect every such mutation to be deleterious, or at least not helpful. In fact many mutations – probably most of them – are deleterious. But mutations can make small, subtle changes in the structure of a protein, and some of these may really be improvements. This is because proteins are polymers and *a mutation can change a single amino acid at a time*. For instance, the difference between alanine and serine is just a single oxygen atom and the difference between aspartic and glutamic acids is just a single $-CH_2-$ group:

Serine

Glutamic acid

If a mutation directs a cell to insert a serine instead of an alanine in one place, its effect will be to *add only one oxygen atom*. That is a tiny, subtle change! Substituting a glutamic acid for an aspartic acid will only add a $-CH_2-$ group to one particular protein, leaving the thousands of other atoms in the protein as they are. Other changes are more severe, of course, but it is the potential for making such minute changes in the structure of a protein that allows proteins to be gently, gradually edited generation after generation so they have functional shapes.

Determining the amino-acid sequences of hemoglobin A from different species shows many slight variations. The functional explanation is that each species is adapted to different conditions, but it is unlikely that *every* difference in amino acid sequence really makes a difference in the life of the animal. Some of the changes that have occurred in the amino-acid sequences of proteins over the eons are too subtle to have any significant effect on protein structure and function. Much of the variation in populations is *selectively neutral*, so two or more alleles of a gene may be maintained in a population simply because there is no selection against any of them. However, any of these changes *could* have a distinct effect on fitness if circumstances change. Human blood groups such as M and N appear to be selectively neutral, though the more familiar ABO blood types may not be – type O people are slightly more susceptible to stomach and duodenal ulcers than type A, and the reverse is true for stomach cancer.

sickle-cell hemoglobin as an adaptation

The rest of the story of sickle-cell hemoglobin is fascinating for a different reason, as another fine example of adaptation to a particular environment. Sickle-cell anemia is relatively common in Africa, southern Europe, and other malaria-ridden areas, because heterozygotes who have one *Hbβ* gene and one *Hbβ*^{S} gene are unusually resistant to malaria. When their cells are infected by the malaria parasite, which is carried by mosquitoes, the parasite starts to reproduce in their RBCs. The malarial infection progresses as those cells release parasites, which infect vast numbers of other RBCs. While growing inside RBCs, the parasites lower the concentration of O_2 and cause the cells to become sickled. These misshapen cells are destroyed, along with their enclosed parasites, by scavenger cells that are part of the body's defense system. Consequently, where malaria is rampant, natural selection favors individuals with one copy of the $Hb\beta^S$ gene because such individuals are resistant to the malarial parasite. Of course, people unfortunate enough to have two copies of $Hb\beta^S$ have sickle-cell anemia and are poorly adapted to any environment. So the heterozygotes are fitter than either homozygote. A. C. Allison found that in some East African populations the frequency of the $Hb\beta^S$ allele is about 0.2 and that the relative fitnesses of the normal homozygotes, the heterozygotes, and the sickle-cell homozygotes are 0.8, 1.0, and 0.24, respectively. About three-quarters of the sickle-cell individuals die before they can reproduce, but heterozygotes have an advantage of 25 per cent over normal homozygotes.

how little changes can make big differences

People tend to think of fitness with dramatic and romantic ideals. Mottos such as the "struggle for existence" or "nature red in tooth and claw" call up images of bloody battles between predators and their prey, where greater fitness means an ability to run faster or to win a battle to the death. In reality, fitness depends mostly on subtle factors, such as the kind of small changes in protein we have just examined, which confer different metabolic abilities; or the ability to live at particular temperatures or oxygen pressures; or small changes in form.

Thinking about evolution is also plagued by the popular myth that adaptations are of no value unless they are fully developed; an eye, for instance, is said to be of no value unless it is fully formed, so there could be no selective value in acquiring any of the minute changes necessary to make an eye little by little over a long time. Modern studies of evolution, however, show how important very small changes can be. Peter and Rosemary Grant have conducted extensive studies of the wonderfully varied finches of the Galápagos Islands off the coast of Ecuador, often called Darwin's finches because they had such a great influence on Darwin's thinking when he visited the islands as a young man aboard the *Beagle* in 1835–36. These islands are subject to severe changes from very wet to very dry years. The Grants have shown that in very dry years the best-adapted Ground-finches, which eat seeds, are those with the largest, strongest bills, which are able to open the large seeds that become most common in these conditions. However, the average difference in bill dimensions between birds that survive the drought and those that die is only about half a millimeter, out of a length of about 10 mm. So the Grants' data show that a subtle difference in form can make an enormous difference in fitness.

Similarly, Craig Benkman and Anna Lindholm studied Red Crossbills, finches whose bill tips cross and make an excellent tool for removing the seeds from Western Hemlock cones, on which the species thrives. They cut off the bill tips of seven captive crossbills, an operation that doesn't hurt the birds since the bills have no nerves; in this way, they asked whether this highly specialized adaptation has adaptive value only in its fully developed form. The birds with uncrossed bills were able to remove seeds from dry, open hemlock cones but were helpless with closed cones. However, as their tips started to grow back and become slightly crossed, they were able to start extracting seeds from closed cones as before, and the birds became more proficient as their bills grew longer and more crossed. This experiment showed that a mutation in an ancestral population that produced even the slightest bit of crossing must have been advantageous and gave those birds superiority in occupying a distinct ecological niche.

living here may be different from living over there

So far, I've been trying to develop a picture of a natural population as a variable group of individuals that may differ significantly from one another, yet whose similarities and pattern of interbreeding with one another make them recognizable as members of a species. Every genotype represented in a population has a certain fitness, but it is important to see that fitness is not an absolute value that will never change. Fitness is measured relative to particular environmental conditions, and if there is any certainty about a natural environment it is that it will eventually change.

Polymorphism gives a population greater potential to maintain itself in spite of conditions that change geographically and in time. Even in a small area, differences in very local habitats may require different characteristics; organisms also have to adapt to changing weather conditions and other events. A population shows *balanced polymorphism* when it maintains the genes for two or more forms because selection favors each form in a different situation.

The value of polymorphism in different habitats emerged from a classic study of the British land snail *Cepaea nemoralis* by A. J. Cain and P. M. Sheppard. Snail populations are highly variable, with base colors of yellow, pink, and brown overlaid with various banding patterns and different colors of the shell lip. The base colors are due to three alleles at a single gene, with brown dominant to pink and pink to yellow. Another gene determines banding, the unbanded condition being dominant, and at least one more gene determines the banding pattern. Why all these different forms? Cain and Sheppard showed that they are associated with patches of different habitats. In woods with a carpet of brown leaves, the unbanded brown and unbanded or one-banded pink snails are particularly common. In hedgerows and rough green areas, the banded yellow snails are abundant. The critical factor in the regional distribution of morphs is their visibility, especially their visibility to the Song Thrush, *Turdus philomelos*, which preys on them. Thrushes bring snails to "thrush anvils," large rocks where they break open the shells to get at the soft body inside. This habit makes it easy to study predation, because the broken shells left around a rock show what kinds of snails have been eaten; the thrushes obviously eat the more visible snails in each patch, and visibility changes with time – for instance, as the background changes from winter brown to the green of spring.

Thrushes are clearly a major selective agent in determining the genetic composition of the snail population. The population of snails survives very well in spite of the thrushes because of their balanced polymorphism. Snails of a single color and pattern might survive precariously in a restricted habitat, but that way of life would be dangerous because the habitat patches are small and ephemeral. The species actually adapts to a much broader habitat by producing individuals that are camouflaged against different backgrounds. The snails pay a genetic price for this (it has been called a *genetic load* that the population must bear) by producing individuals with the wrong patterns in each habitat, but they buy survival in a varied environment by maintaining a variable gene pool.

fitness generally changes geographically

The organisms occupying a certain niche are, by definition, well adapted to that way of life, but the features required for occupying the niche may shift over a species's geographic range. (Some biologists might say that the niche is changing geographically, but if the species continues to play essentially the same role in its ecosystem throughout, I prefer to describe this as a single niche with different genetic requirements.)

In the 1940s, Theodosius Dobzhansky and his colleagues studied genetic polymorphism in wild populations of the fruit flies *Drosophila persimilis* and *D. pseudoobscura* in the southwestern United States and Mexico. After finding that these populations carry many different chromosome inversions, they performed a detailed study of 27 inversion rearrangements in the third chromosome. Figure 5.4 shows the gradients of genotypes that Dobzhansky and Carl Epling found. For unknown reasons, the Standard chromosome has a high fitness in California, but Arrowhead makes for

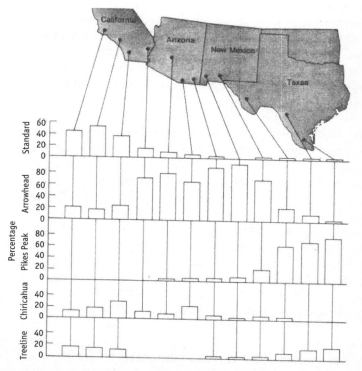

Figure 5.4 *Populations of* Drosophila pseudoobscura *from several places in the southwest U.S. have different frequencies of certain inversions of the third chromosome.*

much better adaptation farther to the east, Pikes Peak has some advantage still farther east, and Chiricahua provides better adaptation in Central Mexico. The frequencies of these chromosomes change gradually rather than abruptly, presumably because the critical environmental variables also change gradually.

The mere fact that the species harbors so many inversions is remarkable, and the geographic distribution of inversions shows that each chromosomal difference can make a difference. You might think that any sequence of genes would be as good as any other, but this isn't so. The expression of a gene may be influenced by its position, and the gene arrangements in *Drosophila* are obviously critical.

As the seasons change, so do the fitnesses of certain gene complexes, as shown by the frequencies of four inversion types of *D. pseudoobscura* at Piñon Flats, California. The Standard type is most common overall, but the Arrowhead and Chiricahua gene complexes provide better adaptations during the spring, for their frequencies increase in spring while that of the Standard gene complex decreases. In summer, the frequency of the Standard type rises again as the Arrowhead and Chiricahua types decline. (Some laboratory observations show that Standard is more advantageous in crowded populations, which may develop during the summer.) The relative fitness of each genotype clearly varies with time, and – as in the story of the snails – the population as a whole survives by maintaining several forms that are adapted to different conditions.

These studies often showed the superiority of heterozygotes, with some clear indications that flies heterozygous for a pair of inversions were more fit than either homozygote. This increased fitness is another reason populations maintain several different inversions.

Leopard Frogs in North America also show geographical change in phenotype. Though designated *Rana pipiens*, the frogs may actually be distinct species spread across eastern North America. These frogs are clearly adapted to the average temperature where they breed. Frog eggs taken from the northern part of the range can tolerate a temperature of 5°C and can develop in temperatures up to about 28°C, whereas those from Texas, Florida, and Mexico can tolerate nothing lower than 10–12°C and can develop up to 32–35°C. These differences in temperature tolerance must reflect distinct gene complexes that adapt each population to local temperature conditions.

Distinct features, such as color, size, and other aspects of form, may vary along different geographic gradients. Thus, a species might show a cline in size along a north–south line and a cline in color along an east–west line. Each of these differences shows an independent response to a different environmental pressure.

pushing the edge

Let's reconsider the bacilli that Ogden Edwards studied. I emphasized that it would be rather easy for bacteria to evolve resistance to higher and higher temperatures because we can so easily find mutants with restricted, or extended, temperature ranges, both cold and hot. Now imagine a species adapted to mid-range temperatures, say around 40°C or a little less, but living near a much hotter spot. As usual, some mutants arise in this population that can weather slightly higher temperatures, say up to about 43°. Some of them happen to be on the edge of the population, closer to that hot spot, and since most of the bacteria can't grow there, the mutants find themselves in unoccupied territory, and they begin to grow very well. Then in this population of somewhat heat-resistant mutants, another mutation occurs that provides even slightly better heat resistance, perhaps up to about 47 or 48°C. Any mutants of this kind who are living still closer to the hot spot will find themselves in a place where their relatives can't grow, but they will be able to grow there very well. You can see where this is leading, of course. We can expect that, little by little, a mutant population will develop that can occupy quite high temperatures, and along the way it may also develop other distinctive features, so we will want to call it a different species from the parents we began with.

I use this example because it is so simple. But we can generalize it to say that this is probably one common way for evolution to happen. Let me go back to Dave Milne's image of the bug population living in a niche represented by a (slowly moving) pool of light. I extended the metaphor a bit by imagining that the bugs in the center of the spot are best adapted to this niche and that those living toward the edge are less well adapted and most likely to fall into the surrounding darkness of extinction. Now those edge-dwellers are less well adapted because their genomes don't carry the combinations of genes that are optimal for this particular niche, but those genomes may give them some increased ability to occupy a related niche. As with the bacteria, it is easy to picture individuals living on the edges of their niche – whether geographically or in some other sense – whose genomes give them the ability to push the edges of that niche, to move into conditions that other members of their species cannot tolerate. And this may be a common factor in the origin of new species.

We have now seen how communities are made of distinct species living together and interacting, and how each species occupies a distinct niche, defined as a certain role or a certain place. We have seen that each species becomes adapted to its niche by means of distinct adaptations – chemical, morphological, behavioral – and that adaptation may be as subtle as the tweaking of a critical protein into a distinctive form. Now it is time to look into the meaning of this word "species" more carefully and to think about the general process of speciation, the origin of new species.

making new species

The idea of evolution developed as an answer to various questions that were puzzling naturalists of the nineteenth century, such as how to understand homology in the light of a separate creation for each species, but a general question requiring a naturalistic answer was, "How did there get to be so many different kinds of living things in the world?" In contrast to the traditional answer, the naturalistic alternative was that each species had arisen through gradual evolution from distinctly different ancestral species. In chapter four, we considered a preliminary answer to the question of just what a species is. It is now time to revisit the issue in the light of the background we have developed about evolution and ecology, since the complications about defining and delimiting species are the result of evolution and are best explained on the basis of evolutionary history.

some difficulties in defining species

The biological species concept, as explained on page 54, is that a species consists of a group of organisms capable of interbreeding with one another. To get one possible point of confusion out of the way, it will be clear that this conception of a species applies only to those that reproduce sexually. Although that includes the majority of species, huge numbers of asexual organisms occupy every habitat. They generally reproduce by one individual dividing in two, by the two dividing again to make four, and so on, to form a *clone*. Many plants also reproduce this way, by sending out shoots or buds. A group of asexual individuals can only be called a distinct species by virtue of their common features. In this endlessly branching pattern, individuals will gradually diverge from one another. There is no firm criterion for including or not including an asexual individual in a species, and an asexual "species" is merely a convenient category, a collection of independent but very similar individuals.

A second side issue arises regarding species of the past. In drawing phylogenetic trees, we sometimes put different species names on a single line to indicate different "species" succeeding one another. This implies that speciation has been occurring, but it really reflects both a matter of taxonomy and incomplete knowledge. The taxonomic problem is that humans like to assign different names to fossil forms that may be members of a continually changing series. As we see in chapter eight, in the last two million years of human evolution, different fossil forms that have been given the names *Homo habilis*, *H. erectus*, *H. sapiens*, and others may all be stages in a single, unbranching course of evolution, or they may have been distinctive forms that arose one after another in a series of rapid speciations. If we had the fossils of all the individuals who lived during this time, we would probably find it difficult or impossible to draw lines separating them into different species. Since the existing fossils preserve only a tiny fraction of the individuals who ever lived, the populations of the past are conveniently broken up into segments, which have been called *paleospecies* to distinguish them from contemporaneous species.

Returning to the question of species living at the same time, remember that a species is initially defined morphologically, as a group of organisms that have essentially the same form. But every population is variable because its gene pool contains allelic variants of many, if not all, genes. According to the most commonly used conception of a species, the most critical feature is that all the members of a species are actually or potentially capable of interbreeding with one another, so in effect they share a common gene pool. That's why all humans are members of the same species even though we don't all look alike. Some examples will show how relying on morphology alone leads to great difficulties.

a. distinct species that are virtually identical

Any serious birder in North America could point to the problem of the *Empidonax* flycatchers. The "empids" are a challenge and a frustration to birders because they are so much alike. These small grayish-yellow birds are distinguished from other flycatchers by their distinctive eye-rings (a circle of light plumage around the eye) and by two prominent light bars on the wing. At least five species are recognized in eastern North America; experts can learn some features of plumage that are likely to distinguish one from another, but in general observers have to rely on a bird's voice and its habitat. Thus, the Least Flycatcher inhabits farms and open woods, and its call is *che-BEK*. The Yellow-bellied, though yellower than most, is best identified by its habitat in coniferous woods and bogs, and by its rising *chu-wee* call. The Alder, of swamps and wet thickets, says *fee-bee-o*; the Willow lives in wet or dry thickets and brushy pastures, and it says *fitz-bew*. There is no evidence that these birds hybridize with one another. They remain distinct, though confusing to human observers, and are a good example of *sibling species*.

b. geographic variation in a species

Many species of birds are fairly widespread, with ranges that cover large portions of North America or Eurasia, yet each one remains quite uniform within its range. A bird of this kind observed in one region will not be noticeably different from one of the same species observed far away. But other species of birds are divisible into quite distinctive *subspecies* that can be recognized morphologically. The Song Sparrow, a common bird throughout North America, has been divided into about twenty-five distinct subspecies. Throughout the east, the sparrows have backs of a moderate brown color streaked with black and lightly streaked breasts with brown lines that converge to a spot in the middle. But birds in the deserts of the west are distinctly lighter, as if bleached out by the sun, and birds of the Pacific Coast are much darker and have much rustier plumages, changing into still darker and larger forms as one goes up the Pacific Coast into British Columbia and Alaska. Because birds of neighboring populations interbreed with one another, they are all considered one species, but it is called a *polytypic species* because it includes populations with distinct morphologies.

c. different forms within a single population

On almost any flat beach along the southern Atlantic coast of North America you will find pockets of little clams called Coquinas at the water's edge. As each wave washes over them, they open to receive the fresh water and then squirm and burrow a bit into the sand. In only a few minutes you could collect clams with quite a variety of colors and patterns on their shells: light blue, streaks of tan, purple and tan, rings of red-orange, and so on. Many populations include two or more obviously different forms, or *morphs*; if species were defined only by morphology, the Coquinas might be classified into three or four different species, but all these forms are just different morphs of one species, *Donax variabilis*. We noted that every species harbors a lot of genetic variability and is genetically polymorphic; this is just a more striking example of polymorphism. Similarly, the Eastern Screech-owls (*Otus asio*) of North America contain two color morphs: reddish-brown and gray individuals, in the same population and even the same brood, just as humans have different eye or hair colors, even in a single family.

problems with the criterion of interbreeding

If we can't rely strictly on morphology to delimit a species, we might at least pin our hopes on the criterion of interbreeding. Other examples, however, show that interbreeding alone is not necessarily a good criterion for populations being members of a single species. The orioles of North America are spectacular orange and black birds. For a long time, the official AOU list recognized two widespread species, the Baltimore Oriole of the east and the Bullock's Oriole of the west. However, the two populations hybridize in a region of the midwest, and on this basis they were combined several years ago into a single species, called the Northern Oriole, much to the dismay of easterners, especially Marylanders, who were very fond of their own species and the Baltimore baseball team named after the bird. Now, one tool available to the modern taxonomist is DNA analysis. When Stephen Freeman analyzed the DNA of several oriole species, he discovered that they are related as shown in Figure 6.1. The DNA evidence shows that the Baltimore and Bullock's are not even one another's closest relatives. They don't hybridize with other orioles that are more closely related, and yet they do hybridize with each other. (They have now been elevated to their old species status, much to everyone's relief.) This kind of example is used by advocates of other species criteria to argue that hybridization should not be used as a criterion of close relatedness or for species definition.

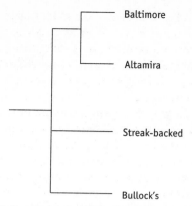

Figure 6.1 *Evolutionary relationships of four North American oriole species.*

In spite of the difficulties we sometimes encounter in applying the biological species concept, it is still fundamental to our thinking. A hallmark of modern biological thought is recognizing that a species is not just an arbitrary collection of organisms but has objective boundaries defined by reproduction. This is one of our legacies from Darwin. The question of defining a species is not primarily interesting because biologists want a catalogue of the world's organisms, but rather because the idea of a reproductively independent unit is so important. Unless a unit – a species defined biologically – becomes genetically independent of other groups, it can't go on to produce other, more diverse groups in another evolutionary step, and it is questionable whether it can become a stable part of a community.

the mechanism of speciation

All these difficulties in defining a species neatly make life tough for cataloguers, but they are a delight to the student of evolution because they show evolution in action in all its randomness and complexity. This will become clearer as we examine the general process of speciation, the process in which new species are formed. This general model of speciation through geographic isolation is due largely to the work of Ernst Mayr in the 1940s. The model is based primarily on studies of birds and insects. It undoubtedly applies to many sexually reproducing animals, and it applies to plants to a degree, although we will have to discuss special mechanisms in plants later.

The Song Sparrow example shows how a single species may vary geographically, and such variation is common; as a species spreads out across a wide range, its populations often acquire many differences. They may become so different that one is tempted to call some populations distinct species, but as long as neighboring populations can interbreed, genes are still flowing from one to the other and they are still all one species. It is only meaningful, of course, to consider reproductive isolation if the populations in question are positioned so they *could* interbreed. Two populations are *sympatric* (*sym-* = together; *patra* = fatherland, thus homeland) if their ranges overlap, *parapatric* (*para-* = next to) if their ranges are adjacent, or *allopatric* (*allo-* = different) if their ranges are separate. Clearly, we can only talk about reproductive isolation with populations that are sympatric or at least parapatric; with allopatric populations, there is no way to ask the question.

The present conception of speciation begins with a widespread species, often a polytypic species in which individuals living in one region are already genetically distinct from those in other regions. The species then becomes divided into two or more populations by some kind of geographic barrier. Maybe the Earth enters a period of glaciation, and the two populations are separated in different glacial pockets. Perhaps they occupy a lowland habitat but spread out to different sides of a mountain range. Perhaps they are a woodland species, and a grassland develops in the middle of their range. Perhaps they come to occupy different islands – a situation we will examine in more detail later. Whatever the cause, two or more populations become allopatric and unable to interbreed with each other. While they are isolated, they undergo separate genetic paths as they become adapted to local conditions. And they remain isolated long enough to become significantly different genetically and to acquire *reproductive isolating barriers*, which keep them distinct.

Reproductive isolating barriers could operate either before mating occurs or afterward. The difference is important. If two individuals mate and produce zygotes that die or reproduce poorly, they have both wasted much of their reproductive potential, perhaps all of it. So there is strong selective pressure to stop hybridization before mating can occur. The following are some isolating barriers, beginning with the premating.

habitat isolation

Two species may occupy such different habitats that they don't come into contact and thus never have a chance to hybridize. The Red Oak (*Quercus coccinea*) is adapted to swamps and wet bottomlands; the Black Oak (*Quercus velutina*) lives in drier, well-drained upland regions. Hybrids between these species are sometimes found in intermediate habitats, showing that they lack physiological incompatibilities to interbreeding and are kept apart only by their ecological specialization.

temporal isolation

Two species may breed at different times, so there is little chance of hybridization. Two closely related types of plants often release their pollen at different times, so there is little or no chance of cross-fertilization of one by the other.

behavioral isolation

Many animals engage in elaborate courting and mating rituals, which help to ensure that the wrong individuals don't mate. These behaviors are genetically encoded, so the final act of mating only occurs between individuals who share genes that give them compatible behavior patterns.

structural isolation

The reproductive structures of two species may be incompatible. The genitals of animals may not fit together properly so a male can't effectively inseminate a female of the other species. In plants whose flowers are pollinated by animals, two species of plants may become isolated by acquiring different flower colors, thus attracting different pollinators, or the flowers may develop different shapes, so they become specialized for pollination by different species of insects.

The next four barriers operate after mating.

gametic incompatibility

The gametes of the species may fail to function together. For instance, the sperm of one species may not be able to fertilize the egg of the other.

hybrid inviability

A hybrid zygote may die because it is weak or deficient in some other way. A zygote with two different chromosome sets may fail to go through mitosis properly, or the developing embryo may get incompatible instructions from the genetic programs of the maternal and paternal chromosomes, so it eventually aborts.

hybrid sterility

The hybrid may develop into a sterile adult. Sterility generally results from complications in meiosis when different chromosome sets are unable to form viable gametes. The chromosomes of even closely related species may be different enough to make meiosis in a hybrid very difficult.

hybrid disadvantage

Even if the hybrids are viable, their offspring may be inviable or have much lower fitness than the nonhybrid offspring of each species alone. Hybrids are often at a disadvantage because each species is adapted (or is becoming adapted) to a different way of life, so hybrids, with a mixture of gene complexes, generally are not well adapted to either way of life. Imagine two populations that are incompletely isolated and are becoming adapted to different niches. In each population some individuals – call them the "hybridizers" – have genes that tend to promote mating with the other population. If intermediates between the two populations have reduced fitness because they are not well adapted to either niche, the hybridizers will be putting their genes into a reproductive dead end, and genes that dispose their carriers to interbreed will be gradually eliminated from both species. The genes that remain in each population will tend to discourage interbreeding. Exceptions to this tendency, however, are quite common among plants, and successful hybridization often leads to the formation of new plant species.

after separation, the test

The next step in speciation is for the populations to expand their ranges and become sympatric again, and now we can apply the critical test: have the formerly isolated groups acquired reproductive isolating barriers or not?

One possibility is that the populations have achieved full species status and won't interbreed. So speciation is complete, and now each species has the potential of going its own evolutionary way, perhaps to divide again in the future. The other possibility is that the populations have become somewhat different but not different enough to prevent interbreeding, so they continue to interbreed. Many examples of this situation are well known. Among the most common birds of the North American woods are large, brown, ground-feeding woodpeckers called Northern Flickers. A startled bird will fly off with a roller-coaster motion, flashing a patch of white rump feathers. In the east, you will see flickers with bright yellow feathers under their wings and tails, and black mustaches adorning the faces of the males; in the west, your flickers will generally have salmon-red feathers and red mustaches. They were once called two different species, the yellow-shafted and the red-shafted flickers. However, intermediate forms occur quite often, especially in the middle of the continent: birds with orange feathers, sometimes sporting one red and one black mustache, or with some other combination of features. In other words, the various populations of flickers are still exchanging genes regularly. The red-shafted and yellow-shafted forms are not distinct species but geographic variants of a single species. They provide a fine example of animals in an intermediate or incomplete state of speciation.

Organisms such as the flickers can give biologists fits because people like to put organisms into neat boxes and give them unambiguous names. But nature isn't so simple, and this can be frustrating. One difficult situation arises when the populations are allopatric; they show some morphological differences but are clearly related, and yet we are not in a position to test their interbreeding. In this case, we call the populations *semispecies* or *allospecies*, and the whole group of semispecies is a *superspecies*. After an extended period of isolation, the semispecies may start to expand their ranges and become partially sympatric again. Then their species status can be determined. The Northern Flickers are at this intermediate stage in evolution, and the two types are still subspecies or perhaps morphs, since they are not well limited geographically.

There is no way to predict just how populations will change as they spread out into different areas. The flickers present a simple case of an intermediate stage of speciation. But some situations aren't so simple. Traveling from the southern California coast up into the mountains, you will encounter several kinds of plants known as Monkey Flowers of the genus *Diplacus*. Many of them are easy to identify and name with the aid of a field guide, but one group may give you some problems. The moist coastal areas support tall, red-flowered shrubs named *Diplacus puniceus*. The drier foothills are home to shorter bushier plants that usually have orange flowers, called *Diplacus longiflorus*. Still higher, in the very dry mountains, are very short plants with yellow flowers, named *Diplacus calycinus*. The names show that these plants are considered three distinct species. However, over a wide range *puniceus* and *longiflorus* grade into one another, so they appear to be mere varieties of a single species, and populations of plants with the form of *longiflorus* can be found in which the flowers are either red, orange, or yellow. Yet at some places in the Santa Ana Mountains, *puniceus* and *longiflorus* grow together and are clearly distinct, with no interbreeding. Are these distinct species or not? Complicated relationships between populations may develop during evolution, and different degrees of separation may evolve in different places. The difficulty of applying names to such organisms is quite unimportant compared to the lessons they hold about evolution: that organisms in different places will have genomic differences, which cause them to behave in different ways in reproduction.

The Monkey Flowers and other complex situations reinforce the point that the biological species concept, with its criterion of reproductive isolation, may run into difficulties because populations may change in complicated ways. Sometimes a species cannot be delimited neatly because we are trying to apply a simple, idealized concept where it may not fit. The Buckeye (*Junonia lavinia*), a common American butterfly, illustrates the difficult situation of a ring of races. Buckeye populations interbreed with one another around the Gulf Coast from Florida through Texas, Mexico, and Central and South America as the members of a species should. But where the ring closes in the West Indies, populations from Florida meet those from South America, and they will not mate with each other. Suddenly they are different. We don't really know how to apply names to these insects. Circles of races showing such complications are actually rather common. A similar situation exists in the North American west with the Deermouse *Peromyscus maniculatus*. In Glacier National Park, Montana, two subspecies meet with no evidence of interbreeding, partly due, no doubt, to their inhabiting different habitats. But elsewhere these populations are connected by races that interbreed with one another.

Although we catch some organisms at intermediate stages of speciation, it is clear that speciation can occur very quickly. For instance, some cichlid fishes were isolated from their parent populations in Lake Victoria, Africa, only 4000 years ago, and they have clearly become distinct and reproductively isolated in that time. Stanley describes this situation and others where speciation may have occurred in even shorter times.

evolution as opportunism and *bricolage*

George Gaylord Simpson did much to put evolution in perspective in his book *The Meaning of Evolution*. His Chapter 12, on the opportunism of evolution, is itself a paean to rationality and biological wisdom, for he begins:

> Over and over in the study of the history of life it appears that what can happen does happen. There is little suggestion that what occurs *must* occur, that it was fated or that it follows some fixed plan, except simply as the expansion of life follows the opportunities that are presented. In this sense, an outstanding characteristic of evolution is its opportunism. "Opportunism" is, to be sure, a somewhat dangerous word to use in this discussion. It may carry a suggestion of conscious action or of prescience in exploitation of the potentialities of a situation. ... But when a word such as opportunism is used, the reader should not read into it any personal meaning of anthropomorphic implication. No conscious seizing of opportunities is here meant, nor even an unconscious sensing of an outcome.

Simpson went on to point out that the opportunities available to organisms are always limited, and that the evolution of one type of organism always presents a limited range of opportunities for those of other kinds. The evolution of land plants, for instance, created a variety of new habitats for land animals to occupy.

We noted in chapter three that a critical feature of organisms is their historicity, and Simpson noted that "Evolution works on the materials at hand: the groups of organisms as they exist at any given time and the mutations that happen to arise in them. The materials are the results of earlier adaptations plus random additions and the orienting factor in change is adaptation to new opportunities." Every new structure is made by modifying existing structures, and each generation survives if its structures merely "make do," not if they achieve some ideal standard of perfection. Again and again, we see organisms operating with mechanisms that are clearly modifications of ancestral structures, that work, but which could be replaced by much better structures.

Now it is easy to read something like design or destiny or purpose into the history of life – particularly if it is viewed superficially, and most especially if it is done with an anthropomorphic attitude. An antidote to this tendency comes from an unexpected source, from the anthropologist Claude Levi-Strauss, who provided the image of primitive humans operating through what the French call *bricolage*. *Un bricoleur* is a workman who creates by tinkering with what he has available and coming up with a contraption that "makes do," even though someone with more resources might create a better device. All the evidence of biology is that if there is some cosmic intelligence behind biological structure and function, that intelligence operates as *un bricoleur*, not as an all-powerful inventor making the best possible design. One famous example is the panda's "thumb," as explained by Stephen Jay Gould. Pandas live exclusively on bamboo shoots, which they prepare with their hands using a kind of thumb-like extension that works against a paw with the normal five digits. The "thumb" is actually an enlarged radial sesamoid bone, one of the normal bones of the vertebrate wrist, which moves with only a slight modification of the muscles that move the true thumb in other verte-brates. Thus, pandas have become adapted for their unique diets through biological *bricolage*, by modification of the available struc-tures to make a pseudothumb that works. A truly intelligent designer, having created the pandas and set them in the midst of a bamboo forest with instructions to be fruitful and multiply, could have supplied them with a much more efficiently designed hand.

I began chapter one by noting that North America and Europe host a multitude of very similar little sparrows and buntings, so one must wonder at their variety. Simpson observed that if this historical view of evolution is correct, one must expect to find multiple solu-tions to adaptational problems, and he explored the idea by refer-ence to the wonderful variety of antelopes in what was at that time the Belgian Congo (Figure 6.2).

Now there must be some one type of horn that would be the most effective possible for antelopes, with some minor variation in pro-portions or shape in accordance with the sizes or detailed habits of the animals. Obviously not all of these antelopes have the "best" type of horns, and probably none of them has. Why, for instance, with their otherwise rather close similarity, should the horns of the

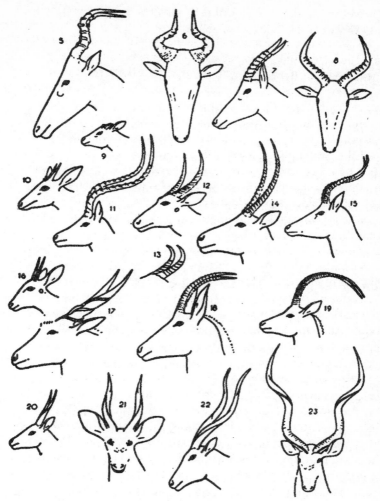

Figure 6.2 *The heads of several species of African antelopes.*

reedbuck (14 in the figure) curve forward and those of the roan antelope (18) curve backward? Do not the impala (11) and kob (15) horns with their double curve, seem to achieve the same functional placing and direction as the reedbuck horns (12 and 14) with a single curve, but to do so in a way mechanically weaker? Even though the animals themselves are small, are not the duiker horns (9 and 10) too small to be really effective, and are not the tremendous kudu horns (23) unnecessarily unwieldly?

Viewed in the light of opportunism and *bricolage*, however, this variety of antelope species makes good sense.

speciation and opportunism on islands

The Hawaiian Islands are inhabited by an unusual collection of little red and yellow-green birds, which are distinguished by an amazing variety of bills. They are now classified in a single, unique family, called Drepanididae, known as Hawaiian honeycreepers. The diversity of honeycreepers contrasts sharply with the typical birds of large land masses. Each continent has many families of birds, each one containing species that occupy very similar niches. For instance, sparrows and finches have short, conical bills and are adapted for eating seeds; woodpeckers are adapted for digging into wood to catch burrowing insects; warblers are small, nervous, insect-eaters with thin bills; and thrushes have moderately heavy bills that are used for eating fruit, insects, and other small invertebrates.

Even though the internal anatomy of the Hawaiian honeycreepers shows that they are closely related, they occupy very different niches and show enormous external differences, especially in their bills (Figure 6.3). The chunky yellow and brown chloridops uses (or used, for unfortunately many of these species are extinct now) its tough, massive bill for crushing the seeds of the naio plant. The ou looks like a parrot and feeds on fruits just as parrots do in the American tropics, using its hooked bill to scoop out the insides of the ripe ieie fruit. The koa finches and Laysan finch also fed on fruits, and the koas could split the tough twigs of the koa tree and eat grubs that lived inside them. The akialoa feeds like a woodpecker, probing its long bill into crevices in trees and sometimes peeling off bits of bark to find grubs and insects. The mamos used their long, curved bills to suck the nectar out of deep flowers, while the iiwi takes some nectar but prefers to eat the caterpillars off flowers. The apapane's narrow bill is suited for its diet of insects with a bit of nectar. As a whole, the Hawaiian honeycreepers seem to have found most of the ways in which land birds can live, and the members of a single family have diverged enough to occupy the kinds of niches that are taken by whole families of birds elsewhere.

The Hawaiian Islands lie far from any continent and have few native land birds other than the drepanids. Sometime in the past, perhaps a few million years ago, a few birds that were ancestors of

Figure 6.3 *Although they are very closely related, the species of Hawaiian honeycreepers exhibit very different morphologies as adaptations to distinct ecological niches, especially in the forms of their bills. (Plates from* A Field Guide to Western Birds, *2nd ed. © 1990 by Roger Tory Peterson. Reproduced by permission of Houghton Mifflin Company. All rights reserved.)*

the honeycreepers must have wandered to Hawaii. Finding few other birds competing for such foods as insects and nectar, they adapted to using these resources. The islands provided a particularly suitable stage for speciation, because as the founding colony multiplied, it spread out over the islands where small populations became isolated from one another. Starting with slightly different founder populations, and given isolation and time, these differences became accentuated. Thus, a colony on one island developed into seed-eaters while those on another island developed bills useful for eating insects. There is some reason to think that the founders were the red and black types that live primarily on nectar, that some of them evolved into the yellow-green insect-eaters, and that others developed later into the fruit-eaters.

The Hawaiian honeycreepers are another excellent example of opportunism. The founders were faced with many opportunities for making a living, and their descendants eventually evolved ways to take advantage of many of them. By means of genetic variations that conferred particular advantages, they seized the opportunities that arose for living in new ways.

adaptive radiation and genetic drift

The pattern of evolution in the honeycreepers is called an *adaptive radiation*, because one original population radiated out in several different biological directions (perhaps also different directions geographically) as its subpopulations took advantage of new opportunities. A general way of life to which a species can become adapted is called an *adaptive zone*. In the honeycreeper case, we may characterize insect-eating, nectar-eating, and fruit-eating as three general adaptive zones, with species in each zone specialized in their own particular niches. Given the right conditions, every species has the genetic potential to divide into more species, thus creating greater diversity. The term "adaptive radiation" is applied both to small episodes of evolution, as in the honeycreepers, and to large episodes, such as the divergence of the many basic types of birds or mammals. Thus, paleontologists speak of the adaptive radiation that happened during the Cambrian era to produce so many phyla of animals, or of an adaptive radiation in the Triassic era that produced so many types of reptiles, including the various lines of dinosaurs.

As species divide and radiate out into new adaptive zones, populations may be most likely to fail during transition times. But remember the point made in chapter five that even a small change in a structure can make an important difference in fitness. We must not imagine that one of the specialized bills of a contemporary honeycreeper was useless until it acquired its modern form, nor were plants inviable while their flowers were intermediate between the forms we now see. Still, a rapid transition would seem to be advantageous. To become a successful new species, a population might have to cross a nonadaptive zone or a zone already occupied. To use the niche-spotlight model again, a population initially shares a patch of light with its parent population. A short distance away are unoccupied patches in different adaptive zones, but to reach them it must cross a darker zone.

It may therefore be important that new species are frequently founded by small populations in which *genetic drift* may occur. Genetic drift might carry a population quickly from one patch to another. The genetic make-up of a small population can change much faster by drift than by selection, and possibly in directions different from those in which selective forces would lead it. Isolated subspecies (semispecies) could acquire different habitat and niche preferences through genetic drift, and these small populations may drift to genotypes that are quite different from the typical genotype of their parent population. A special case of genetic drift is the *founder effect*: an isolated semispecies is founded by a few individuals whose genotypes are quite untypical of the main population, so the new population begins with an unusual average genotype and evolves further from there.

plant evolution through hybridization and polyploidy

For reasons that are not yet understood, hybridization is an important mechanism in plant evolution, even though it apparently plays a much smaller role in the evolution of animals. Edgar Anderson has emphasized the importance in plant evolution of *introgression*, a process in which some genes of one species work their way into the genome of another through hybridization. The hybrids between two species generally are less viable and fertile than their parents, but the progeny made by repeated backcrossing to one parent are intermediate varieties, with only part of the genome from the other parent, and they may be quite hardy and well-adapted to existing conditions. Introgression results from this sequence of hybridization, backcrossing, and selection of certain backcross types, and it is an important source of new variability in plant species. It tends to reduce sympatric species back to semispecies status, and sometimes leads to the emergence of new types.

Introgression is prominent in some of the irises, or flags, which are so abundant and diverse in the lowlands of southern Louisiana. Around 1938, Herbert P. Riley found hybridization between the elegant blue *Iris giganticaerulea* and the brilliant orange *Iris fulva*. The two species are sympatric, but *I. giganticaerulea* is adapted to the waterlogged soil of marshes and *I. fulva* grows in the drier soil of banks and woods. The two only hybridize where the habitats have been broken down by human interference, and there Riley found a number of populations that show various degrees of hybridization, as measured by seven characteristics that mark one parental type or the other. Some populations appeared to be basically *giganticaerulea* with various amounts of the *fulva* genome resulting from continuous backcrossing.

New plant species may also develop more directly by the creation of *polyploid* individuals that have more than the usual diploid number of chromosomes. *Autopolyploidy* results from an abnormality in meiosis, resulting in diploid ($2n$) gametes instead of the usual haploid ($1n$) gametes. This sometimes happens in a plant that can pollinate itself. Self-fertilization, which is rare in animals, permits an unusual $3n$ (*triploid*) or $4n$ (*tetraploid*) zygote to be made, and the apparently greater plasticity of plant development allows many of these zygotes to grow into perfectly good, fertile plants. In fact, polyploids are generally larger than their parents and produce larger fruits; many of our domestic plants, which are cultivated for these features, are polyploids. Triploids are generally sterile because their three sets of chromosomes are unable to engage in the usual processes of meiosis and produce normal, viable gametes. (Triploids such as bananas are valued by humans because they have no large seeds. And, amazingly, aquaculturists have now been able to breed triploid oysters, which don't spoil their culinary value by making large egg masses.) In a tetraploid, the four homologous chromosomes generally seem to avoid irregularities, so such plants tend to be viable and fertile.

Polyploidy may also result from a breakdown of interspecies barriers. In *allopolyploidy*, two diploid sets come from different but closely related species. This may begin with haploid pollen from one species fertilizing haploid ova from another. The diploid hybrids are sterile because their chromosome sets are too different to form viable gametes, but the plants may reproduce vegetatively (asexually). Then later one of these plants may become tetraploid as in autopolyploidy. Allopolyploids may have some advantages in nature because they combine some characteristics of both parents. They may be superior because of *heterosis* or *hybrid vigor*: for various reasons, hybrids are often superior to both of their parents in strength of growth or in general vitality. Hybrids may be suited to a slightly different niche from that of their parent species.

It has been estimated that nearly half the speciation events in the evolution of flowering plants have involved polyploidy. One documented example is the salt-marsh grass *Spartina*. *S. maritima* ($2n = 60$) grows along European coastal marshes, while *S. alterniflora* ($2n = 62$) is found along the North American coast. The American species was accidentally introduced in Britain around 1800 c.e., and it started to grow in patches mixed with its European cousin. In about 1870, a sterile hybrid between them was identified and named *S. townsendii*. It is diploid and also has 62 chromosomes (indicating some minor chromosomal alteration from the expected number of 61), but can only reproduce asexually by extending rhizoids (runners). Then around 1890 one of these plants apparently changed into a fertile allotetraploid, named *S. anglica*, which has 122 chromosomes. *S. anglica* is a very vigorous grass that is now spreading around the coasts of Britain and France, replacing its parental species.

Modern bread wheat, *Triticum aestivum*, also arose through hybridization and allopolyploidy (Figure 6.4). Because of their distinctive forms, wheat chromosomes can be traced back to those of wild grasses, involving two episodes of hybridization followed by

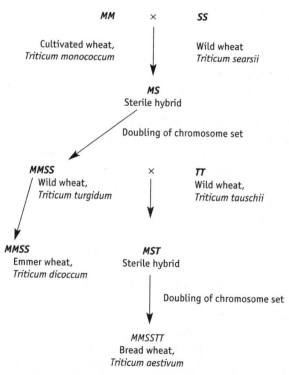

Figure 6.4 *Different species of wheat have arisen through a series of hybridizations followed by duplications of the whole chromosome set. Each of the large letters S, M, and T represents a set of 14 chromosomes characteristic of one initial species.*

duplication. The ancestral wheats have been preserved – einkorn wheat that is grown especially on poor soils in Europe and emmer wheat whose proteins make the excellent gluten needed for pasta.

These regimes of hybridization and selection can produce *sympatric speciation*, without the need for geographic isolation. New species might also arise sympatrically through strong selection for adaptations to different habitats. In Britain, a variant of the grass *Agrostis tenuis* is genetically lead-resistant and is able to live on soils contaminated by the lead-rich tailings of some mines. The original, lead-intolerant populations often grow only a few meters away on uncontaminated soil. Hybrids between the two types grow poorly on both types of soil, so the lead-resistant plants seem to constitute a new species that has arisen within the range of its parent species, perhaps because of only one or a few genetic changes.

In spite of its difficulties, the concept of a species as a group of organisms that can actually or potentially interbreed with one another seems most satisfactory. But from the viewpoint of humans who are eager to put organisms into neat boxes and give everything an unambiguous label, speciation may be messy. We must expect to find populations at intermediate stages. In general, geography seems to be the principal factor in dividing a species into new species, and speciation happens quite prominently in island groups, with their natural barriers to movement. Plants, however, commonly change through hybridization and related processes.

development and macroevolution

It is relatively easy to look at the differences in form of species undergoing speciation and see how those distinct species could arise. If the difference between, say, red-shafted and yellow-shafted flickers lies merely in the colors of pigments, just tweaking a gene or two could account for the distinction, and we can easily see how one gene complex could predominate in the east and the other in the west. The differences among the various Hawaiian honeycreepers are greater, of course, but we can easily accept the idea that some changes in genes for pigmentation combined with some for the length of the bill could account for these different species. But then we stand back and look at the whole animal kingdom, for instance. The obvious enormous difference between a roundworm and an insect, or between a jellyfish and a mammal, seem overwhelming. It doesn't seem to help to recognize that this evolution has occurred over about half a billion years. The great issue is not having enough time but, rather, the more fundamental questions: *How* could these enormous differences have developed? What are the mechanisms involved?

The question could not have been asked – let alone answered – in a satisfactory way until just a few years ago, because it depends upon recent progress in developmental biology and especially in developmental genetics. Every multicellular organism – plant, animal, fungus, or other – begins as a single cell, which then proliferates: it grows and divides into many cells, and this multicellular mass develops a specific shape and form. Along the way, its individual cells differentiate into a variety of more specialized cells; a complicated

125

animal such as a mammal consists of at least a hundred different cell types, such as a variety of neurons in the nervous system, skin cells, heart muscle cells, liver cells, various kidney cells, and so on. Remarkably, each type of cell develops in the correct place. With very few rare and unfortunate exceptions, every newborn human, for instance, ends up with everything so placed that it looks like a normal human.

Evolution operates on the process of development. The change from a lobe-finned fish to a primitive amphibian involved (among other changes) small modifications of the bones in the fins, near the end of development, so they became more functional for movement beyond the water. All the evolution of complex organisms entails changes in growth to make slightly different structures. The remarkable advances of the past few decades in understanding these processes have provided some insights into their evolution in many distinct types of organisms.

As you read this chapter, please remember a point I have tried to make several times: nothing in evolution predestines success, and the existence of such a multitude of wonderful organisms, humans included, is just the result of a long series of lucky accidents. If early animals, during the first few million years of their evolution, had not hit upon certain valuable mechanisms and structures that provide enormous flexibility for future evolution, we just wouldn't have come into existence to sit here and ponder these matters.

being multicellular

The simple unicellular organisms that lived before about a billion years ago (and whose descendants we still find in our waters) differ fundamentally from the multicellular plants and animals that followed. Single cells are almost entirely at the mercy of their surroundings. They proliferate or perish according to accidental events that supply plenty of water or make a pond dry up; that supply the right amount of salt or too much; that supply organic nutrients or none at all. Unicellular organisms can regulate some movement of molecules across their cell membranes and partially control their internal conditions. Many unicells evolved mechanisms of motility – flagella, cilia, ameboid motion – so they can swim to more suitable environments, perhaps avoid droughts and search out sources of nutrition. Still, their resources for survival are limited.

A multicellular organism has potentially greater resources for survival in a hostile world. John Gerhart and Marc Kirschner have expressed this difference in the twin features of conditionality and contingency. Conditionality means that individual cells within the organism have the potential to control the conditions of their surroundings, since the entire organism is at least partially protected from its environment and from the random changes that can occur there. Contingency means the ability of cells to respond to particular conditions, both extracellular and intracellular, and thus to regulate themselves; in particular, cells have the potential to differentiate into specialized cells with specific functions. Unicellular organisms can often respond to environmental conditions by changing their physiology, even changing their forms, and these responses are subject to natural selection. Such changes within a multicellular organism give the organism as a whole much greater flexibility and potential for survival.

how to build an animal

The most obviously diverse creatures on Earth are animals. They originated sometime around a billion years ago, and (as outlined briefly in chapter three) diversified quite suddenly (in geological terms) around half a billion years ago. We now recognize about thirty distinct phyla, related generally as shown in Figure 7.1. For our purposes here, we will ignore the most primitive types (sponges, corals, anemones, and their relatives). We will try to understand how simple animals such as roundworms could have descendants as different as a fly and a mouse. Let us consider how animals are built.

A roundworm is basically a tube within a tube. The outer tube is its body wall, the inner tube an intestine running through the body from the mouth to the anus. This is a fundamental animal form, lost or modified in only a few phyla. It is made quite easily from the initial zygote. The zygote begins to divide into smaller cells: into two, then four, then eight, and so on until it becomes a small ball of cells. Then the cells on one side push inward, to start forming that inner tube; it is similar to pushing your fist into a very soft but strong balloon, and the hole your wrist lies in will be either the mouth or the anus, depending on the phylum. This indented ball will continue to elongate into a body, and eventually the hole at the other end of the intestine – anus or mouth – will break through. Although the

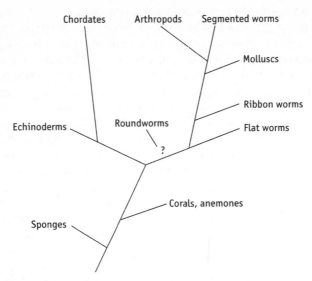

Figure 7.1 *A phylogenetic tree showing the relationships among the principal phyla of animals.*

details vary greatly, that is the fundamental way of making the basic animal form.

To be functional, the tube-in-a-tube must be modified for the typical animal way of life. Animals are predators, either on vegetation or on other animals. The animal way of life is to move around in search of food (and, incidentally, to avoid becoming food), requiring that one end, the head, must go first. The head becomes specialized for its function by acquiring sense organs (eyes, ears, receptors for taste and odor) to detect food and dangers, a mouth for ingesting the food (and perhaps chewing it up), and sometimes special appendages for grabbing the food and stuffing it into the mouth. The head also acquires some specialized nervous tissue (a brain of sorts) for processing signals from the sense organs and controlling the actions of the other parts. The process of acquiring such a specialized head end is called *cephalization*.

This animal needs two other structures, aside from its head. Although a concentration of nervous tissue in the head is important, this tissue has to serve the entire body, so a nerve cord is extended to the tail end. Also, the cells of the body need to be nourished with food and oxygen, while their wastes are removed. In the smallest animals, these exchanges can often take place through direct diffusion to and from the surroundings, but beyond that minimal size the animal needs a circulatory system, with tubes to carry blood to and from all the tissues and a heart to pump it. In the simplest animals, the blood may pick up its oxygen directly from the outside and deposit its wastes there, but the circulatory system generally acquires two appendage systems: a special place for gas exchange, such as gills, and a special place for excreting other wastes, such as kidneys (made of units called nephridia).

I don't mean to gloss over the animal's primary function from an evolutionary point of view – to reproduce itself. But that is a some-what special business requiring that the reproductive (germ) cells be segregated off somewhere and that a simple device be made to help ensure fertilization.

Going beyond roundworms, the primary rule for making more complicated animals seems to be, "Start with identical segments." If a genome can be devised that instructs the formation of a functional piece of an animal, that piece can be repeated as many times as necessary to make the entire animal, of any length (Figure 7.2). (As an analogy, it is similar to the principle that enormous polymers such as proteins and nucleic acids are made by adding more and more similar or identical monomers.) The process is called *metamerization*, and the individual segments of the body are *metameres*. Our model is a humble earthworm, whose body consists almost entirely of very similar metameres.

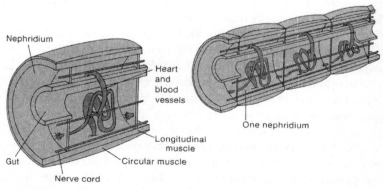

Figure 7.2 *A unit animal consists of a gut inside the body tube, with other organs such as a heart and segment of a nervous system. A whole basic animal can be made by repeating this segment several times.*

Given this basic formula for making a basic animal body, we have to consider how genes can produce it and, especially, how changes in those genes can produce functional animals of such diverse forms.

the idea of proteins that regulate genes

It has been obvious to biologists for a long time that every gene in a genome isn't expressed in every cell; "expressed" means that the gene is turned "on," so its protein product is produced. Although many genes (often called housekeeping genes) are expressed in all of the cells in the human body, each cell type is characterized by its particular proteins (which also give it a particular form). Thus, only red blood cells produce hemoglobin. Only muscle cells produce the proteins such as actin and myosin that form the tough muscle fibers, which pull on one another to produce muscle contraction. Each type of gland makes its distinctive hormones, and only specialized cells in the intestinal tract produce their particular digestive enzymes.

The story of discovering genes that regulate other genes is told in the *Genetics* book, but the general process is easily summarized. Expressing a gene means transcribing a messenger-RNA (mRNA) from it. Let me unpack that complicated sentence by reviewing some points from the section on nucleic acids in chapter three. The genes are DNA regions, located in the chromosomes in the nucleus (except in procaryotic cells, but the general principle applies to all cells). The factories where proteins are actually made are little particles called *ribosomes*, which occupy much of the cell's cytoplasm. The information is carried from the genes to the ribosomes by messengers, which happen to be distinctive RNA molecules. For a gene to be expressed, the enzyme *RNA polymerase* attaches to a region near the gene, a region called the *promoter*. RNA polymerase opens the DNA double helix and begins to move along one strand of the DNA, the so-called template strand, while it synthesizes an RNA molecule. The enzyme operates just as if it were replicating the DNA, except that it is producing RNA instead of a complementary strand of DNA. Nucleotide by nucleotide, it constructs an mRNA molecule with a sequence just complementary to that of the coding strand, and this process is called *transcription*; the resulting mRNA can then move out to the ribosomes, where its sequence is *translated* into protein molecules. Each protein is built sequentially, amino acid by amino acid, as the ribosomal mechanism reads the sequence of the mRNA.

A gene will not be expressed unless it is transcribed. Transcription can be regulated either negatively or positively, by means of other proteins. In bacteria, the regulation is often negative; a distinctive protein called a repressor binds on or near the promoter of a gene and prevents RNA polymerase from starting to act there. In eucaryotic cells, the regulation is more commonly positive: a distinctive protein, or more often a complex of several distinctive proteins, must bind to the promoter and initiate transcription. The exact method used isn't important here. The fact of there being gene-regulatory proteins is important.

Many regulatory proteins, called simply transcription factors, promote transcription by binding to promoters. But genes are also associated with regulatory regions called *enhancers*, and transcription factors may also bind to the enhancer of a gene to promote its transcription. In fact, some genes have several enhancers, and their transcription may be stimulated by various combinations of transcription factors binding to these enhancers. I mention these details only to show that there may be many ways for a gene to be turned on or off.

Every gene can easily have a distinctive promoter. Since every position can be occupied by 4 different nucleotides, there are over a million sequences of only 10 nucleotides, and using 20 nucleotides provides over 10^{12} possibilities. By means of their distinctive sequences, promoters – and thus genes – can be put into classes. So all the genes that encode specialized muscle proteins, for example, could be given a unique promoter sequence and then turned on by a unique regulatory protein that recognizes that sequence. A regulatory protein that selects certain genes to be turned on is naturally called a selector protein, and the gene that encodes it is a selector gene. We will see that the essential function of a selector gene is to confer *positional identity* on a cell; that is, selector genes tell each cell where it is in the body and therefore what it should eventually become. They say, in effect, "You lie in the middle of the thorax, and you are destined to become part of the heart."

Many selector genes have now been identified, especially in the fruit fly *Drosophila*. In general, genes are discovered and identified by means of mutations that happen to occur in them, and they are named by the characteristics of the mutants. Geneticists' senses of humor are revealed when they name new genes. For instance, a gene responsible for producing a distinctive #7 cell in the eye is called *sevenless* (*sev*); related genes found later were then named *seven-up* (*sup*), *son of sevenless* (*sos*) and *bride of sevenless* (*bos*). And you'll see some other funny names as we go along. By the way, gene names are always italicized; the names of proteins are in roman type and are commonly capitalized.

making heads, tails, and segments

The most important basic features of a typical animal are its cephalization and its metamerism. It is instructive to see how these features are created genetically in *Drosophila*, although the early development of fruit flies has some features that aren't shared by all animals. *Drosophila* eggs develop in an ovary surrounded by several nurse cells, which give it special properties well before fertilization; in most animals, the egg develops more by itself, and the head-tail axis is determined in other ways. Nevertheless, the nurse cells of *Drosophila* put two kinds of mRNA molecules into the egg: one at what will become the head end for the protein Bicoid and one at the tail end for the protein Nanos. When these mRNAs are translated, the embryo contains a gradient of Bicoid protein that is most concentrated at the head end, and a similar gradient of Nanos protein, most concentrated at the tail end. In this way, the cephalization of the embryo is determined, and the ground is laid for dividing the body into segments that will eventually take on distinct forms.

The first effect of the initial regulatory proteins is to turn on a series of *gap genes*, so called because mutations in these genes produce embryos with certain segments missing. Each of these genes, with names such as *hunchback, krüppel*, and *knirps*, identifies a region of the body, about ten regions in all. The protein products of these genes are all transcription factors, and their effect, in various combinations, will be to turn on a second set of genes, called *pair-rule* genes because the effect of a mutation in any of them is to delete either all the even-numbered or all the odd-numbered body segments. Some of the *Drosophila* pair-rule genes are *hairy, runt, even-skipped, odd-skipped*, and *fushi tarazu* (Japanese for "too few segments"). These genes lay down the basic metamerism of the body. Geneticists who study them can apply specific stains to the embryo fly to locate each type of pair-rule protein, and a stained embryo always shows a series of colored bands dividing the body

Figure 7.3 *A fruit fly embryo stained to reveal one distinctive protein involved in regulating development shows that the protein has been produced in a series of bands along the body.*

into its 14 characteristic segments (Figure 7.3). Finally, the products of the pair-rule genes activate a third set of genes, called segment-polarity genes, such as *wingless* and *engrailed*. Each body segment is divided into an anterior and a posterior half, which often have quite different structures. Each segment-polarity protein occurs in one half or the other, thus creating this division. Through a complicated logic of repression and activation of genes, this series of genes produces body segments identified by position and ready to differentiate into various structures. How does that happen?

homeotic genes: producing the organs of the body

The homeotic genes were discovered through remarkable mutations that make the segments of the body very similar (*homeo-* = similar) or else substitute one structure for another; the *Antennapedia* mutation, for instance, creates legs on the head instead of antennae. As a class, they are now called Hox genes. Mutant insects lacking all the Hox genes have identical segments instead of distinct segments. *Drosophila* has eight Hox genes that determine the identities of the segments, in one cluster (*Antennapedia*) that determines head structures and another cluster (*Bithorax*) determining structures of the thorax and abdomen; remarkably, their sequence on the chromosome is identical to the sequence of their action from head to tail in the animal.

After the *Drosophila* Hox genes became known, investigators looked for similar genes in other animals. Roundworms have four of them. Mammals have four sets of Hox genes corresponding closely to the *Drosophila* set plus a few more, as if the basic set had been doubled twice: once when the first vertebrates evolved and again after the fishes had evolved. Again, the sequences of these genes on their chromosomes are identical to the sequence of their action from head to tail in the embryo.

These genes determine what specific structures will form at each point along the head-tail axis. In flies, for instance, the second thoracic segment bears a pair of wings and the third has only a pair of balancing organs, called halteres. In early experiments, Ed Lewis was able to make four-winged flies, with wings instead of halteres on the third segment, through a combination of mutations in the *Bithorax* complex. In vertebrates of all kinds, a fin or forelimb forms at the anterior boundary of the region where *Hox-c6* and *Hox-b8* are expressed. The Hox genes act as selector genes, determining in each region which other more specific genes will be turned on or off to create specific structures. The growth of a vertebrate limb, a fin or a leg, then entails complicated interactions among several genes expressed in different parts of the limb bud as it grows out of the body, and again some of these interactions involve specific Hox genes.

M. Akam and his colleagues have suggested how a series of duplications and diversifications of Hox genes among arthropods could account for one important line of evolution. Start with an ancestral arthropod having only three Hox genes that determine a head, several identical body segments, and a tail segment:

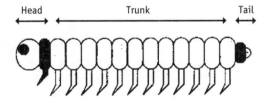

A duplication then produces a gene such as *scr* (*sex-combs reduced*), generating the maxillipeds (MP) of the myriapods (centipedes and millipedes):

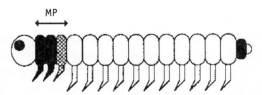

Another duplication produces a gene such as *Abd* (*abdominal*), creating a primitive insect with a thorax and abdomen:

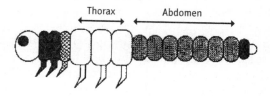

A further duplication can then produce a gene such as *AbdA* (*abdominal-A*), which directs the formation of wings, to generate a fly:

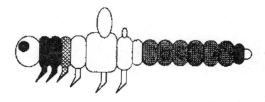

Such examples indicate how Hox genes, because of their fundamental roles in determining structure and their versatility, allow us some insights into how such a great variety of animals could have evolved. The origin of such genes in the most primitive animals seems to have opened a most fortunate series of opportunities for the later evolution of quite diverse forms.

As another example of this flexibility, the vertebrate body plan differs from that of typical invertebrates in the relative positions of major organ systems; in vertebrates, the nerve cord lies along the back (dorsal) but in arthropods and other invertebrates it runs along the belly (ventral). The two body plans are so similar that some classical zoologists debated the question of whether one type of animal could be turned into the other just by inverting one of them. In a sense, this is what has happened through interactions of the regulatory genes that determine the dorsal-ventral axis of the animal body, similar to those that determine the head-tail axis. Arthropods and vertebrates have parallel sets of genes and proteins. The *Drosophila* protein Decapentaplegic (Dpp) defines a dorsal compartment of the body and prevents the formation of nervous tissue there; in the ventral compartment of the body, the protein Sog (*short-gastrulation*) antagonizes Dpp and allows formation of the nerve cord. The vertebrate homologues of Dpp are BMP2 and BMP4, which are present in the ventral compartment of the embryo, where they block formation of nervous tissue. The vertebrate homologue of Sog is the protein chordin, which is produced in the dorsal region of the embryo, where it induces the formation of the nerve cord. So this regulatory regime has the intrinsic potential of producing quite different-looking animals by means of very similar chemical interactions.

flexibility and stability

It should be clear that evolution could not produce such a great variety of animals unless a certain flexibility were built into the operation of the genome. Mutations in regulatory genes must be able to change developmental processes to produce organisms with different forms, but the resulting changes must be viable – the resulting novel organisms must have at least some chance of survival. A common objection raised against the possibility that such complex systems could evolve is a crude analogy with a mechanism such as a watch; if you made some random change in the structure of a watch, it simply wouldn't work at all. So the actual processes of development must not be stubbornly watchlike. They must produce stable, functional structures but with a built-in flexibility.

One feature of development that creates such flexibility is compartmentalization. We have seen that the developing body is divided into distinct compartments, within which specific genes act to produce distinctive structures. Thus, the effects of many mutations will be limited to small compartments and the resulting animals will differ in small ways from their ancestors.

Another mechanism that provides potential flexibility is the combination of a single regulatory protein and its receptor. The image here may need sharpening: any molecule, which we generally call a *ligand*, might bind to a protein. The ligand might even be another protein. The binding of some ligand may then change the protein's shape so as to change its function. For instance, many enzymes have a specific binding site where some small molecule may bind to them; the enzyme alone may be active but becomes inactive when the ligand is bound, and the ligand then functions as a regulatory inhibitor. Or the regulation may work the opposite way: the enzyme might only be active when a specific ligand is bound to it, so the ligand becomes an activator. Proteins called *receptors* have the function of receiving and responding to signals. Some important receptors in animals are exposed on cell surfaces, and the ligand that binds to them may be a hormone. If a specific event stimulates a gland to release its hormone into the blood, the hormone is carried to some remote cells that bear receptors for the hormone, and the binding of the hormone to its receptor initiates some process, which stimulates the cell into a specific action.

By the way, the gene-regulatory proteins we have been discussing bind similarly, but here the "ligand" is generally a specific site on DNA and the function of the protein is to change the DNA temporarily.

Among the most important systems in this regard are enzymes called *protein kinases*. A kinase is an enzyme that can attach a phosphate ($-PO_4$) to some other molecule, and a protein kinase is one that attaches the phosphate to a specific protein. The remarkable finding is that merely attaching a simple phosphate to a protein can change its properties so drastically that it shifts from inactivity to activity (or vice versa), and it has become clear now that a great deal of cellular regulation occurs by means of protein kinases. Some regulation occurs through chains of reactions, called *cascades*, in which enzyme 1 becomes activated, perhaps by a hormone, and attaches a phosphate to enzyme 2, which then becomes activated and activates enzyme 3, and so on. Cascades are biological amplifiers, because at each stage of activation, more and more molecules are activated, producing a large final effect.

Studies of development have revealed several pairs (or trios, or more) of proteins that act as ligand and receptor. In *Drosophila*, for instance, the Hedgehog protein interacts with a receptor protein called Patched and also with protein kinase A. Each of these combinations of interacting proteins is a *regulatory module*, and such modules may be employed in several different developmental processes in a single animal. Modules afford the animal both stability and flexibility. Operating as a single regulatory unit, the module is stable. But it also provides the potential for novelty; for instance, a regulatory mutation might change the time or place for expression of the module, opening up new developmental possibilities. Remember, too, that novelty is commonly introduced through gene duplication and diversification. Genes for some of the important modules appear to have been duplicated several times, producing whole families of similar regulatory proteins with specialized roles.

Regulatory modules are used commonly in pairs to provide a kind of stability (Figure 7.4). For instance, cell 1 produces protein A

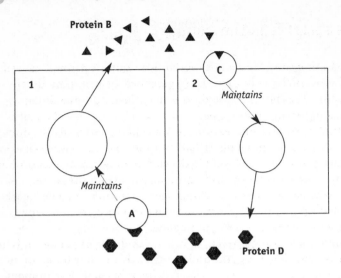

Figure 7.4 *Regulatory modules may be used to maintain two cell types in a stable condition where each cell produces a receptor for a protein produced by the other cell.*

and secretes protein B; cell 2 produces protein C and secretes protein D. But A is a receptor for D, and C is a receptor for B, and binding of a receptor to its ligand stimulates the cell to maintain its condition. So the two cell types maintain one another through their interaction. In other instances, module X activates module Y which in turn activates X, producing a wave of differentiation that may pass through a structure, as in development of the fruit fly eye.

Flexibility is also built into regulation by means of redundancy and overlapping mechanisms. If a process is controlled by two or more mechanisms, which duplicate one another in part, then removing one mechanism through mutation may have little final effect; but – like the opportunism provided through gene duplication and diversification – if one mechanism is changed, it has the opportunity to evolve in a useful direction while the unchanged mechanism continues to serve its original function.

The actual processes involved in growth and regulation are far more complicated than I have been able to show here. (The book by Gerhart and Kirschner, cited earlier, will provide some insight into their complexity.) As developmental biologists elucidate these processes, they make it easier for us to understand how such a wonderful variety of organisms has evolved in the past few billion years.

the secret is in the timing

In addition to all the genetic mechanisms outlined above, one general process allows us to explain a great deal of evolution: the timing of events. Development obviously takes time. A human infant develops for nine months before it is even born, and it then takes approximately twenty years more for a child to achieve full adult size and form. (And the changes that continue to occur – well, we won't dwell on those!) Every event in development begins at a set time and continues for a set time, and a great deal of evolution can be accounted for by means of changes in this timing. For a popularly written, comprehensive exposition of the subject, the book by Kenneth McNamara is recommended.

What is the difference between a tall and a short person? It is primarily in the lengths of the limbs, especially the long bones of the legs. These bones begin to grow early in embryonic development, and throughout childhood they elongate as new tissue is laid down at growth points near the ends of the bones. The genes that determine the timing of these events can shut off growth early or late, producing people of different heights. Now consider the neck of the giraffe. All mammals have seven cervical (neck) vertebrae, and giraffes are no exception. Giraffes do not differ in having more vertebrae but in having much longer vertebrae, bones that were allowed to grow considerably in length before their growth was terminated.

Many anatomical features can be accounted for through extension of this idea. The biologist D'Arcy Thompson pointed this out years ago by showing how one can lay a grid over a drawing of one animal and then, by systematically shifting the grid, convert it into a drawing of a different, but easily recognizable animal (Figure 7.5). Thompson showed that in this way he could account for the forms of related species of fish, for instance, merely by assuming that growth in one species had changed in a simple, systematic way. Here, then, is another general factor for evolutionary forces to "play" with. As this line of inquiry in development grows over the next few years, we can expect to learn how significant changes in form can be made merely by letting a structure grow for a longer or shorter time.

Developmental biologists are just now revealing the intricate genetic mechanisms that regulate the growth of a fertilized ovum into a mature organism. Already, though, we can see many points at

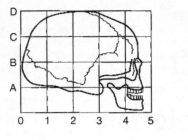
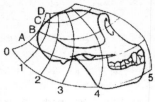

Human skull   Chimpanzee skull

Figure 7.5 *A rectangular grid is drawn over one anatomical drawing and then transformed. The process shows how the skull of a modern human can be derived from that of an earlier primate simply through regular changes in the growth of each region, by relatively greater growth toward the back of the skull.*

which organisms with distinctive forms can be made by mutation or by the production of a new gene through duplication and diversification. Readers who are ready for a challenge may plunge into the intricacies of the matter through some of the books cited in the list of further reading.

human evolution

Victorians who were shocked by Darwin's ideas might have been willing to accept them if only they did not apply to us. As one well-born lady is reported to have said, "Descended from the apes! My dear, we will hope it is not true. But if it is, let us pray that it may not become generally known!" Contradicting the Bible was bad enough, but implying that God's noblest and finest creation, the human being (or at least the well-born male European human being), was not created specially and lovingly as the centerpiece of his Universe, well, it was just ... just too much.

The fact, however, is that *Homo sapiens* is a mammal and a primate, a member of the Class Mammalia and the order Primates that includes the monkeys, apes, and their kin. Desmond Morris called us the "naked ape." We share over 98 per cent of our DNA sequences with chimpanzees, who are clearly our closest living relatives. And although no fossil record is ever quite as complete as a paleontologist might wish, we have quite an extensive fossil record showing how the evolution of certain primates over the past ten million years or so produced humans. This record resides in many precious skeletons and fragments of tooth and bone in museums around the world. The forces of evolution that operate on other kinds of organisms have shaped humanity just as inexorably, and they continue to do so today, however slowly.

To understand humans and human evolution, we need to stand back and take a historical and ecological look at ourselves. An animal's structures say something important about the kind of life it is fitted for; we are not primarily fitted for swinging bats and tennis racquets, poking computers, and driving little vehicles around city streets. We will understand human anatomy and physiology in the light of our ancestors' lives.

primates

Writing about the order Primates, the British anthropologist W. E. Le Gros Clark noted that:

> It is peculiarly difficult to give a satisfying definition of the Primates, since there is no single distinguishing feature which characterizes all the members of the group. While many other mammalian Orders can be defined by conspicuous specializations of a positive kind which readily mark them off from one another, the Primates as a whole have preserved rather a generalized anatomy and, if anything, are to be distinguished from other Orders rather by a negative feature – their *lack* of specialization.

The earliest mammals were quite restricted ecologically, while terrestrial niches were so strongly occupied by reptiles. Le Gros Clark considered that early mammals were probably already adapted to an arboreal (tree-dwelling) life and that primates have retained and emphasized adaptations for this niche, while other orders have taken up various ways of life on the ground, or flying or swimming. Many mammals have highly specialized extremities; hoofed mammals are superbly adapted for running, but they can do little else with their hooves. The marvelous flippers and fins of aquatic mammals, like whales and seals, make them excellent swimmers, but they lead a restricted aquatic life. But for their generally arboreal ways, primates have remained quite generalized mammals. They are characteristically frugivorous (fruit-eating) or omnivorous and are best adapted for living on leaves and fruits among the small branches at the extremities of trees, where their major competitors are bats and frugivorous birds. Later, a few species, such as humans, became adapted to life on the ground.

For their arboreal and largely omnivorous life, primates have evolved several critical features.

arms and hands

The primate hand retains basic mammalian features but has an *opposable thumb*, which moves more freely than the other digits and can be pressed against the fingers to make a fine grasping tool. (Most primates also have an opposable big toe.) All primates can use their hands in a *power grip* for climbing and grasping tree branches – the grip you use to hold a hammer; later-evolved primates, such as apes and humans, also have a more delicate *precision grip* for manipulating small objects – the grip you use to hold tweezers. Chimpanzees and humans use their precision grip to make and use tools; it is a key factor in cultural evolution. Primates also have flat nails instead of the claws of ancestral mammals. This leaves a bare, protected working surface at the ends of the digits, a surface rich in nerve endings that make it very sensitive and contributes to manual dexterity.

Primates typically have very long arms, useful for reaching to the extremities of trees to grasp fruit – another use for an opposable thumb. The primate arm also rotates very freely. With a flip of the wrist, primates, especially humans, can rotate the hand at least 180° relative to the upper arm, while also rotating the upper arm bone (humerus) in the shoulder socket. Just watch a gibbon swinging from the bars in a zoo or a child on a jungle gym, and you'll see the value of these features for a tree dweller.

teeth and jaws

Much of the story of mammalian evolution can be told through teeth. A paleontologist searching for our ancestors has the advantage that jawbones and teeth are among the most common finds in fossil beds, and they show diagnostic dental patterns and other features of hominoid evolution.

We mammals have four types of teeth: *incisors* in the front of the jaw that are specialized for cutting; *canines* just behind them, which are generally sharp tearing instruments; and then *premolars* and *molars* behind, which often have large surfaces for crushing and grinding, but may become specialized for cutting in the more carnivorous mammals. Anatomists describe the dental pattern of a mammal with a set of four numbers, the number of each type of tooth in order for half of the upper jaw, over another four for half of the lower jaw. (The left and right halves are identical, of course.) The generalized mammalian formula is 3.1.4.3/3.1.4.3. Early in primate evolution, the incisors were reduced from three to two in each jaw. New World monkeys have the pattern 2.1.3.3, as did the oldest primates; the formula of Old World monkeys, apes, and humans is 2.1.2.3. Primate premolars and molars have retained their forms for crushing and grinding, although some of the premolars have been lost. On the whole, primate dentition remains quite unspecialized, as befits their omnivorous eating habits.

In differentiating humans from their apelike ancestors and relatives, the structures of teeth and jaws become critical. The jaws of apes are U-shaped, with parallel sides containing the canines, premolars, and molars, connected by a rounded front bearing the incisors; in strong contrast, humans have parabolic jaws, wider at the hinge than at the chin, in which all the teeth lie on a gentle curve (Figure 8.1). The canines of apes, particularly upper canines, are large and pointed; human canines are quite small. When apes' jaws are closed, the large upper canines overlap the lower teeth, accommodated by small gaps in the lower tooth row. This locks the jaw for holding prey but does not allow a sideways movement useful for grinding vegetation. The modern apes also have a distinctive *simian shelf*, a plate of bone across the lower jaw in the region of the canines. A feature that becomes interesting in examining the fossils of young animals is a difference in times of eruption: the canines of apes only erupt after the second molar does, while human canines erupt before the second molar.

The structures of molars and premolars are especially complex. Their biting surfaces have small cusps or cones. A generalized mammalian molar has five cusps. The ape lower premolar has one large cusp, but in humans it has become a bicuspid tooth with two. The

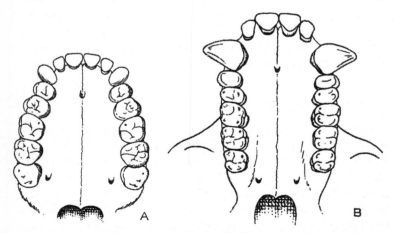

Figure 8.1 *The palate and upper teeth of a primitive hominid (an australopithecine), left, compared with that of a gorilla, right.*

molars of apes are generally high, and they do not wear down, but human molars generally wear down to an even grinding surface. Also, the early ancestors of apes had only four molar cusps; a fifth cusp evolved later.

vision

Primate vision is one of the strongest adaptations for an arboreal life. Think of the challenges facing an animal that has to move quickly through a maze of limbs and branches, deciding instantly where to grab a handhold, how to swing Tarzanlike from a branch here to a limb there. Such an animal needs stereoscopic vision and depth perception, which is achieved by locating the eyes on the front of the head where they can focus on the same object from slightly different angles. (Horses and mice, with their eyes directed to the side, have little or no depth perception; it isn't essential for their ways of life.) In addition to the light-receptors called rods, the retina of a primate's eyes have cells called cones for color vision and greater visual acuity, with a *fovea*, a central area about a millimeter square in humans, that is the point of clearest vision. The fovea contains only cones, not rods, and the lens of the eye focuses an image directly on it. Moreover, the other cellular layers that normally lie over the retina are displaced to the side in the fovea so light striking there doesn't have to pass through them. Portions of the primate brain that process the high-resolution information coming from the eyes are enlarged, as are other areas that control the sensitive hands and process the information coming from them. The sense of smell (olfaction) is less useful to primates, however, and their olfactory brain centers are diminished.

posture and bipedalism

A major trend in primate evolution has been toward more upright posture. Even monkeys sit in upright, human postures, and all higher primates hold their heads high, presumably a general adaptation for getting a better view of their surroundings. Upright posture not only affords a wider range of vision but also is a prerequisite for bipedalism – walking on two legs – which frees the sensitive and dexterous front limbs for carrying things, such as tools and babies. Because bipedalism is such an important and uniquely human trait, we will return to questions about it later.

large brains

Intelligence in mammals is correlated with the ratio of brain mass to body mass, and primates on the whole are big-brained. The increase in brain mass becomes most obvious in the evolution of humans, but all primates have relatively large brains, probably to process all the information needed to move through the trees with such agility.

Finally, primates have fewer offspring than do many other mammals, and their young are dependent on the parents longer. Some of the arguments about the evolution of bipedalism relate it to juvenile development. A relatively long, intense period of adult – child interaction is essential for the evolution of culture as a way to transmit survival skills, a practice that is most strongly developed in humans, who transmit culture via language throughout an extensive childhood.

anthropoids and apes

The order Primates is divided into two suborders:[1] Prosimii includes the little tarsiers and lemurs, and Anthropoidea includes the simians: monkeys, apes, and humans. In his huge, brilliant study *The Life of Vertebrates*, J. Z. Young commented,

> The outstanding characteristic of the anthropoids might be said to be their liveliness and exploratory activity, coming perhaps originally from life in the tree-tops necessitating continual use of eye, brain, and limbs. With this is associated the development of an elaborate social life, based not, as in most mammals, on smell, but on sight.

The anthropoids include separate families of Old-World and New-World monkeys, and a superfamily Hominoidea that includes the families Hylobatidae, the gibbons; Pongidae, the orangutan, gorilla, and chimpanzee; and the human family, Hominidae. (So "hominid" means a member of the Hominidae and "hominoid" is a broader term encompassing the whole superfamily.) We and the pongids share ancestors that lived about 20–10 Myr ago. From these common ancestors, one line of evolution led to several extinct species of prehumans; only a single species of modern humans, *Homo sapiens*, has survived.

Anthropoid apes are distinguished from monkeys by having a short tail or none at all, by distinctive tooth structure, and by a somewhat more upright posture than monkeys. Apes commonly move through the forest by *brachiation*, swinging from branch to branch with their arms overhead, a movement made possible by their long arms with extremely mobile swivel joints. Brachiation has resulted in a reduction in size of the hind limbs and somewhat reduced thumbs on the hands, so that the hand becomes less a grasping instrument and more like a hook that can be slapped over a limb and then released quickly.

The largest apes, however, spend much of their time on the ground. They are clumsy walkers, since the form of the ape pelvis requires them to swing the leg outward to move forward and gives them a crouching, bent-over posture. The hominid pelvis, in contrast, provides full upright posture and permits a bipedal gait – that is, walking erect on two legs. But apes do walk. Chimpanzees and gorillas get around by *knuckle-walking*, putting some weight on the knuckles of their hands from time to time, and this posture allows them to run while carrying things in their hands.

early anthropoid evolution

The geological time-scale for charting hominoid evolution begins in late-Oligocene time, before 24 Myr ago, and continues through the Miocene period from 24 to 6 Myr ago. The Pliocene era extends from 6 to 2 Myr ago, at which time the Pleistocene era starts. The end of the Pleistocene is placed somewhat arbitrarily at 10,000 years ago.

The Fayum beds of Egypt have yielded some remarkable simian fossils of Oligocene age, around 38 Myr ago, including the bones of *Parapithecus* and *Apidium*. These were generalized anthropoids, about the size of a small monkey, with three premolars like more basal primates and New World monkeys. Somewhat larger apes from the later Oligocene, named *Propliopithecus*, were about the size of a modern gibbon and had teeth similar to those of a gibbon, with the 2.1.2.3 dental pattern. They also had certain other dental features that make them appear quite hominoidlike: lower molars with the five cusps of hominoids and incisors set vertically rather than jutting forward. *Aegyptopithecus zeuxis*, very likely an early hominoid, had teeth very much like those of a modern ape, with large molars increasing in size from front to back, elongated front premolars, and large canines. Living in typical arboreal ways in tropical forests, these

Oligocene primates were probably frugivorous or omnivorous. The infamous "coming down out of the trees," which popular thought associates with human evolution, was several million years off. However, the animals that came down out of the trees were not humans but the ancestors of a large part of the hominoid branch.

As the Miocene climate grew cooler and drier, tropical forests in Africa and Asia gave way to subtropical forests and to extensive steppes (large grassy plains) and savannas (plains with scattered trees). The first horses appeared that were adapted for grazing in grasslands rather than browsing leaves. In early-Miocene times, some hominoids also moved into a new adaptive zone, living on the ground in the grasslands, out of competition with arboreal primates, replacing (or supplementing) their diet of fruit and leaves with tough foods such as nuts and roots. (Modern chimpanzees, though basically tropical forest animals, have a similarly varied diet, and some are as omnivorous as humans.) These were the *dryopithecine apes*, *Dryopithecus* and its relatives, whose fossils have been found over a vast area from southern Europe through East Africa, India, and China. Dryopithecines were generalized apes ranging in size from a small gibbon to a large modern ape. Though lacking the huge, protruding canines of later simians, they had strong jaws with more heavily enameled teeth, attached to the skull so as to permit the rotary grinding motion – instead of chomping – useful in chewing tough foods such as roots. The dryopithecines on the whole present a difficult complex of features. David Pilbeam has divided them into two groups: the dryopithecids, whose dentition and other anatomical features suggests their ancestry to various great apes, and the ramapithecids, whose dentition suggests they might have been hominid ancestors. In spite of their food habits, the teeth of some ramapithecines show less wear than do those of *Dryopithecus* and modern apes, suggesting that their permanent teeth emerged later, as in modern humans, and implying a longer period of development. The lack of wear also suggests that they used their hands a great deal, rather than tearing all their food with their teeth, and thus the beginnings of a more upright posture.

These Miocene ape fossils extend from about 20 to 10 Myr ago. The first definitive hominids, dating to about 6 Myr ago, walked fully upright. During that period of about 4 Myr, still largely dark to us, transitional hominids were acquiring bipedalism and other features of later australopithecines. A few fragmental fossils from this period are starting to emerge.

australopithecines, the "southern ape-men"

In 1924, the skull of a hominid child was discovered in a limestone quarry at Taung, South Africa. The anatomist Raymond Dart immediately recognized it as something special and named it a new species, *Australopithecus africanus* ("southern ape man from Africa"); he noted that the skull had many of the features of a bipedal hominid: the rounded shape, relatively large cranial capacity for its overall size, shape of the jaw, and position of the foramen magnum, the large opening at the base of the skull where it attaches to the spine. During hominid evolution, the foramen magnum has moved forward to a more central position, so the skull rests with better balance on the vertebral column as the animal sits or stands upright.

The many australopithecine fossils discovered since clearly reveal hominids with protruding jaws and heavy brow ridges. Comparing the skulls of a typical australopithecine and even a semimodern human of the genus *Homo* will show how different they must have looked and how paleoanthropologists can distinguish skulls, even skull fragments, of the two genera. Don't think of australopithecines as looking like primitive – perhaps rather hairy – humans. They still had the long, sloping faces of apes: broad across the eyes, but narrowing to jaws that we might even call muzzles. Their skulls contrast sharply with *Homo* skulls, which have a generally flat, vertical face with a protruding nose, like modern people. It is more accurate anatomically to think of them as erect, bipedal apes, not humans. (Several recent books about human evolution have excellent drawings of the various hominids, but those in Colin Tudge's *The Variety of Life* convey a striking sense of the changes in our ancestors and cousins.)

During the 1970s, Donald Johanson and his associates unearthed an extensive series of australopithecine fossils, 3.8–3.0 Myr old, in the Afar Triangle of eastern Africa, including the now-famous skeleton of a young female that they named Lucy. Johanson and Timothy D. White established a new species, *Australopithecus afarensis*, to include these fossils and specimens that had been found to the south, at Laetoli, by Mary Leakey. When first described, *A. afarensis* was remarkable because it showed clearly that hominids were bipedal and stood fully upright almost four Myr ago, even though their brains were still small (about 400–500 ml). They were probably no taller than 1.2 m and weighed 25–30 kg. Their jaws and teeth were similar to ours, except for their larger, sturdier molars, and the hinge between jawbone and skull permitted the rotary chewing motion that had begun with the dryopithecines. Evidence from the pattern of dental wear and from animal bones associated with their bones indicates they were omnivores and may have eaten some meat, as modern apes do. The rest of the australo-pithecine skeleton shows adaptations for bipedalism. Their arms may have been somewhat less mobile than ours, but their ankle bones – intermediate between human and typical ape forms – seem suited for bearing weight in bipedal walking. The general structure of their thighs and hips seems well adapted for erect standing, walking, and running, but also for an arboreal life of climbing by grasping trunks and large branches. Their pelvic structure may be an exaptation, which evolved initially as an adaptation for climbing trees and was just incidentally suited to bipedalism. Australo-pithecines probably divided their time between the ground and trees, perhaps sleeping in trees at night as modern chimpanzees do. Like chimps, they probably lived in small groups – extended families perhaps – of a few dozen individuals.

A. *afarensis* undercut the formerly popular view that large brains evolved along with erect posture, based on the idea that bipedalism evolved to free the hands for tool use, which would require a larger brain. But bipedalism clearly evolved in hominids with rather small brains. Modern human brains range from about 1200 to 1800 ml, with an average of about 1400 ml. This large organ supports all the complex activities that humans engage in, and its development from the australopithecine brain was a major feature of hominid evolu-tion. Australopithecines had brains of about the same size as a modern gorilla's brain, but remember that intelligence is correlated with the ratio of brain size to body size, and the gorilla is a much larger animal.

As more evidence that the australopithecines were bipedal, a team led by Mary Leakey described a series of footprints in volcanic ash at Laetoli apparently made by a male and a female of this species walking side by side about 3.7 Myr ago. These tracks are particularly poignant, as they capture for posterity two of our ancestors, probably a mated pair, engaged in a simple activity that men and women still share today. So while they lacked the appearance of humans, in behavior and perhaps in their mental life they may have been very human.

A. *afarensis* was apparently ancestral to at least two distinct australopithecines that coexisted between about 3 and 1.5 Myr ago, along with some early representatives of *Homo*. But just how many species there were is a matter of controversy. Paleoanthropologists studying these fossils have tended to be "splitters" rather than "lumpers"[2] and to assign more distinct species names – and even generic names – to their subjects than other paleontologists do; the several distinct "species" may or may not deserve the names. Some dated between about 3 and 2 Myr ago are known as "gracile" australopithecines, in contrast to "robust" forms that appeared later. The gracile fossils have been named *A. africanus* and *A. aethiopicus*, the latter sometimes assigned to a genus *Paranthropus*. *A. africanus* appears to have been very similar to *A. afarensis*, although perhaps a little taller and with less sexual dimorphism. Robert Broom and Louis and Mary Leakey later described robust forms – designated *A. robustus* and *A. boisei*, but sometimes assigned to *Paranthropus* – whose fossils are dated between about 2.3 and 1.5 Myr ago. They were taller (up to 1.5 meters), had more massive teeth, and were probably vegetarians.

In 1995, Alan Walker and Maeve Leakey found fossils dating from 4.2 Myr ago, which they described as a new species, *Australopithecus anamensis*. These were small hominids; they had jaws of the typical U-shaped ape form but had more humanlike teeth with thicker enamel. Perhaps most significantly, their tibias show the features associated with bipedalism. In 1992, White discovered fossils dated 4.4 Myr ago that pushed the hominid line back still farther. He gave the species defined by these fossils the name *Ardipithecus ramidus*, deeming it worthy of status as a separate genus, and bones assigned to the same genus have been found in strata back to 5.8 Myr ago, virtually to the point sometime between 10 and 5 Myr ago where the hominid and ape clades diverged. *Ardipithecus* was described as "the most apelike hominid ancestor known." (However, some anthropologists are skeptical of its status as a hominid.) Although fossils aren't yet available that would show whether *Ardipithecus* walked upright, the jaw and arm fragments are clearly those of a very early hominid that retains many features of a typical ape. The thin enamel covering on its teeth, for instance, suggests a diet like that of modern chimpanzees. Although no anthropologist talks seriously about "the missing link," some were willing to say, jokingly, that *A. ramidus* comes about as close as one could wish to being such a link.

why did our ancestors stand upright?

I said that the discovery of *A. afarensis* put to rest a previously popular view that bipedalism evolved along with large brains as the use of tools, made possible by that brain, required the hands to be free. It is clear that quite small-brained hominids were fully bipedal. Then the mystery remains: why did they stand up on two legs?

In his book *Lucy*, Donald Johanson presents quite an extended argument from C. Owen Lovejoy to explain the origin of bipedalism. You might want to consult it, for its detailed, illustrated explanation, but I want to examine it here, too. The argument contains an interesting point about the idea of causality in science. If you stroke a cue ball against another billiard ball so it takes a predictable path and drops into a pocket, it is easy to talk about the motion of your cue stick and the cue ball being causes of the motion of the other ball. But an animal is a complicated critter with many structures and features; it interacts with its environment in complicated ways, and the course of its evolution must be determined by many intertwined factors and forces. So in evolution it is difficult, and probably simplistic, to pick out single factors and say, "This is the cause of that." Rather, a complex of several features evolve together to meet certain ecological requirements and to shape a species for a certain ecological niche and way of life. In spite of the following argument about reproductive strategies, another possible explanation for the advantage of bipedalism is that it provided better heat balance under the hot tropical sun. And perhaps other factors were important, too.

Organisms exhibit two general strategies of reproduction. One is to produce enormous numbers of potential offspring, even though only a few will actually survive; the other is to produce only a few offspring and invest much time and energy in protecting and nourishing them. Primates clearly use the second method. Each female produces only one or a very few young at one time and spends a long time nurturing them to independence and maturity. Hominids were pushed toward this method by the evolution of larger brains, which required infants to be born early, before their brains and skulls had grown too large for the birth canal; such very immature young require a longer period of development overseen by their parents. Now, Lovejoy sees this way of reproduction as a potential ecological trap: that the survival of a species is tenuous if it reproduces itself so slowly because parents can raise few offspring at a time. However, the primate way of life could have changed to improve the chances for survival. One way would be to enhance a mother's ability to nourish her infant without leaving it exposed to predators. A female ape cannot carry her young around with her very well as she forages for food in the trees; its hands are growing into good devices for brachiating through the trees but are not well adapted for holding on to her body. So if she is to forage for food, she must leave it alone on the ground for a while, where a predator could easily grab it. There are at least two ways around this dilemma. One is for the species to develop a much stronger social structure, so individuals share food with one another and so the infant can be left in the care of other members of the troop – female relatives, perhaps – while the mother is out gathering food. Another is for males and females to become increasingly bonded to one another, to form the sort of strong pair bonds that characterize human relationships, so the father has reason to bring food to the mother and infant.

Another way to enhance a species's survival is to increase its rate of reproduction, and this can be done by changing the strictly sequential way of primate reproduction to an overlapping way. Primate females have estrus cycles, so they are only fertile and receptive to mating for limited times each year. To reproduce, such a female must be impregnated by a male during this critical time; she then carries the baby to term and nurtures it for a time after birth. And during that time, she is infertile and not receptive to mating. Only after she weans her newborn does her estrus cycle start again, so she can conceive again. If this is a kind of reproductive trap, one way out is to gradually extend her fertile period until she is fertile much of the time – in other words, to transform the restrictive estrus cycle into the human menstrual cycle, which makes a woman potentially fertile most of the time.

The change to the human type of reproductive cycle means that a female is receptive to mating during almost the entire year, except perhaps during her menses. This has the particular advantage of promoting pair-bonding between one male and one female; the pair-bond develops and is maintained by frequent copulation combined with the male giving his mate gifts of food. This complex of behavior patterns is common in many species of birds and mammals, and it is sensible to postulate its evolution in hominids, too.

The picture that emerges from these considerations is one of females having more than one infant to nurture at a time, as human mothers commonly do, and thus needing to use her hands to hold them and care for them; and at the same time, for males having a need to use their hands to carry food to their mates and offspring. This provides a reason for the evolution of an increasingly upright posture with bipedal movement and freeing of the hands.

the first members of *Homo*

From somewhere in the sea of australopithecines, the earliest members of the genus *Homo* emerged between about 2 and 1.5 Myr ago. Although the situation is somewhat confused at present, the skeletal remains of these hominids are often associated with tools.

People make things. It may be our most significant non-anatomical feature. We are not the only tool-making species; one of Jane Goodall's most interesting discoveries was that chimpanzees fashion simple tools, such as probing sticks with which they fish for termites. Now and then, a bird is observed to use rocks or other objects in a tool-like manner, but these are rare. No other species makes tools so consistently or of such complexity as we do. As we begin to talk about our own genus, we naturally look for evidence of primitive tools and the evolution of tool-making.

Human evolution has been characterized by anatomical changes and by the development of an extensive culture, culminating in the use of language. But language – and most of culture in general – does not fossilize and cannot be dug out of the rocks. What we can dig up are tools. Appearing first in strata of about 2 Myr ago, they become more common, varied, and complex up to the present. Until quite recent times, they are the sole remnants of hominid culture. Each collection of tools and other artifacts, along with the ways they are made – a *tradition* or an *industry* – is named for a locality where typical remains are found. However, since we don't unearth hominid hands grasping those tools, we have to infer who the tool-makers were, based on their associations with hominid remains.

In Olduvai Gorge, south of Lake Victoria in Tanzania, Louis Leakey discovered primitive stone tools that represent the oldest known tradition, the Oldowan. The original Oldowan tools seem to be little more than chipped pebbles, and some of the evidence for their being tools is that they must have been carried to the stratum where they were found. In fact, these pieces are apparently just the cores from which flakes, the actual cutting tools, were chipped. Anthropologists experimenting with this technique, in which a flint rock is just hit with another rock, have shown that the large flakes that fall off the core really make quite efficient scrapers and knives. In 1964, Mary Leakey found bones of the species now called *Homo habilis* (literally, "handy man") at Olduvai. The Leakeys placed these animals in the genus *Homo*, for their bodies appeared to be smaller than those of their contemporary australopithecines, coupled with astonishingly human teeth and a large brain capacity (650–700 ml). This find dates to about 1.75–2 Myr ago, about the same age as the Oldowan tools, making *H. habilis* a likely artificer of the Oldowan tradition. In 1972, Richard Leakey reported a new series of fossils from Koobi Fora, east of Lake Turkana (formerly Lake Rudolf) in Kenya. The prize of this collection, a skull numbered KNM-ER (for Kenya National Museum-East Rudolf) 1470, became something of a celebrity among human fossils. It was originally identified as a *H. habilis* skull, but with a brain capacity of 750 ml. Its anatomy is very human. Furthermore, the KNM-ER 1470 bones were associated with artifacts that are more advanced than those of the Oldowan tradition. Some paleoanthropologists who have analyzed these and more recent finds in the Koobi Fora region have judged them to show too much diversity for a single species, so they have assigned some fossils such as KNM-ER 1470 to a species *Homo rudolfensis*. By this definition, *H. habilis* had a narrower face and a brain capacity of 500–700 ml, compared with 700–800 ml for *H. rudolfensis*. Whether one species of *Homo* or more existed at this time, they were distinguished from australopithecines by having larger brains, the foramen magnum quite centrally placed in their skulls, and pelves that permitted an easier upright stride. With hands similar to ours, they were developing greater manual dexterity. They made simple tools. There is no evidence that any australopithecine made tools, perhaps indicating a difference in intelligence that explains why *Homo* eventually won out.

Specialists in hominid anatomy and evolution must be the ones to define early hominid species, but part of learning to think about evolution is maintaining a certain broad perspective. First, keep in mind just how variable a population can be; our own modern species shows enormous variation, even in brain size. Furthermore, think about the process of speciation as discussed in chapter six. Some early representatives of the genus *Homo* were clearly living over a broad area of Africa during a period of several hundred thousand years. Had we observed these early humans, we might have been inclined to call them different subspecies or different semispecies living in neighboring regions, but we probably would not call them separate species. We would certainly look at them ecologically with Gause's principle in mind and would wonder just how many ecological niches might have been available in the Africa of 2 Myr ago for an intelligent, tool-using, bipedal hominid. More than one? In any case, classification of the sketchy *Homo* fossils of this period is still controversial.

To add to the *habilis-rudolfensis* issue, a remarkable, almost complete skeleton named the Turkana Boy was unearthed from a 1.6-Myr deposit west of Lake Turkana. He was judged to be about nine years old when he died; apparently he fell into a swamp and was buried, so his body was not disturbed by predators, as was so typical of other hominid fossils. This fossil is now taken to represent a species called *Homo ergaster*, although many anthropologists consider the *H. ergaster* fossils merely to be early African representatives of *Homo erectus*.

Muddy as the current picture may be, there is evidence for two to four types of hominids coexisting in Africa between about 2.5 and 1.5 Myr ago: one or two types of australopithecines evolving from the *africanus* to the *robustus* type and at least one species of early *Homo*, whether it is named *habilis*, *rudolfensis*, or *ergaster*. The stage was set for the development of the next human species.

Homo erectus arrives

About 1.5–1 Myr ago, *H. habilis* and whatever other "species" may have coexisted with it were replaced by *Homo erectus*. Eugene Dubois described the species in 1891 from specimens he discovered in Java, and named it Java man or *Pithecanthropus erectus*, meaning "ape man that walks erect," for features that were considered remarkable at the time. *H. erectus* people stood about 1.5 meters tall, with a skeleton much like ours, but a skull more like that of earlier hominids. Their cranial capacity of 800–1100 ml approaches the modern human range, but they retained massive teeth and characteristic heavy eyebrow ridges. *H. erectus* was widely distributed throughout Africa and Western Asia. Fossils assigned to *erectus* may reach back to almost 2 Myr ago but certainly to 1.5 Myr ago; the youngest specimens are as late as 300,000 years ago. Similar fossils dating from around 600,000–250,000 years ago are found in Europe, and anthropologists commonly assign them to a separate species,

H. heidelbergensis, named after a fossil jaw discovered at Heidelberg, Germany. The argument is that the *heidelbergensis* skull is more "inflated," that its heavy brow ridges are more individually arched above the eyes, and the back of the skull is more rounded, along with certain facial features. But, to avoid becoming tedious on the subject of defining hominid species, I'll refer to them all as "erectus" people.

The *erectus* people left clear records of a developing culture. They were omnivorous hunters and gatherers. Large herds of animals, which must have provided plentiful food, roamed the extensive steppes and savannas of their middle-Pleistocene world. The camp-sites of these people contain vast bone remnants of deer, antelope, and large, ferocious animals such as bears and elephants. They may have killed these animals with pointed wooden spears and probably depended upon techniques used by contemporary aborigines. A hunter can stealthily creep up on his prey, and bipedalism allows him to dog his prey at a steady trot for hours or even days, until it is too exhausted to resist. Primitive hunters may also have used the aboriginal American technique of stampeding herds of animals over a cliff to their death.

The *erectus* people left extensive collections of stone tools that define the Acheulean culture, characterized by both core and flake tools. Crude as they are, the choppers and tear-shaped hand-axes of this culture are clearly an improvement over those made by previous hominids because they are carefully worked into functional devices, rather than just being chipped along one edge. They must have been used for domestic purposes such as fashioning wooden tools or cleaning and cutting the carcasses of animals. This stone tradition defines a long period, the Lower Paleolithic (Old Stone Age), that lasted until about 200,000 years ago in Africa, and to perhaps 150,000 years ago in Europe and Western Asia.

Like contemporary tribes of hunter-gatherers, the *erectus* people were probably nomads who roamed widely in small bands and returned to the same base camps periodically. At some point, they also learned to use fire, for evidence from both Hungary and China clearly shows that they were cooking with fire 500,000 years ago.

The *erectus* humans lasted for nearly a million years, at least 40,000 generations, and during that time both they and their environment changed. At first, while the climate was still relatively warm and they were quite unskilled, they probably went naked and lived in the open. But the Pleistocene climate was growing colder, and by 600,000 years ago a series of ice ages began, during which extensive areas of Eurasia and North America were covered by glaciers. The people of these times began to clothe themselves with animal skins, and some moved into caves. By domesticating fire, they could heat those cold, damp spaces and keep wild animals out.

The development of language is a key aspect of human evolution, since human culture could not have developed far without speech. Language offers a great selective advantage, as it is applied to developing a social structure and hunting cooperatively, since social solidarity depends upon named classes of relations that cannot exist without language. Familial relationships, for instance, are passed from one generation to the next by language, whereas nonlinguistic primates must reestablish dominance relationships every generation. The primate brain had been evolving linguistic capacities for a long time. Contemporary apes have considerable linguistic ability; gorillas are reported to communicate with 22 distinct sounds, and chimpanzees have an even larger natural vocabulary and are highly communicative. (Whether chimps can learn to use an artificial language as humans do is a controversial issue, but at least they can communicate well, if not creatively.) Clues from artifacts and from skull morphology, which shows the size and shape of various brain areas, indicate that *H. erectus* probably used a kind of rudimentary language.

With culture, a new mechanism of natural selection appeared that could shape behavior much faster and more effectively than purely genetic selection. Cultural requirements also put a premium on a larger brain for storing and processing information, so it is no wonder that in less than a million years of evolution the human brain increased so enormously.

Neanderthal and later humans

By 250,000 years ago, the human skeleton was well established and was modified very little in further evolution. Between 250,000 and 150,000 years ago, *H. erectus* was replaced as the dominant hominid by people much like us, generally designated *H. sapiens*. The earliest fossils define Neanderthal humans, named after the Neander Valley in Germany where the first fossils were found. They have been named a subspecies, *H. sapiens neanderthalensis*, but were they our ancestors? Are there Neanderthal genes in the modern human genome? The answer, according to analyses of mitochondrial DNA (mtDNA), now seems to be No. Some investigators have obtained samples of mtDNA from Neanderthal fossils and compared it with modern human DNA; they are clearly quite distinct, and one group of investigators estimated that Neanderthals must have diverged from the ancestors of *Homo sapiens* between 365,000 and 850,000 years ago. Also, studies by Brian Sykes and his colleagues on the diversity of mtDNA in modern human populations show only small differences, consistent with common ancestors about 30–40,000 years ago, but certainly no more than 80,000 years ago. This work leaves no room for Neanderthal genes that might have been combined with *sapiens* genes. So it is reasonable to designate them a separate species, *H. neanderthalensis*.

Although they were not our ancestors, the Neanderthals are fascinating. Averaging about 1.7 m in height, they were considerably more robust than our ancestors but had large cranial volumes, averaging about 1600 ml. The major anatomical differences between Neanderthals and *H. sapiens* lie in facial features, since a classic Neanderthal skull has a markedly receding chin, heavy brow ridges, and a sloping face and forehead, in contrast to the slight brow ridges, higher foreheads, vertical face, and more angular chin of *H. sapiens*. Some anthropologists, however, regard the classical, heavy-browed western Neanderthalers as a subgroup whose facial features may have been an adaptation to the cold, like the heavy brows and flat noses of contemporary Arctic peoples such as Eskimos. Over most of their range, from western Europe through the Mediterranean, the Middle East, and East Africa, most Neanderthals were of the "progressive" type, with skulls much more like ours.

Some time before 250,000 years ago, as *erectus* humans were being replaced by later humans, the Acheulian tradition in tool-making was being replaced by the Mousterian. Hand-axes that had been made by striking chips off a core were now made more carefully by striking a wooden tool held against the core to remove flakes. This method produced sharper, more symmetrical tools. The resulting flakes were delicately shaped into tools such as scrapers and spear points. The invention of a long wooden spear with a sharp stone tip must have been a major advance in hunting. Among Neanderthal artifacts are the bones of many animals. Neanderthal people possessed the knives to butcher animal carcasses and the fire to cook the meat. The cold climate must have placed a premium on these fires for warmth and on animal hides for crude clothing.

modern humans

Virtually all the skeletons dated later than about 35,000 years ago are those of *sapiens* people. Until the issue of Neanderthal genes was settled, the genetic evidence was consistent with various ideas about our origins. But today we are left with the "out of Africa" model: that modern *sapiens* people emerged from a single African source sometime around 100,000 years ago and spread through Europe and Asia, eventually replacing indigenous humans in each area.

The recent discovery of very small human skeletons on the Indonesian island of Flores shows that other species of humans may have been living quite recently along with *Homo sapiens*, although their designation as *Homo floresiensis* raises the usual questions about the definition of a species and the legitimacy of such names. These little people, who lived as recently as 13,000 years ago, stood only about three feet tall when fully grown and had anatomical features unlike those of pygmies, who belong to *H. sapiens* in spite of their small size.

Over the last 35,000 years humans have become a truly cosmopolitan species spread across the face of the Earth, with only small genetic differences among contemporary races. Physical evolution in humans has not stopped, but it is of secondary importance to cultural evolution, which has wrought remarkable changes in a short time.

The first modern *sapiens* humans are known as Cro-Magnon, from the cave in southern France where their remains were found. In the Upper Paleolithic period, from about 35,000 to 8000 B.C.E., they created the foundations of our culture. With ever more refined methods, they learned to shape stones and then bones into excellent tools. We find spearheads and fishing hooks like those made by modern hunter-gatherers, and needles show that they must have tailored clothing out of animal hides. They were probably our equals in intelligence and humanity. They carefully tended their dead, which were sometimes painted with red ochre and buried with various artifacts – evidence of some thought about an afterlife.

They also expressed themselves through painting and sculpture. Some of their carvings rival our own in delicacy and realism; others are clearly exaggerated representations of pregnant women that probably figured in fertility rites. (Fertility was important to people who were constantly threatened with injuries and death; their rate of infant and childhood mortality must have been enormous, and no more than 10 per cent of them lived to the age of 40.) Paintings from at least 12,000 years ago in some French and Spanish caves still inspire awe and admiration. These people had learned to make paints from clays and animal fats colored with charcoal and metal oxides; their painted scenes emphasize the animals they hunted, perhaps for rituals and magic to ensure successful hunting or the return of migrating herds, or to boast about past successes.

Contemporary with the Cro-Magnons, similar Upper Paleolithic cultures of hunter-gatherers were thriving in Asia and Africa. But by about 10,000 years ago many had started to settle in permanent communities where food was abundant. At this time, there was a general warming of the Earth, a retreat of the glaciers, and a transition to the so-called neothermal conditions in which we now live. All ecosystems had to adapt to these changing conditions, and people of this time were intimately entwined in their ecosystems. Northern European people, for instance, had long been largely dependent on herds of reindeer, but with warming conditions these herds had to adapt to new food plants and to the encroachment of forests into the European plains. There is also good evidence of very dry periods about this time. These factors forced people to find new food sources. Some tribes settled on lake and ocean shores where they created transitional cultures, known as Mesolithic, with efficient industries for catching fish and molluscs. While these European peoples continued to subsist by hunting, fishing, and gathering, others to the east were inventing something that would change the face of the Earth: agriculture. And at this point we abandon the realm of anthropology and evolution, and move into human history.

notes

1. In another modern classification, the order is divided into two different suborders defined on the basis of nasal structure, but the more traditional classification will be more useful for us here.
2. Among taxonomists, splitters are those who tend to divide taxa into smaller groups, and lumpers are those who tend to combine smaller groups into larger ones.

probability and entropy

This chapter explores a kind of argument often heard from people who have doubts about evolution, including scientists who express what they think are legitimate scientific doubts. The argument is twofold, or perhaps it rather mixes two scientific concepts in a confusing way. The gist of the argument is that it is impossible to imagine anything as complex as even a simple organism arising by chance, and that evolution as commonly described violates the second law of thermodynamics. These arguments raise complex issues. Their advocates don't understand either the concept of natural selection or the principles of thermodynamics, but conclude that there must be an Intelligent Designer who is responsible for the wonderful complexity and diversity of organisms. That is a conventional conclusion, a version of natural theology advanced in many forms over many years by theologians of various stripes. But those who conclude that life is a miracle in the traditional sense – a supernatural phenomenon outside the realm of science – miss a more exciting conclusion: that life is a miracle (though I hesitate to use the word) in a scientific sense. There is a kind of grandeur, a freeing and elevating of the human spirit, in recognizing that the wonderful complexity and diversity of life, which we see in ourselves and in our surroundings, has been produced solely by the interplay of natural forces over long times, without the need for foresight, planning, or intelligence.

the improbability of life

To address the probability argument first, remember that a typical protein is made of a couple of hundred amino acids – 300 is a good average. Since a protein can be made by placing any one of 20 types of amino acids at each position in the chain, there are 20^{300} possible proteins of this size, or approximately 10^{390}. Numbers like this are so absurdly huge that we can only make them meaningful with science-fiction stories. For instance, suppose you had a machine for putting amino acids together in any desired sequence, and suppose it could assemble a protein of 300 amino acids in one second. Suppose you set it to work at the instant the universe originated, around 15 billion years ago, programed to assemble every possible sequence of 300 amino acids one by one, and you waited until it made just one protein of this size with a biologically useful sequence – an enzyme, perhaps. The machine wouldn't have to produce all 10^{390} combinations before it hit on a good one. Maybe it would only have to make half that number. How long would it take to do that, just by chance? One year is about 3×10^7 seconds, so in 15×10^9 years the machine could make 4.5×10^{17} different proteins. That's a pitifully small number in comparison with 10^{390}. (Remember, please, that 10 raised to a power x is only one-tenth of 10 raised to the power $x + 1$, so the difference between 10^{17} and 10^{390} is enormous.) Well, suppose you made a million machines, or a billion, or a trillion, and you had each one making different sequences. A trillion is 10^{12}, so those trillion machines could make 4.5×10^{29} proteins. Still nowhere near the number needed.

Several people, particularly critics of evolution, have made this kind of calculation and have then asked, "Suppose you had a lot of amino acids (or any other random 'parts' of an organism or a machine) on some primitive planet, and you let them assemble themselves by chance. What is the probability that they will form a functional organism, or even a single functional molecule?" Given the kinds of numbers I've just been playing with, the probability is so incredibly small that the scenario is beyond belief. The conclusion is that organisms could not be created by chance; there must have been an intelligent creator to assemble all the parts in a functional way.

Before addressing the probability issue, let's examine this word "functional." Our bodies are made of organs with distinct functions, such as pumping or filtering blood. Their functions depend on having constituent cells with particular functions, such as contracting rhythmically or moving certain atoms and molecules here and there. The cells, in turn, operate as they do because they are built of certain proteins (and other molecules) that interact chemically with one another or with small molecules in their vicinity. The word "functioning" is most meaningful at this chemical level. We easily mislead ourselves if we think that the only functional molecules are those that do the kinds of operations that go on in our bodies, or in the bodies of other living things that we know of. This attitude is terribly myopic. Remember that modern organisms, ourselves included, are historical objects whose functions, whose mechanisms, have been derived from the mechanisms used by their ancestors. There is no obvious limit to the range of chemical processes that could have biological functions. Every protein, assembled at random, will interact in *some* way with the molecules around it, because every chemical structure has *some* affinity for other molecules and interacts with them. Thus, every primitive protein molecule, no matter how randomly it was slapped together by unknown forces, could have had a function. If the proteins of our ancient ancestors had interacted differently with their surroundings, evolution would have taken a different path and we would have quite different metabolisms.

Advocates of the probability argument just don't understand natural selection. I have called natural selection a kind of *editing* process, and that is a key to understanding it. Of course, it would be impossible simply to produce a perfect functional protein *de novo*, out of nothing. But that isn't what actually happens. The process always starts with a structure, which then gets modified. A really satisfying rejoinder to this probability argument would go back to the barest glimmerings of life in the most primitive biological structures and show just how genetic editing could produce a more completely functional structure. But, as discussed in chapter three, the processes that produced the first barely functional molecules, probably RNAs and proteins, are obscure and hard to reason around. So I will skip ahead to the point where some kinds of functional organisms have started to evolve. In fact, we don't even need whole organisms; just some barely functional proteins or RNAs will serve as long as their structure is specified by primitive genomes. Any such molecule will have at least the beginning of a function; or, better, among a collection of molecules produced randomly, there will be some that have the bare beginnings of *functions*, plural. All that means is that they will interact *somehow* with other molecules.

So a primitive organism whose genome specifies any protein with any function at all will have some ability to persist, to function, and to reproduce itself. Its offspring may include some mutants that have variations on the structure. One or more variants may have slight improvements on the original, or maybe slightly different functions. Of course, other variants will be worse versions, and the organisms that make them will be discarded. Further reproduction of the surviving versions will create another generation of variants. Again, many will be discarded, but some may be improvements, and they are selected. The process continues generation after generation, gradually producing better and better versions and more variants with other functions. So natural selection is a process that inherently creates better functions, merely by chance. Richard Dawkins has written about this as a *cumulative* process, one that builds one slight improvement upon another, and it is this kind of process that has generated the wonderfully complex structures we see in ourselves and in the rest of the biological world. So organisms intrinsically are things with an inherent capacity for bootstrap uplifting.

All those variants that are discarded as being worse are important to the process. Garrett Hardin has written "in praise of waste" to emphasize the importance of producing all those inferior versions, which are just thrown away. The process depends on "tinkering," producing random changes with no foresight; then it happens, merely by chance, that some improvements are produced. But tinkering produces waste, and the waste is necessary.

Let me try an analogy here that might help. The situation I've been analyzing is similar to the famous scenario of putting a million or a zillion monkeys to work pecking randomly at typewriters, with the assurance that, given enough time, one of them will eventually type the works of Shakespeare. In a modified version, suppose each monkey is *genetically disposed* to type a certain random sequence and that one of them keeps typing the sequence, "To be or nox to be, tham is the questiop. Whether tis nobles in the dharieaspjeoiesj;rlskjewa;lisejss ..." and the rest is gibberish. We single out this monkey as being on the right track and let it reproduce in an environment that encourages mutation. Then one of its offspring might correct the "nox" to "not," or one of them might change the first bit of gibberish to "mind" and thus get closer to the right sequence. In the next generation, we breed one of the monkeys that types an improved version, and one of its offspring may be a mutant that types a still better version. Of course, given the number of letters and punctuation marks in English and the length of Shakespeare's works, the probability of a monkey producing them by chance is even lower than the chance of making that random good protein; but I've changed the scenario by making the system *genetic* and by introducing selection – not natural selection, but selection by rationally examining what each monkey produces and picking the best sequences. And – at the risk of stressing this too much – notice how critical it is for the system to be genetic.

entropy

The second kind of argument that gets mixed in with the probability argument is about thermodynamics – the science that deals with energy – and the concept of entropy. Entropy is a rather subtle and tricky concept. It can be illustrated in various ways, and I will try a couple of different approaches.

You know about energy. It is the ability to do work, and work means moving anything any distance by applying a force. Suppose you need to do some work – say, moving a piano up to the third floor of a building. If the building has a large elevator, you can use its strong cables and powerful motor to hoist the piano up. If not, you can get a few husky guys to move it. The elevator motor uses electrical energy, which is converted into the mechanical energy of raising the piano. The electricity came from some distant source, such as water falling down through a dam or coal being burned or perhaps the heat generated by radioactive material. If you have to use strong men, they will be expending the energy stored in their bodies to power their muscles – energy that came originally from the food they ate.

In transition from the source to the motor, a lot of energy will be lost. Regardless of its source, the electricity generated will have less energy than there was in the source. At every step of changing one form of energy into another, some energy will be lost as heat. The motor running the elevator will be hotter than it was before. The husky guys will have less energy stored in their muscles than there was in the food they ate; and while sweating and straining, they have produced a lot of body heat. As energy is converted from one form to another, the total amount remains constant – that is the *first* law of thermodynamics. But some *must* always be wasted. The "must" reflects another law of nature. The energy that can be conserved and used for further work is called *free energy*; the wasted energy is heat. The *second* law of thermodynamics says that in every real process, less free energy will be available afterward than there was before, and more heat will be generated. A quantity called *entropy* measures how much energy is wasted. The entropy change in any process is actually the heat generated divided by the temperature at which the process happens.

Besides relating entropy to wasting energy as heat, the idea of entropy can also be understood in relationship to probability. That conception will help enhance the previous argument about the probability of making a functional organism. It is best illustrated with some simple examples.

Example 1: Your bedroom is a little messy. Although you do have some neat piles of clothes, books, and papers, you have others scattered about randomly. If you don't make any effort to straighten the room, do you expect to see the piles degenerating into random messes, or do you expect to see the random messes making themselves into neat piles?

Example 2: You have a shallow, open box with a checkerboard pattern printed on it. You stand across the room with a lot of checkers and throw them one at a time into the box. When you look into the box, do you expect to see (1) all the checkers arranged in a few neat rows on one side of the box or (2) the checkers lying randomly on the pattern?

Example 3: Make a tank that will hold water, divided in two by only a thin barrier. Fill one side of the tank with hot water and the other with ice water. Which of the following do you expect to observe? (1) Heat flows from the ice water into the hot water, so the ice water gets cold enough to freeze and the hot water gets hot enough to boil. (2) Heat flows from the hot water into the ice water until both tanks come to the same medium temperature. (Without getting into a long lesson in physics, it will help to know that when water – or any substance – is hot, its molecules are moving faster. Molecules in a liquid or gas move around randomly, constantly colliding with one another. When a fast molecule and a slower molecule collide, the fast one gives up some of its energy to the slower one, so their energies afterward are more average.)

The answers to these questions are quite obvious. The examples show that the natural course of events is for everything to achieve a less organized, more disorderly condition – in other words, a condition with high probability. Neat, orderly conditions have a low probability of occurring. You know that things tend to become messy as we move around and use them, and it takes special effort to make them orderly again. If you threw your clothes into the room, the probability of them landing in neat piles is essentially zero. In the checker toss, you also expect to see the checkers lying randomly on the squares. It is very unlikely that they would all fall on only a few squares in an orderly arrangement. Similarly, the probability of all the water molecules with high energy – the hotter molecules – moving in the direction of the hot water is practically zero. Instead, the molecules all move randomly in different directions and end up all mixed with each other. Heat simply doesn't flow spontaneously *toward* a hot thing – it flows *away* from a source of heat, and things tend to achieve medium-range temperatures. This is our common experience of the world.

Entropy can be measured by its relationship to heat, and it can also be related to probability. A condition with low probability has low entropy; one with high probability has high entropy. Another statement of the second law is that any system left to itself will run toward a condition of maximum entropy, which means maximum disorder.

the entropy of evolution and of living

Now let's return to evolution. A second kind of argument made against evolution is that it violates the second law of thermodynamics. Critics say, "The laws of thermodynamics say that systems ought to be getting worse and worse – more and more random and run down. The evolutionists claim that organisms are getting more and more complicated and well organized. That simply can't happen." How to answer such an argument? (By the way, remember that the idea of evolution as progress is an illusion, and many lines of evolution have produced simpler creatures rather than more complex ones.)

One answer to the argument is that it just isn't true as stated. The second law says that the entropy of every *closed* system will reach a maximum. A closed system is one that cannot exchange energy with its environment, but an organism is just the opposite of closed. It's quite obvious that if someone tried to make you into a closed system by keeping you from getting any more energy from food, you would rather quickly turn into a system with high entropy – a rather disgustingly high-entropy system that would have to be cremated or interred in a cemetery. You maintain your relatively low entropy through a continuous input of more energy. And the whole world of living organisms also maintains itself only through a constant input of energy, ultimately light from the sun.

Let me amplify that by examining an organism to see how the laws of thermodynamics will affect it as it reproduces. Any old organism will do, but it is most instructive to take a small, simple asexual organism like a bacterium. Here's one. Observe this bacterium as it sits in a flask full of nutrients (sugar and other organic compounds). It grows larger. It divides in two. It reproduces. So do all its offspring. The two divide into four, the four into eight, and so on. After several hours, the flask is getting cloudy with bacteria. Are any laws of physics being violated so far? Well, we might be concerned that the second law is being violated even if no evolution is going on. After all, the flask contained molecules of sugar and a few salts, and now those molecules have been converted into some highly organized biological structures! That, in itself, seems to be a violation. If it is true that matter naturally tends to become less organized and more disordered, how is it possible for the stuff in the flask to become more organized? Isn't life itself a violation of thermodynamics?

This has been an issue in physics, and we have to resolve it before moving on to the larger question of evolution. The general answer is No, the ordinary processes of growth and reproduction don't violate the laws of thermodynamics. Quite a bit of energy is stored in the bonds of the sugar and other organic compounds, the energy source for the bacteria. Quite a bit of energy is also stored in the bonds of the complicated molecules of the bacteria. But a comparison of the two shows that the sugar contained more energy than is now built into the bacteria; in fact, most of the energy that was in the sugar has gone off in the form of heat, wasted energy. Less than half is still in the bacteria. So when we compare free energies before and after, we find less free energy after bacterial growth, and that satisfies the second law of thermodynamics.

Still, a kind of nagging doubt is trying to make itself heard. Yes, we might agree, simply measuring energy will show that there is less in the bacteria than there was in the sugar. But the molecules of the bacteria are a lot more *orderly* than those of the sugar, aren't they? And wasn't an important part of the concept of entropy about order – about bedrooms getting messy instead of orderly, about checkers falling in a messy instead of an orderly pattern? Isn't there still something wrong here?

There seems to be. To solve this puzzle, let's go back to the messy bedroom and think about how we can make it orderly again. Ah, here's a sweater on the bed; pick it up, fold it, and put it in the closet on the sweater pile. Here's a pair of pants thrown over a chair; it looks dirty and needs to go into the laundry. Here are several papers. Ah, this one needs to go into the pile of correspondence to be answered, the next one can be thrown into the recycling basket, the next one needs to go into a certain file in the filing cabinet, and another one needs to go into a different file. That book on the floor needs to go into a certain space on the shelf. Little by little, piece by piece, we can put the room back in order. When we are finished, we will have expended some energy in our muscles and we will have created some order in the room. But how did we know where to put everything to create the order? We needed some *information* – information about the structure of the room and where each item is to be stored. The key to understanding this situation is to understand information, and now let me remind you that genetic systems are all about information: the genetic information encoded in genes. To explore that idea further, let me go on an apparent digression to another situation involving entropy, one similar to the chamber with hot water on one side and cold water on the other side.

When the science of thermodynamics was developing in the nineteenth century, the great physicist James Clerk Maxwell made up an instructive story. He imagined a chamber filled with gas molecules, divided in two with a little gate in the division and a little demon operating the gate. The demon can watch the gas molecules as they move around randomly. The demon watches each molecule as it approaches the gate; if a fast (hot) molecule approaches from the right, he lets it go into the left chamber. If a slow (cool) molecule approaches from the left, he lets it go into the right chamber. Otherwise, he keeps the gate closed. Little by little, he allows fast (high-energy) molecules to accumulate on the left and slow (low-energy) molecules to accumulate on the right. Thus, the left chamber gets hot and the right chamber gets cold.

The demon is violating the laws of thermodynamics. It is decreasing entropy, but the natural course of events is for entropy to increase or at least stay the same. But how can the demon do that? It does so only by obtaining *information* about the gas molecules – by discriminating among them on the basis of their energy. If the demon operates by magic – outside the physical laws of the universe – then it can violate the second law of thermodynamics and reduce the entropy of the chambers. But if it operates within the laws of physics, it must expend more energy to get information about the speed of the molecules than the energy it stores up in the gas, and this makes it physically impossible.

Now we can reconsider the organism that seems to be violating the laws of physics. I said that it has less energy in its structure than in the sugar it uses as an energy source; it seems to be violating the second law by making considerable order out of a chaos of little molecules. The answer again lies in information. First, the information for the structure of the whole organism is encoded in its genome. That genetic information gets transformed into *structural information*, information in the orderly structure of each protein molecule, and those proteins, in turn, are the agents that create the greater order of growth. And now I can reveal the great secret that makes this all understandable: *information is negative entropy*. The physicist Leon Brillouin used the abbreviated form *negentropy*. Leo Szilard, the brilliant Hungarian physicist who was involved in the development of atomic energy, pointed out the relationship between entropy and information in an obscure paper in a German journal in 1929, but, as Brillouin wrote, he was misunderstood. Claude Shannon, whose early work in information theory laid the foundation for much of modern computer science, discovered the relationship again in 1949, although he wrote about entropy in a somewhat confusing way. The interested reader with a background in mathematics and physics can get the details of the idea from Brillouin's book. Like any physical concept, this idea can become very complex, but for our purposes it is enough to reflect on what we have already seen: highly structured objects, containing information, can establish greater order in the world they interact with. Your highly structured brain, for instance, contains some information (in what form, we don't know yet) about where various objects belong in your room, so you can use your brain to create order. DNA is a highly structured object, and the organisms it surrounds itself with (to borrow a biological metaphor from Richard Dawkins) contain other structures that transform the information in DNA into more of their own order. Each protein molecule, being formed with a particular shape to perform a certain function in an organism, creates order as it performs its function.

Evolution can be told as a story about storing up structural information, functional information, in the form of complicated organisms. Because evolution operates in organisms with genomes, which store information that makes for successful reproduction, it becomes a kind of mechanism for organisms collectively to lift themselves by their bootstraps. The instruments – organisms – involved in evolution are intrinsically information-bearing structures, and this gives them a special place thermodynamically. Now, of course, none of this contradicts the second law of thermodynamics. As I emphasized before in joining Garrett Hardin to praise waste, producing every generation of successful organisms wastes a lot of structures (a lot of material and energy) that don't survive. This is the cost we pay for maintaining those that are at least as successful as the previous generation and perhaps even a shade better at surviving the exigencies of life.

I mentioned earlier that Jacques Monod begins his book *Chance and Necessity* with a quotation from Camus's *The Myth of Sisyphus*. Sisyphus, Camus's central figure, was condemned for eternity to roll a huge rock up a hill, only to have it roll back down each time. Camus wrote, "Sisyphus ... too concludes that all is well. This universe henceforth without a master seems to him neither sterile nor futile. ... The struggle itself toward the heights is enough to fill a man's heart. One must imagine Sisyphus happy." So, too, in a world that needs no intelligence to explain its beauty and intricacy, we creations of chance and necessity may look back on our long history with happiness, with even a kind of pride – if the word is not too much – that we have achieved our condition through the operation of the purposeless forces of nature.

the problem of creationism

creationism in historical context

Darwin wrote his great books on the origin of species and the "descent of man" against a background of Christian orthodoxy, with its belief that the world, and all life on it, had been created quite recently as described in the Bible. Although many people quickly saw the logic of his ideas and were won over to them, the immediate reaction in English and American society, including the society of scientists, was shock and disbelief. Several writers (see Further Reading) have summarized this history very well. Briefly, during the latter part of the nineteenth and the early part of the twentieth centuries, the idea of evolution evoked antagonism among the faithful, but not the strong, aggressive reaction that emerged later. The first strong reaction arose during the 1920s among evangelists such as Billy Sunday and their followers. Influenced by their evangelical railing against modern ideas, several states in the U.S. passed laws prohibiting the teaching of evolution in the public schools. The famous Scopes Trial in Tennessee in 1925 was a response to these laws, a testing of the law; unfortunately, although the verdict went against Scopes, the case was dismissed on a technicality, so there was no opportunity to carry the issue to a higher court and thus test the constitutionality of the anti-evolution laws until much later.

The general mood in public education during the 1930s and 1940s, even into the 1950s, was to quietly ignore evolution, largely out of fear of creating a public uproar and violating some of the existing laws.

But this mood ended abruptly in 1959, largely because of Sputnik. Americans had faith in the superiority of American science; Americans knew that their scientists had invented the atomic bomb (quietly ignoring the whole development of modern physics in Europe and the key roles of leading European scientists in the atomic bomb project) and were now creating a beautiful new world of plastics and antibiotics. They had faith in the superiority of American public schools. So the public was shocked when the Soviet Union demonstrated its technical superiority, at least in one arena, by launching the first satellite to circle the Earth. Congress reacted quickly, pouring money into programs sponsored by the National Science Foundation and others to improve science education in the U.S. This new emphasis on science included the production of modern science textbooks for high schools, and the biologists who wrote and consulted on these books naturally emphasized evolution, since it is a foundation concept of modern biology.

The contemporary creationist movement was largely a reaction to this new emphasis on evolution. Though the various creationist viewpoints differ in emphasis, they are all characterized by a horror of evolution, both for strictly religious reasons and for a complex of social-political reasons. Modern Christians, of many denominations, have reacted with alarm to the social changes in contemporary American society: increasing violence, decreasing moral values as shown particularly by more and more blatant sexuality, increasing access to abortion and acceptance of it, and growing lack of respect for traditional values among youth. To traditionalists, it became obvious that subversive elements, including international communism, were destroying American society and its values; these forces had even won a prohibition of prayer and the teaching of religious values in schools, and were generally turning American youth away from family and faith, toward a crude, materialistic culture. Religionists blamed these changes on the emergence of a collection of ideas that they labeled "secular humanism," identifying it as a secular religion that opposes all traditional religious values. And they saw evolution as a kind of sour frosting on this bitter cake.

Although the U.S. Supreme Court has ruled unconstitutional the teaching of creationism in the public schools, under the guise of so-called "creation science," the teaching of evolution is under renewed attack. In opinion polls, about half the adult population profess their disbelief in evolution, making it easier for creationists to win their battles. Many citizens are alarmed by this situation, and organizations such as the American Civil Liberties Union and Americans United for the Separation of Church and State have been waging continuous battles over this and related issues.

Eve and Harrold (Further Reading) have distinguished among types of creationists. The central and most common belief is young-Earth creationism, which maintains that the Earth is only a few thousand years old, and that the world and all life were created as described in Genesis. In contrast, old-Earth creationists accept the dating of geologic events but still insist on divine creation rather than evolution. They may do this, for instance, by noting that the Hebrew word *yom*, which is translated as "day" and used to describe the periods of creation in Genesis, does not necessarily refer to a 24-hour day, so the "days" of Genesis could have been as long as geologic periods. The old-Earth creationists have maintained that by rejecting all the sound scientific evidence for the age of the Earth, young-Earthers are in danger of making the whole idea of creationism look ridiculous. Still, the old-Earthers reject evolution, especially the idea of human origins through evolution.

Eve and Harrold apply the designation "theistic evolutionists" to those who accept the scientific account of evolution but maintain that life was originally divinely created. Theistic evolutionists show clearly that there is no necessary conflict between science and religion in their proper spheres, and no reason for anyone to oppose the teaching of evolution. Some may believe that the purpose of evolution was to create humans and that God chose to do it in this way; a general anthropocentrism has been hard to maintain since the development of modern science, and yet this may be a personal belief to which people are entitled. As a philosophical position, theistic evolution stands outside science, so no empirical evidence can be adduced to support it or oppose it. It is a position held on faith, as are religious beliefs in general. But theistic evolutionists in general are not opposed to the scientific account developed in this book.

beliefs of "scientific creationism"[1]

Leaders of the young-Earth creationists include a small group who have been devising a so-called creation science as an alternative to mainstream contemporary science. Particularly because they propose their science as a legitimate alternative that ought to be given equal time in the public schools, it is important to deal with their claims. People in an open society are free to believe anything they want to. But principles of the various sciences are so closely intertwined that those who try to develop an alternative to mainstream biology are forced to attack other principles of modern science. Thus "scientific creationists" run into serious problems when they come up against modern physics and geology.

Moreover, since creationists claim that everything originated about 4000 B.C.E., it is enlightening to put some historical perspective on this discussion, for they are in conflict with history and archeology as well as the natural sciences. There is good evidence that sheep were domesticated in northern Iraq around 9000 B.C.E., that wheat and barley were domesticated in southwestern Iran around 7000 B.C.E. There was an extensive settlement at Jericho around 7500 B.C.E. Writing began in Sumer and Egypt around 3300–3100 B.C.E. The Akkadian civilization dates from 2800 B.C.E., and the empire of Sargon I lasted from 2350 to 2250. Advancing human civilization was not being disrupted by events that creationists must place during historical times, including unbearable heat and huge glaciers, as discussed below.

the age of the Earth

Young-Earth creationists claim that the Earth is only about 6000 years old, rather than about 4.5 billion. To account for this huge difference, scientific creationism must try to discredit the methods used to determine the age of the Earth and its geological layers. The most important of these methods (chapter two) are radiometric, based on the rates of decay of various radioisotopes. Now radioactive decay is just one phenomenon covered by modern physics, especially quantum mechanics. This fundamental science underlies all the rest of modern science, and its foundations are secure, even though any subject of ongoing research is always open to reexamination. Radioactivity is explained by the so-called strong and weak forces, the forces that hold an atomic nucleus together and allow some particles occasionally to decay into two others. The theory of quantum mechanics established during the 1920s and 1930s holds together with remarkable coherence, and anyone who proposes to attack any part of it has to find some fundamental defect in the theory. No one has tried to do this. It would require a profound knowledge of modern physics, and it would be foolhardy at best for anyone lacking that knowledge.

To try to attack quantum mechanics, some creationists have pointed to something they can understand – the speed of light, one of the primary physical constants governing the universe. They have tried to show that it isn't really constant or that its value isn't really well established; then the fabric of physics will have a small hole in it, and the whole thing may be weakened. If, for example, the speed of light can change, then perhaps other constants related to radioactive decay could change. However, attempts to cast doubt on the speed of light have been quite unsuccessful. More and better measurements in the last few years have just made this constant more precisely known and more certain.

Some creationists have tried to attack the speed of light by reference to the redshift observed by astronomers. This is similar to a Doppler effect but an effect of light rather than sound. You experience the Doppler effect regarding sound when you hear a police siren or a train's horn as the vehicle approaches you or leaves you. As it approaches, the sound waves are pushed closer together, shortening their wavelength and thus raising the pitch of the sound; as it leaves you, the sound waves are stretched out, and the pitch falls. Astronomers of the 1920s discovered a significant shift in the light coming from distant stars, a shift toward the longer light waves at the red end of the spectrum. This redshift is evidence that the stars are all rushing away from the Earth – in other words, that the universe is expanding. This is now a fundamental concept of astronomy.

Creationists have attacked this phenomenon by arguing that the conventional interpretation of the redshift would require the universe to be expanding faster than the speed of light, in violation of relativity. So they have argued that the universe is actually very young and that rapid changes in the speed of light have simply given the illusion of old age. However, this attack shows a misunderstanding of physics. Even though the redshift is analogous to the Doppler phenomenon in sound, the redshift in light reflects the fact that, as Donald Wise has put it, "these wavelengths represent a kind of tape measure embedded in space itself." The light started long ago from the stars, with characteristic wavelengths. But while it has been traveling, the universe has been expanding, so the wavelengths of the embedded light have been stretched, and the longer wavelengths we measure are in effect a measure of how much the cosmos has been expanding in the long term. The point is rather subtle, but it carries the lesson that the coherence of modern science, the interdependence of its various concepts, makes it very difficult to reject a part of science in the name of some special cause without running into difficulties somewhere else.

sedimentary deposits and continental drift

We saw in chapter two how the idea of evolution developed through the combined growth of biology and geology, so "creation science" runs into strong conflicts with geology as well as biology. Some of the principal "creation scientists" have earned Ph.D. degrees in geology, yet without losing their faith in an Earth created according to Genesis. These geologists have to ascribe all the events of sedimentation and fossilization to the Noachian flood and its consequences, and since the Bible says the flood lasted for about a year, they have to cram events into that short time that actually took place over many millions of years. This creates some problems.

Sedimentation occurs as minute rock particles and minute organisms with hard shells fall out of water to form a mud that gradually turns to rock under heat and pressure; limestones are made from calcareous mud – that is, mud made rich in calcium carbonate (calcite) by organisms that make their shells from this mineral: single-celled organisms such as radiolarians and foraminifera, and by animals such as molluscs. The sediments form distinctive layers, one on top of another, to eventually create beds of rock hundreds of feet thick. These beds contain the fossilized remains of animals showing the successive appearance of different types, from small invertebrates through fishes to terrestrial vertebrates such as reptiles, birds, and mammals. Creationists have to explain this. One of their attacks has been to claim that the sedimentation is really much more chaotic than that – that geologists have distorted the stratigraphic record to make it appear regular and defend established ideas about Earth history. (Interestingly, the petroleum industry has no doubts about traditional stratigraphy and continues to pour billions of dollars into exploring the geological column with core drilling.) The best answer to that charge is actually to watch geologists at work, to see how carefully they interpret the layering in each area, and to wonder why the adherents of a whole science would want to delude themselves so badly.

George McReady Price proposed one creationist explanation for the layering of fossils in 1923: that as the flood came on, terrestrial vertebrates (including humans) rushed up the mountains, so they were buried last, while all the simpler aquatic invertebrates were buried in the lower levels. The obvious question is why the aquatic creatures were killed and fossilized at all! The flood must have expanded their potential habitat enormously, giving them plenty of space to live in, and even as the waters slowly receded at the flood's end, the animals could slowly retreat without dying en masse. And why should they have died with the layering we observe? Why weren't fish skeletons or amphibians mixed with invertebrates in the lowest layers? Why do the lowest sediments contain the remains of species such as trilobites that are so different from any animals alive today? And why are there no fossils of all the humans who must have been killed in the flood? There must have been a lot of them, and one would expect at least a few of their skeletons to have shown up in the sediments. (The fossils of early hominid species described in chapter eight were clearly not modern humans who died in a flood.)

Sedimentary beds can be incredibly thick, showing what long times were required to deposit them at the very slow rates of about 1–3 cm per 1000 years that have actually been measured in the deep sea. The chalk cliffs of Dover, for instance, are 1000 feet thick, made of the shells of foraminifera that lived briefly and then settled to the bottom of the ocean. At the lowest rate, 30 million years would be needed to deposit a bed 30,000 cm (about 1000 feet) thick. That is a good approximation to the actual rate, since the cliffs are dated to the Cretaceous period, between about 144 and 65 Myr ago. However, if the Dover chalk beds were actually deposited during a single year, they must have grown at the rate of about 80–90 cm – nearly a meter – per day, which is beyond belief. Imagine standing in the shallow water near the shore of an ocean brimming with minute organisms that are dying and falling so fast that your feet are being buried as you stand there.

Similarly, the Kaibab limestone visible in the Grand Canyon of southeastern United States is 150 m thick. If it had been deposited during the flood year, the organisms that produced it would have made calcareous mud at the rate of 40 cm per day.

To get around the problem of sedimentation rates, the creationist geologist Steven Austin has devised another scenario. Austin postulates that during the 1500 years between the creation and the flood, the atmosphere had a much higher level of carbon dioxide than it does now. During that time, he believes, organisms formed their carbonate shells very rapidly and abundantly, depositing calcareous mud in the depths of the oceans. He then postulates that continental drift – explained in the next paragraph – occurred at speeds of 1–10 km per hour, and these forces hurled mud deposits onto the continents during the flood. He apparently does not explain how all that mud turned to rock very quickly.

While rejecting the bulk of geology, creationist geologists actually believe in tectonic plates and continental drift. It is now well established that the continents rest on huge plates of crust that are floating on a bed of magma, and over very long times they have been changing their positions, at rates in the order of 1–2 cm per year. They were once clustered together in a gigantic continent, Pangaea, which then broke up into a large northern supercontinent and another large southern supercontinent. The northern mass then broke up as North America drifted away from Eurasia, and the southern mass divided into South America, Africa, India, and Australia. As the tectonic plates separate, they create more ocean floor, whose gradual formation is visible in trenches between the continents, as in the middle of the Atlantic Ocean, both north and south. Where one plate pushes against another, the edge of one is generally forced downward, a process called subduction, while the plate on top is folded into mountain chains. This has happened, for instance, where the plate bearing India has pushed into the plate bearing Asia, raising the Himalayas. Even the slow movement of 1–2 cm per year requires enormous forces, but the friction between adjoining plates is so high that they cannot slide past each other smoothly; instead, they build up pressure that is released in sudden starts, which we experience as earthquakes.

The creationist contention that all these continental movements occurred in a very short time naturally leads to some absurdities. You may have been wondering where all the water of the flood went, and the creationist Henry Morris suggested that it all drained away into the ocean basins as the continents moved apart. But if this happened during the last half-year of the flood, the continents must have moved at incredible speeds. The Americas are about 4000–5000 km from Africa and Europe at various points, and to move even 4000 km in, say, 200 days, they were moving at 20 km per day or half a mile per hour! Perhaps realizing that such a speed defies belief, another group of creationists led by J. R. Baumgartner has proposed that after the Earth's core formed (only 6000 years ago!), the convection and friction from the moving plates of crust changed the Earth's mantle from the consistency of rock to the consistency of Jell-O, and the continents, riding on this base, were able to move at speeds of meters per second. One result was that plumes of steam emerged from some unknown source in the Earth and then condensed and created the flood. This scenario ignores the heat of the Earth's formation, which must have raised the temperature of the planet by 2500°C, so it is beyond belief to imagine that it happened within the last few thousand years. Furthermore, if the masses of steam were released that created the flood, their cooling released additional heat. Just how Noah and his family and all the creatures on the Ark survived this heat is not explained. But somehow it was all used to melt the Earth's mantle to the Jell-O consistency so the continents could be moving, though all this was happening underneath the flood waters that for some reason were not boiling away. Finally, at the end of the flood year, all this heat dissipated miraculously, leaving the Earth at its present temperature with no evidence of the heat and with very few hot springs, which we might have expected from the heat in the Earth.

These creationist arguments were obviously devised out of desperation. They are terrible examples (or perhaps excellent examples!) of special pleading, imagining special, unique circumstances that might explain the facts but defy common sense. Austin must assume extremely high CO_2 concentrations in the atmosphere, for which there is no other evidence. He must explain how plants and animals, including humans, that were adapted to those conditions could live in the atmosphere following the flood (and why, by the way, did it change?) with much lower CO_2 levels. He must assume that his high level of CO_2 caused animals to grow and die and produce calcareous muds at unheard-of rates and that the huge tectonic plates on which the continents rest were able to move at unheard-of speeds. Finally, even granting that such incredible movements could have generated the forces to throw ocean sediments onto the continents, he must explain how the sediments were deposited with fossils so neatly arranged in the order we find them.

coal deposits

Creationists don't do any better when they try to explain the formation of coal beds during the flood. According to traditional geology, the carboniferous strata that we mine for coal were formed from the gradual accumulation of 20–30 m of vegetation in swamps; bacteria living in this vegetation removed oxygen from it and left high concentrations of carbon, which then gradually turned into coal under the pressure of overlying rock. The oldest strata are around 320–280 Myr old; others were laid down in Mesozoic or even Cenozoic rocks. In Austin's doctoral thesis on a coal bed in Kentucky, he concludes that the bed had been a mat or logjam of floating vegetation that turned into coal very quickly. So creationists propose that all coal beds had been formed this way during the flood. However, the coal beds of Pennsylvania and West Virginia cover 20,000 km², and they are highly structured from sands and lake beds up through the overlying vegetation. Creationists still have to explain how a logjam of that size could have been formed, how it could differentiate into the observed structure, and finally how it could possibly turn into coal within only a few hundred years to, at most, a few thousand years.

the ice ages

Geologists have adduced overwhelming evidence for four ice ages during the Pleistocene era of the last two Myr. Observers in the nineteenth century began to realize that powerful forces had been moving huge rocks around when they saw that these rocks, some of them weighing many tons, were far removed from their places of origin. At first, their movement was ascribed to the rushing waters of the Noachian flood, but in 1802 John Playfair, a professor of mathematics at Edinburgh, suggested that they had been moved by glacial ice. This hypothesis explained the large scratches on these boulders as well as the huge moraines (deposits of gravel) that must have been deposited ahead of glaciers as they pushed down from the north. Other scientists presented evidence that the glaciers had covered large parts of Europe and North America. In 1840, Louis Agassiz published a study of the glaciers and developed the idea that there had been a rather recent ice age. Then in 1854, Adolphe Morlot discovered fossils of plants between layers of glacial deposits and interpreted this as evidence that there had been two warm periods between three distinct cold periods. The evidence is that subtropical vegetation was overrun by advancing ice sheets, laying down distinct soil horizons. Around 1900, Albrecht Penck and Eduard Brückner studied the Alpine glaciations and established that there had been four major glaciations, which they named Günz, Mindel, Riss, and Würm. Later investigations showed that some of these periods were divisible into subperiods of partial warming and partial retreat of glaciers. The glaciations have been dated in multiple ways. Ice cores cut down through the polar glaciers show thousands of distinct annual layers. Also, the decay of ^{14}C (see Table 1, chapter two) is used to date relatively recent geological events, and measurements of ^{14}C decay of the CO_2 in air bubbles trapped in the ice can be correlated with ^{14}C dating of trees and the patterns of tree rings, and with sedimentation in glacial lakes and the patterns of sedimentation in deep-sea cores. There is also good evidence for much older ice ages, including one in the Precambrian.

Of course, creationists ignore all this evidence. Austin's model for continental drift postulates that the heat released during this process warmed the ocean waters. (I mentioned earlier that the heat would have been so intense as to boil all the water away, but never mind.) Austin then postulates that the warmer oceans would have warmed the atmosphere and, for some unknown reason, facilitated transfer of moisture to the poles. He then introduces another postulate for which there is no evidence: that geologic activity during the flood produced volcanic ash, which reflected the sunlight, cooled the Earth, and produced a very brief ice age, which ended around 2000–2500 B.C.E. Leaving aside all the special assumptions, Austin does not explain how there could have been an ice age during historic times, when there is plenty of evidence for the beginnings of human civilizations without any massive ice sheets.

The creationist geologists have tried to develop other arguments to defend their beliefs, such as their interpretation of the sedimentary layers visible in the Grand Canyon. (The creationist influence has become so pervasive that visitors to the Grand Canyon can now purchase creationist literature giving their own version of how the sediments and the canyon itself were formed.) But by now you should be able to see that creationists can only defend their view of Earth's history by absurd assumptions and special pleadings, which are quite at odds with well-established principles of geology and physics, and with well-established history. Yet this is the kind of "science" they would like the public schools to teach our children.

"intelligent design theory"

Many people who would like to be creationists for religious reasons gave up on naïve creationism long ago, realizing that it is simply incompatible with all of modern biology with evolution as one of its central tenets – indeed, with modern science as a whole, as I have shown above. But the religious tendency made another foray into evolution and biology a few years ago in the form of so-called "intelligent design theory."

Intelligent design (ID) must be understood in its larger context, and for this purpose the collection edited by Pennock is invaluable. In her opening paper in this collection, Barbara Forrest explains that ID is a central factor in a program with much larger goals; in the words of Phillip E. Johnson, the inventor of ID, "we should affirm the reality of God by challenging the domination of materialism and naturalism in the world of the mind. With the assistance of many friends I have developed a strategy for doing this. ... We call our strategy the 'wedge.'" The movement began when Johnson, a Professor of Law at the University of California, Berkeley, underwent personal traumas after a divorce and became a born-again convert to Christianity. Focusing on evolution and creation as a central issue, Johnson gathered a group of sympathetic academics to advance his program. But their goal is not merely to overthrow the idea of evolution; it is to replace the entire naturalistic philosophy and methodology of science with an alternative philosophy, which Johnson dubs "theistic realism": "A theistic realist assumes that the universe and all its creatures were brought into existence for a purpose by God. Theistic realists expect this 'fact' of creation to have empirical, observable consequences that are different from the consequences one would observe if the universe were the product of nonrational causes." With evolution as its focus, Johnson and his followers have been energetically promoting their "wedge strategy," primarily through the Center for Renewal of Science and Culture, a part of the Discovery Institute, a Seattle-based think-tank.

The most articulate proponent of ID, as a would-be science, is William A. Dembski, who has developed some complex arguments based on an extensive historical review. His book *Intelligent Design* is subtitled, "The Bridge Between Science & Theology," and his fundamental motivation, clearly, is to promote theistic realism, though he does not use this phrase. Dembski dismisses scientific naturalism, as I outlined in chapter one, as an ideology that is not essential to science, and he would happily admit supernatural forces, such as gods, into science. (Evidently this is justified by a 1993 Gallup poll of the opinions of Americans about evolution.) But he does not realize – or at least admit – that such a move destroys the essence of science.

Naturalism entails the determination to restrict science to things and phenomena that can be investigated empirically. No one has ever seen electrons, but we can posit their existence because we can perform experiments that determine that they exist and have specific properties. But we cannot (scientifically) posit the existence of a god because there is no way to test such an idea empirically; you can imagine a god who has any characteristics you choose – one who loves beetles or hates homosexuals or prohibits the eating of milk and meat together – and belief in such a god can only be sustained through revelation, authority, and faith, not through investigation.

Dembski tries to develop a modern, sophisticated version of natural theology. The natural theologians of the nineteenth century put forward arguments for the existence of God based on their observations that the natural world is wonderfully complex and orderly; as the Anglican minister William Paley put it, if one found a watch in a field, one could immediately infer from its complexity that it had been designed, and by the same argument, the beauty, harmony, and order we observe in the world leads us to conclude that it must have had a designer – God. Dembski willfully misunderstands the genetic nature of organisms and the process of natural selection – he calls it an oxymoron. He denies that useful information can be generated by natural forces, though this is precisely what does happen as a result of mutation and natural selection – Monod's chance and necessity. He argues that the only explanation for the wonderfully organized, complex creatures we see around us, including ourselves, is design. Design then implies an Intelligence, a deity with the knowledge and power to have created everything. He develops a sophisticated argument that we can recognize design in nature by certain criteria, principally complexity and what he calls "specification." His notion of specification is difficult and far from clear, but the argument becomes more substantive when he relates it to the arguments of the biochemist Michael Behe.

In his book *Darwin's Black Box*, Behe argues that many biological systems are characterized by what he calls *irreducible complexity*, by which he means that they consist of essential parts so interrelated that removing a single part will destroy the function of the whole. His examples of such complex biochemical systems include the blood-clotting mechanism of vertebrate blood, the immune system, and the little motor mechanism that drives bacterial flagella, which I used as an example in chapter one. Behe doesn't have to dig very far for complicated mechanisms on which to base his arguments; organisms in their chemical detail are incredibly complicated. From this observation of complexity, Behe reasons that such systems could not have come into existence through a gradual evolution but must have been created in their fully functional form by an intelligence.

The scientific aspects of the issue raised by Behe and Dembski are far too complicated to examine here; my role is to guide the interested beginner into the fray, with a warning that it is intellectually taxing and not to be entered lightly. The counterargument to Behe, that even the most complex structures can be explained plausibly by means of known evolutionary processes – and perhaps similar processes yet to be discovered – has been developed by several writers, notably Richard Dawkins in such books as *The Blind Watchmaker*, whose title is a direct challenge to arguments of the Paley type. The issue, scientifically, comes down to a set of questions that need to be answered empirically and theoretically: for each specific biochemical mechanism, can one designate a plausible scenario for its evolution through ordinary evolutionary processes, without any need to invoke design or a designer? Though some investigators have given positive answers to the question in certain cases, it remains fundamentally open, a challenge for continued work.

Although Dembski and his colleagues propose to pass off their ideas as legitimate scientific theory, ID fails as science. Johnson, in the quotation above, expects theistic realism to have "empirical, observable consequences" that are different from those predicted by classical biological theory. Well, such consequences exist, but unfortunately for ID, the observations favor classical theory and call for the rejection of ID. I noted in chapter one and again in chapter six that all the evidence favors the random formation of new species and structures by opportunism and *bricolage*. Organisms actually have all kinds of defects in their structures and operations; had they been created by an intelligent designer, they would be designed much better than they are. Dembski and Behe evidently postulate an intelligent designer who is very good at making complicated biochemical systems but who makes all kinds of silly mistakes in constructing other systems, such as eyes and the pharyngeal apparatus that sometimes confuses breathing and swallowing. One ID response to such criticism is a version of the theodicy argument, that we simply do not know the mind of God, and what appears to us to be ugly, dysfunctional, and nonideal is perfect and beautiful from God's point of view, with his cosmic perspective. But if ID purports to be science, this argument takes it outside the boundaries of science. ID fails the empirical test: it no longer has implications for observations or experiments that could challenge it. It becomes unfalsifiable.

But the ID argument fails as science in a second way. Science is an open-ended program of determination to seek answers to questions of Why and How about the universe. The Behe–Dembski program represents abandoning that quest, giving it up. That is one of its fundamental difficulties. (I'll get to its other, more serious difficulty in a moment.) We see some extremely complicated mechanism operating in an organism, and the spirit of the scientific quest demands that we seek an answer to its origin: explain how, step by step, protein by protein, this mechanism could have come into existence through ordinary biological processes. That is an open challenge, and evolutionary biologists must meet it in instance after instance. But the ID proponents write a period where there ought to be a question mark; they shut the door on scientific inquiry by giving a pat, unsatisfactory answer: "God designed it. That's the answer, so forget it and go about your business."

I have shown that "scientific creationism" is a pseudoscience because it must pervert science to conform to an ideology, Christian fundamentalism. But ID is a pseudoscience of a much more dangerous sort, because it would not only pervert a limited arena of science but would pervert science as a whole, as a human enterprise, to satisfy the same ideology. Dembski's book *Intelligent Design* purports to be developing a richer science and to be creating a link between science and religion; but the science Dembski would create by rejecting naturalism would be distorted and ultimately unrecognizable as science, an enterprise subservient to the Christian theology so prominent in his book. Dembski, Johnson, and their colleagues make no secret of their strategy to gradually wedge Christian theology into science. However, we now have a history – a sad and frightening history – of sciences perverted and repressed by ideologies, extending from the persecution of Galileo by the Catholic Church to the long suppression of genetics in the Soviet Union in the name of communist ideology. In the past few years, critics have cited instances of science being perverted and ignored in the U.S. by the current administration whenever it conflicts with the administration's political ideology. The last thing any secular democracy now needs is a pseudoscience based on the belief "that the universe and all its creatures were brought into existence for a purpose by God."

The ID supporters expect to extend their ideology into the operation of American society, and eventually world society, by making

ID a part of public school science education. Thus their program is a real danger to all secular, democratic societies since it threatens to replace democracy with theocracy. Unfortunately, ID is very seductive to those who are scientifically and philosophically unsophisticated, including most educators, who cannot have had extensive study in science and philosophy on their way to becoming teachers and administrators. Then, given a public already skeptical about evolution and school boards made of equally ignorant citizens whose personal agendas often include introducing religion into the schools, the wedge cohorts have potentially fertile ground for their program. Although the U.S. Supreme Court has ruled against the outright teaching of creationism in the public schools, the battle to keep education free of ID will depend upon articulate and philosophically sophisticated advocates to argue before courts that may be unable to comprehend the subtleties of the issue.

Those who still believe in democracy rather than theocracy will have to be constantly vigilant of their legislatures and their local school boards. Fundamentalist legislators may introduce bills mandating the teaching of creationism or ID in their states' schools; though such bills may make little headway in the busy legislative process, citizens need to keep an eye on them and be ready to oppose them. I hope this book can serve as a citizen's handbook for those who need to marshal their arguments before legislatures and school boards. As the judiciary that might stand against this movement becomes more politicized, we cannot rely on it as an ally in the fight for democracy and rationality. Only a highly educated, activist citizenship can ensure the health of democracy as we know it.

notes

1. Much of the argument in this section is taken, with the author's permission, from Donald U. Wise's paper "Creationism's Geologic Time Scale." I thank Dr. Wise for giving me permission to use his paper so extensively.

references and further reading

Note Books are listed under the chapter in which they are first mentioned, but some are relevant to more than one chapter.

general

Dawkins, Richard. *The Blind Watchmaker.* New York, W. W. Norton, 1986.

——— *River Out of Eden.* London, Weidenfeld & Nicholson, 1995.

——— *Climbing Mount Improbable.* New York, W. W. Norton, 1996.

——— *The Ancestor's Tale: A Pilgrimage to the Dawn of Evolution.* Boston, Houghton Mifflin, 2004.

Dennett, Daniel C. *Darwin's Dangerous Idea: Evolution and the Meanings of Life.* New York, Simon and Schuster, 1995.

Irvine, William. *Apes, Angels, and Victorians: The Story of Darwin, Huxley, and Evolution.* New York, McGraw-Hill, 1955.

Norman, David. *Prehistoric Life: The Rise of the Vertebrates.* New York, Macmillan, 1994.

preface

Johanson, Donald, and Maitland Edey. *Lucy: The Beginnings of Humankind.* New York, Simon and Schuster, 1981.

chapter one

Huxley, T. H. "We Are All Scientists." Reprinted in *A Treasury of Science* (Harlow Shapley, ed.). New York, Harper & Brothers, 1958, pp. 14–20.

Malinowski, Bronislaw. *Magic, Science and Religion and Other Essays.* New York, Doubleday Anchor Books, 1954.

Salmon, Wesley C. *Scientific Explanation and the Causal Structure of the World.* Princeton, Princeton University Press, 1984.

Toulmin, Stephen. *The Philosophy of Science.* London, Hutchinson, 1953.

chapter two

Cutler, Alan. *The Seashell on the Mountaintop.* New York, Dutton, 2003. An excellent biography of Nicholas Steno.

Dampier, Sir William. *A History of Science* (4th ed.). Cambridge, Cambridge University Press, 1948.

Jacob, François. *The Logic of Life.* New York, Pantheon Books, 1973.

chapter three

Gould, Stephen J. *Wonderful Life: The Burgess Shale and the Nature of History.* New York, W. W. Norton, 1989.

Guttman, Burton S. *Biology.* Dubuque, IA., McGraw-Hill, 1999.

Morgan, Elaine. *The Descent of Woman.* New York, Stein and Day, 1972, p. 96.

Stanley, Steven M. *Macroevolution: Pattern and Process.* Baltimore, The Johns Hopkins University Press, 1998.

Tudge, Colin. *The Variety of Life.* Oxford, Oxford University Press, 2000.

chapter four

Boyd, W. C. *Genetics and the Races of Man.* Boston, Little, Brown, 1955, pp. 234–235.

Darwin, C. *On the Origin of Species by Means of Natural Selection.* New York, Dolphin Books, Doubleday & Co., pp. 65–66.

Kingdon, Jonathan. *The Kingdon Field Guide to African Mammals.* London and San Diego, Academic Press, 1997.

Monod, J. *Chance and Necessity.* New York, Knopf, 1971.

Page, R. D. M. and E. C. Holmes. *Molecular Evolution, A Phylogenetic Approach*. London, Blackwell Science, 1998.

Williams, George C. *Natural Selection: Domains, Levels, and Challenges*. New York, Oxford University Press, 1992.

chapter five

Berry, R. J. *Inheritance and Natural History* (Collins New Naturalist Series). London, Bloomsbury Books, 1977.

Fogleman, James C. and William B. Heed. 1989. "Columnar cacti and desert *Drosophila*: The chemistry of host plant specificity", in J. O. Schmidt (ed.), *Special Biotic Relationships in the Arid Southwest*. Albuquerque, University of New Mexico Press, pp. 1–24.

Gould, Stephen Jay and Elizabeth S. Vrba. 1982. "Exaptation – a missing term in the science of form". *Palaeobiology* **8**:4–15. Reprinted in D. L. Hull and M. Ruse (eds), *The Philosophy of Biology*. Oxford, Oxford University Press, 1998.

Grant, Verne. *The Origin of Adaptations*. New York, Columbia University Press, 1963.

Lack, David. *Darwin's Finches: An Essay on the General Biological Theory of Evolution*. Gloucester, MA., Peter Smith, 1968.

Weiner, Jonathan. *The Beak of the Finch: A Story of Evolution in Our Time*. New York, Knopf, 1994.

Whittaker, R. H., and P. P. Feeny. 1971. "Allelochemics: Chemical interactions between species". *Science* **171**:757–769.

chapter six

Gould, Stephen Jay. *The Panda's Thumb*. New York, W. W. Norton, 1980. Also reprinted in Pennock, *op. cit.*

Levi-Strauss, Claude. *The Savage Mind*. Chicago, University of Chicago Press, 1966.

Mayr, Ernst. *Systematics and the Origin of Species*. New York, Columbia University Press, 1942.

Simpson, G. G. *The Meaning of Evolution: A Study of the History of Life and of Its Significance for Man*. New Haven, Yale University Press, 1952.

chapter seven

Buss, L. W. and M. Dick. "The middle ground of biology: Themes in the evolution of development", in P. R. Grant and H. S. Horn (eds), *Molds, Molecules, and Metazoa*. Princeton, Princeton University Press, 1992.

Gerhart, John and Marc Kirschner. *Cells, Embryos, and Evolution*. Malden, MA., Blackwell Science, 1997.

McNamara, Kenneth J. *Shapes of Time: The Evolution of Growth and Development*. Baltimore, The Johns Hopkins University Press, 1997.

Thompson, D'Arcy. *On Growth and Form* (Abridged ed.). Cambridge, Cambridge University. Press, 1961.

chapter eight

Leakey, Maeve and Alan Walker. "Early hominid fossils from Africa", in *New Look at Human Evolution, Scientific American* special issue, 2003.

Le Gros Clark, W. E. *History of the Primates*. London, British Museum (Natural History), 1950, p. 28.

Montagu, A. *Man's Most Dangerous Myth: The Fallacy of Race*. New York, Columbia University Press, 1945.

Sykes, Bryan. *The Seven Daughters of Eve*. New York, W. W. Norton, 2001.

Tattersall, Ian. *The Last Neanderthal*. New York, Nevraumont Publishing Co., 1995.

Wong, Kate. "Who Were the Neanderthals?", in *New Look at Human Evolution, Scientific American* special issue, 2003.

Young, J. Z. *The Life of Vertebrates*. Oxford, Clarendon Press, 1950.

chapter nine

Brillouin, Leon. *Science and Information Theory*. New York, Academic Press, 1956.

Hardin, Garrett. *Nature and Man's Fate*. New York, Rinehart, 1959.

chapter ten

Behe, Michael J. *Darwin's Black Box*. New York, The Free Press, 1996.

Dembski, William A. *Intelligent Design: The Bridge Between Science & Theology*. Downers Grove, IL., InterVarsity Press, 1999.

Eve, Raymond A. and Francis B. Harrold. *The Creationist Movement in Modern America*. Boston, Twayne Publishers, 1991.

Garraty, J. A. and P. Gay (eds). *The Columbia History of the World*. New York, Harper and Row, 1972.

Nelkin, Dorothy. *The Creation Controversy: Science or Scripture in the Schools.* New York, W. W. Norton, 1982.

Pennock, Robert T. (ed.). *Intelligent Design Creationism and its Critics.* Cambridge, MA., MIT Press, 2001.

Wise, Donald U. "Creationism's geologic time scale". *American Scientist* **86:**160–174, 1998.

index